Tartts 2

incisive fiction from emerging writers

edited by

Joe Taylor

with

Debbie Davis, Gerald Jones, and Tina Jones

Swallow's Tale Press
an imprint of Livingston Press
The University of West Alabama

All stories are held in copyright to the authors
Copyright © 2006 Joe Taylor
All rights reserved, including electronic text
ISBN 0-930501-32-2, library binding
ISBN 0-930501-33-0, trade paper
isbn 13 978-0930501-32-7, library bindbinding
isbn 13 978-0930501-33-4, trade paper
Library of Congress Control Number 2006927117
Printed on acid-free paper.
Printed in the United States of America,
Publishers Graphics
Hardcover binding by: Heckman Bindery
Typesetting and page layout: Angela Brown
Proofreading: Margaret Walburn, Amanda Peabody,
Tricia Taylor, Mettie Seale, Alexius White, Lauren Snoddy,
Donmonique Gracie, Brittany Lovette, and Betsy Compton
Cover design: Joe Taylor
Cover Layout: Jennifer Brown
Cover photos: Tina Jones (with thanks for the loan of Chris Hawkins's hand, the slender one, and Joe Taylor's fried peach tart, the greasy one)
Acknowledgements: These stories appeared first in the following magazines: Joe Benevento's "Rebirth on Richmond Hill" in; Catheleen Calbert's "Greece" in *Southern Review* (Autumn 2003); Christopher Chambers's "Carl, Under His Car" in *Gettysburg Review*; Jocelyn Jane Cox's "Blue Balls" ("So Cinnamon") in *JANE*; Wendy Dutton's "The Engaging and Sometimes Repulsive Way of the Natural World" in *The American Voice* #42; J.A. Grow's "What Girls Leave Behind" in *Other Voices*; Jimmy Carl Harris's "Hot and Sunny on the Fourth" in *ByLine*; Mona Houghton's "The Woman Who LIved in the Avocado Grove" in *Anyone Is Possible* by Red Hen Press; Meg Moceri's "Eclipse Tonight" in *Natural Bridge;* Sandra Novack's "Conversions on the Road to Damascus" in *Iconoclast*; Jan M. Stinchcomb's "Norman's Girl" in *Words and Images*; Jim Tomlinson's "First Husband, First Wife," in *Five Points;* Susan Vita Weiss's "Dresses for the Melons" in *Rosebud.*

Special thanks to the Alabama Epsilon chapter of Alpha Chi at The University of West Alabama for being the proud sponsor of the award money for the Tartt Short Fiction Prize.

These are works of fiction.
Surely you know the rest: any resemblance
to persons living or dead is coincidental.
Livingston Press is part of The University of West Alabama,
and thereby has non-profit status.
Donations are tax-deductible:
brothers and sisters, we need 'em.
first edition
6 5 4 3 3 2 1

Table of Contents

Introduction		vi
Philip Cioffari	Gun Hill Road	1
Naomi Benaron	Love Letters from a Fat Man	13
Joe Benevento	Rebirth on Richmond Hill	26
Louella Bryant	Dare's Tractor	35
Cathleen Calbert	Greece	42
Christopher Chambers	Carl, Under His Car	49
Jocelyn Jane Cox	So Cinnamon	61
Wendy Dutton	The Engaging and Sometimes Repulsive Way of the Natural World	68
J.A. Grow	What Girls Leave Behind	75
John Hanft	J.J. and the Dried Man	85
Jimmy Carl Harris	Hot and Sunny on the Fourth	94
Mona Houghton	The Woman Who Lived in the Avocado Grove	99
Scott McWaters	Developing Story	108
Meg Moceri	Eclipse Tonight	121
Sandra Novack	Conversions on the Road to Damascus	141
Elizabeth Orndorff	The Ginkgo Tree	153
Michael Schiavone	Skin	162
Jan Stinchcomb	Norman's Girl	170
Jim Tomlinson	First Husband, First Wife	181
Valery Varble	Moving Scars	197
Phil Walzer	The Cantor and the Milkman's Wife	212
Susan Vita Weiss	Dresses for the Melons	224
Biographies		234

Though there were fewer entries this year than our first year, the judging was much harder, since the level of writing overall was more intense. In consideration of this and in consideration of the American obsession for being first and only first, plus the accompanying phobia of finishing as a finalist, we have initiated three changes for this anthology. First, we took both published and unpublished stories, to open the field. Second, we considered all the stories entered, not just those of the "finalists." That word is placed in quotation marks because we had no formal finalists as such—hence the third change. (See the previous comment about America's obsessions and phobias.) These changes have made this second collection of Tartts a very strong and varied one indeed.

~the editors

TARTTS 2

Philip Cioffari

Gun Hill Road

The girl had burst into the diner in a hurry but once inside she had taken her time settling into a booth, spreading her things on the seat—an overstuffed knapsack, a leather jacket, a set of keys—then sipping two cups of coffee, one right after the other, with deliberate restraint. She sat by the window beneath a neon sign, OPEN 24 HOURS, the bright orange light of the letters directed toward the street and the ghostly, moonstruck tombs of the cemetery on the far side. Her eyes kept drifting to the window as if she might be expecting someone. Finally she lifted the knapsack onto the table and began to undo the straps.

It was nearly three in the morning and there were no other customers to distract Molly, the owner, a large woman with a round, hard face who leaned behind the counter studying the girl, directly across the aisle, for whom she had developed an instant dislike. "That bag," she said, "off the table. I keep a clean place here."

"Yeah, like the neighborhood."

"I can't help what happens outside. But in here I don't let things fall apart."

"Good for you," the girl said with a sharp edge, but she set the bag down on the seat beside her. "Another coffee."

"That'll be your third cup."

"Is there a limit?"

Another smart-mouth, Molly decided, moving around the register toward the booth. They came in after school from P.S.

12 for doughnuts and soda. Noisy and brazen, the girls often behaved worse than the boys, no traces of what once had been referred to as "breeding." If they were unruly enough, she refused to serve them and they would jeer and curse at her from the street. This one was older, though, out of school. She reached for the cup, saw the girl was thinner than she had thought, more fragile, despite the attitude. " 'Least drink de-caf, for god's sake."

"I need the caffeine. It keeps me alert. For whatever's out there." The girl glanced at the street, a busy thoroughfare by day but quiet now, the stores on either side of the cemetery shuttered with metal grates. "For whoever's coming to get me."

Molly stood at the coffee machine, her back to the girl, and worked the lever. "And who's that?"

"That's for me to know."

Something coy had slipped into the girl's voice, but Molly was in no mood for games. "Have it your way," she said, watching the dark swirling motion in the cup.

"You had more business in this place, you'd leave your customers in peace," the girl said with another hint of playfulness.

Molly shut the spigot, glanced at the girl: the too-thin face, the pale skin, the drawn look around the eyes. She'd be old at twenty-five. "You and peace don't look like best buddies."

"That's your point of view."

"That's my point of view." Molly brought the coffee to the table, extra creamers on the saucer, but the girl insisted on drinking it black. She pointed to the girl's middle where her black T-shirt—too short and tight, if anyone wanted Molly's opinion—rode an inch or more above her jeans. "Acid's gonna tear the bottom outta your belly."

For a March night it was not particularly cold, but the girl rubbed her bare arms then leaned toward the mug to warm herself. "It's my belly."

"For a while," Molly said. She walked by, shifting her weight side to side, returning to the counter where, beside the register, she stood guard over her world: the street door directly opposite her; the wide plate glass window and counter along the right side of the room; and on her left the narrow hall to the rest rooms with its row of cigarette and candy machines.

The girl gave her a sideward glance, part smirk, part smile. "What's it to you anyway?"

Molly heard something in her tone, something softer, as if the tougher she made herself out to be, the more the cracks in that toughness exposed themselves. She couldn't have been more than eighteen. A pretty girl really, despite her gaunt look and the unwashed blonde hair pinned up hastily. "You remind me of someone, that's all." She stared out at the street lamp's ghostly blue shadows. Sirens wailed in the distance. "Same attitude."

"Yeah? What's that?"

She turned back to the girl. "Screw it before it screws you."

"Sounds like good advice."

"I hope it doesn't get you where it got her."

The girl, sipping from the mug, glanced at the street. The sirens faded, replaced by the low rumble of traffic. "And where's that?"

"Dead."

Beneath the table the girl's left leg jiggled nervously, her knee bare where the denim had ripped away. "Hey, we all gotta go sometime."

"She was twenty," Molly said in a flat voice.

"Live hard, die fast."

"That's what she would have said."

A thin smile played on the girl's lips. "She got what she wanted, then."

Molly felt herself bristle, her dislike of the girl flaring in her eyes. But the girl didn't seem to notice. "You can make sure that coffee thing is filled, 'cause I'm gonna be here a while. I'm celebrating; it's my re-birthday." She rushed on in a breathless voice: "I escaped. Co-op City. My boyfriend lives there."

How much of this girl's life did she want to hear? But on slow nights like this when nothing broke the silence save the dull buzz of the electric clock or a siren's scream, she fell prey to distractions of any kind.

". . . I was suffocating, asthma of the soul," the girl was saying. "Like, he makes me stay in the room with him all day while he conducts his business. He's got eight phones. Different colors." She gripped the cup in both hands, grinning at Molly sheepishly, apologizing for something. "He doesn't let me answer them, just wants me there where he can, like, see me, feel my butt, you know, if he gets the urge. If I go into the bathroom or the kitchen, anywhere he can't see me, he panics. And all night, *every* night, he talks to me, he won't let me sleep, talk talk talk, telling me stories, childhood stories, *terrible* stories. He tells me his nightmares too, not just recent ones, but all the way back to when he was five. He remembers them all."

Molly, having heard something in the story she didn't like, began wiping the already gleaming and spotless counter, working the rag in quick, overlapping circles across the surface. Think moonstruck snow with flecks of gold, the salesman had described it when showing Molly the samples; and, since having it installed, she'd been determined to keep it *pure* as snow. She lifted the pie case and wiped clean the area beneath the base. "This guy. He deals?"

"If you can suck it, fuck it, snort it or pop it, he sells it."

Molly stopped wiping and dropped the rag in the sink, tightening her nostrils against the biting smell of ammonia. She stared at the girl's empty, smiling face. "You a hophead?"

"Hophead." The girl smirked. "How quaint."

"*Are* you?"

"I do some pills." The dumb smile gone now, she pulled at the sleeves of her jersey, her mouth tight, her face drawn in on itself. "For the pain. Mental pain."

"What makes yours so special?"

"Don't rag on me." She wrapped both hands around the mug, holding it tightly and lowering her head as if in prayer. "I'm trying to kick it. That's why I have to get away." From her bag she removed several stacks of fifty-dollar bills, bound with rubber bands, and dropped them on the table. "Hector doesn't believe in banks."

Molly stared in disbelief. "You dumped him *and* you robbed him?"

"I want to be sure he knows I'm gone."

"There are easier ways to commit suicide."

"I'm free. That's what counts." Fingering a stack of bills, she leaned back triumphantly in the seat. "He said I didn't have the guts to leave him. He said I wouldn't make it to the end of Gun Hill. Well, I did. I'm here. The end of Gun Hill Road." She smiled and gazed into the street. "You're my witness. You and those tombstones out there."

"Your cheering section."

"And if this runs out, I've got other things to cash in." She pulled a cellophane bag of white powder from her knapsack and set it down next to the stacks of fifties.

With both hands, Molly gripped the silver rim of the counter and leaned forward fiercely. "What's *that*?"

"Domino Sugar. What's it look like?"

"Get it outta here." Her chest heaving, Molly came quickly around the register, reached for the bag and tried to wrestle it from the girl's grasp.

"Hey, gimme that." The girl half-rose in her seat, holding tight to the bag.

"Get it out, goddammit!" She was bigger than the girl three times over, but the little twit just wouldn't let go.

The bag ripped, its contents spilling out in powdery rills. "Jeezus!" the girl said, "all right, all right!" She was half-standing in the cramped booth, hugging the torn bag to her chest. Molly stepped back, breathing hard, and watched her bend low to sweep the spilled powder from the table, brushing the loose grains into the bag with her cupped hand. "You know what this stuff's worth? You know how much this stuff costs?"

"I know what it costs. Now get out." Molly bent forward, wheezing, hands on her hips. "It cost my daughter's life."

The girl suddenly stopped gathering her things. "Your daughter O. D.'d?"

"Yes," Molly said, settling heavily on one of the counter stools. It creaked beneath her, the stiff cracked vinyl cushion in need of replacement. "But she was already dead by then."

The girl stood and hoisted the knapsack over her shoulder. "I'm sorry."

"So am I. Now get out."

Jacket in hand, the girl stayed in the aisle. "I'd like another cup of coffee."

"Get it somewhere else."

The girl reached inside her pocket and pulled out several loose fifties which she slapped on the counter.

"I don't want your money," Molly said, without so much as a glance at the bills.

"You can't afford to turn away business."

"I told you to get out." They stood in a face-off until Molly pointed toward the wall phone in the hall. "The 4-7 might be interested in that white stuff in your bag."

"I'll flush it down the toilet before they get here."

Molly started for the phone. "Go ahead then." But the girl made no move toward the rest rooms. "No cops," she said.

"Then go." When the girl turned toward the door, Molly saw again how childlike she was, a wisp of a thing, spindly legs and arms, skin so pale it looked unhealthy.

At the door the girl hesitated, eyes cramped with fear, and she turned back. "I can't go out there. I'm scared."

"You should have thought of that before."

"You're so cold."

She looked genuinely disappointed—even hurt, as if Molly had reneged on a promise. Briefly, Molly felt herself wavering but damned if she would give in. "So what are *you*? Miss Warm 'n' Cuddly?"

In the doorway the girl hovered moth-like, eyes flitting from the street to Molly. "Just let me stay till the sun comes up."

"Same thing's waiting out there, dark or light."

"One cup. I'll leave then. I promise."

Molly sighed and returned to the register. "I'm too old for promises."

The girl stepped toward her, halfway between the door and the counter. Her eyes, pale-blue and moist, had lost their defiance; in the overhead light's glare, they looked washed-out. One hand holding her jacket, the other gripping her bag's shoulder strap, she spoke so softly Molly had to strain to hear. "Pretend I'm your daughter."

"My daughter's dead."

"I know, but—"

"So leave her out of this."

The girl shifted her knapsack. "If she had needed a place to stay a while. Wouldn't you have wanted someone to help her out?"

"What do you know about it?" Molly heard the sting of accusation in her words, but she was asking the girl for something, too—though exactly what she was asking she couldn't have said.

"Nothing, I—" Her face flushed and she stared at the black and white squares of the tile floor. She was trembling now, her voice quaking too. "But if she needed something—"

"I guess she got what she needed," Molly said with such weariness that the girl raised her eyes.

"So, can I stay?"

Molly poured a mug of coffee and set it on the counter. "Sunrise, you're outta here."

The girl's name was Ash. Ashley, really. But she had shortened it because she couldn't stand the name, *Ashley.* She said this while she sat at the counter, holding the mug as if to warm herself. She asked Molly if she liked working the graveyard shift and Molly, resting back against the sink, her hands flat against the cool rim, said it wasn't a matter of liking or not liking, it was just better than lying in bed awake all night and the girl nodded as if she understood. She, too, felt safe here, she said. Nights, driving by in Hector's car, she had seen Molly serving customers or sitting alone reading the newspaper. On the dark street, the bright yellow lights had seemed inviting, had made the diner seem so warm and cozy. Molly said she was a fool. "You stole money and drugs from some low-life scum who's gonna come after you. How can you feel safe?"

Ash slumped on the stool. "Why are you so mad at me?"

"I don't understand you, that's why."

"You sound like my mother." She turned on the stool and tried to hide swallowing a pill with her coffee but Molly, catching her reflection in the window, leaned across the counter and spun her around.

"How long you been putting that junk in your body?"

The girl shrugged. "Three, four years. No big deal."

What the hell was wrong with these kids? "Where was your

mother all that time? Where is she now?"

Ash waved her hand in dismissal. "My mother lives in another world."

"Where's that?"

"Her bedroom." She began pulling sugar packets from a plastic tray and lining them along the counter. Molly pushed the tray out of reach and scooped up the line of packets, one by one, setting them back in the dispenser, patting them top and sides until they were neat again. Ash swiveled around to stare at the street. Something had caught her eye. So Molly watched her thin, narrow shoulders and beyond that the dim outline of her face in the window glass until the girl turned back. "She got sick when I was twelve," she said in a voice emptied of feeling. "Lupus. I used to think she was going to turn into a werewolf. I'd look to see if her fingernails had grown, or if she had hair on her palms." She forced a smile. "But she just stayed in her room, getting high on *legal* drugs, to kill the pain. After a while, she didn't even try to get out of bed. Just gave me money whenever I asked. Anything, so I'd leave her alone."

Molly leaned heavily on the register, watching the girl as if she were estimating something. Farther east on Gun Hill, a police siren uncoiled into the night. "Your father?"

"Gone."

"Your mother know where you are now?

"No."

Molly pointed to the phone. "Call her. Tell her send somebody to get you."

"Nobody in that country club world's gonna come get me in the Bronx. They wouldn't be caught dead here." The girl looked toward the street again where a gang of boys, voices raised, ambled past the cemetery fence. She turned back to Molly with a faint, apologetic smile. "Besides, they all hate me. She hates me."

"That why you need pills?"

"They make the world less ugly."

Molly shifted her weight. Her legs were killing her but she wouldn't let herself sit. Not now. Not with the girl here. "The world's what it is. Ugly or not, you decide."

"Is that what you told your daughter?"

Grabbing the rag again, Molly searched the counter for stains. Finding none, she moved farther along the surface, pushing the rag with short brush strokes, applying so much pressure its moisture seeped between her knuckles. "I told my daughter a lot of things. But she was too busy annihilating herself. Like you." She stopped pushing the rag and glared at the girl. "I want to know why you put that junk in your body."

Ash's fingers fidgeted on the cup, her leg jiggling beneath the rim of the counter. "What do you want me to say?"

"I want a reason." Molly came back along the counter, the pain in her legs sharper now, slowing her down. "One reason—"

"I don't know." She slid from the stool, her face drained of color and looking, for the moment, on the verge of tears. "I hate her, all right? For leaving me, for driving my father away. I hate being alone and afraid all the time. Is that what you want to hear?"

Molly shuffled into the aisle, breathing hard, face to face with the girl. "You don't have the guts to—"

"—What?"

"*Feel.*"

"I feel plenty."

"When it's easy. The rest of the time you're a zombie. The walking dead."

"You think you know everything, right?" Ash, backed into the hall, stood between the cigarette machine and the restrooms where she held her ground, shoulders pulled forward, hands jammed into her jeans. "But you don't even know why your daughter O.D.'d."

Molly turned slowly and made her way back behind the counter, standing with her feet spread and her arms crossed. "She was a coward."

"She wanted to kill the ugliness once and for all."

Excuses. She was so sick of excuses. "A coward. Like you," she hissed.

Ash screamed: "You don't know what it's like!"

Molly lowered her head and closed her eyes; she was tired, a lifetime's worth of tired, and she figured when it was her time to go it would be from exhaustion, not some disease. When she opened her eyes she found, staring back at her, her reflection in the coffee urn—her face, with its close-cropped gray hair and lusterless skin, a ditch from which all life had been drained. It was smeared across the stainless steel like graffiti. "I think I know," she said softly.

The clock buzzed into the silence. On the street a car sputtered by noisily.

The way the woman leaned against the counter, staring at the floor, at nothing, the resignation in her voice, brought the girl hurrying back to her bag. "I'm sorry, I'm sorry," she said, propping it on the stool and digging inside. "I want to show you something." She held out a photo. "My dog," she said, thrusting it toward Molly. "When I was a kid. He was the best part of—" A car revved loudly on the street and she glanced up. A black Lincoln had pulled into the curb directly across the street. "Oh,

God. He's here."

"Hector?" Molly had come instantly to life, straining for a view of the street beyond the window's glare. The car waited, lights on, motor running, its interior impenetrable behind tinted glass.

"I thought I'd have more time." Half-crouching, her face turned away from the street, she had backed against the cigarette machine. "To talk, I mean."

"Talk's not gonna help you now." Molly moved quickly toward the door, locking it. "I'm calling the cops."

"Please, no. He'll kill you," Ash said, following Molly down the hall where the sweet smell of cleaning agent seeped from the rest rooms. Molly already held the phone in her hand but the girl, eyes wide with fear, shouted to wait.

"How long's he gonna sit out there?"

"Five minutes, maybe. He'll give me time to come out."

"You don't have to go."

Crying now, Ash leaned against the wall paneling, shaking her head no. "You don't understand."

Molly reached toward the rotary dial. "I'm calling the cops."

The girl moved closer to her, trembling, her eyes looking bruised from the way her make-up had smeared. "You'd do that for me? Risk your life?"

Holding the phone to her chest, Molly drew herself to her full height and stared hard at the girl. "I locked my daughter out of the house because I couldn't watch what she was doing to herself. The doctors and counselors said yes, cut her off. Don't enable her. If you want to help her, let her go. So I did. I threw her out on the streets. She was dead within a week. My only child." She raised the phone and began to dial. "So don't get all dewy-eyed. I'm doing this for myself."

Ash flattened her hand against the rotary dial. "You don't know the whole story. I've done this before. Run away like this. I always go back." She waited until Molly set the phone in its cradle before she withdrew her hand. "I can't. I can't turn him in."

"You said you wanted to be free."

"I do, but—"

There was a whining quality to the girl's voice that Molly hadn't heard before. "Give him back what's his then. Throw the bag outside. Maybe he'll leave you alone."

"He needs me. He—"

"You'll find other men to need you."

"*I* need *him*." She moved to the window, staring above the cigarette machine at the street, at what she could see of the black Lincoln. "To keep me company nights. When I can't sleep. To talk to me so I'm not alone."

"You said he kept *you* awake," Molly said behind her. "You said *he* couldn't stand for *you* to be out of *his* sight."

"I—lied."

"So this is some kind of game? You take his money *and* his dope. Of course he's gonna come after you. Guaranteed. Tell me, you feel loved now, with him waiting out there?"

The girl, eyes flared, whirled to face her. "It's not a game."

"Prove it. Leave him." Molly reached for the wall switch and the diner went dark, except for the faint glow of night lights behind the counter. She pushed the girl past the restrooms toward a screen door. "Out the back. There's a hole in the fence. Cross two yards, then one street over. You can hide in my house till morning. We'll figure what to do then."

"You make it sound easy." The girl shook free of her, framed against the screen, and pulled something from her pocket. Molly knocked it from her hand, the pill's gelatin casing clicking against the tile floor.

"I can't leave him."

"You mean you won't leave him."

A car horn sounded outside. Ash shrugged. "Have ta go."

But Molly moved quickly ahead of her down the hall. At the counter she bent beneath the register and pulled out a baseball bat. "Don't be crazy," Ash said, behind her, "they have guns."

Unlocking the front door and swaying unsteadily on the outside step, Molly brandished the bat at the street. No traffic: the street quiet enough to hear the drone of the blinking light at the corner. In front of the cemetery the Lincoln waited, motor running. "Come on out here," she yelled at the darkened windows. "Come out here where I can see your face, you son-of-a-bitch. Leave her alone." She drew in her breath and yelled again. "*Leave her alone!*" For a moment she rocked on the step, gripping the bat with both hands, watching the car pull away from the curb. When it had turned the corner at the blinking light she came back in. The girl stood inside the door, clutching her bag.

"You see? That's how much he loves you. He just drives away." The girl wore a smug smile that Molly wanted to slap away.

"He'll be back. I know him."

"Out the back door. Go on. Hurry." Molly pushed her again but this time the girl pushed back.

"You can't just order people around. I need time. Things take time. Don't you see?"

Molly stood holding the bat, feet spread, blocking the door. "How *much* time?"

"Time," the girl said.

"Another excuse. Another lie."

She was shaking her head, saying *no no no no*. "You threw your daughter out. She wasn't ready. Look what happened to her."

The brief hope that had lifted Molly's spirits dimmed. She felt light-headed. It seemed for a moment her legs would give out and she teetered against a booth. "I *know* what happened to her." Another of life's oddities, she thought: she had never wanted to be a mother, had staunchly believed children were a woman's worst mistake; yet she had come to love her mistake more than herself. And here she was again, fooling with someone else's mistake this time, as if life had taught her nothing.

"She needed time, that's all," Ash was saying. "To work it out." A car horn broke the silence. The black Lincoln had reappeared, this time parked right in front of the diner. "Have ta go."

"Go then." Molly reached for the wall switch and flooded the room with light; she moved unsteadily to her roost behind the counter. The bat clanked against something metallic when she released it.

"Thanks," Ash said, standing between the counter and the door. "For talking to me. For letting me stay. I had to get away a while. Feel what it's like being normal." She came around the counter and stood close to Molly. "Can I give you a hug?"

Molly stood rigidly, mouth tight, hands braced on the Formica. When the girl reached to hold her, Molly felt herself stiffen but she didn't move away.

The girl smelled of smoke and flowers. "Can I come back sometime?"

"Sign says we're open twenty-four hours."

"I don't want you to be mad at me." In the new light the girl's face had a brighter look, despite the smeared make-up.

"I'm not mad at you."

"Disappointed, then."

"Yeah, I'm disappointed." She stood locked in place, staring ahead at the reflection in the plate glass window: the moon-white counter with its flecks of gold, the silver machines along the wall behind her.

"I want to give you something." The girl was thrusting something at her, the color print of her dog. "Me and Teddy. I look so happy here." When Molly made no move to take it, or even look at it, the girl's hand wavered. "I'll leave it right here," she said, sliding it onto the counter.

The car horn sounded again, more impatient this time. Ash slung her bag over her shoulder, turned toward the door but hesitated. "Your daughter. 'Least you cared enough to take a stand. You tried to help her. That's more than my mother did."

The low, uneven buzz of the wall clock filled the space between them.

"Close your eyes, okay?" Ash said.

Molly stared vacantly at the windows, as if the girl had already left. "What for?"

"Just for a second."

"I don't like games."

"Just this time."

"I like to see what's coming at me."

"Just for a second. Just this once, all right?"

She leaned against the counter to ease the burden on her legs. The first scissoring pains of a headache had already begun invading her temples. It had been a long night and the long day coming up would be broken by only the few hours' sleep she'd manage when the morning shift came on. But this was her life and she'd chosen it—most of it, anyway. In the girl's eyes she saw the buoyancy that passed for hope in the young. She was tired of fighting, thinking—tired. She lowered her head and closed her eyes.

"Think of your daughter," Ash said. "Sometime nice. When you were holding her in your arms. When she was smiling."

For several moments there was nothing but darkness behind her eyes and then out of the darkness Becky came running toward her—it was summer, their back yard—and Becky was seven, maybe eight. No, she was eight, she was sure of it because of what she was wearing: the blue overalls and pink jersey Molly had bought for her birthday. And she was running, running, the morning light streaming behind her, her blonde curls jiggling, her smile as wide as her arms and Molly held her and held her and held her. "I forgive you, Mama," Ash's voice whispered. "I forgive you." Somewhere a door opened and closed and when Molly opened her eyes her hands gripped the metal rim of the counter and the girl was gone, a shadow on the steps outside, running toward the street.

Naomi Benaron

Love Letters from a Fat Man

From: misslman51@aol.com
Date: Fri, 20 Feb 2004 04:20:51 EST
Subject: Greetings from Tucson, AZ
To: marleneinfo@marlenedietrich.com

My Dear Marlene,
 Forgive me for resurrecting you from your eternal rest, but I feel I must communicate my thoughts. As a sufferer of chronic and incurable insomnia I often ingest the fare of late night movies. Tonight I watched a double header of your films—*A Foreign Affair* and *Touch of Evil*—and was deeply moved, not so much by the films as by your beauty.
 My name is Otto, coincidentally (or not) the third name of your father, Louis Erich Otto Dietrich. You must excuse my nosy nature; I have spent the past two hours discovering you on line. To use a phrase that has found its way into the English language since your passing, I have "Googled" you. It is amazing to me the series of parallels in our lives that draw us together.
 I am a slim man and, I am told, handsome. My hair is blonde, imperceptibly silvered, with the hint of a wave. Until my son died and my wife began to reclaim her affections morsel by

morsel, I had the build of a barnyard rooster, all sinew and bone. However, I seem to have swallowed a whale. Otto Orca am I. The last time I tipped the cargo scale at my physician's office, I weighed in at 433 pounds, and blubber accrues at an alarming rate. I can no longer ambulate with ease, and caring for myself has become impossible. The simple task of tying my shoes requires the most undignified contortions.

Although *Touch of Evil* seemed quaint and moralistic, *A Foreign Affair* was of great interest to me. I was surprised by the empathy shown to the people of post-war Berlin. I watched enrapt, moments passing before the risk of losing consciousness compelled me to breathe. You will understand this when I tell you that my father was from Dresden. While he was occupied defending the *Vaterland,* his first wife looked up one night to see the sky become a storm of fire. I imagine her, transfixed by this terrible beauty, the air around her igniting as bombs screeched to earth, her arms around my two unknown half-brothers, all movement suddenly beyond the realm of possibility. Incineration would have been instantaneous, their ashes fusing with the rubble of the building—an eye for an eye.

I was a late edition, a second thought, born to the American nurse who cured my father of typhoid in a DP camp. My father became a good American citizen. Fascinated by the electrical nature of things, he earned a PhD in Electrical Engineering. He decried the pursuit of war and worked for a well-known firm in the peaceful applications of his profession. He kept the insignias of the Reich hidden in a pouch of velvet. I found them after his death, tucked away in a dresser drawer. When I hold them in my hand, Marlene, they burn holes in my skin.

In contrast to my father, I have been at liberty to find employment in a military field. I am a physicist, studying the perfection of skin. Not the vulnerable covering of viscera and bones, the lunar whiteness that shimmers from the divine curvature of your legs. I study the skin of missiles. I strive for a combination of strength and slipperiness, if you will. A skin that will glide without friction, that hides from the searching eyes of radar and remains cool and intact despite unimaginable forces, to deliver its cargo to the upturned faces of mothers who watch with their young children tucked beneath their arms. An eye for an eye.

Due to my current condition, I have taken a leave of absence. The last time I attempted to drive my car, I did irreparable damage to vehicle and psyche. The space between stomach and steering wheel had become infinitesimal, leaving little room for the expansion of diaphragm that occurs with the intake of breath. Late for work and in a fury, I planted my feet and gave a violent backward thrust. I am a very strong man. My father, at age 75, was crowned the Strongest Man in the World, in the age category Seventy Plus. Fueled by adrenaline and a boiling anger at my recently departed wife, the poor seat was no match for my tantrum. I somersaulted backward, seatbelt, chair and all, into the rear of my SUV. There I dangled, helpless and upside down, my sausage legs and arms waving: a monstrous insect from a late night horror film. It is the strangest feeling, Marlene, to have tears streak up your forehead and soak your scalp.

I finally extricated myself, pushed the car back into the garage and closed the door, leaving the seat where it had landed —a twisted memorial to human rage. My breath came in violent shudders, and my heart had the sound and feel of a wrecking ball careening into my ribs. I trudged into the kitchen and turned the deadbolt. I made a vow: *Here Otto shall remain, until they lift his lifeless form from the floor with their crane.*

If anyone can understand this decision it is you, Ms. Dietrich. You who spent the last years of your life locked away in your Paris apartment, poisoned by the perceived ill will of humankind, drowning liver and kidneys in a gourmet alcoholic stew. Although I do indulge in a glass or bottle or two of fine wine with my meals, this shall not be my Weapon of Mass Destruction. I have embarked on a journey to eat myself to death. No fan of cheeseburgers and french-fries, the sword I turn against myself is of well-honed, quality steel. I shall annihilate myself one steak Diane, one French-vanilla ice creamed raspberry tart at a time.

    Yours in spirit and in flesh,
    Otto

From: misslman51@aol.com
Date: Sat, 21 Feb 2004 08:27:37EST
Subject: The Spirit of Opportunity
To: marleneinfo@marlenedietrich.com

Dear Marlene,

By now you are blinking in your newly awakened state and wondering what has become of the world. Here on earth events catapult toward unimaginable conflagrations; nothing new in that department. We continue to invent excuses to destroy ourselves, and improve the weapons with which to accomplish this. Certainly I am as guilty as any, earning my bread as I do from optimizing methods of destruction. But beyond the reaches of our floundering planet the news is better.

On January 4th an adorable little rover named Spirit landed in the crater Gusev on the surface of Mars. His brother, Opportunity, landed in the vast plain of Meridiani Planum on January 25th. It is here that scientists believe they have the best chance of discovering evidence of water on Mars. After some initial problems, both vehicles are prattling about, happily gathering samples and snapping pictures.

I have read of your heroic performances at the front lines during the closing year of WWII. The exploration of new frontiers by our brave robots gives me the same tantalizing flicker of hope that the soldiers you entertained must have felt. To a universe of death you brought light and life and a pair of legs that were out of this world. In the midst of a drought of human kindness, two creatures of engineering genius ignite the hope of finding water on a desiccated and deserted planet.

    Yours in anticipation,
    Otto

From: misslman51@aol.com
Date: Mon, 23 Feb 2004 05:01:30 EST
Subject: Marta
To: marleneinfo@marlenedietrich.com

My dearest Marlene,
How are you? I am well, thank you, as well as can be expected. You are probably asking by now, how does such a fat man accomplish suicide by haute cuisine when surely he barely fits in his own kitchen? How does he chop vegetables for his sauté, pound veal for his Weiner schnitzel when his stomach protrudes like the prow of a ship before him? You are right to wonder, and please, have no fear of being frank. All that remains of my feelings is a hard-packed square of mud left to bake in the sun's heat. My wife, may she be eternally blessed, saw to that. And as we are on the subject, I have made a surprising discovery of my own! You, my Goddess of smoldering perfection, suffered from bouts of chubbiness yourself. The temptations of all aspects of physical pleasure, it seems, hovered around you like a shadow. If I were inclined to reverse my own pitiful condition, I would do as you did and lie down on the floor for hours, turning the wheels of an invisible bicycle with my legs.

I digress. In answer to your question, a wonderful and shockingly beautiful young woman named Marta cares for me. From her name you would presume her to be of Spanish descent, but she is as pale as an Icelandic goddess. Her father, a lazy man, barely literate, filled out her birth certificate, and for expedience or ignorance or exasperation, left out the 'h', and so it stands. Marta is tall, even when she slips off her platform heels and glides about the house in bare feet. She is thin; my eyes can trace the articulation of bones beneath the silvery shell of her skin. Her hair, like yours, is bronze.

Marta is between husbands, and so was glad for both diversion and employment. When she met me her eyes widened as she calculated dollars in my bank accounts and days until my impending death. But we have come to an agreement on this account.

Marta, as she confessed in the lateness of an evening, her tongue slippery from several glasses of an excellent Medoc, finds her mates through the obituaries. She looks for older women whose final farewell is celebrated in the more fashionable funeral homes. She memorizes vital statistics, researches pertinent information on line. (Marta has the MO of a brilliant scientist—she's a woman after my own heart.) Black-silked to the gills she approaches the grieving and vulnerable husbands.

"My mother went to school with your wife," she says. Or, "Your wife was my fourth grade teacher. I remember. . ." And so on and so forth until she slides inside the poor sot's grief and asks if she can bring him a meal.

At this point, let me testify, it is all over. I have felt the tingle of her fruit sorbet against my teeth; the fiery caress of her Chicken alla Diavola has brought tears of desire to my eyes and an uncontrollable sweat to my brow. Were she to deny me, I would crawl across coals to lick a morsel of home-baked buttered bread from her fingers.

I have taught Marta to play chess. She is a quick learner and has a fiercely competitive nature. As I march toward her king her skin ignites, and her brows furrow together in a delightfully seductive 'v'. Lately I have been forced to bring out the timer, as without this distraction she would soon beat me. Last Wednesday she revealed a bold strategy, tricking me into thinking she would pursue a simple mate when in fact she sacrificed her queen and threatened me with disaster. Fortunately, somehow flustered by her success, she made a blunder on the next move and allowed me a merciful checkmate, rescuing a battered intellect from further blows. Marta forgave my conquest by presenting me with a bold Bolognese for dinner: buttons of porcini mushrooms crowning a mound of fresh linguine, salade Niçoise and a loaf of bread shimmering with olive oil and roasted garlic on the side. For dessert she served cheese cake drizzled with intertwined ribbons of caramel and chocolate.

On Saturday I reserved the film *The Blue Angel* and a biography of the same name from the library. The Internet is a wonderful thing, Marlene! Truly one can live one's whole life with no more effort than the flick of the wrist, the click of a finger on a mouse. It is my prediction that future generations will develop the blinking watery slits of mole eyes, the pallor of salamanders wiggling about in caves. Marta picked up my treasures this morning and brought them. This afternoon I caught her sitting next to the window, bare feet pressed against the glass, skirt sliding up her sun-warmed thighs, reading the story of your life. She did nothing to reclaim her modesty when she saw me. She merely pursed her lips and wrinkled her nose.

"Did you know Marlene Dietrich was a lesbian?" she asked.

Her hand, supporting the open book (she had devoured nearly half!) rested in a fold of blue cotton pouched between her legs. I must admit to a flush that warmed my cheek, a drop or two of sweat that seeped into the furrows of my neck.

"I would appreciate your asking before you abscond with my books," I said, shuffling off toward the safety of my office.

"I was the one got it," she called after me. I imagined her fingers casually brushing across the folds of her skirt as she readjusted her legs.

Tonight I will watch the most famous of your films, a bowl of buttered popcorn by my side. Hungarian paprika sprinkled on top provides a tantalizing addition, melting in red streaks that add a hint of sweetness and fire to the kernels.

But first I must ask you—is it true? I have heard of your affairs with men, but never a word of other diversions sampled. Of course I am open-minded, Marlene, but you must understand my history. My father was Aryan down to the mitochondria of his cells. Any tendency toward what he considered feminine weakness was answered with a belt. Sometimes, it seemed, he failed to remember who had lost the war. Well, enough. The stress of memory on my weakened heart causes uncomfortable palpitations; a gentle warning squeeze informs me it is time to cease. I shall bid you *gute nacht*.

    Yours in admiration,
    Otto

From: misslman51@aol.com
Date: Tues, 24 Feb2004 06:00:16 EST
Subject: Cuckold Doodle-Doo
To: marleneinfo@marlenedietrich.com

My dear Marlene,

How I weep! Were this letter pen and ink, blue rivers would flow from the page. I have watched *The Blue Angel* three times, and would have watched it a fourth had not my heart trembled with a weight of sorrow, threatening to burst from its "mortal coil." Your portrayal of Lola-Lola, cabaret singer and femme fatale, has left me clawing for a breath of air.

In the four o'clock stillness of my bedroom, my life takes on the shadowed cast of the Blue Angel's world. There is no sound beyond the groan of walls and floors struggling to bear my bulk. No breath of child, no sigh of wife. To attempt sleep is useless; the ghost of Lola-Lola's unlucky Professor Rath squats on my shoulder. Like this saddest of protagonists, I am a cuckold and a clown.

I had a wife, Marlene. My wife was beautiful. She was taut: an ungrounded wire leaving a trail of sparks in her wake. She had a boy's haircut, bangs falling coquettishly over her eyes. She had the narrow hips of a young man and tiny feet. Did she marry me for love or money or my Germanic beauty? Who knows. She was no cabaret singer, no Lola-Lola perched on a stool. She was a teacher of high school mathematics, but like Lola-Lola, she wove an inescapable web. I saw how men orbited around her, snared in her gravitational fields.

Was I like Professor Rath—a lonely, awkward man imposing his will on the world, peeking secretly into the sordid corners of life, undone by desire for a woman as indifferent to him as a mongoose to her prey? In the beginning, no. I was slender and tall, a crowing rooster, a leading man. But events beyond my control (perhaps) undid me, and I began to eat. In the end a fat man can be no more than a diversion, a freak amusement.

I had a wife, and she left me long before she left me. As punishment for my sins she began to deny me, one sweet taste at a time. I became a victim of starvation smothering in patés and mousse. I followed her from room to room, kissing her shadow. I cooked her elegant dinners and waited till eight, till nine, drinking wine at the table, playing Chopin, listening to the unanswered ring of her phone. I consumed her portions as well as mine and stewed in my own rage. I devoured desserts. Late at night, when she came home, I watched her from darkened doorways, a cigarette nearly burning her fingers while she read a book, traced the arc of a circle with her toes. I sniffed at the air for the hint of a man, the soured perfume of an embrace.

I had a wife, and could have killed her or, like Professor Rath, I could have died of grief. We make our choices; we lie in our beds. When Rath discovered his Lola-Lola with another man he crowed like a rooster until crowing consumed him, transformed him into a beast of rage. He could have killed her then. The balance of plot could have tipped either way. Instead he willed himself to die alone in a darkened classroom, stretched across the desk from where he taught when his life was still his own.

Oh, where is Marta? I am in need of an omelet. With fresh asparagus and a salty cheese—a Feta or Gorgonzola—to mask the taste of tears.

        Yours in flesh and desire,
        Otto

From: misslman51@aol.com
Date: Fri, 27Feb2004 03:58:46 EST
Subject: In Your Image
To: marleneinfo@marlenedietrich.com

My dearest Marlene,
 Felicitations. I am fairly well, thank you, although I have noticed a new shortness of breath—a chortling that accompanies the intake of oxygen—and my fingers have grown puffy. Now that I am at peace with my decision, I observe these changes with scientific curiosity, as insignificant as a fly on the wall. Marta, who knows nothing of my plan, has become alarmed and vowed to eliminate salt and red meat from my diet.
 My rover friends, Opportunity and Spirit, have returned pictures of a Martian sunset. From the surface of Mars the sky appears indigo and is filled with dust. Soil samples collected from Opportunity have a much wider range of colors than previously seen, but no evidence of water yet.
 You will be pleased to hear that Marta is quite enamored of you. She has acquired a collection of movies and books that are now strewn about the living room. She demanded reimbursement, which I don't mind. This obsession of ours injects purpose and direction into the stale atmosphere of the house. Although the universe expands, my own world becomes smaller daily.
 Marta has taken to plucking her eyebrows into a thin arch that accentuates the almond shape of her eyes, and this morning she appeared wearing a pantsuit, tie and fedora. She called me into the kitchen, and for a moment I thought she had conjured up your physical being. I took a step back, the floor reeling unsteadily beneath the two boats of my bedroom slippers. There you stood, illuminated by sunlight drifting through the drapes, your face a play of light and shadow as if a director's spotlight had been perfectly placed. You turned to face me and thankfully became Marta once more, a mirror in hand.
 "It's perfect, don't you think?" she asked.
 She did a slow spin. Pebbles of sunlight speckled face and suit. I remained speechless. She showed me the pictures of you parading around Hollywood in similar garb. How courageous you were to expose soul and spirit at a time when our sexual nature was kept in a well-locked closet. Hollywood was a far cry from the delicious decadence of pre-war Berlin.
 "I found these at the thrift store. Twenty-seven dollars. She twirled the fedora on her finger and replaced it at a provocative angle. "Two bucks for the hat. I thought you wouldn't mind."
 Frankly, I was delighted and amused. My fingertips tingled, abuzz with desire to reach out and touch her skin.

It was after a breakfast of steel-cut oats with fresh strawberries and whipped cream (Marta is taking the issue of my health far too seriously!) that the oddest thing happened. She cleared the dishes, brought an armful of books to the table and plopped them down. While flipping through pictures she suddenly stopped, her finger resting on a portrait of you with your daughter Maria. Confronted with the sultry gaze of your eyes, speech leaves me, and from the slackness of Marta's jaw I knew she was similarly affected. Your daughter stared out at us with a look of ill-controlled fury.

"She's jealous, that little one," I said.

Marta withdrew her finger as if burned. She looked at me, but said nothing. Stupidly, I continued.

"Jealous of the world for stealing her mother's love."

With those words, Marta slapped me. Her fedora flew from her head, and her pinned hair escaped to tumble over her shoulders.

"What do you know about it?" she said and walked out, leaving the fedora where it fell.

I sat for a moment, a beached whale, contemplating the act of hat retrieval. I picked up the book and went to my bedroom, my finger marking the page where an angry girl stared.

Beyond my bedroom window a family of Gambel's quail parades past, scratching seeds from the dust. In my imagination they are faithful to each other until death do them part. I have propped up the photograph of you and Maria on my desk beside a picture of my father, my mother and myself. The same pouting mouth and smoldering eyes stare back at me from my young visage. My father is straight-backed, as if preparing to salute the inspecting Führer. His arm is placed on my shoulder, but my body leans away.

Do not feel guilty for leaving the care and affection of your daughter to others, as you so often did. In the end, my Marlene, we are all abandoned.

And so, *auf wiedersehen*, my dearest.

    Yours, as always,
    Otto

From: misslman51@aol.com
Date: Sun, 29Feb2004 23:06:27 EST
Subject: Duped?
To: marleneinfo@marlenedietrich.com

Dear Marlene,

As you can see, today is a rather special occurrence, the 29th day of February. The sky as well maneuvers into a portentous configuration. In three weeks time, five planets will be in alignment. Mercury, Venus, Mars, Jupiter and Saturn will thread themselves across the evening sky. The moon will hang from this string of jewels like a pendant.

Today was also an auspicious day in my own tiny universe. Today, in chess, Marta had me. She opened by setting up a risky Queen's gambit. As usual I played the aggressor, pouncing on all pieces offered. But when we progressed to the endgame and she laid her finger lightly on the bishop, I saw with horror that mate in two moves was inevitable. She looked at me and smiled. She lifted her finger and responded with Kt X P check, a ridiculous move that allowed my knight to penetrate the territory of her king. I am troubled, Marlene. Deeply troubled. Had she not seared me with so pointed an expression, I could easily have dismissed her mistake as a lack of attention, an inability to follow through with an attack. But those eyes—your eyes—pinned me for the cuckold that I am.

How many men (and women) fell victim to your gaze? How many unwitting clowns, Marlene, crowing with a cry of presumed conquest found themselves fluttering helplessly at your feet? It is always too late when we discover that freedom of movement is an illusion. We are maneuvered into alignment by a pair of irresistible eyes, a pair of legs with skin as luminescent as the moon.

    Yours in deepest admiration,
    Otto

From: misslman51@aol.com
Date: Thurs, 04 Mar2004 05:05:12 EST
Subject: The sins of the father
To: marleneinfo@marlenedietrich.com

My Marlene,

I have been in bed for 3 days, too heavy to move. I swallow sorrow like bread. I expand beyond belief. Marta has finally rousted me, chasing me out with her dust cloths and vacuum cleaner. She claims my lair has become exquisitely foul, overrun by droppings of food that have turned into brightly colored colonies of fungus and mold. I attempted to communicate by laptop, an odd expression at best, for not even the most slender of Internet Surfers places it there. But the word for me is particularly meaningless. Any semblance of a lap has been long buried by the geology of fat.

In the year 1944 you slept with American generals and sang to the soldiers of the *Vaterland*, concluding your broadcasts with a dedication to the Allied forces that you boasted were on the brink of destroying the Reich. Did my father, hunkered down on the frontlines, hear your throaty German drinking songs and curse you? I would like to think so. In the year of my birth, 1951, you already had two grandchildren and appeared for what you were, a fading cabaret beauty, in *Rancho Notorious*, another in your string of failed Hollywood films.

   In the year 1979, a year after your last film, *Just a Gigolo*, a child named Marta had a child of her own, a little girl. Had she kept her, she would have named her Amber. She told me this two days ago, perched on the edge of my bed, nibbling at a fingernail. When her father noticed the bulging belly behind her billowing shirts, he beat her until she prayed she would miscarry. She did not, but at her own request she never saw her daughter. She wonders now about the color of her eyes, the cut of her hair, and perhaps, although she did not say, about the woman she has always known as her mother.

   In 1992, the year of your death, I had a child: a son. Like his father he was a late edition, born to an aging father with a young woman as his prize. But unlike me he was not an afterthought. His eyes were hazel and his hair was brown with an auburn hue. He walked at ten months and began to read before the age of four. Perhaps it was wrong, but we let him sleep nestled between us when he was terrified by dreams.

   I had a son, and when he was seven my wife left him in my care while she attended a conference. He had a delicate nature and was prone to exaggeration. A nick on a finger became a war wound. So you can understand why I assumed he had a touch of flu, an insignificant sniffle. My own father drove me from my bed when I shivered with fever; it was all I knew.

   I had a son, and when he was seven he developed an infection, and the infection went to his heart, and beneath his pale and sweating skin his heart silently expanded until it no longer had the strength to pump life through his body. I had a son and my wife left him in my care and she barely had time to kiss him goodbye before he sighed and left us childless. When I held him in my arms he was as weightless as a little bird.

   On March 2nd, 2004, eleven years and ten months after your death, and one year, four months, 3 days and some odd hours after my wife, who never found it in her own diseased heart to forgive me, left me for more promising and fertile (and slimmer) ground, a little robot named Opportunity, equipped with all manner of scooping and digging tools, discovered strong evidence of flowing water on Mars. This conclusion was reached after analysis of rock samples showed the presence of sulfates and niches where crystals form, implying a wet environment.

   The material seen inside these niches was shiny and bright. Here on earth, in Tucson, Arizona, in a desert in the midst of a drought, the forecast is for rain.

My Marlene, née Maria Magdalene Dietrich, pray for those of us who shuffle along on the skin of this planet you have left behind. I remain yours in affection and am attempting the faintest flicker of hope in a hopeless world, *meine liebe*.
     Otto

From: misslman51@aol.com
Date: Wed, 24 Mar2004 08:00:01EST
Subject: Water on Mars!
To: marleneinfo@marlenedietrich.com

My poor Marlene,
In the end you could not sustain the illusion, nor could the illusion sustain you. You were nothing more than a play of light and shadow arranged beneath a spotlight. You amassed the weight of years as I amass the pounds of human suffering. You consumed scotch at 10:00 in the morning. You stumbled and fell onstage, lacerating legs, fracturing femurs. In the end, the freedom that had sustained you imprisoned you. Terrified that a photographer would capture your traitor skin on film, you withdrew to your apartment and drank yourself to a lonely and furious death. Perhaps I am ready now to return you to your sleep.

Forgive my silence of twenty days, but here on the planet of Otto much has happened. World events continue to deteriorate, and the War Machine clamors for my services. My telephone rings off the hook.

Marta has discovered the Marlene Dietrich Collection at the Film Museum in Berlin, and she is determined to go. There are 15,000 photographs and more than 300,000 leaves of written documents on display, as well as countless personal effects including 50 handbags, 150 pairs of gloves, 400 hats, and 440 pairs of shoes. *Meine liebe* Marlene, your closets must have shuddered under the weight of your vanity!

Since Marta is perpetually short on funds, she has decided that I will accompany her on her quest, and of course provide an all-expenses-paid vacation. She has calculated that I could be stuffed into an airplane seat if I lose 100 lbs. Amused at her request and ignorant of the capacity of her resolve, I acquiesced. She has rolled up her sleeves and gone to work. She threw out gallons of ice cream and absconded with wheels of fine French cheese. She divides steaks into infinitesimal portions, denies me butter on my baked potato, searches out the caches of Belgian chocolate hidden beneath my mattress, and hunts for evidence of illegal crumbs. I am forced to feed on troughs of salad with a tasty (although low-fat) vinaigrette. The final humiliation occurred when she brought the stationary bicycle of one of her departed husbands and set it up in the living room facing the television. I was terrified that I would upend the contraption or collapse the insufficient frame with my initial mount, but it has proven surprisingly well engineered. We have set up a stack of your movies, and I pedal and sweat as I watch you in your various incarnations of Marlene-hood slink across the stages of your life.

It is your last film, *Just a Gigolo*, that I return to most often. Surrounded by an entourage of handsome, cravat-adorned young men, you stare out with your black-lined and hooded almond eyes and say, "Dancing, music, champagne: the best way to forget." In the darkness of a deserted café you stand next to a piano player whose silhouette fades into shadow. The ruinous brushstrokes of well-lived years have been erased by the feathery touch of a black veil and the flickering shadows from a wide-brimmed hat placed at a provocative angle. With white-gloved hands clasped and a gold broche fastened at your throat, you belt out your final song, the title song of the movie. From the deepest wells of human resolve you drink in the strength to sing as you have never sang before. *Life goes on without me*, you proclaim, the slightest quiver in your voice, and so it does, and so it shall when the terrible bulk of me goes up in flames to leave behind a simple pile of ashes weighing nothing. I read in your biographies that tears flowed from all who watched the filming.

From the planet Mars the news overwhelms me. My friend Opportunity appears to have landed on the shoreline of an ancient sea! The latest photographs of rock show bedding planes with ripples and discordant angles which, to the best of our knowledge, form only in the presence of flowing water. I have magnified the pictures, traced my finger along the delicate curves, and I concur. The possibilities for life, I learn, are found in the most surprising places.

       I shall remain yours,
       Otto

Joe Benevento

Rebirth on Richmond Hill

> "I am in all hearts
> I give and take away
> Knowledge and memory."
>
> —*Bhagavad-Gita*

In her forty years in Richmond Hill, Louise Domenico had seen more than one transformation occur on Liberty Avenue, the main commercial thoroughfare of her part of southeastern Queens, but nothing could have prepared her for Bimal's Bombay Market, or, more accurately, for its proprietor, Bimal Das. Louise had been utilizing the convenience store on Liberty and 125th Street (she lived on 125th Street, just six houses east of Liberty) since its days as the Torelli Brothers Market, and right through its time as a Puerto Rican "bodega." She saw no reason to stop getting her milk and other sundries there just because some Indians had taken over the spot. Certainly these Indians seemed a little more foreign than the Hispanics (her speaking fluency in Italian had given her a working comprehension of Spanish) and her son and son-in-law both claimed that they smelled badly, but these were hardly reasons enough to walk five blocks out of her way to the next alternative. She was as disinterested in goat's meat and curry powder as she had been in the previous owners' plantains or "cuchifritos," but she still needed an occasional carton of milk, and the new owners seemed capable of at least a merchant's English; she saw no reason to switch.

Anyone entering Bimal's Bombay Market would first not fail to notice the clutter. In additon to all the staple items one might expect to find in a small grocery store: milk, eggs, bread, butter, soda, coffee, there were not only Indian specialties, but an assortment of other ethnic foods, ranging from jalapenos to Halvah, with which Das had stocked his store. Unlike so many other small, ethnic market owners in New York, Das by no means wanted to limit his clientele to his own race or creed. In addition to food, he sold tee shirts and caps, mostly with New York motifs, for any potential tourists; most of this merchandise was arrayed just outside the store proper. Inside, Indian statuary and jewelry were also displayed, both for decoration and sale.

Bimal Das himself, a short, elderly, though ageless man, with dark reddish-brown skin, deep black hair only moderately streaked with grey, and a shiny black mustache, was ever present and ever ready to talk to anyone in his vicinity. And so Louise Domenico, no matter how little her interest in India, in Bimal Das, in anything but the bread or milk she came out for, could not avoid getting acquainted with her new neighbor.

It would be unfair to say that Louise Domenico was unfriendly, even less accurate to label her reclusive. Since her husband's death ten years earlier, she had lived alone in the house she and Sam had moved to from Brooklyn with their two children, in search of a quieter, less crowded neighborhood and home. Now Louise's children both wished her to live with them, in safer Westchester and Suffolk counties, respectively, but she could not bear to leave her husband's last home, though she was now one of the few white people left on her block (several of the first wave of blacks and Hispanics who had displaced the whites had themselves since moved on to "better" sites). Her world consisted of visits to and from her children and grandchildren, and the many memories locked safely behind the doors of her home—the comfort of her own clutter. Louise had kept everything: old clothing—hers and her family's—a bewildering assortment of knick-knacks and statues, old furniture and appliances, antique radios and black-and-white TV's that still worked. She lived through the valued memories she kept stored in those items, and so had no need for anything new, except for those things that refused to keep, like eggs and butter and milk.

By her first few visits to the Bombay Market, Louise had already found herself introduced not only to Bimal, but to his son, his son's wife and a few of their children. She decided that she liked all of them well enough; they were polite, hard working and smelled just fine, and, besides, it never hurt to have some friendly faces nearby in that neighborhood. (The muggings had diminished considerably since most of her neighbors were Asians, but racial tensions, of as many varieties as there were races in New York, still made the streets too often unsafe.) Still, Louise wondered why Bimal himself seemed so particularly attentive to her, especially when there were so many other customers in need of charming.

On perhaps her tenth visit, just before closing, when only Bimal was behind the cash register, she found him more loquacious than ever, and wondered if she would ever escape with her quart of milk.

"Louise, I see that you have some interest in these figures. Do you like them?"

Louise had only been glancing at the statuary which was prominently displayed on the counter, just to the left of the cash register, to avoid the almost hypnotic effect of Bimal's brown eyes. To be polite, though, she responded:

"Yes, it's . . . well, it's very different."

"Do you wonder what it represents?" he himself wondered.

"No, no, not really," she honestly responded. He seemed a little offended by her lack of curiosity, so she hastily added (she wasn't certain why) "Oh, but if you have the time to explain."

"Yes, it would be a pleasure. You see this is a statue representing Vishnu, the Preserver, one of our most important gods, and his consort Lakshmi."

"Who's who?" she asked, her curiosity up a bit.

"Well, you see, Vishnu, he is the larger one with the four hands—you can tell it's him because he holds the mace in one hand—see it—and the conch in the other. At his feet on this bed of snakes is his consort, the goddess of good fortune. She has you see, her one palm down—that symbolizes prosperity—and her other hand up to give a blessing. I hope she will continue to bless our endeavors. This statue has been in my family for hundreds of years."

"That's very nice," she said, sincerely. She was particularly impressed by the age and family value of the statue, something her own children never seemed to appreciate, when they kept invoking her to "get rid of some of this junk," but then she remembered who she was and had to add: "but I was raised Catholic; we only believe in one God."

"So do we, really, Louise. You see we have, much like you Catholics, a trinity of Gods. Brahma is the creator, not unlike your God the Father, then we have Vishnu here, the Preserver, and Shiva the Undoer, and all the the rest of our gods you might compare to your own saints. So, we have many gods, but we believe not only that there is but one God, but that there is really but one reality, and we all are part of one whole. We believe that we all have to go through many lives, reincarnations, to get closer and closer to the one truth, the one God."

"That's very interesting," Louise said, though really she found it confusing, even troubling, but she had no wish to denigrate another's faith, not even this odd man and his weird religion. "Very interesting," she repeated.

"Yes, well I suppose it's quite strange to you, isn't it? But, it's like your Shakespeare said; 'There are more things in life than are dreamt of in your philosophy.' Do I have that right, Louise?"

"Oh, I'm sure you do," she responded, sure at least that she had no clue about anything Shakespeare might have had to say, and wondering how a man like this, someone her son might call a "monkey" or a "Gunga Din" could. Her puzzlement was too great. She smiled and merely said, "Thanks so much, good night now."

Louise Domenico walked home with almost a bit of fear at her side. She was not so much troubled by what Bimal Das had told her, but more by the memory of his magnetic eyes. Yet she was not so troubled as to discontinue her trips to the Bombay Market.

II

Over the next several weeks Louise Domenico learned more about Bimal Das and India. She discovered that his certain command of English had come from a college education in Bombay and a career as a personnel manager in that same city. He had left India when his firm had been closed for "political reasons" and when his own safety was jeopardized by those politics. He had been unable to take much out of India with him; he had had to live with a cousin in Brooklyn for a number of years before finally having enough to get his own store and the apartment above it on Liberty Avenue. He was a widower five years; his wife just had not been able to adjust to America, to all that was so new; he himself had eventually found all the mixing of culture and the many opportunities exciting, in spite of his age. Louise came to admire his spirit; he seemed to enjoy her common-sense, honest approach to life, to understand her respect for the past, and so a friendship began. Still, Louise did not make much of it, particularly to her children, for fear they would make too much of it and disapprove.

Louise left Queens for a week in April; her daughter Bettina had a week off from work and insisted that her mother spend it with her in Westchester (Scarsdale, specifically, where Louise's son-in-law was prominent in dermatology); Louise enjoyed her time there well enough, but was happy to return to her own house. In among her mail, though, she found an unexpected note; it was from Bimal Das.

> *Dearest Louise,*
>
> *This is the first week since we opened our store that you have not graced it by your presence. I hope I did not presume too greatly in trying to telephone you, but since I received no response I have decided on this note. I'm hoping you are well and will soon return. I look to you as a personal Lakshmi, a goddess of good fortune, since we have had nothing but good luck since you began frequenting our humble market. May you be always well.*
>
> *Cordially,*
>
> *Bimal Das*

Louise did not know whether to be charmed or alarmed by this letter. To be compared in any sense to a goddess made her want to giggle. "Louise, now you're a goddess," she laughed to herself as she looked in the mirror and saw an old woman, a mere 5 feet tall, squat, with thick glasses, her grey hair in a simple bun, a dark blue dress older than her time in Queens, a face weathered by the loneliness of time—what kind of goddess could she be? And yet no one had used such words in describing her ever before in her life, not even Sam, when she had been young and not unlovely; somehow she found the present image flattering, but opposed to the preservation of her dead husband's love. "Me, a goddess," she repeated, both puzzled and amused.

But Bimal Das did not share her amusement when she presented it to him a few days later.

"Do not deride the spirit of my concern, please," he petitioned, more offended than she could have imagined possible, as she spoke to him in a corner of the store:

"Oh, I'm sorry, it's not your concern I was talking about, just the goddess thing. I'm a little old to be a goddess, don't you think?"

"I thought I had told you, in my faith time and space are meaningless commodities, less real, less lasting than the milk you purchase. As a matter of fact, and I have hesitated to tell you this, in the wisdom of your eyes, even now when they are laughing, you remind me very much of a woman I knew when I was a very small child in India, and within the boundaries of my beliefs, you may be that woman, reborn. You may be unaware of past lives, but your eyes remind you of them, in spite of your laughter."

Louise wanted to laugh again, but his words were too serious, too troubled to allow it. His words had a passion that startled her, that seemed to suggest an interest beyond a friendly proprietor's province. She thanked him for his concern and hurried home.

A few days later she found in her mailbox a small package contained inside a plastic bag from "Bimal's Bombay Market"; inside was a statue, deep cerulean, less than two feet high, of a man with a bull's head. A note from Das explained the gift:

> *The god Shiva is often represented in this form. He is the 'Undoer' a translation I prefer to 'Destroyer' because he is not evil; sometimes we need to undo the old, to make way for the new. This statue was a gift to me from my wife; it is precious to me, but I would like you to have it, and consider the role of Shiva in our lives. Would it perhaps be too forward of me to invite you to an Indian dinner—there is a very authentic restaurant not far from here; you would honor me if you said yes. You touch a strange chord in my heart; I cannot even explain why, except that perhaps I understand your pain and the way you reverence your past. I may seem foolish to you, but I believe we each carry the gifts of many lives; we should not be overwhelmed by the details of any one of them. I say too much—I will await your reply.*
>
> *Bimal Das*

Unfortunately for Das, it was a Saturday, the day when Louise's son Tony and his wife Alice came to take her to the supermarket. When Tony got a look at the statue and the note which he grabbed from his still distracted mother, he flew into a rage:

"The nerve of that nigger! Where the hell's he come off asking you out?"

"He's not a nigger, is he, Mom?" Alice corrected, "He's Indian, right?"

"Oh, I beg your pardon, what's with this Sabu then, this curry powder punk asking her out? These people are unreal! First they take over the neighborhood, buy all the houses and live twenty in a house, like animals, they stink up the neighborhood, and now he's got the nerve to want to get his dirty hands on my mother! I've got a good mind to walk over there and remind him that there's still a few white people with something to say in this part of town!"

"Stop, stop!" Louise shouted, "I'll tell him myself, you just stay out of this," she implored, crying.

"Well, sure, sure, Ma, okay," Tony responded to her tears. "I just don't want him bothering you. We'll make sure we really stock up on groceries this trip so you don't have to go in the middle of the week anymore. You know if you'd let me get you a new refrigerator like I've wanted to, you could keep milk more than three days."

"Yes, yes, okay," she responded, absently, the somehow eternal image of Das's eyes turning her to stone, the deeply glazed blue stone of the bull-man she still held in her hand.

III

Louise Domenico waited three days before getting up the nerve to go to confront Bimal Das, to tell him to leave her alone, to let him know she would not be buying any more milk from him, to give him back his statue. She waited until almost 9PM, closing time, when he would be there by himself and at most a customer or two would be around. She carried the statue in the same plastic bag she had received it in and thought of what she might say: how she respected him and his culture but how he had to realize they were too old and too different; how she had been raised to stick to her own kind; how she had no interest in any man of any kind, anyway. But when Louise and her courage got close to the Bombay Market, she looked up and saw an inordinate number of people milling around the entrance; a few of them were police officers. She somehow managed to get close enough to see inside where Bimal's family was trying to console him, as they stood in the midst of knocked over merchandise and broken shelves and statues. Das had lost his normal, placid countenance; he was screeching alternately in English and in a language foreign to Louise. What he seemed most concerned about was the statue of Vishnu and Lakshmi that was shattered in many pieces on the floor, with the rest of his good fortune. "Why, why would they do this? What have I done to them?" he lamented, and Louise thought she heard in that lament, in the indignation of sorrow and misuse, a voice from the distant past, the voice of her father's father, who had also cried out "Why?" ("Ma, perchè, perchè?") when the front windows of his modest home in Brooklyn had been shattered by rocks hurled by young Irishmen who did not want a "Wop" in their neighborhood. A stunning sense of what she had heard others call "deja vu" engulfed her; her imagination, her shock made Das sound just like her grandfather. She overheard enough of the conversation around her to discover that a group of young, marauding white "punks," perhaps Italian, had decided to "make a statement" at Bimal's market. That statement of unexamined hate followed Louise back home; she knew she could not return Das's gift, repel his advances, while his plight so closely resembled that of a family member, a memory of her past.

IV

A week later, in the early morning, when few customers yet graced the Bombay market, which had been back in business two days after the attack, Louise Domenico held that same plastic bag she had meant to take to Das the previous week. She seemed as determined in her resolve to deliver the contents of the bag to the market's proprietor.

When Das saw her and what she held in her hands, he asked her to step into a room away from the customers, the better to talk to her:

"Oh, Louise, it's been so many days since I sent you my gift and my invitation. I meant to call, but, I don't know if you know, we had, some, some trouble here, and I've been so busy trying to recover and so, sad, really, about the trouble, and about not hearing from you, and now, now I see (he indicated the bag) that I was right to be worried about your response."

"No, no this . . ." she stammered, searching for an articulateness to match his and finding herself failing,"but this isn't what you think, I, ah, well, here, take it."

She gave him the bag and inside was a statue, about the same size as the one he had given her, but of an entirely different sort. It was not the representation of a Hindu god, but of a young Catholic saint, a woman, with a benign smile and her hands folded in prayer.

"Who, who is this?" he questioned, both charmed and amazed.

"It's Saint Fortunata. She's not a big saint or anything, but she was the patron of our old church, our old parish in Brooklyn, where Sam and I lived before we moved here, where we got married; I almost forgot I had it. I don't know much about her; she was a martyr, a virgin, but I know her name, Fortunata, is Italian, for, you know, luck, the fortunate one, so I thought, since I saw you lost your other one, well, this can't replace that, you had it so long, but, well, I wanted you to have it."

Bimal Das said nothing, in part because he was overcome by the grace of the simple gift he held in his hands, and in part because he could see Louise was still struggling, had still more she wanted to say.

"And listen," she continued, "I don't know if I'm ready for Indian food, it might be too spicy, but, especially since you've had all this trouble, why don't you let me make you dinner, come over for pasta; I not only make the sauce homemade but the macaroni too—my own grandmother's recipe, and you could maybe bring the dessert if you want. Do you have good desserts in India?"

"Well, of course we do, Louise, don't you remember?" he smiled.

Louise Domenico surprised herself once more that morning by getting Das's joke, something about reincarnation, she rightly reckoned, right there in Richmond Hill, Queens, and she laughed, looking back to Bimal with an eternity of understanding and good will.

Louella Bryant

Dare's Tractor

When Dare turned the station wagon from macadam onto the logging road, Homer lifted his head and whined. Linea grabbed the door handle as the car staggered in and out of ruts dried from mud season's thaw and then bumped over rocks and roots as the path grew narrower. She looked out the window and frowned at new growth sprouting thick as whiskers along the drive.

At her feet, the thermos sloshed and the lunch bag rattled. She thought about the pungent crunch of dill pickle. Coming out to Dare's land always made her hungry.

The car lumbered into the meadow, and Dare cut the engine. Most of his fifteen acres were treed, but Dare, who liked order in the midst of chaos, had cleared a lower slope and mowed it with the tractor.

Saturday morning sunlight spread over the grass like marmalade. Ferns uncoiled under maples, sticky with new leaves.

"You ready?" Dare had his door open, a leg out of the car. Homer was already trotting toward the woods, nose to the ground. Every weekend for the three years they'd been married—every weekend there was less than a foot of snow on the ground—they came to cut trees from the ridge where Dare planned to build a house someday, a dream he had before he met Linea, a dream in which she wondered if Dare considered her at all.

"Ready-Freddy." Linea got out and stretched, then pretended to look for spring migrants, trying not to let on she was really watching Dare open the wagon's back end and spread a towel on the ground. He slipped off his loafers and stepped on the towel. In one motion, he pulled his belt loose from the buckle, unbuttoned his khakis, and let them slip down. He folded the pants twice and placed them in the trunk. He liked to keep his city clothes clean, in case they stopped somewhere for dinner on the way home. The dungarees, black with grime, lay atop the toolbox, and Dare slipped them on over his plaid boxers. Cruddy as the jeans were, Linea liked the way they fit him, gripping his behind affectionately. He had a nice build for a man nearing middle-age. Working the land kept him fit. After he'd changed into his flannel shirt and tucked it into the pants, he sat on the bumper and pushed his feet into the old work boots.

Linea knew the routine. Next he'd be sliding the tarp off the tractor, starting her up, prodding her toward the house site.

"I'll head on up," she said.

"Want a ride?" He grinned.

"No thanks." He liked to tease her with the tractor, even though he knew she didn't like the noise of it, the brutishness. If she'd admit it, she was jealous of the thing. Dare had gotten the old Case from a Bristol farmer, who had bought it used and worked it thirty summers. Every spring, if he were lucky, Dare needed only to charge the battery, but if he wasn't, he'd have a flatbed haul the whole business all the way to Bridport for diagnosis and physical therapy. Dare kept its orange metal polished and rode it like a prize thoroughbred.

"Come on, Homer," Linea said. She started toward the path she and Dare had cut last summer, him with the chainsaw while she followed, swinging a machete at berry bushes. Now the swath was broad enough for two, although uneven and mottled with rocks.

Near the spring, she hopped over wet leaves and soggy ground. At the first brush pile, the climb got steeper. She took off her sweatshirt and tugged the sleeves into a knot at her waist. Overhead she saw a flash of red—a cardinal—and somewhere a white-throated sparrow chirped. Below, the tractor growled to life and Linea broke into a jog.

Just as she reached the house site, Dare came over the rise perched six feet above the ground, neck craned to check the tractor's tiny front wheels bumping over rough trail. The rear wheel treads left giant chicken tracks in the soft soil. He pulled the thug toward her, and she jumped out of its way.

When he turned off the engine and hopped down, she said, "You bring the saw for me?"

He plucked the handsaw off the tractor and handed it to her. "Watch yourself," he said. "Last time a tree hit you on the head, remember?"

It had been a thin sapling, but she'd forgotten to push the trunk away from her as she cut so the tree would fall in the other direction. The tree hadn't hurt her much, just startled her, but she was glad for Dare's concern. Once in a while she felt the tiniest pinprick of suspicion that he had married her for her cooking, her housekeeping, her good-natured sweating weekend labor on the land.

"Any particular area?" she asked.

Dare looked around and pointed to a grove of young growth.

"Start in on those," he said. "You can haul branches down here when I'm finished felling." He peered at the dog. "Keep an eye on Homer, okay?"

Dare had rescued the scrawny beagle from some hooligans in the north end of town, a pellet wound in the shoulder and another in the hip, as if they'd been using him for target practice. Linea had tried to get Dare to deposit him at the Humane Society, but he insisted on nursing the dog back to health first—it had been through enough, he'd said. She drew the line at the mutt sleeping on the bed, and it took to the rug on Dare's side. When it was perfectly healed, not even a limp, Linea said she'd be glad to drive the dog to the shelter. But Dare said, "What's the point?" and the canine had stayed.

Linea's sneakers pressed into dewy moss. Two dead apple trees stood like black bones among the younger saplings, their branches snapping off with barely a touch. She picked out a tree whose trunk was no bigger than her wrist, gangly as a teenager, and bent to dig the saw teeth into the base. It would take another year of weekends to open the view to the mountain ridge. Linea was just as happy with brick and cement, streetlights and shopping centers, but Dare said he preferred the morning alarm of squawking crows to city sirens. "Celestial," he said of their caws. Nuisance, Linea called them, but she'd never tell Dare that. He had not solicited her preferences when he sketched the house design. She would have liked a big country kitchen, a walk-in closet, a deep laundry room, not the austere bungalow that outlined its floor plan under his pencil lead. She supposed she could hang her clothes on hooks, if need be, and wash her laundry in the kitchen sink, if that's what it took. At her age, she understood compromise.

The tree gave way, catching on limbs as it tumbled. Linea took the saw and severed the last tendon of bark holding to the stump then grabbed the base of the trunk and dragged the tree to the brush pile. She swept herself off and arched her back to pull the muscles back into place. At least she was firming up, her arms getting definition. The work was good, the air fresh and clean.

The smell of the chainsaw's exhaust invaded the aroma of pine needles. Linea hiked to the ledge to check on Dare. Here was a man—legs braced, chainsaw gnawing and spewing fumes—a warrior on a battlefield, tree trunks scattered around him like the mortally wounded. She enjoyed a moment of pleasure, of ownership if she allowed herself, before figuring she'd better get back to her task.

Forgetting where she'd put the handsaw, she headed toward the grove to look for it. When she passed the tractor, its engine ticked, cooling. What did Dare see in this old thing, anyway, pocked with pebble dents and scratches he'd filled in with touch-up paint? She walked behind the giant rear wheels and punched the rubber.

The grinding of the chainsaw stopped. Her watch said it was not yet noon, too early to break for lunch. Maybe Dare was ready to have her haul severed limbs. From somewhere, Homer howled. She'd forgotten to look out for the dog. Down the slope, she found him next to Dare, who was on the ground, cradling his right knee.

Why hadn't she insisted on that cell phone? But, then, they were up a road that was no road, and she wasn't sure she could even have given directions to their spot. How many miles off Route 116? How far down the dirt road? She could recall no landmarks for the turn onto the property. And neighbors? What neighbors? She always worried about him with that saw—one distraction and he could lose a leg.

But she was wasting time and Dare was hurt. She slipped coming down the hill and took her time getting up. She had to be careful, couldn't sprain an ankle or they'd both be stranded. The smell of exhaust swirled with the stench of composting leaves and the fragrance of sawdust, confusing her.

When she reached him, she did a quick scan and found no blood—a good sign.

"Dare!" she said, but his name was lost under Homer's barking.

"Quiet," she yelled. Had she kicked the dog? The beagle backed up and yelped.

Dare winced. "Think I snapped a tendon."

"Here," she said. "Let me help you to where it's flat. Can you walk?"

"I don't know." He flipped himself over, balanced on hands and the good leg, like a sprinter about to take off. "Better get me a stick to lean on."

Running up the slope, she noticed how the moss changed under her feet. Below the ridge it looked like tiny spruce trees, but up top it was tight clumps with needle-sharp spikes that pricked through her sneakers. She wished she'd worn leather boots.

When she brought him a branch from the brush pile, he put

his weight on it and limped toward the tractor, grimacing.

"I wish you'd wear a hardhat," she said, walking ahead of him—he didn't like to be helped. "It's dangerous working way up here, no one within screaming distance. Did you ever think of that?" They'd been through all this before, but she needed to hear herself talk, the sound of her own voice nurturing her confidence.

When she realized Dare wasn't answering, she turned. He was lying on the embankment, spread eagle, as if admiring the view.

She thought for a minute he might be playing a trick on her, as he had the first spring they were together, when he made the bent nail look like it had gone through his finger, dribbled with blood-colored paint. She had fumbled for the keys and had him halfway to the car before he started to laugh, as if her concern had made her foolish.

"Are you okay?" she asked.

"The knee's bad," he said.

A strange indignation flushed through her. How dare he injure himself, leaving her stranded on this wild hillside.

"I'll go for help," she said.

"Where?" He tried to laugh, flinched instead.

She could drive back toward town—there was a phone at the general store where they always stopped for a cold drink. Or she could keep driving, pick up a bottle of good wine on the way. At the townhouse, she could make a nice salad, and, later, sort through Dare's clothes, making piles for the secondhand store, for the trash, then make some excuse Monday morning when the electronics store called to ask why he hadn't shown up for work. She would be as she'd been before Dare, which wasn't all that bad, really. The coyotes and foxes and insects would deal with Dare, and, eventually, the saplings would grow up again, and what was left of him would be lost in the jungle of his property.

But, no. She had this mess to deal with, her two-hundred-pound husband with a busted knee. She wouldn't be able to carry him out—they were three or four hundred yards from the station wagon. She looked around for Homer and heard him yipping off in the distance. She hoped Dare hadn't seen her kick him.

"You'll have to get the tractor," he said.

"The tractor?"

Years ago, farmers used horses to pull out rocks and plow a field. A horse made sense—you could talk to a horse. But this machine had no soul. Unless she wanted to count the soul Dare had put into it. Tinkering with the engine, filing the plugs, catching oil drips in a pan, covering it with the tarp each time they left the land. Dare had said the first thing he wanted to build was a shed for the tractor. She'd run better if she had a shelter, he'd said. Sometimes Linea believed he loved that brute more than he loved her.

She trudged up to the Case, put her foot on the L-shaped step, grabbed the steering wheel and pulled herself up. Her butt swung around and flopped onto the seat, which was curved to match the shape of a man's derriere, with a little lump in the front between the legs like a Western saddle. The gearshift lever came up between her knees, and there were two foot pedals—brake and clutch, she supposed. But which was which was anybody's guess. The back wheels bulged like big thighs, and she reached out and rested a hand on a fender, as Dare did sometimes when he drove. The steering wheel bent slightly to the left so it looked as if you were heading toward the right when you were really going straight. The throttle was just behind the wheel, a lever for giving it gas. It seemed simple enough.

Dare had left the key in the ignition, and Linea reached for the starter button. When she stomped on the left pedal and pressed the button, the engine coughed, then erupted into a chorus of grunting pigs. The gear rod was cold on her fingers, but she gripped hard and yanked toward what she hoped was first, guessing it worked on a standard H format, and let out the clutch. The machine lurched forward, and she had to jerk the steering wheel to avoid a pine tree. The left front wheel came off the ground, and then the tractor righted itself.

Going down the steep incline, she nearly swallowed her tongue. She kept her foot on the right pedal, which looked like a brake and must have been because she managed to keep it under control.

Below, the ground leveled out, and this is where she headed, assuming it would be easier to get Dare down the slope than up it. She found neutral and let the engine idle while she went to him. When she lifted his foot, he sucked his lips in between his teeth and crab-walked, dragging his rear end over the moss. At the tractor, she paused to figure out the best way to mount him onto it. She considered draping him over the engine, using her sweatshirt to tie him around the tractor's nose, but the heat might burn him, or something might fly loose and kill him. He'd have to get up on the thing, lean on the fender next to her, using his arms to keep the weight off the leg.

She propped him against the engine, got her shoulders under his bottom and hefted him onto the tractor. He wedged himself behind the seat, leaning against the fender.

"You all right that way?"

He nodded, his eyes dark.

"Jesus, Dare," she said. "You've always been so careful—how'd you manage to hurt yourself?"

Dare stared at the treetops, where a black crow watched, head tilted in curiosity.

Linea took her place on the tractor and heaved a deep breath. "You hang on, you hear?" She was talking to herself as much as to Dare.

Jamming the rod into gear, she coaxed the tractor forward, between two maples, onto the winding path. She was getting the hang of it, almost enjoying herself.

Coming around the last corner, the trail took a left up a hill before it opened into the meadow.

"You'll have to downshift to get up this pitch," Dare yelled over the motor.

Which way was down? When she muscled the lever, the engine sounded as if it were choking to death.

"Back and to the left, nice and easy," he said.

While she was trying to distinguish left from right, back from front, her foot slipped off the clutch and the tractor bolted forward. Homer, gray rabbit dangling from his jowls, stood rooted in the way. Linea knew he wanted Dare, wanted to show him the prize, but how to get to him? The dog apparently figured the best way was straight ahead, and he shot toward the tractor.

The path was too narrow to turn, too narrow for the dog to run alongside.

"Brake!" Dare said.

Which was the brake? She hit the right pedal and only after the big rear wheel bumped over the dog's body did she realize she should have pushed in the clutch as well.

Somehow Dare was on the ground, kneeling beside the dog, bad leg appearing to give him no trouble. He lifted the dog's body, draping the limp carcass over his arm. Homer's tongue hung from his mouth, a drop of saliva clinging to the tip.

"I'm sorry, Dare," Linea pleaded. The dog's glassy eyes stared at her.

After a minute Dare looked up from the lifeless pup.

"You never liked Homer, did you?" he said, incrimination in his voice.

"I'll bury him," she said, "after we get you to a doctor."

"I don't need a doctor," he said, getting to his feet, cradling the dog against his chest like a sleeping baby.

Overhead, a crow laughed a grating, mocking screech.

Linea got down from the tractor. Then she walked toward the station wagon, leaving Dare by his tractor, on his land, his dead dog in his arms.

Cathleen Calbert

Greece

It was my wife's idea. Perhaps that's worth emphasizing. She was the one who suggested a baby. I just complied. Voilà: blue-line, pink line, success. I brought home champagne and oysters to celebrate.

Even so, the pregnancy seemed hard on her, a shock to the system. Well, she'd spent thirty years alone in her sleek body. I'd call her streamlined. The kind of woman who does things quickly. Walks fast, gets in a lot of talking before breakfast, sorts out paperwork like a postal worker on speed.

It wasn't that she slowed down or gained weight or anything. In fact, she grew even thinner the first couple of months. I told her I hoped she wasn't carrying Rosemary's Baby: a little comic relief. I knew it must be rough trying to make it through her long days and not look like some demon seed was sprouting inside her.

The doctor said that she should spend the last few months in bed. Time to lie back for a change, watch some TV. She just had to recline and let the baby do its thing. And that's what happened. Her face turned shiny and pink, freckles melted back into her skin, and her stomach swelled underneath her nightie.

She was in labor for over thirty hours. I helped with her breathing and let her scream. I didn't say anything when she bit me. But it took me aback. When you marry a woman, you don't look ahead to a day when she will try to rip the flesh off your hand with her teeth.

Then it was over, and we saw what we'd achieved: a beautiful baby. I beamed at my wife, and she beamed back at me, and we both beamed at the baby. On the way home from the hospital, my wife chattered happily about painting stars and clouds on the ceiling of the baby's room, how much she loved the baby, how much she loved me, how great it would be to stay home and take care of the baby.

Because that was the plan. Everything was ready. Shirts the size of handkerchiefs hung in a neat row. We had gotten the books, the bibs, the booties, and we'd set up the state-of-the-art crib, little lambs hanging overhead like woolly clouds.

We devoted the first weekend exclusively to the baby. We tried to bathe it in the kitchen sink until it started screaming and my wife started weeping. Then we folded the baby into the white blanket trimmed with blue bears and pink hearts and lay beside it on the living room rug, holding hands. There we were: a happily married couple with our new baby.

Monday morning, I went back to work. I made myself some breakfast, knotted my tie, and kissed my wife, who lay dozing in bed, the baby's mouth suctioned to her left breast, which looked shiny and swollen sticking out of her nightie. I stroked the smooth skin, and she moaned, putting her hand to her forehead. I wanted to climb back in bed with her, but I closed the door behind me, giving her a chance to start the day slowly.

At first, everything went swimmingly. By the end of that week, she was adept at sticking the little arms into the little shirts, and by the end of the second she could tenderize chicken breasts with one hand while the other held the baby's head to her nipple.

That was another thing. My wife started cooking. I thought we'd rely on take-out or delivery like we did before. But my wife picked up a few women's magazines, the kind she usually didn't even bother to paw through in checkout lines. By the end of the third week, she was subscribing to five of them. I'd come home, and there would be Chicken Paprika, carrot curls and rose radishes on the side, Lemon Whip for dessert. I told her she didn't have to, but she said it was interesting. She thought I was interesting too. She'd pour me the wine that she couldn't drink. Then she'd watch me.

"Is it good?" she'd ask the moment I got a mouthful of food in.

"It's great," I'd say. It always tasted fine to me. Home-cooking was a treat.

"So what happened today?" she'd say. "How'd it shake out with Spinelli?" That sort of thing. I'd talk while she jiggled the baby.

I don't know when everything started to get balled up.

To be honest, I didn't see that much of the baby. I'd propped a heart-shaped frame with the baby's picture on my desk, but that was from the first weekend of the baby's life, and it looked more like one of those blind newborn mice than anything. I didn't see my wife that much either. But it's not as if I abandoned her. I was usually home by eight. We'd have Swedish meatballs and fresh-cut green beans or whatever. Before long, the baby would fuss, then all the Goodnight, Baby rituals. I tried to help, but I was all thumbs. Too big or loud or clumsy. Besides, I never knew where she kept anything. Still, I don't think that bedtime behavior was good for her, or for me, or for the baby. After my wife twinkled up the "Mary Had a Little Lamb" number half a dozen times, she'd kneel beside the crib and whisper, "Please. Please. Please. Please. Please." I don't know. Is that supposed to help? It didn't sound helpful to me.

Before long, she stopped exercising with Renée on TV. My wife told me that herself. It wasn't like I checked her thighs for cottage cheese. She said that if she saw Renée's perky face again, she'd scream. I laughed. She said that if she saw Renée's perky butt again she'd knock over the TV. Well, I laughed. I thought she was trying to be funny. Except she wouldn't quit. If she saw Renée on the street, her life wouldn't be worth a hill of beans.

Then there were the cakes.

We'd been having dessert after dinner ever since the magazine thing got going. Date bars, peaches and cream, instant pudding. She tried a "White Cloud" cake from scratch, but its layers didn't rise beyond the height of three fat pancakes. We tossed it. No big deal. It wasn't like I said I had to eat cake or I'd go crazy. The night following the White Cloud defeat, she served up one of those supermarket bargains with ice cream. The cake was okay. It's not as though it was a big topic of conversation. It disappeared from the fridge in what I'd say was the normal time span for cake disappearances, nothing alarming.

But the day after she tossed the empty cardboard, a new cake appeared. Another grocery store job yet bigger, fancier, with sliced almonds around the sides and dollops of chocolate circling the rim. Then they started coming in a steady stream: bundt cakes, carrot cakes, orange cakes, spice cakes, Boston creams. We'd have a slice after dinner, then, boom, the cake was gone, another taking its place the next night.

After a few weeks of this, I poked my head in the fridge to find a huge blue box from the upscale French bakery. Everything had been shoved aside to fit it in. I opened the carton, and stood there blinking at an enormous, whipped cream concoction, all peaks and cherries. It was the biggest cake I'd ever seen.

"My God," I said.

My wife came in behind me and peered over my shoulder. "It's something, isn't it?"

I lowered the lid and closed the refrigerator door without saying anything.

When she called me in to dinner, I found thick white slabs on our dinner plates. It must have been a quarter of the cake each. My wife pulled her napkin out of the elephant napkin ring, flicked it in the air, and gracefully laid it in her lap. Then she forked a mouthful.

"Honey," I said.

"Yes?" she said, her voice creamy.

I didn't have the heart to say anything, but I knew something was going on. And I was right. That was the end of her cooking. Instead, she took to weeping.

"She's been trying so hard," my wife wailed when I walked through the door. I handed her a Kleenex from the box she'd placed on top of the TV. The commercial about a distraught woman with waxy build-up ended, and another with skillet dinners began.

"You've been cooped up for awhile," I said. I patted her bare knee, which looked good to me; it wasn't as if I could see the cakes reappearing in her body. "Maybe you need to get out more. Take in a movie."

"But the baby," my wife said, looking up at me, sniffling.

"The baby's not old enough to go to the movies."

Apparently, once again I hadn't said the right thing. She stared at a commercial for feminine protection.

"What if someone else looked after the baby?" I asked her.

"You?"

"No, no," I said. "Someone who could help with things. Regularly."

She began ripping up her pile of tissues. "I don't know," she said. My wife could look very young when she shrugged, especially when she wasn't dressed. "Another woman?"

I ran my hand up her thigh. The thigh looked pretty good too. Renée or no Renée. I said, "Wouldn't it be nice to have someone in who knew what she was doing?"

"Like I don't?" She pushed my hand away.

I looked around the place so she could see I was looking. It wasn't neat as a pin anymore. I'd written "Dust me" on the TV with my finger, and the screen stayed that way. Then I glanced at my wife to show that I'd noticed the mismatched socks, the stained nightgown, the lopsided ponytail of uncombed hair.

"I take good care of the baby," she said and jutted her chin out at me.

That was true enough. Whatever else, the baby got its due. "But the baby's clothes," I said quietly.

"What's the matter with the baby's clothes?" she said. "I spend a lot of time on those clothes."

I lifted the baby out of its playpen, confronting her with the black satin pantaloons, the tiny maroon cape tied below its chin, the red velvet hat on its head.

My wife turned back to the TV.

"I'll call an agency in the morning," I said. "Okay, sweetheart? Let me do this for you?"

"You can jerk off for all I care," my wife said, and she didn't usually say such things.

I knew I had to get on this one in a hurry. I made the initial calls from the office and got the ball rolling. My secretary, Bev, interviewed the women because my wife wouldn't have anything to do with the project. Bev came through for me before the end of the week. "I think I've got her," Bev said. "I think she's what your wife needs."

When I told my wife, she threw the *TV Guide* at me before she ran into the bedroom crying. Of course, I followed her. I did the usual back-patting, there, there, baby.

"So is she some hot babe?" she asked me.

"Some hot babe?"

"She'll come into my home and take care of both of you?"

"You're thinking of a movie, honey." Laughing, I held her in my arms and kept patting. But she'd gotten me going. I pictured Giselle, Danielle, Justine. Some lithe nineteen-year-old with slender thighs and pert breasts that peeked out of her clothing as she stretched and stooped around the house. She'd be French. She'd be lonely. She'd look up to me. I put my hand between my wife's thighs, and she finally let me.

It turns out, her name *was* Danielle, and she was good-looking. Not wispy French though. Dark brows and light brown skin. Cropped brown hair. She looked hearty. The kind of woman who has calves, like she could run a marathon and afterwards make everybody something to eat.

My wife stayed in the kitchen while I gave Danielle the tour. Then I took her to the baby.

"Here's our darling." I gestured toward the crib.

Danielle reached in, scooping up the baby, who was dressed in a black-and-white striped jumpsuit, a black-and-white pillbox hat on its head. She laughed, holding the baby out to get a look at the get-up. It took me a few seconds. Then I understood. The baby was a jailbird.

"So," I said, a proud papa smile plastered on my face. "Everything okay?"

She brought the baby to her chest and looked at me. "Sure, we'll be fine."

"Honey, I'll leave you and Danielle to get acquainted," I said to the bathroom door.

"Go fuck your mother," my wife yelled. "And leave me the hell alone." This last part also was screamed.

When I walked into the living room, Danielle was seated on the couch, cradling the baby, her mouth in a downward smile.

"I'm sorry," I said. "My wife is . . . uneasy."

"I understand," she said. "It'll be okay."

But it wasn't okay. My wife wouldn't let Danielle near the baby again. She got one of those front-packs and strapped the baby to her chest. She vacuumed with the baby, dusted with the baby, and washed out the tub with the baby against her breasts.

Danielle called me at work and said she wondered if she was doing any of us any good. I told her it did a lot for me just to know she was there. I said she should meet me for coffee, we could talk about things. She said she'd be happy to at the first opportunity. I said that for the time being she should sit back and relax. And that's what she did. When I came home, Danielle was eating Cheeze Doodles, her muscular legs taking up the couch. It seemed to me with legs like that she should be running up and down the street, but she just smiled at me cheesily. I heard the roar of my wife's devotion to her domestic duties coming from the bedroom.

But a person can only keep up with something so long. Monday morning, my wife couldn't get out of bed. She'd brought the baby in some time during the night, and it lay sleeping on her chest. I was surprised she hadn't glued it to her. When she heard me, she tried to lift her head from the pillow. Finally, she gave up.

"I can't do it," she said, a woman defeated.

I called Danielle in from the other room. She put down her donut and followed me.

"Take it easy," Danielle said as she lifted the baby out of my wife's arms and into the crook of hers. "I'm here to help you."

I closed the door behind me.

When I came home that night, they were watching TV, the baby plunked in its crawler wearing a pink tutu and a rhinestone tiara.

"Well, hello," I said. "There's my . . . baby." I hesitated at the outfit but didn't want to disturb the peace, so I chucked the baby under its chin. "And my two favorite ladies."

Danielle smiled and offered me some Nachos. My wife didn't say anything, but she let me kiss her cheek.

The next night when I came home, the television was off. Female laughter floated from the kitchen along with the smell of cooking. I found my wife chopping salad greens while Danielle rocked the baby, who was dressed in Farmer John overalls and waving two small red cows in the air.

"Dinner's almost ready," my wife told me.

"Great," I said. "You ladies are going to spoil me." I beamed at the two of them. "What are we having?"

"Salad and spaghetti," my wife said. She began slicing up a loaf of Italian bread.

"Great," I said. I yawned nonchalantly and opened the fridge. No cake. "Great."

The following night I almost fell over the coat rack when I came in. The place was pitch-black. After I managed to hit the lights, I looked around for a message, but there wasn't any. It occurred to me that my wife and baby had been home every night since I'd had them. I mean, since we had our baby. I made myself a martini and waited. Checked my watch. Checked to make sure the phone was working. Turned on the TV. Made myself another martini. I ended up passing out on the couch. When I woke up, it was morning, my wife asleep in our bed, the baby asleep in its crib.

"Honey," I said, shaking her. "Did you go out last night?"

"Mm hm," she said, turning away.

"How come?"

She mumbled into her pillow.

"What?"

"Everybody wanted to go dancing."

"What are you talking about?" I said, but my wife was snoring.

The night after that, I opened the front door cautiously. The lights were on. I smelled something warm and cheesy. "Hello?" I called. When I walked into the kitchen, no laughing women greeted me. I opened the oven: two trays of lasagna. A slow dread settled into my stomach as I cracked the refrigerator door. Still, I sucked in my breath as I saw a blue box from the French bakery. I slit the tape and looked in: Mocha Swirl.

"Honey," I shouted. No answer. The bathroom door was open. Empty. The bedroom door was closed. I quickly pulled it open. Empty. I looked in the baby's crib. No baby. "Honey," I said, but I wasn't really calling anymore. "Danielle. Baby."

I made a pitcher of martinis and brought it into the living room. As I sat down on the couch, I noticed a white rectangle taped to the TV. I got up, pulled it off, and read, *Everybody wanted to go to Greece. We left you something to eat.*

I turned on the TV and poured myself a drink. I thought about the whole thing. I could see Danielle. Those legs were meant for a Mediterranean shore. I could even see my wife: the kind of woman who does things quickly. But I wasn't sure it was fair to include the baby. After another couple of drinks, I figured that maybe the baby had wanted to go to Greece. Who was I to say?

Christopher Chambers

Carl, Under His Car

Carl, under his car on a Saturday morning, stares at the bell housing of the automatic transmission that has settled heavily onto the left side of his chest, and he thinks about the conversation he had with his wife this morning. The argument was not unusual. This time Angel, their sixteen-year-old daughter, wants to go on a school trip to Washington, D.C. Carl is sure this is not a good idea—a bunch of hormone-crazed teenagers on a three-day trip to a big city with only a handful of chaperones. Three days also means two nights the kids will spend in a hotel. It isn't just the money, though that is no small consideration. The thought of his Angel in a hotel room causes Carl to squirm, and when he does, a sharp pain shoots through his left side. Jesus Christ, he winces. Somewhere deep within him there is a twinge of guilt almost tinged almost imperceptibly with pleasure. Or vice versa. Sometimes it's as if he'd never left Holy Cross High School.

Gloria left this morning in a huff to spend the day shopping at the local mall. Carl retired to the garage to work on his project—a 1972 Buick Gran Sport in an early stage of restoration. A repair manual lies open on the workbench, grease-smeared fingerprints mark the page for automatic transmission removal and installation. Step 14. Remove the bolts that attach the transmission bell housing to the engine. Step 15. While using a pry bar to ensure that the torque converter stays firmly mounted to the transmission, pull the transmission off the engine.

Carl doesn't recall what the next step is. He does remember that the manual states that installation is basically the reverse of removal. And he is sure the manual does not have specific instructions for removing a transmission that is wedged between the engine and a hapless shade tree mechanic, effectively pinning him under the car. He hears his dead father's voice, the sneer in it when he says the words shade tree mechanic. Carl's father, the auto mechanic. Carl, Sr., a real auto mechanic with a closet full of blue work shirts, long and short sleeve, with the Mr. Goodwrench patch over the left pocket and his name, Carl, in script above the right.

The garage door gapes open to a mild, sunny day, and Carl worries that one of his neighbors might happen by, see him under the car, and stop to chat. He does not want to chat with any of his neighbors right now, and as much as he would like to be out from under his car, he doesn't much like the idea of asking, say, Bruce Edelbrock for help. He knows he would never hear the end of it. He imagines Bruce down at the Town Tap. There he was, I tell ya, pinned to the floor under his own car like a goddamn bug. I don't know what woulda happened to him if I hadn't stopped by. Huh. Huh. Huh. That laugh.

The pain is not too bad, Carl thinks. From where he is pressed to the oil-stained concrete floor, he can see the corner of his workbench, the open toolbox, a wooden shelf bowing under the weight of a row of old baby food jars filled with nails, cotter pins, assorted nuts and bolts. He sees the Ridgid Tools calendar hanging on the pegboard among the hand tools and extension cords. Even though it is late March, Miss February still smiles warmly in an orange bikini. She stands in glossy living color next to a new Ridgid pipe threader, one hand on her bare hip, the other caressing the sleek machine. Carl looked ahead, into the future, and found Miss March, sultry with a twenty-four inch pipe wrench, somehow less aesthetically pleasing, and so has been content to remain in February in his garage.

Carl has worked a pipe threader like Miss February's. His brother-in-law, a heating and plumbing contractor, has a similar threader, though his is filthy with cutting oil. It resembles the one on the calendar, well, about like Gloria resembles Miss February, Carl thinks, and immediately he feels a twinge of guilt that is not at all like the pain in his shoulder, nor tinged with pleasure of any kind. Carl loves his wife. He has worked with her brother since being laid off from the canning company, where he'd worked since high school, as he'd always expected to. He lugs the machine from and to the truck during the week, and has come to resent the heavy threader.

The underside of the Buick smells of used motor oil and automatic transmission fluid. Smells that remind Carl of his father. Carl, when underneath cars, has never quite shaken the feeling that his father is watching critically his every move. This causes him to try too hard with ratchets and pry bars, to lose his cool when a bolt won't loosen or a wrench slips. Gloria teases that he can't seem to change the oil on one of their cars without barking the skin off his knuckles. And she's more right than Carl would like to admit. All the way back to auto shop. The sight of his blood trickling from a scrape, mixing but not mixing with the oil on his hands, the pain. There is something to this, flesh meeting metal. But Carl doesn't analyze it. He finds peace in the garage, under his car. More and more, it is the only place in his house where he feels at ease. With Angel older, in high school now, Carl has become an outsider in a house of women. He never has understood women, he admits to himself, and they become more and more mysterious to him as time goes on. Carl's mother died when he was a child, of a weak heart, his father told him.

Carl feels fluid trickle slowly from his shoulder to the inside of his arm and into his armpit. It tickles some, and he hopes it's transmission fluid, a bright viscous red that doesn't look at all like blood. He's afraid to move his arm. He grimaces at the tickle, and imagines how he must look, under his car, grimacing while transmission fluid runs into his armpit, and he laughs, triggering a sharp pain in his chest, like the one he felt when he first tried to move after the transmission slipped off the floor jack onto him. The transmission didn't really fall on him. He'd been almost snug beneath it, trying to free the torque converter with a pry bar when the jack kicked out, and the transmission, a Turboglide, settled into him like a bowling ball into a cheap mattress. Not to imply that Carl is anything like a cheap mattress, though Carl Sr. used to bowl league every Wednesday night at the Stardust Lanes.

Carl closes his eyes to think. The concrete is cold beneath him, and he can hear small sounds. A whir that he identifies as the electric clock on the garage wall. He stole the clock from the plant when he was laid off after twelve years of faithful service. Grudging, but faithful. That was what, ten years ago now? How has it come to this? he wonders, the years flying by like mere passing thoughts, like faraway dreams.

In the distance he hears a voice, constant and vaguely familiar. It's Harry Carey, he realizes. Someone in the neighborhood is listening to the Cubs game. They're playing the Reds today. Preseason. Carl thinks the pitching staff is looking better this year, but he isn't too hopeful. Being a Cubs fan, he knows, means maintaining a stubborn glimmer of hope in the face of almost certain disappointment. He tries to make out the radio broadcast, but Harry's words seem to be carried along on the breeze, and only the sound of them is blown into the garage. It would be nice to be able to hear the game while he lays here, he thinks. Carl is not given to panic, and he has not yet begun to worry. Not too much. He is short of breath, but Gloria will be home eventually. He can't see the clock, or the wristwatch on his immobilized left arm, but he figures it is close to noon. Which reminds him that he hasn't eaten since a coffee and Danish this morning. His stomach rumbles.

Carl tries to figure where Gloria might be, to determine when she might be coming home. He pictures her leaving the house this morning. It must have been around ten. She would drive down Palisade to the thrift store, maybe pick up some work clothes for him, an alarm clock for her collection. Half an hour or forty-five minutes there. Then on to the mall. Carl loses her at the mall. He goes there once a year, at Christmas, and it gives him heartburn just to think about it.

Hell, he has no idea where she is, or how long she'll be. She might be out with Jennie Hurst for all he knows. Maybe she and Jennie are at the Continental Lounge across from the mall right now, drinking White Russians and talking about their husbands. Carl doesn't want to think about that possibility. At the last neighborhood cocktail party, Jennie came up to Carl where he stood by the hors d'oeuvres, and ran her long, manicured fingers lightly down his arm and smiled.

"When is that hot rod of yours going to be ready for a test ride, Carl?"

All the while, Henry, her husband stood across the room watching, leering at them. And Hurst, the school psychologist, was one of the chaperones for the D.C. trip. Which gets Carl back to thinking about Angel. His Angel. Carl remembers like yesterday the day she was born, a little pink bundle in his wife's arms and him feeling like he'd just come awake for the first time in his life, that everything up to this moment suddenly meant nothing. Everything beyond this moment an unwritten book. The universe shifted, and he was no longer at the center of it. This soft little bundle was. When he held her, he realized this was the most important thing he'd ever done, and he swore that he would always be there for her. Always.

But now his Angel is like a stranger to him, listening to that goddamn hip hop music. She rolls her eyes at him when he remarks on the music and the baggy pants, her bare midriff and the blue anodized ring in her pierced navel. She spends hours on the phone, and can't utter a sentence without using the word "like" a half a dozen times. He knows he sounds like his old man, but he can't help himself.

When some kid appears at the door to pick Angel up for a date, Carl makes a point of trying to scare the hell out of him. A dark look, a crushing handshake, his shirt sleeves rolled up over his tattooed, muscled biceps. He knows what is on these boys' minds and he doesn't like it one bit. He remembers getting the same treatment from Gloria's old man when he was their age, and it pains him to remember how ineffectual it was, how he had his hands up under her sweater, or wedged between her legs before they were two blocks away.

Carl had another GS back then. The love of his life. Red with white stripes. All the factory options. The big block 455. Early one February morning coming back from Wisconsin, where the drinking age was still eighteen, going too fast, he missed a curve on a wet country road and rolled the Buick three times. It only recently occurred to Carl that surviving the wreck was something like a miracle. The car was totaled. Carl and Bruce were both thrown free. Carl awoke half-buried in the wet soil and corn stubble, staring up at a fingernail moon and the white blur of the milky way arcing across the night sky. It took him some time to remember who and where he was. When he pulled himself up from the muddy field, he saw the twisted ruin of the Buick upside down above him, its headlights still dimly reaching out into the darkness. He felt as if he had died. Bruce lay back in the ditch, still drunk, and laughing. Laughing like an idiot.

A lifetime later, Carl saw an ad in the paper for a restorable Gran Sport, and it seemed like the answer to something. His desire for the car was more need than want, and he borrowed from the savings account for Angel's college to get it. A long bad time with Gloria over that.

An almost full can of Old Style sweats just beyond Carl's reach. He picks up the half inch ratchet handle with the extension and carefully extends it toward the beer can. He feels the pain in his chest again, and he lets the ratchet fall. He turns his head slightly and looks up to Miss February, still blessing the threader.

A small crack of sound in the distance. At Wrigley Field, a baseball arcs high away from a swung wooden bat. The sound of Harry Carey's voice rises in volume and intensity. Carl holds his breath, hoping that it means good news for the Cubs, a homer, runs scored at the least, a game-winning rally. But he can't make out the words, and the sound subsides to a low murmur, color commentary, the lull between batters. For Carl, the long fly ball continues to hang in the sky, its flight unresolved.

When he has calculated the reach, the foot-pounds of pull required to slide the can across the floor without tipping it, he again grasps the ratchet handle, reaches out, and slowly draws the can toward him with the care of a master machinist.

When Carl has the can in his hand, he revels in its cool wetness a moment before tipping it over his mouth. Beer spills down his chin and soaks into his shirt as he drinks. He thinks again about lunch. The fried chicken left over from last night is in the refrigerator. He likes leftover fried chicken.

He can see out the garage door a square of driveway, his mailbox, the top half of the duplex across the street, blue sky above. The Shelby kid rolls by delivering papers from a skateboard. *The Saturday Tribune* skips across Carl's drive and into the holly bush. He almost yells after at the kid, but decides against it. This is not the time to get into it with the paper boy. Carl wonders where Gloria is now. How long can a person shop? He knows that in Gloria's case unfortunately, the answer is a long goddamn time. He closes his eyes. The faint murmur of the ball game continues in the distance. The long fly ball still soars deep in center field. The clock on the wall whirs. Down the street a dog barks. And he hears footsteps coming down the sidewalk.

Carl holds his breath. The footsteps stop, and then start up again, coming closer. He says a prayer-like, please, oh god, but the footsteps come up the driveway. He opens his eyes. In the narrow gap between his feet and the gas tank of the Buick, he sees a pair of legs, faded blue jeans, athletic shoes, one untied, shuffling toward him. Not Bruce, he hopes. But it is Bruce, and now he hears the chuckle, low and suggestive. The sharp slap of an open hand on the top of the Buick.

"The fuck you doing under there?" says Bruce.

"What do you think?"

"Taking a nap? Huh huh."

"Maybe." Maybe I'm dreaming thinks Carl, under his car. All of this a dream, dream-like as it is. Only to awaken. To awaken, refreshed.

"Listening to the Cubs?"

"Yeah."

"Yeah?" Carl imagines Bruce looking around, seeing the radio on the workbench, unplugged for the cord to the trouble light. The light hangs from the underside of the open hood, hooked into one of the ram air induction scoops, and it casts a yellow light down around the big block v-8. Carl, with the exception of his right arm, is in the shadows.

"I was. A while ago."

"I couldn't stomach it neither. Got no pitching at all this year." Bruce belches, and shuffles over to the workbench. Carl can see the back of his head as he leans over to get a closer look at Miss February.

"Wouldn't mind running some pipe through that threader." Bruce whistles. "Know what I mean."

"What do you mean, Bruce?" Carl says. Sharply.

"You know, man. I mean . . ."

"Forget it. I know what you mean."

"What's up? You sound kind of weird like."

"Yeah?"

"You need a hand?"

"No. I'm thinking."

"Thinking about what?"

"This tranny . . . and shit."

"Turboglide, right?"

"Yeah."

"Them are good trannys."

"Yeah."

All I have to do is ask him to roll that floor jack back under here, Carl thinks, and we could get this thing up enough for me to get out from under it. But for some reason, he can't ask. He and Bruce went to high school together, played on the conference champion baseball team together, even dated a couple of the same girls. Carl remembers Bruce bragging once about tearing the clothes off that skinny little Muldowney girl in the bushes at a keg party, how she was so drunk she couldn't walk or talk. And Carl remembers not saying anything, and has never forgotten this.

Carl remembers sitting up in a muddy field and staring at the wreck of his car, feeling like his life was over, and Bruce's laughter ringing in his ears. That was what, twenty years ago? Christ, he says to himself.

"I'm going to the Tap. Come with and have a cold one," Bruce says. He squats down and peers under the car at Carl, squints at him there in the shadows under the Buick.

Carl looks at the big, sideways face of his old friend and feels a powerful urge to flail at it with the heavy ratchet that lays by his hand. The urge is to hurt. To cause bodily harm. He takes a deep breath. Exhales. Carl, calmly:

"Nah. I'm in the middle of this here . . ."

"Tranny?"

"Yeah."

"All right. Anything you need under there before I go?"

Carl thinks about the cardboard bucket of fried chicken in the refrigerator, the cordless phone, which could be anywhere in the house, the Cubs game and the unplugged radio. He thinks, for no reason at all, about Angel.

"No. I'm all set," he says.

Bruce shuffles off down the driveway and down the street to the Tap where the usual crowd sits at their usual places at the bar, watching the Cubs win or lose another game. Gloria, meanwhile, browses through paperback classics at the Books-R-Us outlet. Carl, still under his car, hears from a couple blocks away the deep thumping of a high-power car stereo system with the bass pushed all the way up. A buzzing begins on the workbench as the thumping gets closer. The tools in Carl's garage begin to vibrate. Carl feels the low frequencies pulse through the transmission, through him, and through the concrete slab on which he lies. That Puerto Rican kid that Angel's been seeing, no doubt.

The kid drives a gleaming old Chevy Impala low rider with thirteen coats of hand-rubbed candy-apple lacquer, a trunk full of Die Hards and one of those hydraulic lift kits that drops the chassis down to within inches of the pavement and causes the car to hop up and down obscenely at stop-and-go lights. Carl can tell by the clatter of lifters from under the hood and the blue-black smoke from the tailpipe that the motor is on its last legs. He wonders what kind of person would paint a car that barely runs. The batteries and the shocks are likely worth more than the whole goddamn car. Stomach acid gurgles and threatens to rise in his throat.

He refuses to learn the kid's name. Ralph, he calls the kid. Or Rudie. Ra-hoolio, if he's in a good mood. What does Angel see in a skinny, sorry-ass kid with the crotch of his pants hanging down almost to his knees. She's asserting herself, Gloria tells him. Let them be. They're just kids. That's what worries Carl. He and Gloria were just kids, too. But they weren't this stupid. Were they?

The Impala bounces to a stop at the curb outside Carl's house. The kid knows enough to turn the music down here, but Carl can still hear the insistent, muted thump of it, and the buzz and rattle of door panels and window glass. A car door opens and closes with a thunk. The sound of sneakers skipping up the sidewalk. Angel. The front door slams shut. Carl imagines her dropping her jacket on the floor in the hall. She will never learn. She runs to her room, maybe. He has always been uncomfortable there, and will only stand in the doorway trying not to look too closely at anything in the fragrant, jumbled room. So much color and life. Carl hears water running through the pipes inside his house. Noises in the kitchen. The side door opens.

"Daddy?"

"That you, Angel?" Carl's voice breaks slightly.

"How's your car coming?"

"Fine, honey."

Carl can see her feet. Pink canvas high tops poised. Her jeans taper and end mid-calf, revealing a hands width of thin leg, the graceful curve of ankle below. Carl has a great and sudden desire to hug his daughter, to hold her tightly in his arms for a long, long time.

"Me and Raul are going to the park. To hang out, okay?"

She's lost to me, Carl thinks, and he feels his heart breaking, the weight upon it almost unbearable.

"Okay," he says.

Angel skips toward the open garage door, and the sun-drenched, dangerous world. Carl struggles to follow the pink shoes in their carefree dance away from him.

"Angel," he calls out.

She stops. Turns back, pink shoes pivoting. "Yeah?"

"Be careful, honey."

And then she is gone. Carl lies under his car, eyes closed. The clock whirs. The world outside turns. It is Saturday, and spring is near. At Wrigley Field, relief pitchers warm up in the bullpen. Carl breathes and tries not to think about anything.

Carl looks up and sees Miss February move. Her head turns slightly so that she is looking down at him. She continues to smile, but in her smile is a look of pity and tenderness that he has not noticed before. The pipe threader beside her turns slowly, whirs smoothly, masking the far away chatter of the Cubs game. Miss February steps down from the workbench and moves toward Carl, her bare feet gliding over the cold concrete. A warm glow fills the garage.

She bends down beside the Buick, reaches under the car toward him. Carl in turn reaches out to her, his right hand outstretched, seeking her touch with neither thought nor hesitation. His right hand. He stares at her, transfixed by the vibrant, tanned skin of her arm, her hand, her fingers. Flawless, he thinks. Impossible. She touches him lightly, and in her touch Carl feels the sure knowledge that everything will be all right. He relaxes, and only then realizes that he has been holding tension in his body, fighting against the weight that is upon him. He gives in to it. Accepts it. And it is lifted from him.

Later, when the pilgrims arrive to kneel in Carl's garage at the shrine to Our Lady of Skokie, as Miss February is christened by the media, Carl drives to a bar in another neighborhood where no one knows him, and watches the Cubs with strangers. The Buick sits home in his driveway in an arrested state of partial restoration, covered with a tarp. Gloria sits inside the garage door in an upholstered chair she brought out from the family room, making change, and crocheting another afghan, or a sweater for Carl. The pilgrims pay five dollars to kneel at Carl's workbench and pray to the Ridgid Tool calendar.

Some of them believe they see Miss February's smile broaden, a light brighten in her eyes, a slight, sympathetic downward nod of her head as she looks upon them, one hand on her erotic, virginal hip, the other on the holy threader. Some reverently touch the stain on the garage floor where Carl lay pinned beneath the Buick before he was saved by Our Lady. They anoint themselves with the slick trace of the transmission fluid that coats the tips of their fingers. Some purchase small souvenir wrenches adorned with an enameled picture of the Virgin Mary (after consulting with the parish priest, Gloria decides against using the image of Miss February on the souvenirs; a letter from the Ridgid Tool company threatens legal action if their calendar, or their model is used in any type of marketing campaign. The church itself withholds judgment on the alleged miracle, issuing an ambiguous statement confirming that God does indeed work in mysterious ways, and that anything that increases faith is good, whether or not it is officially miraculous).

Gloria takes the money to the Savings and Loan to deposit into the account for Angel's college education. For the first time in years, Carl and Gloria do not argue about money, or about Angel. Carl gives Angel his blessing to go on the trip to Washington, D.C. He sees her off to O'Hare, and hugs her for a long time in the terminal while the rest of the kids crowd toward the boarding gate. Angel hugs him back.

Carl, back to work with his brother-in-law, threads pipe and daydreams. On the job site, Carl runs the threader with a new proprietary air. He savors the smell of the cutting oil, the faint metallic taste in the back of his throat. Sometimes he stands next to the threader with his hand on the filthy motor casing in the same manner in which Miss February stands beside her threader.

By August, the pilgrims will have dwindled away, or Gloria will be forced by the city council (already the neighbors are complaining about the traffic and parking) to close the shrine. The Buick, freshly painted and rebuilt, will be back in the garage where Carl will work on the interior. A new headliner, carpeting, the seats reupholstered. Carl will install a new radio himself. He has a glow-in-the-dark statue of the Sacred Heart of Jesus for the dashboard. He will take Gloria for a drive on a Saturday night in the fall, park by the lake where they can smell the water and hear the hush of it lapping at the beach.

Tune an oldies station in low. Her head on his shoulder, her hand on his chest. Carl will close his eyes and feel what it is like to have everything he ever thought he wanted, and then realize that it somehow isn't like he imagined it would be. And still it will be all right.

Or perhaps Gloria arrives home from the mall and walks into the garage, her arms filled with shopping bags. She sees Carl, under his car. She frowns at the Ridgid Tools calendar hanging above the workbench.
"Why is your calendar still on February?"
"Huh?" Carl, shaken from a bizarre reverie. "Gloria?"
"Are you all right?"
"Gloria . . ."
"Just a minute. I have to set these bags down before I drop something."
Gloria goes into the house and Carl hears her shoes click across the linoleum. The radio comes on. The Rolling Stones singing "You Can't Always Get What You Want." Carl hears Gloria singing along. Her voice gives him chills. She will return soon. She will position the floor jack to lift the transmission up off him. She will stay calm. He has always admired her ability to handle a crisis.

In high school when the Weber kid almost drowned in the pool, when everyone else stood there staring at the limp body on the stark, white concrete, it was Gloria who rushed up, knelt down and breathed the life back into him. Carl thinks this might have been the moment when he fell in love with her. He remembers being paralyzed, the smell of chlorine, water running down his face, his chest, his legs. And the image of Gloria, her slim, graceful fingers clamped over Weber's nose, and spread flat on his thin chest. To place her mouth over his, in front of God and everyone. To breathe into him. Her wet hair flat against her head, clinging to her freckled shoulders. A drop of chlorinated water hanging off the end of her nose like a jewel. In between breaths she straightened up, counting, oblivious. Her bathing suit was blue. Her breasts small and nearly perfect rose and fell, and with them a new ache in Carl's chest. The desire to be saved by her. A wail from far off like a siren. Yes, Carl thinks. That was the moment.

Gloria will insist on calling an ambulance, and she will ride in the back with him. While he waits for her to return to the garage, he thinks to ask her to bring along the bucket of leftover fried chicken. He can see by the change in light out the garage door that the sun is setting. It will be dusk by the time an ambulance arrives. He imagines lying under a clean, white sheet on a stretcher, looking up at the reflections of the lights flashing on the roof of the ambulance.

The morphine is working. The i.v. drips slowly, each translucent drop hanging like a textbook curve ball before dropping down into the graceful tube that arcs into Carl's arm. The ambulance driver has the Cubs game on the radio, turned down low, under the static of the two-way radio. It's the bottom of the ninth, all tied up. José Cardinal steps up to the plate. My man, José, Carl cheers silently. Gloria sits beside him, and holds a cold drumstick to his mouth. He takes a bite of the chicken leg, and chews slowly. The taste is incredible. Heaven. It's as if he has never truly tasted anything until this moment, and he thinks that maybe everything will be this incredible from this moment on, out from under his car, saved.

Or perhaps Carl, under his car, still, thrown from the Buick as it rolled and flipped into a cornfield in northern Illinois on a cold night in February, 1978. In the terrible, suspended flight, he saw in flashes of vivid imagination his future and all that it would have held, lived this life in the brief moments before he came to rest in the damp soil and corn stubble where he would lay pinned beneath the car he loved and had destroyed, thinking about his father, about Gloria and their plans together. He would wait for a beautiful woman to save him. An angelic woman filled with light who would reach out to him a graceful flawless hand, lift the heaviness weighing upon him, fill him with her miraculous breath, and raise him up, up, and up.

Jocelyn Jane Cox

So Cinnamon

I'm always replaced by redheads. In the workplace, in line at the supermarket, everywhere. I don't know if they're real redheads or if they massage the pigment into their scalps on a regular basis. I don't know if there are more redheads now than there used to be. I don't know the per capita ratio of redheads in this state versus others in our venerable union. I do know that they are somehow drawn to me—it must be something chemical—and that a statistical analysis of my footsteps correlated with those that trace them would come up: 100% redheads.

My boyfriend Randy and I went bowling a week ago on a whim. I hadn't been bowling in years, and had forgotten how hard it is to find a light enough ball with large enough finger holes.

"Try over there," Randy suggested, pointing across several lanes to some balls I hadn't yet sized. I'd gathered several balls in our corral, but none of them were quite right. Because I didn't want to spend the rest of this life with a bowling ball attached to my hand and because I didn't want to fling my arm off with a ball I couldn't control, I headed across the alley in search of the perfect fit.

The lighter balls are generally lavender or pink and clearly targeted to eight-year-old girls and those thin-fingered women whose rings tend to slip off. Balls with more generous holes have a heft to match. They are traditionally black and nondescript, dulled by all that high-speed, action-movie contact with the pins. These are geared toward everyone else. How about a middle-ground gray or tasteful maroon for those of us who eat three meals a day, don't believe in free weights, and who, with a little luck, can pull off a strike but rarely a spare? For having absolutely no training and little technique, I'm an all-right bowler. *If* I have the right equipment.

   I left Randy sitting in front of the scoring computer in one of those yellow plastic seats that take butt cracks into account. He'd easily found a ball and was now creating three-letter pseudonyms to represent us on the screen. Randy is amazing. He thinks my theories about redheads are hilarious, that my "paranoia" is a hoot, which might seem condescending if a long line of *really* unsympathetic suitors hadn't already passed through the turnstiles. They used words like "schizophrenic," "psychotic," and one guy, the zookeeper, twirled his index finger by his head, like he was making an imaginary circle around his ear: "Loopy" he said, and walked on through, into the open arms of a redhead. The last guy, an astronomy grad student who played the guitar for me after sex, soft and mellifluous, went to the fish market to buy some lobsters we could smother with butter for our three-month anniversary. She was waiting for him behind the counter, her apron all smudgy with sea water, her hair like a beacon. Now they eat scallops, salmon, all manner of crustaceans for no particular occasion.

   I've recently started sending postcards. *Told You So*, I draw with my calligraphy pen, with less resentment than you might think. I'm someone with a hypothesis; I've gathered a fascinating set of observations and, if nothing else, I feel I deserve some credit.

   But maybe Randy would be different. That night, we'd already had a good dose of fun. We'd gone to It's A Wrap, and ordered whatever we wanted.

   "Money's no object," Randy said, pulling wadded, one dollar bills out of what most would call a change purse but what he claimed had once been an ideal receptacle for drugs. He's a landscaper. In his spare time, he's writing a how-to book about fatherhood, even though he's never been one. He says his dad is the anti-example and argues, quite convincingly, that this is sufficient research. He's a confident man. He's comfortable with himself and knows how to unwind after a hard day of work. We'd each halved our wraps, like little tubes of food, then traded. We ate this lunch-ish dinner on high chairs that felt dangerous, around a table that seemed no bigger than a coin. I'd perched in that exact spot before, by myself and with other men, but it wasn't nearly as entertaining. When we left, I was so enamored with Randy that I didn't even look back to notice who sat at our table after us, or note for my records, the color of her hair.

Likewise, I headed across the alley without wondering who Randy would date next, without scanning the place for her crimson locks. In fact, I felt the best I had in a long while. The worn, treadless soles of my rented shoes combined with the carpeting in a way that pleased me, in a way that made me think that life was something smooth and carefree, something to slide through.

My mother can pinpoint the exact moment she fell in love with my father. They were on a road trip, winding through the Rockies. In a clearing, the sun reflected off the snow, which reflected back and forth across the mountains, then off the passenger window mirror, and finally hit my mother's retina in a way that made her tear ducts flow with pleasure, and filled her with an incredible longing for the fellow at her side.

"It's just that random," she assured me long ago, leaning dreamily against my bedpost. And even though they've loathed each other for many years now with the intensity of a thousand suns, I believe in the power of that one monumental—if entirely random—moment. I gazed back at Randy, still hunched over the scoring computer.

Filled with the image of him, and all the wraps we'd share in years to come, I took off at an exuberant trot and slid my slippery, rented shoes across that industrial carpet with the elation of a woman who is at last, truly and unsuspiciously in love.

As if in honor of this moment, the rack of my destination cradled two intriguing specimens: a green and a royal blue. This was a day to remember, all right, a collection of perfect sensations to someday recount to our own lovely daughter. I even pondered the physical similarity between a lane and an aisle.

Unfortunately, despite their colors, these balls were only a shade better than the rest, and I stood there lifting the heavy blue ball then popping my fingers in and out of the green, snug holes. Both were an improvement on anything I'd yet found, but could not be carried simultaneously all the way back to lane 14. I chose the blue first and transported it across that vast space as if it were a child or planet in the safe crux of my forearms.

When I returned, Randy was cooling his palm in the air jet; he'd already taken his practice turn. I saw that the scoring screen labeled the opponents as HUN vs. NAP.

"Thanks for waiting, *Hun*," I said, unashamed of my penchant for afternoon naps.

"Found it?" he asked.

"Not quite," I said, "but this and another are as close as I'm going to get. Be right back." I swiveled around to complete part two of my mission only to spy someone else hovering over my rack and fingering the green ball. There was a point when I might have been shocked, taken aback by what I saw, but this was merely another link in a long chain of controlled coincidences. I stood and took her in: her slim frame hosting uncommonly large breasts, her speckled complexion, and her full head of red hair.

I've studied so many of these women: unpacking their books in a library chair still warm from my flesh, pulling down a roller coaster's safety bar still damp with my sweat. I've even trained one or two of them long before their promotions into my desk seemed remotely possible. The thing is, their hair is never actually red, artificially enhanced or not. It's usually more of a rust shade. It's the color of bus and dentist upholstery and, yes, we were right in grade school: carrots. I could almost feel sorry for them, but pride prevents me. After all, men attribute to them a certain worldly innocence, an earthy exoticism that couldn't possibly be found in a mere brunette.

This one was testing the green ball by inserting her two fingers and thumb then letting it hang at her side exactly as I had only a few moments before. I don't directly blame these women; I'm not sure they even realize the inextricable nature of our fates. But sometimes I just get overwhelmed with frustration. Like the handmaiden who tastes food for the queen, I blaze trails, break in men and bosses, and pick bowling balls with a precision and care they'll never appreciate. I turned back toward lane 14 because I knew it was the best ball she was going to find and I didn't want her to glance over and see *my* Randy sitting alone.

Besides, it was high time we got this game rolling. I was anxious to impress Randy with my bowling savvy. If my memory serves me correctly, there have been one or two men who have been inspired by my game, and one or two others who have been intimidated by it. A compromise between the two would have been nice in Randy; a little intimidation and inspiration seemed as ideal a way as any to commence this life-long journey.

"What gives?" Randy asked.

"Never mind," I said, hoping he wouldn't look over in the rack's direction.

"Did you see that redhead?" He gestured toward her, apparently taunting me.

"Sure," I sighed. "She of course took the other ball I wanted to try."

"I actually know her," he said, enjoying himself. "She runs at the track." Randy's a sporadic jogger. He says he just likes to commune with nature, but the high school where he goes doesn't have any grass—even the oblong donut hole of the track is concrete. And there are only two trees, one of which seems to have slipped into a coma.

"She explains a lot about your new *training* regimen," I said, as caustic as possible. Truthfully, I had no reason to believe he'd been going over there more frequently than usual, I've just been so thoroughly conditioned to be suspicious. I couldn't tell whether he was serious about knowing her, or not.

"Don't worry," he said, then kissed the ski slope of my neck, which gave me a chill: the good, not the creepy kind.

"She probably smells like . . ." I paused, trying to think of something reddish and rank. "A barn."

"Well I'll never know." He kissed the flatland of my shoulder. Sometimes we talked about fate. He was fond of making the berserk argument that humans have control over their destinies, as if the future is a lawnmower we push out in front of us. I didn't buy this, but also I realized it was ridiculous to let her ruin our outing, so I vowed to cut her out of my mind, like a mere blade of grass.

Randy had listed himself first on the scoreboard. While I did a series of torso twists and shoulder rolls, Randy plunged his fingers into the only black ball in our corral. He stepped over and lined himself up with the lane, then stood with the ball curled up by his chin. He remained quite still for a while, as if the ball was whispering last-minute tips. I sat down and admired the view; oh, how I'd come to know the exact gape and fold of that denim and the striped drawers underneath.

Finally, he took three steps and unleashed the ball. It curved toward then veered away from the gutter in a long, shallow arc. Randy cocked his head left, as if this had an influence on the outcome. Birds look like this after they fly into windows. The ball crashed into the phalanx of pins throwing two of them head over heels into the back wall, knocking another two on their sides like felled trees, and leaving the rest to teeter then regain composure.

"Damn!" Randy said, grinning. He aired his clammy palm in the stream of the air jet.

"Forty percent, Hun!" I exclaimed, just to bug him.

When the ball came spitting out of the black hole, he lined himself up again, meditated just as long, and threw. The ball traveled a deeper lobe this time and upset the remaining six pins all at once. He blew on his knuckles then rubbed them on his chest, the same gesture I planned to employ after my turn.

"Madame . . ." He presented the lane to me with satisfaction.

I strode confidently to the corral. This was a good day to be alive. This guy was all mine. And he could bowl. Not because he'd practiced, or ever been on a league, but just because he could. This was going to be a great game.

As I spun my recent acquisition to find the holes, I thought of blueberries, skipping blissfully through sun-splashed fields of them wearing a white nightgown. When I slipped my thumb then middle and index fingers into the side of my ball and hefted it with a jerk of my right biceps, I realized I'd made the wrong choice: the holes did not automatically catch on my joints so I had to bend them in order to maintain grip. I would have been much better off with the smaller holes of the green. But that ball was in different, freckled hands now. I supported the blue ball with both arms, like Randy, right below my chin. After my eyes traveled the length of the wooden aisle before me, envisioning a straight line, I continued to pose there, allowing Randy his due opportunity to admire the view. Then I peeked around to confirm he was looking. Indeed, he stood directly behind me; arms crossed, feet apart, eyes appreciatively peeled.

I hugged that leaden blueberry a little closer into my chest, inhaled, and began my promenade, the physical action that would wow Randy, prove I was fun and sporty and in complete control of my limbs. This would clinch his undying affection. My arm unfurled like a frog tongue catching flies, swung beyond my hips like the pendulum of a grandfather clock, and picked up the power of a cannon—

Then the ball slipped prematurely from my medium-sized fingers. It projected behind me with a velocity I am unable to calculate and Randy would rather not. The impact shuttled him several feet backwards and bent him in half like a broken stick. He shrieked then curled in on himself, his face contorted and unfamiliar. The ball lolled slowly under one of the seats and I knelt quickly at his writhing side. "So sorry. So sorry. Sorry. Sorry. Sorry." But these syllables were a sorry match for that kind of pain.

A crowd formed. Men winced. The wail of a siren neared. And I scanned the sphere of people around us for the redhead, wondering when she would appear in order to administer her TLC. I craned my neck and took a panoramic look around the whole alley. While doing so, I glimpsed the green ball still on top of that faraway rack; she hadn't chosen it after all. I blinked and looked for her again, but couldn't see her anywhere. I shook my head in amazement. It was as if, right there, on the waxy floor of the bowling alley, the cycle had finally been broken.

"I'm going to die," Randy whimpered.

"You're not." I rubbed his arm giddily. Control had been given to me like a gift. "We're going to be fine!" I said, accidentally including myself. "Fine!" I exclaimed, jogging alongside the stretcher.

On the way to the hospital, Randy squeezed the feeling right out of my hand. A numbness danced up my arm and throughout my body. This, I understood, was the tingling sensation of mutual ownership. We might hurt each other over the years: throb, ache, even scream, but we were together, and nothing else mattered.

Randy lived. He was given painkillers for the severe bruising. He'll eventually, with the help of therapy, be able to enjoy the splendors of sex again and probably even test his theories on fatherhood.

His ER nurse was kind and soulful. Her white shoes squeaked along with everyone else's on the emergency room linoleum. Of course her hair was red, or more the shade of apricots, and probably smelled as sweet. As she bent over to adjust the pillow behind his head, sure enough, they launched a lengthy discussion about the weather—its ebb, its flow, the necessity of a sweater.

Randy didn't notice me walking away. Chemistry, like so many other sciences, is not confined to laboratories.

Before taking the bus home, before dipping the tip of my calligraphy pen in its little well, before finally tearing open the box of *So Cinnamon* hair color hidden in the depths of the cabinet underneath my bathroom sink, I paused just outside the hospital's entranceway. I stood next to a miniature sandbox, a play-space for discarded cigarettes, and watched the automatic glass doors move back and forth on their track, over and over again. Those doors have a way of insulting as quickly as they accommodate; they slide open then shut without bothering to shield you from what transpires inside.

Wendy Dutton

The Engaging and Sometimes Repulsive Way of the Natural World

My Life as an Eskimo
Doc makes a big production out of giving me my first flashlight. He says, "Roy Boy, when I was a little, my mother would spank me if she caught me reading under the covers at night. Well, son, this is for you." And he hands me a huge flashlight, the kind that could light half the universe.

My dad is not a doctor-doctor. He is a doctor of philosophy. When my mother died of cancer, he sold our house in Seattle, quit his job at the university, and moved us to Ketchikan, Alaska. It was just a dot on a map at first. Then it was a dark wooden house covered in snow.

He says from this point forward my whole childhood will be one big adventure.

I tell my aunt Twyla HE'S TURNING WEIRD. Twyla writes back a letter that says so long as I have inner peace, I will feel centered no matter where my father takes me. I also write letters to my old friends that say how I have been tracking grizzlies with Doc. It's all part of my life as an Eskimo. The truth is we watch a lot of videos.

Here in Alaska the sun is only up four to five hours a day in the winter. It's like the whole state of Alaska is sleepwalking. People just go about their daily lives in the dark. But they get mad easy.

At school, fights break out all the time. Doc says this is because they are frontier children, coming of age in a lawless land. "They just don't know how lucky they are."

"But there's nothing to do here," I complain.

"Nothing to do! See here, we got supplies. A VCR, a Nintendo, we got everything. And look, look, WE GOT CHIPS."

I don't understand how this happened. One minute I was living a normal life with a mother and an equal balance of light and dark. And the next minute it's like I am stuck on a camping trip with my father, a camping trip that will never end.

The Baboons of Gambe

Doc tramps into the house with tennis racquets strapped to the bottom of his boots. His enormous red jacket is zipped so that only his spectacles and new walrus mustache peek out. When he unzips, a pile of magazines and catalogs topple to the ground. "Handy stuff," he declares. "Can act as a wind guard." He has made another trade with Mrs. Yamick.

HE'S OBSESSED WITH CATALOGS, I write to Twyla.

"You can't mail order happiness," Twyla writes back.

I grumble from inside my fort. I have scooted all the furniture in the living room close together and draped the arrangement with blankets. The TV gives off a weird blue glow inside the furniture cave. I am watching another animal special on public television. I am a big fan of the specials on account of Grubb.

Grubb is half my age, maybe five years old. He is the son of Jane Goodall, the famous animal lady. Grubb has lived all his life in Africa. His father is the photographer who makes all the movies. They specialize in chimps, though I have also seen their movies on wild dogs. This one is called "The Baboons of Gambe."

In "The Baboons of Gambe," Grubb takes off all his clothes and leaps into the lake where a baby baboon named Pumpkin also happens to be taking a swim. The announcer explains how Grubb has been taught to coexist with wild animals, but under no circumstances will he interfere with their natural lives. This is to say if a little monkey was abandoned by his mother and starving to death, Grubb wouldn't be able to give him a sandwich. It would mess everything up.

Grubb and Pumpkin paddle and splash and swim in circles side by side, never getting very close to each other. Lately I think about Grubb all the time, this boy who swims side by side with baboons, this boy who has a mongoose for a pet. That, I think, is true adventure. This is adventure with a twist.

The Breasts of the Mango Sisters

"Roy Boy," Doc begins, "I've got something to tell you. Tomorrow is the day my special order arrives. Very special. We've got to be down to the station by 8:00. At 8:00 tomorrow our new life begins."

I thought this was our new life," I grumble from inside my fort.

"New lives are coming to us all the time, son. This is Alaska, the final frontier. Anything is possible."

I remember the day Doc made the special order. We were outside in the snow, testing Doc's new telescope which he also mail-ordered. Doc is sitting cross-legged in a snow saucer at my feet, flipping through a girly magazine. I pretend not to see. I zero in on Mr. Kerchenko's trailer. "He's feeding his dogs," I report. "Gross: he's got a dog biscuit in his mouth, and he's making the dog jump up and get it."

Doc gasps. When I look down, he is ripping out an advertisement. It has a picture of a topless woman wearing a necklace of flowers strategically placed. I only catch a glimpse before Doc tucks the advertisement in his wallet. Later that night when I look inside his wallet, the advertisement is already gone.

At the bus station we meet a woman. She is tiny and round and has long black hair just like in the ad, but she is fully clothed. Her dress is so bright red she seems to vibrate when she gets off the bus.

It looks out of place beneath her shabby trenchcoat. The coat is not nearly warm enough. Doc trades with her. "There," Doc says, zipping up his big red down jacket. "It matches your dress."

With his hand on the zipper at her chin, they gaze at each other.

About a thousand years later they remember me.

"So," Doc says, "this is my new wife, Mango Blossom."

You can't mail order happiness, I think.

Mango Blossom pinches my cheek. This shocks me. I thought cheek-pinching went out a long time ago. It soon becomes apparent that this woman has some idea that I am a lot younger than I am. When we get home, she speaks to me in a high squeaky voice like you use with babies.

"Are you an Eskimo?" she says to me. "Is this your igloo?"

"House!" I practically shout. "This is a house."

Mango Blossom stands up to her full height, which is just about an inch taller than me, including her spiked red boots, caked with slush. A shadow comes over her face and she says in her sand voice, "I know what a house is. I know English, little boy."

"Roy," I holler before diving into my fort. "I'm Roy."

The first thing she does is pick up our dirty dishes. Out of a corner of the fort, I watch her. She leans against the boxes we never bothered to unpack and takes off her wet high heel boots. Then she throws them on the floor hard and stares at them for a long time.

I have to admit she is beautiful. I picture her growing up with the Mango sisters on some tropical island like you see on fruit juice commercials. And the Mango sisters wear nothing but grass skirts and flowers. They have perky brown breasts that don't even seem x-rated.

They are not tits or knockers or boobs. They are just the breasts of the Mango sisters.

After two days of living with us, Mango Blossom makes an announcement. Doc and I are at the table, waiting for her to serve us steaming plates of rice and curry. The sauce is practically fluorescent.

Normally I wouldn't eat anything fluorescent, but it beats hot dogs and chips. Mango puts the plates down before us, and immediately our faces are wet from the steam. We bow our heads and pretend to pray.

"Look," Mango Blossom says right in the middle of it, "would you please stop calling me Mango Blossom?"

Doc's face gets all confused.

"It's Roberta. Mango Blossom is just my pen name, the one I used for the service. I didn't even make it up myself. My real name is Roberta Wiggins."

Doc and I look at each other. "Roberta Wiggins," we repeat.

"I grew up in Sacramento. My mom was half Hawaiian. But that's about it."

"Oh," I say, disappointed.

"This is a wonderful meal, Roberta," Doc croaks.

Fire #1

The first time Doc caught on fire it was an accident. An oil lamp exploded in his hands. Luckily he was outside when this happened.

Otherwise he would have burned the house down. This is the one fact Mango Blossom keeps repeating over and over.

Mrs. Yamick comes over with sheep poop. She shows me how to press the poop into patties, which I am supposed to hold onto Doc's burns. The second-degree burns are on Doc's hands, all blister and puss: gross.

The first-degree burns are on his arms and neck.

"He could have died," I say to Mango Blossom in the kitchen.

"He could have burned the house down," she says back. She is smoking at the kitchen table, flipping through a catalog while she talks on the phone. Mango Blossom has an amazing amount of friends for Alaska. They call on the phone and sometimes even come over.

Mango Blossom's friends are mostly men. They are not ordinary men.

They are great big oil men. Their arms are full of tattoos. One guy has a thermometer on his arm, and when he flexes his biceps it turns into a hard penis. Every time he sees me, he makes a big production of showing me this.

Doc lies in one room, and Mango Blossom lies in the guest room.

Sometimes she even takes an oil man in there. You can hear them laughing. You can hear other things too. I sit with Doc and hold the sheep poop patties against his arms while he holds some more in his hands. We are so busy with the sheep poop that we have no choice but to sit there and listen to all the noise on the other side of the wall.

We never talk about it. We just listen.

Mango Blossom doesn't sleep with Doc anymore. She says the stink is too bad. I am used to it. I lie with Doc. He is stiff all night long, but awake. He listens to Mango Blossom leave, and he listens to her come in again. Sometimes she is not alone when she returns. Once I awoke to the sound of a man growling. I could quickly see it wasn't Pop. He was lying stiff beside me with his head turned toward the guest room wall, listening.

The Loaded Gun

The first thing Doc does when he gets better is go out to the tool shed and get his gun. He comes stomping toward the house, yelling, "If I can't kill her, I'll kill myself"" As it happens, Mango Blossom is splitting a beer with a big bald man, and they watch Doc from the kitchen window.

"This is loaded," he wails. And he's swinging the gun around. They just watch him. They don't even get up.

"She's driving me crazy!" he hollers.

Nothing.

After getting no response, Doc goes back and puts the gun away in the tool shed.

I am frozen in my hide-out beneath the porch. I mean, I pretend I am really frozen like one of those woolly mammoths some men in town found frozen in ice. And when the woolly mammoth unthawed—and it took several months—they ate it.

Fire #2

For the second fire, part of the house did burn, and all of Doc, as he ran after Mango Blossom, ablaze. They say he lit himself on fire just to get Mango Blossom's attention, though I can think of a zillion better ways to get someone's attention.

HE'S DYING, I write to Twyla. But she doesn't believe me until she comes. This time the burns are all over his body. Some of his veins have melted shut. He can hardly breathe. It seems like the bandages that cover him also keep him from breathing. But the doctor says his veins have partially melted shut. The burns give off a bad-bad smell, much worse than before.

Twyla has nothing to say. This is unusual. I wait for her to talk as we stand outside Doc's hospital room. She has just gone in to see him. Now she is standing in the hall of the hospital, shaking.

The Difference Between Alligators and Crocodiles

At home, Mango Blossom is packing.

"How's your dad?" she says, clacking into the kitchen with a cigarette in her mouth. She's got her red high heel-boots on again. She doesn't even seem to notice the ash all over the floor. There's still puddles in the corners from when the firemen came.

"Bad" I say.

"I'm sorry about that." she says, and I turn on the TV. It's like a sign from God: an animal special is on.

"There is a big difference between crocodiles and alligators," the announcer begins. "Some alligators are docile and live in places like the Florida Everglades. But crocodiles are more of an aggressive breed and live in places like Australia." It's true, their faces are monster faces. They have those puny, mean eyes and that long warty snout.

"Let me give you some advice," Mango Blossom says. "Never get married. No matter what. On the day you get married, remember me and what I said."

I appreciate her confidence. I mean the part about me getting married some day. It never occurred to me before.

Mango Blossom goes back into the guest room. She comes out with her matching blue plastic suitcases. The phone starts to ring. It rings and rings. "It could be the hospital," Mango Blossom says.

"Could be," I say.

"It could be about your dad."

"Could be," I murmur again.

I just keep watching the special. The phone keeps ringing. The door bangs shut. That's Mango Blossom leaving. She comes back in to say one more thing. "Oh, I'm taking the coat." Doc's red down one.

The announcer says, "This is a scene most people have never seen."

Then they show the crocodile lifting a turtle out of the water in his jaws and shaking it. The turtle is pretty big. But the crocodile shakes it so violently that his shell comes whizzing off. And then the crocodile is just munching the body of the turtle. There isn't any blood. The turtle's body is just meaty. But you can see its little head, poking out as it is being devoured.

"This may seem gruesome," the announcer continues, "but scientists assure us it is all part of the engaging but sometimes repulsive way of the natural world."

J.A. Grow

What Girls Leave Behind

    Pink plastic pearls from a broken elastic bracelet. Like these I'm holding between my fingers. Pretend jewels, or princess dreams all fallen apart. I still find them, left over from years ago, pill-sized shocks of truth. These silly reminders of what little girls are like, this is what makes me start thinking again. I imagine all those beads rolling away, like escapees, scurrying to places small and safe, away from a vacuum.
    How did the rubber band bracelet snap? I don't remember, but I can picture it in my head. Hear it. All the confusion, a swirl, a smash. Noisy girls running in my apartment, my daughters on visitation. Afterwards, a string of things left behind: purple socks and stains, a blue, fuzzy bumble-bee and soggy pretzel sticks, plastic juice cups half filled with red Kool-Aid.
    Those nights, weekends—when sometimes I was drunk and sometimes I was angry—those nights are caught in the amber of blackouts and scotch. My memory has condensed the years into slow-moving stick-figure cartoons, like the kind we drew when we were kids. The outlines of motion. Occasionally, I remember a startling fragment that makes me jump as if a bug

has flown in my mouth and is caught in my throat. I don't want to swallow it.

But this comes back to me: a clear moment one evening, an undrunk feeling. I was boiling frozen corn for dinner and drinking scotch when an unclouded notion of myself bubbled up in the boiling water. I was a wilting woman, a drunk, slicing the corner of a plastic bag and pouring frozen corn kernels into a pan on the stove. This is who I am, I thought. Wilt, wilting, being wilted.

(Or this: Wilt disease. A highly infectious disease of some caterpillars in which the *carcasses liquefy.* I learned this from the glossy *World of Insects*, an elementary encyclopedia the girls left here.)

Maybe something else washed by. A sense that there were layers to this existence, invisible but real; that some larger life was taking place in my own living room where the girls played Barbies and sang and painted. The *living* room! A place I couldn't see from the kitchen. "Something is going on here," I said to the corn. Then it passed. I gulped my scotch and called them to dinner.

"Sit at the table!" I yelled too loudly. Everything was a chore of impossible weight. Getting all the food to finish cooking at the same time, for instance. And then, having the girls sit down simultaneously. We'd eat. Yellow, red, brown, the color of dinner: corn, catsup, and fish sticks. Or else I'd sneak home leftovers from the caterer where I worked. Crab dip and a couple of slices of somebody's wedding cake for dessert.

"I'm a good mother. I'm a very good mother; just tired right now," is how you lie in your head.

The girls would leave purple Magic M arkers around the house, and bobby pins, white underwear with violets and bows, lost socks, and wet bathing suits peeled off in a hurry, stuffed bears and monkeys, and pillow cases, and glass jars with dead bugs, and tears, and love notes, and baby teeth, and fear of jumping from the diving board. I taught them to dive one summer, how to jump in head first. Those were good days.

I remember this as I crawl on my hands and knees, a sad animal, feeling about in dark corners for old toys and beads and things I've forgotten. It's late afternoon, the sun is weak through the blinds. I want to find more pink pearls. I want to see my girls young again. Because I had not been paying attention or else I'd been hearing and seeing the wrong things. I miss them, *missed* them while they were jumping around the house and squeaking and playing and crying and splashing each other in the bathtub. I can hear it, the swoosh and slap of water against the sides of the tub. Slappp. Solid. I can hear that with my hand.

Some days I was sick and couldn't lift my head from the pillow, and some days I was moody and strong as the wrong side of a hurricane.

They'd play games with each other. "You be the vampire this time, but NO biting."

"O.K." Then, two minutes later a scream.

"Ouch! Stop it!" one of them would cry, usually Missy, the oldest. "You don't play right!"

"I'm sorry," Janine would answer in a baby voice, but it would be too late for the fat rubber band snap of my patience. A broken rubber band stinging the skin, that was my voice, the tone of my unpredictable anger.

(When I was pregnant, no one ever told me—no one ever touched my elbow and pulled me aside and said, "I just want to tell you this. Children are hard." Which is what I would say, now, if anyone asked.)

Believe me.

I'd paint pictures with them, and we'd laugh and pull out fancy clothes and hats. We'd play dress-up-girls with my shoes and slips and lipstick. My baby would walk around with pantyhose on her head like long, floppy ears. We wore gloves. I had a box full of gloves, soft, flat palms. The girls would pull out more and more of my clothes until I got tired. "That's enough," I'd announce before they were through. It would be fun to a point, and then suddenly I wouldn't have the energy to move.

"Hey!" I'd frown and snap my fingers. I used to sit in a corner of the room with my back propped against the wall and drink from my favorite glass. My faux crystal glass filled with scotch.

"Don't run! Don't walk down the steps in my high heels!" Because someone always falls, someone *always* gets hurt.

"Put. It. Down!" I'd glare when they were shoving each other and bickering over the same hat. My hand coming down hard and flat on a table top. My eyes humorless and mean, my mouth a tight, straight line. There are not too many pictures of me smiling. I didn't like my teeth showing.

I still don't smile much, I realize, as I sit in the corner of my room, my back propped up against the wall, a bottle within my reach. I hold a box of photographs on my lap and narrate. "Here's one of me holding my daughter when she was a baby, my first," I say. "Well, no, actually, that might be my second. And here's this one, I was so young. This is of me and my ex-husband when we got married. Look how smooth my skin was. This is taken on our wedding day. I mean, we are really smiling dumbly. No idea what was coming." I pretend I'm showing my daughters or my mother or a woman down the street who walks her boy to school.

"Look here," I say to all of them. "The photographer posed us near the doors, and next to us is the church suggestion box. See that?" I point. " 'Suggestion Box' in our wedding picture! Ha!" I've often wondered, for years, what little pieces of paper were jammed inside, what kind of advice? Maybe something like: these two people shouldn't get married. Or have children. Or drink.

"For the record, I am not the only one who fucked up," I explain to the photographs. But no one answers and says, "Yes, I know."

In theory, I got married when I was seventeen so I could move to California. My husband, who was just a kid when I think about it, promised to take me as far away from my mother as possible. Get all the way away. As it turns out, all we did was move to the other side of Baltimore.

We were so naive, so full of expectations. Once, soon after we were married, we went for a car ride to Pennsylvania. My husband was going to treat us to a weekend away in the mountains, and I couldn't wait. I wore a brand-new wool dress. The first time in my life I was really going somewhere. It snowed tiny flurries as we left the city. Small, gray strays that would never amount to anything. ("You will never amount to anything!" my mother used to hiss. She was the smeary picture of gin. To this day, I don't drink gin.) As we drove further north, a half an hour, the snowflakes kept falling, more and faster, until we had to turn around on an exit and come home. We never even left the state.

I remember snow blindness and silence on the drive back, a kind of deafness. My husband was concentrating so hard, his knuckles were white on the steering wheel. I felt burning needles in my toes because the car heater didn't work. "There's nothing to cry about," he said. So I stared out the window, trapped and disappointed, angry, cold; and this is how I took my first few drinks, to take the chill out of life.

I used to make our bed every morning and cook dinner when I got home from my job. That's when I was working as a receptionist for a doctor. He was good to me; he'd give me pills for my nerves. My husband had a job, too, selling rivets or something, and every night he'd recite his plans for us. "After you have our first kid, we'll move into a bigger house," he'd say, as if it was fool-proof. His grip was on everything: he had the mortgage worked out, the car payments, the timing of my pregnancies. He picked out what clothes I should wear, the food we'd eat, the friends I should make. I lived in a glass jar with holes poked in the lid for air.

My ex-husband is a piece of work. I don't even like saying

his name, stuck with it as I am. He used to wear a gold cross around his neck like a saint, like someone who is never wrong. King of the super humans. Most of the time he walked around shirtless, as if he were Atlas, so busy holding up our world. Why did he have to squeeze it to death? To plan every move? That's like trying to figure what path a tear will take down your face. Maybe it gets stuck, maybe it drips off your chin. You don't know. Let me tell you, it's no fun being married to Atlas.

I made friends with the girl next door, Evelyn, who liked to drink and was three years older than me. She had a baby already and lived with this guy who worked where my husband worked, and things were fine. We had cook-outs with hot dogs and beer, and we'd laugh. I can still picture the crinkled scar near her eyebrow when she smiled, her fake diamond earrings swinging wildly from her ears. She was always losing them. We wandered the floors of her living room, kitchen, bedroom, the supermarket and liquor store on our hands and knees looking for her earrings. "It's here somewhere," she'd say, and we'd drop to the floor as if her jewels were priceless. We flirted with everyone. I developed a big laugh and a smile. I became friendly with strangers.

I'll never forget it. Evelyn and I were at the corner bar one afternoon, there were only two other people in the place, when we heard sirens screaming outside. The bartender was a dreamy man who stared out the window as he smoked cigarettes. He said, "Hey, there's some commotion on your block," as nonchalantly as if he'd said, "Hey, close the screen door, you're letting in flies." We finished wine and walked outside, blinded at first by the scorching sun.

("Ladybug, ladybug fly away home, your house is on fire, your children are alone." I sang that with the girls a few years later, when they were old enough to play by themselves in the backyard. They'd dig up worms and pull them apart, save them in a bucket with dirt and wait for the worms to re-generate. One afternoon they found a butterfly struggling to free its wing from a cocoon. The girls pulled the sack open, but it didn't help. The butterfly panicked and fluttered in circles, heavy and lopsided.)

It was Evelyn's house that burned down that afternoon while her baby was sleeping.

"Who would do something like that? Leave a baby alone?" the neighbors asked. I knew; I was standing right next to her while she cried and the police took her into custody. I stepped aside as they lead her away, and I never saw her again. Our friendship ended on the spot.

For months afterwards, my husband didn't foresee that I'd

become so restless, that the dishes would pile up, that something inside me would stop. My heart, maybe. It clicked shut like an iron door.

"It's hard to give a shit these days," I sang to myself like a country-western classic. I still went to the bar.

My husband became rageful and jealous; he'd throw dirty plates against the wall and jerk me by the arm to scold me; grab my hair to keep me from leaving. I got bruises. Some might say, on his behalf, it's hard to live with a drinker. I know this to be true myself. For a while, I thought it was love, so I stayed. But inside my head I sang even louder. I made promises and wishes to myself, and then I stopped coming home. My mother, she used to pull me like that. She left marks. She had long, sharp fingernails the color of tobacco, and she teased her hair. "She doesn't mean it. She's sickly," my aunts told me when I was young. I dreamed I was Dorothy, throwing water on the wicked witch and watching her melt.

I don't have any pictures left of myself as a child, but I think my girls look like me. My baby has my straight, thin hair. If I had different hair, I might be beautiful. "She's cursed with my hair," I say to other mothers, proud in a way that my girl has something of me besides fear. She's got round eyes that smile or cry in a blink. She's a bubble with a round tummy, fat knees with dimples, a red mustache from drinking so much juice. This is how I still see her.

I pull out the next picture and look in the mirror to compare us. "Look at this," I say. "The oldest one has my sharp nose and the long curve of my eyebrows. She stands just like me, with one hip jutted out, her fragile fist propped on it like a dare." I don't say out loud how she pokes her finger at her sister with tense meanness when she's angry. "Where do you think she got that from?" my ex accuses. This child is serious, so serious. Those dark eyes of hers have absorbed every detail, every speck. She has thoughts she will not let go of.

I'd try not to say mean things to my girls about their father, but words would slip out. "Girls, you're father is a jackass with no poetry in his soul," I sneered a couple of times. After all, I sang to them and read books, while he was as plain as a fact, black and white, no nuance; his heart a thick metal square.

"Their father is an unfeeling bastard, a son of a bitch," I say out loud. "He's lied. He's taken my daughters away from me and exaggerates things about me which he refuses to understand. He says I'm a bad influence, that I've left handprints, scars on my daughters. I ask you, what kind of mother would do that?"

I'm sitting on the floor, the phone next to me, and I'm talking to a woman, someone I don't know, from an alcoholic hotline I dial when I'm lonely. "But he won't listen. For instance, once there was a blue and purple bruise on my youngest daughter's thigh from when she fell against the table leg. It was purely an accident. But he's unforgiving." After a while I forget she's there, the woman on the phone. I don't hear what she says back to me.

Sometimes I'd ask the girls questions when I didn't mean to, like: "How's your father's new girlfriend? Is she nice?" Fine, they'd answer. No hints. They were so young and already knew how to keep secrets.

If they were here right this minute, I'd say this. "I apologize for the day you wanted to go swimming and I didn't take you." They would forgive me, I know.

They begged me to take them to the pool, "Teach us how to dive again!" They pleaded with me to put on my bathing suit. "You look fine, Mom," they said, but I didn't like what I saw in the mirror. My stringy hair and slumped shoulders, a bloated stomach from booze. I felt too ugly, so we stayed home while I sat on the end of the sofa and watched my stories and drank. It was a hot, quiet afternoon, dark with the blinds pulled down. They were playing quietly, but somehow my fingernail polish was spilled on the carpet.

"Goddamn girls!" I screamed, this voice of mine bursting delicate ears like the loudest monster of all dreams. The worst kind. Where does this *voice* come from? "All these spills I have to clean up! Goddamn It!!" I grabbed at something, an arm. I was pulling my oldest girl at an odd angle from her armpit, dragging, yanking her with my fist. I squeezed harder.

"I *told* you girls *NEVER* to touch *anything of mine* without asking first!! You don't *Listen* to *ME*!! You n*ever Listen* to *ME*!!" These words pounded my girls, pummeled and bruised them until they lost the air to breathe. A force was inside me that had nothing to do with fingernail polish. Thrill and terror. A scream inside my head, and outside, and my pulse not recognizing the difference. I don't know the difference.

"Jesus Fucking Christ! Go get a towel!" I said, disgustedly, and let go of her arm. She stood up slowly and put her hand on the sore spot where my fingerprints tattooed her skin. The youngest one stood up, too, and they said something to each other with their eyes. There was that millisecond that I saw between them: swallowed hatred. One of them rushed out of the room to get a towel, and the other one couldn't look at me. She went, too.

"You need a *wet* towel," I cried when they came back. "A wet towel!"

"I told you," I heard one of them barely breathe to the other. They hurried to leave me.

I slumped to the floor on my knees and swallowed the rest of my scotch. I wanted it so much I could've licked the inside of the glass.

"I tell you this because I need to explain," I say to the photographs, to the images who might be listening. "I heard the only fear we're born with is the fear of loud noises. So I'm sorry. This is how sorry I am."

Sometimes my oldest girl would follow me around with a pink, plastic pale of water because she didn't want me to burn the house with my cigarettes when I passed out. It wasn't always like that, though. We brushed hair and sang and ate popcorn and cake for breakfast. We slept on the floor in a huddle underneath our blanket tents when it was cold, when the electricity got turned off. There was the time one of my boyfriends took us out to play miniature golf, except the car broke down on the way. He left to find a garage, and we sat in the car waiting for him to come back with a gas can. Long, hot hours, and then it rained. We rolled up the windows and breathed stuffy air and watched giant drops fall on the windshield. "There is nothing to cry about," I said when my baby began to sniffle. She had hot tears rolling down her cheeks, and her thumb was in her mouth. We sat in the car on the side of the road like sweaty, dead fish in a dried-out aquarium. A fish tank with all the water on the outside.

After they left me behind, there were spills I couldn't clean up for a few days because they made me too sad to try. Pudding sat in a puddle on the table and made the wood turn white where it seeped through. There was a half-eaten bowl of ice cream turned to soup, hair brushes and Band-Aids, dinner dishes piled in the sink with dried catsup and crumbs. Spills of my own I haven't cleaned up, one boyfriend spilling into the next and so on. I made a mess of it. Around me are the remains of all that's been broken, and everything I walk on feels like sharp slivers.

I used to have a favorite glass, sparking with cut grooves at the base, until it was shattered. I sat it down for a second, just one second, on the edge of the table when it got knocked off by my oldest daughter, Missy. I can see her in my head. What is she doing? She's swirling or something and singing. "Mom," Janine said, "Help me get this unknotted," and she held up a shimmering tangle of old necklaces. So I put my glass down for just a second.

Some things, I didn't mind if they got ruined, and some things, they made me mad. My daughters didn't know the difference. So, my glass fell on the floor and a triangle the size of an arrowhead chipped off. I felt like I'd been pierced. Not all the scotch spilled out, *but I couldn't drink it.* Glass chips floated in the scotch, so I had to pour it out. This might not mean much to anyone else, but it broke my heart. I couldn't even yell before I began to sob. "We're sorry, Mom," they whispered, and their small hands patted my hair, so light like careful spiders. So light, afraid to touch me. All three of us cried, and I will always remember that part. Sitting Indian-style on the floor, and then all of us wiping our noses on my sweatshirt. I said, "Why are you guys crying?" and they answered in soft voices, "We don't want you to get mad." I cried even harder. My girls are quiet when they talk. They're beautiful.

Since then, I get a few weeks here and there. Nine and a half months, once. Sober. I almost made it. I call those hotline people on the phone and they do what they can. Let me tell you, it's hard. Remorse follows me like a cloud. I'll try again one of these days, but I can't stand the emptiness.

The little-girl-sounds are gone. Their father took them away. I said, "You can't do that, I'm their mother." It's unusual for the courts to take them away from the mother, but anyhow. All the paperwork and lawyers and court dates are a blur. The details mean nothing.

I get school pictures in the mail every year. They've gone from crooked teeth and straight haircuts when they were seven and eight, to braces and training bras and eyeliner and miniature bikinis, size two. Then one day it'll be sex too young with some dumb-ass boy, and pregnancy, fights and screaming, then divorce from another s.o.b., and no children. The silence of that, of children taken away.

What's left is the sound of water dripping. I hear the bus thunder down the street, an occasional siren, the cats fight in the alley, the pipes from the apartment next door, the constant tick of my alarm clock. Late at night, my eyes open in the dark, click, click, click, click, click.

"It could be worse," I always say.

The box of pictures is still on my lap, the phone off the hook, next to me. The sun has gone down, and it's nearly dark. I feel around the bottom of the box and find the remains of an old earring and one last photo of me and Evelyn, when I was still pretty and thin. We're in our bikinis by the plastic blow-up pool, and my husband is in the background with the garden hose. Evelyn is holding her baby and waving like a queen. I'd forgotten this, taken near the end of that summer.

One day we were drinking wine, roaming the floor of the bar on our hands and knees, laughing and hunting in the dark, under every barstool, for the fake pearl earring she'd lost. We were feeling our way through peanut shells and cigarette butts, searching for the clasp or the pearls. "Are you sure you lost it here?" someone asked. "You sure you didn't lose it at home?" Then the bartender said, "There's commotion outside, something's going on."

   I recall how dizzy I felt when I stood up. We swallowed the rest of our wine and smiled. "Your teeth are purple!" Evelyn said, and we laughed. Then we walked outside to see what had happened. I was blind for a split second, the day was so bright. Shortly afterwards, they took Evelyn away. Her baby died, and there was a judgment I made immediately which has stayed. The tightness of her sweaters, the shape of her face, her polished, press-on nails and fake jewels were despicable to me, and I felt disgust in my stomach for days. Since then, I have compared myself to her and I've decided I'm not that bad.

   A few weeks after the fire, an old man from the bar handed me a broken earring. "You lost this," he said, and pressed the plastic in my palm.

   I've never been able to throw it away. I can't wear it, either. I tried to fix it once. For what? Evelyn would leave her infant alone whenever she went out, and I didn't know any better. I was a child myself.

John Hanft

J. J. and the Dried Man

He limped on, alone, walking in the night next to the Southbound where thousands of cars and trucks climbed the pass. The cold cut through him everywhere, but his ears, hands, and feet were the worst. He would cup his ears with his hands, because his ears were so cold, then his hands got colder and hurt more, so he put his hands under his arms for warmth and that worked for a little while. Then his ears felt like they would freeze off, so he cupped his ears with his hands and went over the whole process again until there was a rhythm to it. Of course, all this time, his feet hurt most of all and made him limp.

This wind wouldn't quit, a numbing December east wind blowing twenty-five knots or more straight across the Southern California coast and Highway 101 in one of the coldest winters since the 1930's. Later tonight standing water would freeze. "What a joke," he said out loud. "All those bush gorillas from up North coming from there to here to get warm in sunny Southern California."

When big vehicles hit wind gusts roaring out of the coastal

canyons, you could hear the sounds of compressed air go up half an octave, then back down again once the rigs penetrated and passed through the gusts.

He didn't want to continue walking all that much, but he knew the rules. "The trick is to keep your toes moving or you're going to lose them," he heard those old voices say in his head, those voices first heard years ago.

He still lived with the old voices. He still lived with the memory—the memories were as strong as ever, maybe even stronger now, tonight, in this weird cold winter in California.

When J.J. was young, he loved jazz and fast cars and hated cold weather—the perfect California, in other words. Now he had little music, no cars, no home, and no warmth. "I'm the perfect old bum now," he said.

"You got to play it day to day," the old voices said.

"Play music, you mean; that's funny. Look at me," he said.

"You used to play, J.J. You were good."

"Yeah, wasn't I?" and he heard the sounds of Miles Davis, and Coltrane, the Duke and Kenny Burrell in his head. Then he heard himself play the same licks on his electric before his hands were ruined. His playing days were long gone now, but he still played in his head and used what was left of his fingers to make the runs on imaginary strings of his imaginary guitar. Everyday he practiced in his mind as he was doing now, trudging along, alone, next to the Southbound.

"Just a few more miles to the jungle, J.J.; you can do it — there'll be a fire there, maybe some food, someone to talk to, maybe."

"I hope so," he said and the wind tore the words out of his mouth and the cold cut him to his bones. There was a hill up ahead he recognized; once over this hill and down the other side was the jungle, a half acre of old palm trees left over from a rundown coastal park people called the Hobo Jungle. The park was set aside during the 30's and homeless have lived there ever since. Now there was serious talk of getting rid of the homeless in this town, so sometimes all the homeless were kicked out of the park.

Pretty soon, he would leave the path next to the Southbound. Cars sounded different going down the hill. "A less richer mixture," he thought. He could hear the cars which were out of tune. A good running engine was next to music in his ears, and an out-of-tune engine was like being flat or sharp in music—not right, not good, not perfect like the pitch of the great Miles Davis. To go right you had to have it all together.

A long time ago, J.J. had it all together. When he was just out of school, he worked in an auto speed shop during the day and played jazz in a club at night, but then he got drafted, no deferment for J.J., one of the first to go to the Korean War.

On the way down the hill he saw the bright lights of the city. The lights looked more intense because the air was so clear in the gusty East winds of late December. The lights looked cold.

"All you got to do, J.J.," he said to himself, "is coast on down the mountain, then the jungle, a quarter mile, that's all."

He limped on.

The jungle was empty when he got there. Others, because of the intense cold, had gone off to the Mission shelter or had found an empty house or a hallway or an alley or an abandoned car, something like that, where they could escape the night wind. J.J. found an old yellow mattress and he hauled the mattress to the base of a ten-foot boulder in the center of the stand of trees. Someone had built a fire there away from the wind and left a ring of stones for a fireplace. The coals were cold now and there was no wood about to build another fire. He didn't care. "This mattress gonna save old J.J.'s ass," he said and he pulled the old mattress around him like a blanket and laid there on the ground. "Damn a bear if I'm not halfway warm," he said and his fatigue and hunger started to catch up with his coldness. He felt faint. "Don't let go, J.J.," he pleaded with himself.

He knew the rules. If you start not caring, you go to the edge, so you have to keep moving, you have to hang on to the margin. He played a B.B. King lick in his head and that helped. He remembered his favorite car engine, chromed, ground, and balanced, and that helped, too. But more and more he slid a little towards the edge and it was warmer there—he understood the danger of that. It was more pleasant there, bright and clean and simple and you could give into that warmth if you let go. He had been to that edge before. It was like sleep and wonderfully pleasant at last and your whole body wanted to, but if you didn't fight it . . .

"Seems like ever since that damn war I've been fighting cold," he said and he remembered. He remembered the terrible cold and the fighting to get out of Chosin Reservoir Valley in Korea. The Marines called that place "frozen Chosin." Most other people never heard of the place. J.J. can't forget the place. He was never a Marine, but he was a soldier in the U.S. Army, a stray, rescued by the Marines in Frozen Chosin. "I'm a piece of living history," he liked to say.

He couldn't forget when the Chinese army came out of the hills of Manchuria. No one could believe their numbers—they had hid so cleverly, and no one really knew they massed like that; no one really believed they would invade either, but they did. The Chinese pushed the U.S. south and like a giant herd, the U.S. forces stuck in Chosin, bunched in the passes of the valley, insulating themselves with firepower and air support. The Chinese came from all points of the compass while the entire mass of military energy moved slowly south in the freezing cold. J.J. was there. Every single part of his anatomy reminded J.J. that he had been there. "You never forget it," he said and in his mind he saw the Red Army come out of the hills of North Korea. They swarmed around J.J.'s unit on the east side of the frozen artificial lake called the Chosin Reservoir. Twenty-five hundred U.S. Army soldiers were cut off from the main group and were now in trouble. Gray sky, frozen ground, the flat lake, everything was frozen with snow flurries blowing at fifteen knots, and not a soldier without some part of him frostbitten.

Everybody had to eat snow because canteen water froze solid. Thirst went along with fear, so they ate snow constantly. The few C-Rations left were also frozen, and their teeth cracked if they bit down too hard, and J.J. got that terrible feeling that there was no feeling left in his feet.

Army survivors of the initial attack came under the command of a Colonel who made himself totally visible and wore a crisp uniform and, would you believe, a polished helmet. He held the Army units together as they crawled south.

J.J. remembered the Colonel next to a soldier who was about to give up. "You can make it, man," the Colonel yelled when that soldier nearly went down; he got that soldier a ride in 3/4 truck, warning him, of course, that you could freeze to death in a vehicle unless you kept your feet moving, your circulation working, your head and ears covered. J.J. remembered the rules. Another time the Colonel spotted stragglers coming out of the hills. They had been pinned at the east end of the reservoir but had fought their way out and were not taking fire from enemy positions in the hills. The stragglers plowed through knee-high snow; they stumbled like drunks—the snow kicked up around them; two of them pitched forward, one spread-eagle, motionless in the snow; the other slid down an incline as if he were riding a child's belly sled. When he hit a tree, his slide stopped. He didn't move. The snow around him turned red. Enraged, the Colonel called for an airstrike, and Marine aircraft dropped napalm and strafed the enemy positions. The gray and white of the hills turned orange and black. After that, most of the stragglers joined the retreat down the southern road next to the frozen reservoir.

The Colonel was killed by sniper fire. The Army battalion fell apart when that happened, and they were only four short miles away from a rescue unit which held the Chinese off at Hagaru-ri just down the road. J.J. remembered. He remembered that where he was most of the vehicles had been destroyed and the men behind him were killed or captured and you could see some of the Chinese troops bayoneting the bodies of G.I.'s strewn around the road. Bodies in the destroyed vehicles were bayoneted, too. Many G.I.'s just stood in groups over to the side of the road and they were captured and under guard.

Ahead, J.J. saw Marine aircraft make a new napalm drop which fell short of the advancing Chinese and landed right on the head of the retreating U.S. Army column.

With Chinese in front now as well as in the rear, what was left of the middle column, including J.J., slid down the roadside to the frozen lake. Bullets kicked up snow and ice and J.J. heard bullets whine by, and when he hit the lake he slid on the ice and went down, and when he got up, he fell again, so he crawled and slithered over the snow-covered ice.

The pursuing Chinese stopped at the edge of the frozen lake. No way were they going down there, because the frozen lake was colder than the road. With the wind blowing over the ice and the temperature at 29° below, plus 15° or so as a wind-chill factor, plus fatigue, destroyed summer uniforms, inadequate foot gear, frostbite, frozen limbs, wounds, the terrible slipping-sliding gait of men trying desperately to run away, and pain, terror, panic and finally, total despair, just maybe, J.J. says, you will get a glimpse and some feeling for Chosin.

Then the nightmare mortars fell noiselessly from the gray sky. When they hit the ice, they exploded with deafening cracks and thunder and flames and shrapnel mixed with broken ice. J.J., walking like a crab, shuffled and slid around the fallen. Some wounded crawled slowly and begged J.J. for help but each time he tried to help, he went down, and each time he went down, it got harder to get up. Then the enemy lined the road, and for some inexplicable reason ceased fire on the American soldiers.

Survivors of J.J.'s battalion, one by one, a little more than 300, finally made it out and were rescued by a Marine division. Now there is an axiom that Marines take care of Marines. Even dead Marines were evacuated; bodies were strapped on vehicles, on the barrels of 105's, on tank cannons, on roofs and hoods. Dead or alive, the Marines would all make it South.

The badly wounded were airlifted out at a landing field at a frozen farmer's field scraped smooth and level enough for transport planes. J.J. was told by a Marine officer to report to the airstrip for examination and possible airlift.

Bordering the airstrip and in a line were empty stretchers left behind by wounded Marines. J.J. was given a blanket and was told to lie down on a stretcher, and so he huddled under his blanket and tried to stay warm. He tried to take off what was left of his left glove, but most of the skin wanted to come off with it; he left the glove on. Since his left foot quit hurting hours ago, he was afraid that it was frozen, and when the Marine corpsman asked J.J. where he was hit, J.J. told him he thought his foot was frozen. The Marine passed him by. More seriously wounded Marines were onloaded as soon as they arrived.

"They gonna let me freeze," he said.

Several times the corpsman passed him as soon as badly wounded Marines were brought in and shipped out. Dead Marines were lined up next to J.J. J.J. moaned.

"I'll get to you, soldier!" the corpsman yelled over the whine of the engines but J.J. could see this wasn't going to happen right away. He could die of exposure—he knew that, so he got up off his litter and stumbled away from the airstrip, past the K.I.A.'s, down to where another corpsman worked and over to where the rifles of the wounded were stacked. He found a 30 caliber carbine with three rounds in its clip. Wrapping his left foot in his Army blanket, J.J. shot one round into his foot. No one saw him do it and with the roar of planes no one paid any attention to the sound of his carbine shot. J.J. made it back to the line of litters further down the line where the other corpsman loaded wounded aboard planes bound for hospitals in Japan. J.J.'s elongated footprints in the snow were red.

In Japan, a bowlegged shallow-faced major decided to treat rather than amputate what was left of J.J.'s foot because he didn't want J.J. to get a medical discharge. If he could fix J.J. up enough, he was going to send J.J. back to the war.

"Explain to me again, son, how you got hit on the top of your foot?" the major asked.

"Sir, I've already told you many times that I was on my way back trying to make it on the ice when I got hit in the foot."

"How do you mean on your way back?"

"I fell backward on the ice—bullet hit me in the foot—foot so cold didn't even hurt until later."

"Then you walked with a hole in your foot all these miles?"

"No, sir."

"What, then?"

"It wasn't that far, though it was very hard—don't even remember walking."

"Yeah, I'll bet. You're damn lucky I didn't amputate your foot and fingers—they were pretty badly damaged; you know. Nearly frozen, mostly frostbitten. You're damn lucky you didn't lose anything. You can keep your fingers probably, but I can't promise dexterity."

"But I play music!"

"What instrument do you play?"

"Guitar."

"In time, perhaps."

"When?"

"In time—you're going to have plenty of that. I'm sending you back—not to front line duty, of course, but you're going back."

"But soon I can go home, right?"

"Oh, no you can't."

"Why not?"

"S.I.W.'s don't go home—they go back."

"What's a S.I.W.?"

"Self-inflicted wound."

So that spring J.J. went back and had to start his tour all over again. This time he was assigned to a truck company in grave registrations; he would, in other words, until he was discharged, freight the dead.

The war stalemated. Peace talks began. Still people died, 33,000 all total in that war. And, as a result, J.J. had little time for anything but driving a six-by truck stacked with dead men. After he loaded his truck and slowly drove away from the medical collecting station and down the winding dirt roads next to the Imgin River, he watched, when he could, the bodies roll and bounce, and this made him sick. He never really got used to the bodies.

Ambulance drivers up at the front could get cases of Sapporo Beer from the Black Market. They liked J.J., and when J.J. had to pick up a load of killed-in-action from the front, they always invited J.J. over for a bottle. This group of K.I.A.'s J.J. was to haul was particularly ghastly because some of them had been dead since winter and had only been discovered this spring. Most were covered with blankets and their stretchers were in neat rows on the ground. At the end of one row, one body couldn't keep his blanket on because his arms were outstretched and the wind kept blowing the blanket away. He had turned black and his skin had dried hard and was pulled back tight around his bones; his arms were outstretched, reaching, hardened in this position—no one dared push his arms down, because arms would probably break off, so the black arms reached for you as you looked down at him. He smiled back, the black skin pulled tight away from his white teeth. Hardened eyes like small dried prunes watched you. They followed you when you walked down the rows. An expensive watch hung loosely around the dried man's left wrist. Many had thought about taking the watch but could not face that grin and the eyes that followed your every movement. With his arms stretched out like that and his skeletal black fingers curved inward gracefully, the dried man looked like he wanted to embrace you, and he smiled and smiled and smiled.

  That night the drivers had a party. They all got drunk in the back of an ambulance and they made each other tell about the time they had the best meal of their life and that was fun. One guy wanted everybody to tell about the best sex they had ever had, but no one wanted to tell that kind of story. Then they laughed and hit each other on the legs with their fists, to see if they could give someone the worst charley horse. If you had a big bump swell up on the top of your leg, you won an extra bottle. Everybody got drunk and had bruised legs.

  When the others had gone, J.J. stayed in the ambulance with its driver, a new guy. They set up two litters to sleep on—one on each side with plenty of blankets, but it wasn't cold that spring, a thing hard to remember for J.J. now in his freezing Hobo Jungle next to the California ocean this deadly winter. The new ambulance driver said he wanted to tell J.J. something.

  "Yeah, what?" J.J. said cautiously.

  "The Dried Man?"

  "What about him?"

  "Well, you see . . . well . . ."

  "What, man?"

  "I got his watch."

  "When did you get it?"

  "When I took a whizz."

  "Put the watch back."

  "I can't. I'm afraid."

  "He's dead, man. I mean really dead."

  "That's why I'm afraid."

  "You weren't afraid when you took it."

  "I was drunker. I'm more sober now, and I feel badly about the watch."

  "Give it back to him for Christ' sake."

  "I know, but I can't," he said and started to cry.

  J.J. held the watch closely in his good hand. Now at night in this war you just didn't get a flashlight or strike a match or anything like that to get about—any light might trigger incoming, so J.J. had to feel his way in the light of the crescent moon to the Dried Man's stretcher. The man was there all right waiting with his arms reaching for you and his eyes fixed on you.

  "Here's your watch, mother," J.J. said and he slipped the watch carefully over the black curved fingers, and the skinny wrist and the watch slid down the Dried Man's shrunken left arm until the watch stopped sliding just before the elbow and what was left of the tattered shirt sleeve.

  The Dried Man, of course, smiled and the crescent moon's light glinted from his teeth.

J.J. hauled bodies for six more months after that before he was finally discharged, but none of his cargoes were as bad as the Dried Man. J.J. always had the image of the Dried Man in his mind after the war, even now, year after year. He saw him up close, like that night with the watch; he saw him from a medium distance lying there on his litter with his arms reaching; and he saw him afar when the Dried Man was evacuated, his litter stacked high on top of a six-by's stake racks—he had to be tied down to his litter and since his arms were outstretched like that in that awesome reaching position, he wouldn't fit in the lower rack, so he was secured on the top, more or less alone, turned slightly to one side, staring down at you, grinning. It was the grin that always got you.

Tonight, now, in the Hobo Jungle, that freezing December along the California coast, J.J. saw the Dried Man again, only this time it was different; he had never seen the Dried Man like this before and he told him so.

"Hey, Dried Man, you can move," J.J. said.

The Dried Man was lying next to J.J. as J.J. lay sandwiched in the dirty mattress behind the big rock in the Jungle. Then the Dried Man rolled over to J.J. and widened his reach and grinned more and ever so slowly beckoned with his black fingers for J.J. to embrace him and J.J., reluctantly at first, but then with a strange enthusiasm, moved out of his mattress into those outstretched arms, right next to the grinning face with the intensely white teeth and J.J. looked long into those prune-like eyes and the eyes all of a sudden seemed moist and J.J. felt a full and overwhelming camaraderie for the Dried Man and the arms closed around J.J. until, at last, for the first time really in over thirty winters, J.J. felt warm.

Jimmy Carl Harris

Hot and Sunny on the Fourth

Hot woke up resolved to do something about it. She fixed herself some eggs, then took to the trail that began at her back door and climbed up to the clearest air. She sat on a fallen sycamore beside the trail and thought it through. With her mind settled on what needed to be done, she returned home and put on the necessary clothes. She went out to her truck and ground the starter until it coughed itself awake.

It was midmorning when Hot came down off the mountain. She thought of it as her mountain and was grateful the strip miners had determined it contained too little coal to justify ripping it apart with bulldozers. An early rain had left a ground fog that swirled around the hurrying truck and tried to embrace it like a cool shroud. Near the point where the narrow blacktop curved around an outcrop of ancient rock, an alert doe nudged her curious offspring away from the roadside. The guttural exhaust echoed up the hollow and startled blue jays so they bolted for a higher limb.

Hot slowed when she reached the spot where, in April, a category four tornado had dipped its angry funnel into the hollow and reduced Macedonia Full Gospel Holiness to widely dispersed kindling. She remembered the old church, its bare wood pews worn slick by generations of hand-sewn dresses and 401 overalls. There, on a chilly October day thirty years back, a teenage girl, not yet called Hot, came forward and accepted Christ as her personal savior. The preacher took her the next Sunday at dawn to be washed free of sin by full immersion in the icy creek that ran behind the church.

In 1951, six years after she'd been baptized in the name of the Father, the Son, and the Holy Ghost, she returned from a sojourn up in Nashville. On her first Sunday back, she slipped into a back pew. Throughout the sermon, she endured being glanced at by red-faced men and glared at by hard-eyed women. She left during the invitational hymn and never came back. Still, from then on, if anyone had bothered to ask, she would have claimed membership in the church where she had professed her faith.

Today, Hot saw that several men from the congregation had worked up a good sweat preparing the surviving foundation for a new white frame church identical to the old one. She glanced at the graveyard they had cleared of debris on Decoration Day. She noted the recent graves, the eternal resting places of the four souls whose trailer had been found by the twister. She'd heard, during one of her infrequent trips into Ebenezer, that the adults were found huddled where the bathroom had been but the baby was taken up by the heartless wind and dropped into the creek. She thought of stopping to inquire about a burial plot but decided against it. There'd be time enough later for dealing with last rites. She rumbled on down toward town.

At the intersection with County Route Four, Hot pressed her palm against the steering wheel and spun it in a sharp turn toward Ebenezer. She released the wheel, punched the accelerator, allowed the pickup to pull itself straight. She slammed the gearshift up into second right when her own voice, singing about a lonesome burning soul, spilled out of the speakers. She dropped the shifter hard into third and continued to hold the gas pedal to the bare metal floor.

Her lonesome soul number had been the A side of her demo disk, her get outta this place song the B side. After two years of being just another mountain girl with haunts in her voice and no connections, reality had driven Hot out of Nashville. The bus had dropped her off in Ebenezer. She'd hitchhiked and walked, trudged the way a woman great with child will, up the hollow to the mountain. Back then, her mamaw was still alive and Hot moved in with her. Hot had lived there ever since, raised her son in the unpainted clapboard house with a splash of yellow jonquils to challenge the shadows cast by the upreaching pines. She'd hid her record in a box of quilting scraps. Only recently, she'd had her sides transferred to an eight-track. She'd told the guy making the tape to fill it out with cheating love songs borrowed from Patsy and the rest.

About half-way between the church and Ebenezer, at the point where the valley began to broaden and modest dwellings were more frequent, was the Americal Kwik Sak. The small, green-painted cinder block building was surrounded by coils of concertina wire and had an entranceway constructed of neatly piled sandbags. Over the door were crossed flags, one the red, white and blue, the other the three red stripes on yellow of the Republic of Vietnam.

Hot parked outside the wire. She passed between the sandbag walls and under the flags. She looked around the small convenience store, then called out. "Wheels?"

"Back here. Who's that?"

"Hot. I see you got you some of that coiled-up barbed wire."

A legless man in a wheelchair trundled from behind a display of potato chips. His hair was pulled tight back into a ponytail. He was wearing blue jean cut-offs and a sleeveless, camouflage pattern hunting vest. Attached to one side of his wheelchair was a rifle scabbard encasing a battered but well-oiled Winchester Model 74. "Concertina. Man can't be too careful with his security."

"You expecting an invasion?"

Wheels propelled himself to a point where his bare stumps were six inches from Hot. "Yeah. By my own government."

Hot glanced at the pink, withered remains jutting toward her but held her ground. "Maybe you ought to pay your taxes."

"Maybe I should've gone to Canada. Wha'cha need, Hot Stuff?"

"Smokes."

Wheels spun his chair, rolled behind the counter, and tossed her a red pack of Pall Malls. She nabbed the cigarettes in midair with one hand and put her money on the counter.

Wheels looked Hot over more carefully. "Love your get-up. Where you headed?"

"Ebenezer. Got to tend to some unfinished business."

Wheels looked out the barred window of his store for a long moment. "Sunny."

Hot was already at the door, silhouetted against the glare. She answered before she left. "Sunny."

Wheels lifted a fist to full arm's length and held it there. His shout followed Hot all the way out to her truck. "Right on, Babe, right on."

In Ebenezer, Hot slowed to show respect and pulled into the

funeral home parking lot. She quieted the tape and the engine and slid out of her ride. She stood for a moment in front of the ersatz antebellum splendor of the Bondurant Funeral Home, felt the heat of the pavement through the soles of her boots. She field-stripped her cigarette butt, reduced it to tiny shreds of paper and flakes of tobacco, as Wheels had taught her to do. He said it prevented the enemy from knowing where you'd been. She passed between the white columns and shoved the door open.

Aubrey Bondurant, in gray seersucker, sported a wilted carnation in his lapel. He wafted forth from his office and hovered on the beige carpet, positioned in Hot's path. He uttered something that sounded like, "Kanipye?"

Hot put her hands on her hips. "Say what?"

Aubrey took a deep breath and enunciated, "Can I help you?"

"Where y'all got Sunny?"

Aubrey looked Hot over. He took in her olive drab head rag and her faded black tee shirt with *Walking Dead* stretched across her bosom. He briefly appreciated her denim-encased legs, kept slim by thousands of hours on mountain trails, but winced at the sight of her heavy, polished boots. "You're here for the gentleman the VA brought in?"

"Yeah. Sunny."

Confusion joined the resentment puckering Aubrey's round face. "The VA rep said his name was—"

Hot's interruption drove Aubrey back a step. "When he was little, people said he could light up a cloudy day. They took to calling him Sunny and it stuck. Where y'all got him?"

Aubrey flapped a hand toward a door on one side of the lobby. "The Liberty Chapel. We use it for our veterans." He retreated to his paneled cubicle and his muted television set in time to catch the end of the daytime drama he'd been watching.

Hot strode into the chapel. She paused to adjust her eyes to the gloom, then studied the metal cart where the flag-draped coffin rested. She released the brake on each wheel and pushed the cart out of the chapel. She was maneuvering it through the front door when Aubrey reemerged from his office.

Aubrey was instantly breathless. "What're you doing?"

"Something that should've been done a long time ago."

"You can't just remove the deceased from the premises."

"Watch me."

Aubrey grabbed the push bar of the glass front door. He let go when Hot drop-kicked him in the crotch. He squirmed on the carpet, holding himself, while Hot loaded Sunny into the bed of her pickup. She stretched a rope across the truck bed and knotted it into place so that it secured the flag atop the coffin. She rested her hand on the coffin for a moment, then got into her truck.

The courthouse square was early-afternoon quiet. The Fourth of July sun had driven most sensible citizens to seek some shade or, if they were wiser, some recently air-conditioned space. That evening, the square would fill with families half-listening to overweight men in their fifties ramble on about the good war, about Guadalcanal and Anzio. Parents would still their children with promises of Methodist ice cream and Baptist fireworks. The combined church choir, in harmony for the only time of the year, would belt out a fair-to-middling a cappella rendition of "God Bless America."

Hot slowed when she reached the square. She took her tape out of the player and inserted another. The *I Feel Like I'm Fixin' To Die Rag* blasted raucous into the still heat. She circled the courthouse until the patrol units blocked her front and rear.

"Come outta there, Hot." The sheriff's deputy stood ten feet away from Hot's truck, his right thumb hooked in his gun belt. His fingertips dangled near his service revolver.

Hot did as she was told. She leaned against the rear fender of her truck, put fire to a Pall Mall, flicked her Zippo closed with a flourish, and nodded to the deputy. "You won't be needin' your gun, Hank."

Hank bobbed his head in acknowledgment. "I know that." He kept his right hand near his weapon while he waved at Hot with his left. "What's with the get-up?"

Hot gave her head rag a gentle pat and glanced down at her shirt. "This is stuff Sunny brought back from over there." She jerked her head sideways toward the cab of the truck. "The music was his, too."

"I heard it before. In 'Nam. Sorry 'bout Sunny."

Hot took a deep draw on her cigarette and blew a stream of smoke toward Hank. "What's that y'all said when you got back? 'It don't mean nothing'?"

"Yeah, we said that." Hank tilted his head to one side and looked at Sunny's coffin. "What're you up to, anyway?"

"I'm giving my boy the Fourth of July parade this town never gave him."

Hank laid down the benediction. "Never gave none of us." He came to attention and saluted the mortal remains of the son still in her womb when, more than two decades earlier, she stepped off the bus from Nashville. Then, he asked Hot to please put her hands behind her back.

Mona Houghton

The Woman Who Lived in the Avocado Grove

    Jacqueline lives in a house in the middle of an avocado grove. Her husband, Frank, and her daughter, Pauli, used to live there too, in this house surrounded by the trees with the low and reaching branches, but now Jacqueline stays alone.
    This morning Jacqueline wakes up with tears streaming down her cheeks. It is appropriate. She sits bolt upright in bed and sees herself in the mirror above the dark wood dresser. It is Pauli's twenty-first birthday today. Jacqueline says, "Maybe Pauli will call," but Jacqueline knows this will not happen.
    She finds her own voice comforting, almost like hearing another person. Right after Frank left, hearing herself speak in the silent house startled Jacqueline, but she has grown quite used to it.
    As Jacqueline sits on the end of the bed and pulls on the

faded jeans and tee shirt she wore yesterday she looks at the picture of her mother on the dresser, the one in the silver frame.

Frank, who will soon want to discuss their divorce, called last night. He is coming by for lunch today because it is Pauli's birthday.

"Pauli'll come back." "She's just being a teenager." "They all do crazy stuff sometime." The other parents had tried to console Jacqueline and Frank after Pauli disappeared one day. Sixteen years old. The police insisted on calling her a runaway, one of thousands. The policeman said, "You don't know teenagers."

"But I do," Jacqueline insisted.

And that is what scared her. Jacqueline had taught history at Valley Center High, a school just six miles from the avocado grove, for fourteen years.

She knows teenagers. She knows how they can turn on you, like snakes. "Pauli gives great head." She found it scrawled on her blackboard one day in pink chalk. And Jacqueline was a favorite teacher among the students.

Jacqueline begins to wander through the house, not to visit its rooms, but to look out in each direction into the grove that contains her. She sees Miguel out by the tool shed. He is repairing a section of the drip system. It needs constant attention. The water comes from the Colorado River—dirty water. If Frank lived here he would spend half of every day checking the nipples under each tree, making sure grime had not clogged the inner workings. But Frank no longer lives on the land, and so now bigger sections of the system break down more frequently.

Frank believed Pauli ran away, too. Jacqueline couldn't stand it that he thought this. Jacqueline knew someone had kidnapped Pauli, someone had stolen her.

Pauli learned to walk while Frank and Jacqueline learned to graft one kind of avocado onto another's root system, turning trees that produced watery Zutanos into ones covered with creamy Fuentes, large, roundish Bacons, pebbly skinned Haases. It was spring, a Saturday, when Pauli took her first steps. The family had gone down to the trees growing along the river. Frank prepared the understock, splitting it several inches through the smooth, straight-grained section. Jacqueline, having shaped two of the scions into long and gradually tapering wedges, was easing them into position in the understock when she looked up and saw Pauli with her tiny hands wrapped around the edge of the wheelbarrow, pulling herself up into a standing position. Jacqueline had seen this maneuver hundreds of times before, but on this day her daughter's eyes caught hers. In them was a glimmer, a wonderment, the primitive awareness of a moment when the impossible is transformed and becomes, suddenly, reachable.

Jacqueline whispered to Frank, "Look," as Pauli's little fingers loosened their grip. They both watched as their daughter stepped out into the unknown. Back then that had seemed so exciting.

The screen door slams closed behind Jacqueline as she walks out into the August heat. At the sound, Miguel faces her. He takes a step back, says, "Good morning."

Jacqueline can only nod. On her way over to the sprinkler spigot she feels the blades of grass between her bare toes. Miguel's son is Pauli's age. He works summers at the nursery in town. Frank works there now, too, but he comes to the grove to talk to Miguel. Frank worked these fifteen acres too hard and for too long to simply walk away, or go very far. He lives in an apartment above a tee-shirt store in town. It was supposed to be temporary, but it didn't turn out that way. He moved in there three years ago. When Jacqueline thinks of his apartment, she imagines the old one where he lived when they were students. She will not go to the new one.

Jacqueline met Frank at the Mediterranean coffee house on Telegraph Avenue in Berkeley in 1964. They were both freshmen, but Frank was older; he had been in the army for four years. At the time a lot of boys had stopped shaving, or had never started, and peach fuzz covered their rosy cheeks, but Frank had a real beard, and his black eyebrow hairs met in the middle of his forehead.

Frank had seen Jacqueline on campus, in Murphy Hall. Jacqueline knew because this was Frank's opening line: "Aren't you in Mueller's history class?"

To Jacqueline, Frank seemed mature, sophisticated. He found Mueller's historical perspective "narrow and simplistic." Frank had a room of his own, off campus. Jacqueline had seen the place, a big, old, Spanish-style house with a painting of Castro on the front gate. Some of the people who lived there called it a commune. Frank called it a place to crash.

Frank took her there that afternoon, to his room with the Indian bedspreads billowing down from the ceiling and the candles lining the window sills. A flag hung across the opening to the closet. A water pipe occupied the desk, and books on Buddhism, nihilism, and existentialism covered the floor beside the mattress with the grayish, crumpled sheets.

Frank eased Jacqueline in through the door and asked, "Want a bowl?" as he walked over to the water pipe and picked up one of its octopus arms.

Jacqueline had smoked pot before, but always discreetly, in

thin joints, or in the shells of emptied cigarettes—never in a hookah pipe.

"Come on, let's get high," Frank said.

Jacqueline turned around on the heel of one foot. By the time she had completed her circle, Frank was breaking the buds.

Pauli was smoking pot at twelve. Jacqueline caught her doing it in her room, alone, and had a different reaction than she ever would have expected. She pretended she didn't see it, or smell it. She pretended she didn't notice her daughter's glazed eyes. Pauli used a bong pipe. Jacqueline found it the next day while Pauli was at school, hidden inside a roller skate. Jacqueline never told Frank because she knew Frank would want the three of them to *discuss* it.

Jacqueline hasn't taken any illegal drugs in almost fifteen years. The only buds she worries about these days are the ones on the avocado trees. If blooms come too early, a frost might take a whole crop. But it is summer now, the fruit is set, the avocados are on their way. In six weeks it will be time to pick the majority of the Haases. She finally manages to say "Good Morning" to Miguel.

Jacqueline inherited the land from an uncle, her mother's brother, a man she hardly knew. He had bought the place years before as an investment. Jacqueline had never even been there, to that valley sixty miles north of San Diego and thirty miles inland from the Pacific Ocean. She knew three things about the area: it had mild winters, hot summers, and soil that avocado trees loved. Soon after the title papers arrived she and Frank drove down to see what an avocado grove actually looked like.

As the probate lawyer drove around the perimeter of the property, all the green seduced Jacqueline. She barely heard him, the pluses and minuses: six of the fifteen rolling acres covered in producing trees, flood damage from the heavy rains in '63. Then the lawyer took them down to the end of the dirt drive, to the buildings. When Jacqueline saw these, when she stepped out of the car and stood in front of them, a calm came over her, something captivating. Unlike the other ranches in the valley, the house and the work shed on this property sat in the middle of the grove. Avocado trees enveloped them.

Jacqueline and Frank spent the next five days working their way through the old house, poking into the attic, the basement, the closets, making love on the sun porch. They found magazines from the forties, and a drawer full of crocheted antimacassars. And in the heat of the afternoons, they would go out to the grove, to one of the trees near the house, and they would each grab hold of one of those low, horizontal limbs and pull themselves up onto it. They would each straddle a branch and talk.

Jacqueline gave birth to Pauli the first summer they spent in the valley, and Jacqueline fell in love with her new baby, and Frank and Jacqueline fell in love with each other all over again.

Jacqueline's own mother had died when Jacqueline was six years old, of a brain tumor. Two weeks after the funeral Jacqueline's father gave her the framed picture that stands on her dresser today. In the picture Jacqueline's mother, at twenty-one or twenty-two, leans against the Chrysler Building in New York City. She is smiling. She has on a fashionable forties dress and her eyes look clear and bright. The same day that Jacqueline's father gave Jacqueline the picture, he put all the rest of his wife's personal belongings into the car and drove them down to the Goodwill. The photograph in the silver frame was all Jacqueline had left of her mother. She turns from Miguel and walks toward her house.

In Berkeley, in the house with Castro on the wall, Jacqueline and Frank found out all sorts of things about each other. They spent afternoons, whole weekends, in that bed with the crumpled sheets. Jacqueline loved the sex of it, the sensuality—the smells, the tastes, the sounds. She also dreamed of a little girl, but still she was careful, for Jacqueline also knew how she wanted it to be—for them to have a real house and real jobs, to be a real family.

Frank was spiritual, back then. Jacqueline's soul intrigued him. He found it mysterious, as curious as looking up on a moonless night and seeing the Milky Way, he used to say. He described it as something dark that lurked inside of Jacqueline, between the practical part, the way she alphabetized the books on the shelves under the window, and the secret part, the way she, each night, arranged her brush and hand cream and the silver-framed photograph of her mother on the thrift-shop dresser they had bought the week Jacqueline moved in. It would be years before Frank actually understood he would never be allowed to see into the dark, that Jacqueline would keep him out forever.

Jacqueline and Frank smoked the hookah pipe a lot when they lived in that house. They dropped magic mushrooms, hitched into San Francisco to the Filmore to hear Hendrix and Joplin. They marched against the war, threw water balloons at policemen in riot gear, took bad acid and ended up at the Free Clinic begging for hits of Thorazine. Frank practiced Buddhism for a couple of years—he ate nothing but whole grains and lentil beans and he always smelled like incense. Jacqueline was more focused. She spent most of her free time concentrating on classes—Social and Intellectual History of Europe to 1815, History of War in the Modern World, Comparative Socialism. The subject intrigued her.

Pauli hated history. Pauli hated science, English, art history. Pauli hated school, period. Nor did she like baseball, or after-school ballet lessons. She didn't want to play with any of her classmates, whom Jacqueline would have happily had over any afternoon. To witness her daughter choosing this isolation pained Jacqueline in places she hadn't known before. Jacqueline ended up screaming at her little girl, "Talk to me." Pauli glared at her and turned around and walked away. Frank tried to help. He read books, he talked about boundaries and respect. Jacqueline screamed at him, "Don't interfere." Frank screamed back, "We're talking about our Pauli."

Jacqueline knew exactly how she and Pauli should be together. She had known this since she was eight or nine years old. It was supposed to be like it would have been with her mother—them in harmony with each other and with the world. Jacqueline experienced the need for this primitively, like hunger or desire. And when it didn't happen she felt senselessly terrorized.

But that can only last for so long. In time, Jacqueline stopped feeling anything.

Frank cried in Jacqueline's arms one night after he tried to make love to her. He wanted back into his wife's heart. Jacqueline could only see Pauli, ten years old now, in the schoolyard, her mouth filled with grass, dirty tears streaking her cheeks, three of her classmates around her, jeering, and Pauli yelling back at them, "Sons of bitches."

Standing at the kitchen sink, Jacqueline watches through the window. The rainbird spits water out over the small patch of lawn by the back door of the house. Miguel works at the bench in front of the shed, cutting a piece of plastic pipe with a hack saw. Jacqueline says, "I should help him." But she doesn't move, for she knows she can no longer cooperate. Jacqueline tried to get Pauli's picture onto the milk cartons in L.A. county. Mr. Morley, the man in charge, said, "Sounds like a run-away to me."

The last fun Jacqueline had was on the night in 1985 when the Rolling Stones played the Los Angeles Coliseum. Frank and Jacqueline's best friend from Berkeley, Ted, was visiting. He had arrived that Friday morning. He had been down in Baja, Mexico, fishing, and when he and Frank walked in through the screen door, Ted looking so big and tan and relaxed, his blond hair gleaming, Jacqueline started to look forward to the weekend, to the three of them spending some quiet time together. Pauli, now a surly fifteen, was going to ride up to Los Angeles with a group of friends for the concert and then spend the night at an aunt's house. Frank had called the aunt to confirm Pauli's plans. Jacqueline had been against the trip. "I don't trust her," she had said to Frank. Frank's attitude was more accepting. "She's a teenager, Jacqueline. Cool down." To Jacqueline, Frank sounded like some new-age guru. He didn't understand how wrong it all felt to her—their lives, everything that happened in the house. Pauli had shaved her hair off above her right ear. Jacqueline could hardly bear to look at her. She dreaded being around her own daughter, yet was anxious when Pauli left the house. Still, part of Jacqueline felt relieved that Friday afternoon when Pauli got into the car with her friends and they all drove away.

She breathed the relief out in a sigh as she finished washing the home-grown lettuce she had traded for avocados earlier in the day. Ted was sitting at the breakfast table, a bottle of tequila and a bottle mescal in front of him. He had bought them before crossing back over the border. Ted said, "It's just a haircut, Jacqueline."

By the time they finished dinner Jacqueline and Frank and Ted had worked their way through half the bottle of mescal. Frank and Ted had been at the Stones' Altamont concert in 1969. Drinking shots made the remembering all the more vivid. While Jacqueline and Ted did the dishes Frank dug out all his old Stones albums from 1966 and '67 and '68. Pretty soon "My Sweet Lady Jane" and "Back Door Girl" and "Ruby Tuesday" blared out from the living room speakers. Shot glasses in hand, the three of them sang along with Mick Jagger. They sang at the top of their lungs. For the first time in years, Jacqueline actually lived for a few hours without Pauli haunting her. She looked at Frank and felt turned on. She started twirling around the room. Frank and Ted followed her—the three of them dervishes spinning toward some moment of clarity. They emptied the bottle of mescal and ended up dividing the worm three ways, each eating their piece solemnly, like a sacrament.

Just before dawn Frank led them to the highest point on the property, up to where the trees that made the best avocados stood. Ted picked a tree (he said the tree picked him) and they all climbed up into it. Jacqueline, the lightest, stood on the highest and thinnest branch. She hadn't, in years, looked beyond, hadn't really seen a whole landscape. She felt herself open up inside, hard crusts peeling away, as the three of them, there in the branches, watched the sun rise up over the valley.

After Jacqueline turns the rainbird off, she decides to take a shower, wash her hair before Frank comes over for lunch. She looks at herself in the mirror. With the end of a finger, she smooths out the skin around her eyes. She notices that her lips are getting thinner, her nose broader. In the bedroom, after pulling a comb through her wet hair, Jacqueline finds a pair of clean jeans in the dresser, and a blouse, an ironed one, in the closet. She looks out the window, into the avocado trees, as she dresses.

Jacqueline used to love the trees with their hearty leaves, their long, elegant limbs, and that fruit, tender and seamless. And she used to love the house too. In the summer there was no better place to be in the valley than in this house, cooled by the air under that canopy of green. A little breeze would blow through and the house would swell with the sweetest scents—just hints of earth and trunk, and sometimes, late in the afternoon, a trace of alfalfa, especially if Old Man Walker had watered recently. And Pauli was growing tall and strong. Her kindergarten teacher called her a rebellious child, but this didn't worry Jacqueline. A little rebellion never hurt anyone.

By the time Pauli was seven years old, Jacqueline was driving one hundred miles a day to a special private school for difficult children in Escondido. The counselor at the local grammar school had recommended the institution. Pauli simply made no effort to get along with her peers, her teachers, with anyone. And at home, Jacqueline knew, Pauli refused to participate. At meal-times she wouldn't eat if Jacqueline or Frank insisted she use a fork or spoon or knife, and she could go without food longer than either of her parents could refuse her. And sometimes a day or two would pass when Pauli wouldn't utter a word. Jacqueline's feelings started wrapping around themselves, becoming tangled. Every time she tried to think about Pauli, every time she tried to plan a talk with her, she found herself helplessly confused, up against some wall inside herself that she could not get over. Frank wanted to help Jacqueline; he insisted that somehow the two of them could survive anything—that nothing could stop them as long as they were together. But part of Jacqueline lived behind a barrier, with her mother, in the cloudy childhood corners, in the time before the tumor slowly compressed her mother's brain and turned her wicked. Jacqueline would not discuss this though, not with Frank, not with a psychiatrist, not with anyone.

Pauli came home from The Rolling Stones concert with a tattoo on her arm—a large rose with "I love Mick" in script beneath it. Jacqueline went crazy when she first saw it, some three weeks after the concert. She happened to walk into Pauli's room one afternoon while Pauli was changing her clothes. Pauli tried to hide the scabby mess on her arm. She said, "You didn't knock." When Jacqueline started screaming and hitting Pauli, Pauli laughed at her. By the time Pauli disappeared she had two more tattoos: a snake around her ankle, and a tear rolling down her cheek.

Jacqueline hears Frank's truck rattling its way up the drive. By the time she gets back to the kitchen, Frank, tall and as thin as he was in Berkeley, is standing in front of the work bench talking to Miguel. When Jacqueline opens the back door, Frank turns, as if sensing her. He waves. "I'll be right in."

Today is Pauli's twenty-first birthday. It is the fifth time Jacqueline and Frank have celebrated the day alone. Yesterday Jacqueline picked up a cake at the bakery, a small one. Frank will come inside in a few minutes. They will make tuna fish sandwiches and share a beer as they eat them. Then they will have the cake. Together, they will cry. Frank will hold Jacqueline and kiss her hair and they will feel themselves break again.

This is the last birthday Frank wants to celebrate. He will tell Jacqueline this as he gives her a present: a picture of Pauli in a silver frame. Pauli will be fourteen years old in the photograph. She will not be smiling, but will look beautiful.

Frank and Jacqueline will sit together, without speaking, for a little while, and then Frank will leave and as he leaves Frank will take the rest of the birthday cake out to Miguel and Miguel will eat it in the shade behind the shed. Later, Jacqueline will take the picture in the silver frame to her bedroom. She will stand it next to the one of her mother.

That night, in a dream, Jacqueline will find herself in a fantastic palace. She will be the tattooed woman, every inch of her body covered in an exotic design. When she looks out the leaded windows, she will see her trees, their trunks covered with tattoos like her own. She will walk out to them and stand, like a goddess, arms raised, chin high. When the wind blows, the grove will swell with the sweetest smells. For years people in the valley will whisper about the woman who lives in the avocado grove.

Scott McWaters

Developing Story

1.

Pictures and words are left behind. Scrawled on the walls of a dormitory hallway in black magic marker is the image of a tree with a noose and hanging stick figure surrounded by enlarged genitalia and flaming crucifixes. Epithets written in bold capital letters: "FUCKING NIGGER" and "HOE NIGGER" and "NIGGER GO HOME." The two students who live in the room, Frank and Jason, exhausted from studying for final exams, didn't hear a thing. Frank notices the graffiti early that morning on his way back from the shower. He awakens his roommate. Their fourth floor resident assistant is told and the campus police phoned. The police arrive quickly, take photographs, aren't able to dust for prints because of the surface and the countless number of fingers that touch the wall every day. They instruct the RA to begin washing away the racist mural with bleach and water, not wanting to scare or anger the dormitory's janitors or any of the other residents. Afraid of the repercussions, the authorities are conversing in low voices, walking as if the hallway's carpeting were cracking ice. Half-asleep students who have morning exams are told to mind their own business, that there is nothing to worry about. The two victims are questioned behind closed doors. Shaken up, nervously chuckling, they attempt to shrug the incident off, saying it's just part of life in the South. They don't have a guess as to who would want to do such a thing, no enemies on the hall or in the dorm or on the campus. They are polite freshmen from Selma and Montgomery who have become involved in a local church together, met girls, played intramurals, gone to football and basketball games, and are both hoping to make the honor roll again this spring semester. Frank has already declared engineering as his major, while Jason remains undecided.

2.

One of the nation's 24-hour news stations is on campus assembling a story to be aired in June in connection with the 40th anniversary of Governor George Wallace's stand to block Vivian Malone and James Hood from being the first black students to enroll in the University of Alabama. The report will be about changes that have taken place on the campus (13% African-American enrollment, integrated athletic teams of national prominence, award-winning minority faculty members). The crew is filming Foster Auditorium, getting a close-up shot of the commemorative plaque, which is no larger than a small television screen—a reminder of the event that took place in front of the auditorium's doors. A young, blonde reporter in high heels is searching for students who'll agree to be interviewed for the news piece, when someone walking across the street yells back to her that the *real* story is taking place inside the dorm next door.

Before the police force them to leave, the crew is able to get the names of the two victims and footage of the RA cleaning the wall. The reporter phones her producer in New York City. The irony. They have to go live. She can't believe the luck on her very first assignment—a hate crime, in Alabama nonetheless, out of all the things in the world to cover. They will interview the victims at the exact spot where Wallace stood, if one of them will agree to talk. The reporter reminds herself to relax her lower jaw, conscious that her overbite might be showing, aware of how the camera exaggerates.

3.

In 1963, coming off the largest vote of any gubernatorial candidate in Alabama's history the year before, news of George Wallace's "stand" at the University of Alabama rippled through the country, a flick across a taut white sheet. His campaign slogan, "Segregation now, Segregation tomorrow, Segregation forever!" was still echoing in the nation's ears while Americans stared at footage of the forty-four-year-old Wallace, erect, pointing, haranguing like a Southern Baptist preacher in an attempt to block the national guard from allowing President Kennedy's orders of integration to be carried out.

Still campaigning. Always campaigning? That could be George Wallace's mindset while appealing to the crowd of white citizens of Alabama, to the country that gathered around Foster Auditorium to witness a young man and woman attempt to further their education. Interpreting artifacts makes every viewer an anthropologist on the American dig. Watch the image on film. Study Wallace intentionally stitching himself for an instant to the peripheral camera, because in the future he won't be what people have assumed. Inspect the stand of the public man, the messenger, who recognizes it's all about what is perceived in the moment.

4.

The news has spread. By noon the Black Student Union has organized a "Say No to Racism" rally to be held that evening on the campus quad. They will use candles and revisit old speeches from Martin Luther King Junior, speeches given in Alabama years ago to a different generation, to a different nation. Singing of hymns and prayer are planned. As long as their names aren't mentioned, the two victims have agreed to make an appearance on stage. Also, Prince Leigh, an Alabama football alumni and now a pop music star, will make a special guest appearance. Leigh's already in Alabama visiting his elderly father in a Birmingham hospital. He knows the president of the Black Student Union from their old neighborhood and talks to her over the phone that afternoon. "I guess it's all rising back to the surface again, Sister. Just when they want to think it's dead in the Heart of Dixie," he pauses. "If Dad were feeling better, I'd bring him with me to talk about carrying white men's golf bags for your whole life. He's got stories I still haven't even heard."

5.

It's a racially mixed dormitory. But the rooms within it are rarely integrated—a color by numbers picture. Frank originally was assigned a white roommate back in August but each of the boys requested a room transfer, and a week later the white student moved in with a friend. The police interview this former roommate, who for the entire school year has been living on the floor below. He was sleeping last night, hasn't really seen or interacted with his old roommate much, but doesn't have anything against him. He feels bad about what has happened, that someone in the twenty-first century would act like that. They really haven't talked since those first few awkward days when they lived together, annoyed by each other's CD collections, clothes and taste in movies. They had difficulty finding something to talk about until they discovered that they both shared an interest in architecture; both hoped to help construct bridges and tall buildings in the future.

6.

The news crew is banned from reentering the dorm. They stalk around the outside of the five-story brick building getting footage. The reporter's jaw is aching. Soon they will go live. While telling the cameraman not to miss the Confederate flags substituting as shades in some of the dorm room windows, she can't help but feel proud about what her parents did back in the 60's when they left New York for a summer and worked as volunteers, registering Mississippi blacks to vote. They helped to change things, helped change this country like she is doing now. These images of Confederate flags are about to be broadcast out to the entire nation and the world quicker than the time it takes someone to turn on a television.

7.

Outside Memphis, Corley Schock has just returned home from an afternoon spent donating plasma. For the past three months he has been going twice a week and saving his cash in an empty coffee can. Ever since his back was injured while working a construction job to repair part of the Memphis Country Club, Schock has been waiting to begin collecting his disability checks. It's a complicated system, but his boss assures him the money will arrive soon.

Schock is a hard, honest worker. In a worn orange chair that used to belong to his deceased father, he reclines himself to a position that relieves his pain, and then calls for Rex to jump into his lap. His girlfriend, Rose, gave him the puppy for his birthday last month. Rex is a pound dog, a mix with the distinct markings of a Dalmatian spotted across his fur. Corley is bandaged at his right elbow. He rotates his arm and flexes the large forearm muscles of a man who's spent the majority of his life building things. Large veins make intimations along Schock's dark skin. The ladies at Aventis tell him that he was made for donating. He grabs the remote control from atop an unopened box and turns on the television. Scratching Rex behind the head, he again wonders what they do with plasma, where it actually goes. He always forgets to ask because he's nervous having a needle in his arm, watching his blood being pumped out and then put back in again, but he will remember during his next visit. A young, blonde reporter is standing in front of a building as they cut to a commercial. Corley hopes plasma goes to help victims in need like blood donations do.

8.

The Kappa Alpha's, the KA's as they're known, are a fraternity at the end of the campus's Old Row. One impotent cannon guards the house's large front lawn. A statue of Robert E. Lee stands in the foyer and a large Confederate flag hangs from the roof. One of the KA's former pledges, a newly inducted member, had an English class last fall with Jason. The two were assigned as partners for an essay on cause and effect. Because both of the students had busy schedules, they had trouble finding a time to meet in the library in order to research a topic and gather information. They ended up each writing part of the essay on their own and then cutting and pasting their ideas together. They made a C- on the paper.

9.

The media works like a grater on life, runs stories back and forth, back and forth until everything is left in pieces.

10.

At Innisfree, a pub in downtown Tuscaloosa, white folks, mainly lawyers, are sipping happy hour drinks after work, talking under the glow of two mounted televisions. When the report coming from the University airs, the crowd gets quiet. They gaze at images of the blonde with full lips. Her overbite is only visible if the viewer knows what to look for. The patrons don't notice. She is doing a good job keeping her jaw relaxed while interviewing one of the anonymous victims. They stand in front of Foster Auditorium. Once the interview is over, footage is shown of the preparations for the upcoming rally, microphones and speakers being assembled. Prince Leigh's name is mentioned and then his picture is shown. Next, in a taped interview, the leader of the Black Student Union is asked about racism on campus. "It's here. Definitely exists. A burden we're always carrying, but just different than it used to be," she pauses and looks into the camera. "Little quieter than when Governor Wallace stood at this exact spot and let all his views be known. But hate is still here. It's always around us."

11.

At Déjà Vu, a bar in Ithaca, New York, students wait for the news with eager anticipation. Cheers and clapping erupt when the report from Alabama is aired. Just last year they were in school with this reporter, drinking cosmopolitans at this bar together, selecting songs from the jukebox in the corner. Everyone is quiet when she begins to interview the nameless victim. "Her lips look fuller on television. Oh, but her overbite is showing." Everyone sighs when they see footage of Confederate flags covering windows. The people in this bar see the situation down South as being totally black and white. "Rednecks!"

someone screams. "The war's over!"

A few girls cheer when Prince Leigh is mentioned. "He's hot!" They are all proud of the reporter. They drink to their friend and the great job she's doing, and then return to talking about their plans for the summer, internships in Manhattan and an August trip to Cape Cod.

12.

Corley Schock has been dating Rose since Christmas time. They met online. Corley's sister encouraged him to try to find someone in cyberspace since the forty-four-year-old bachelor hadn't had any luck on the ground. So he started going to the library, learned how to use the Internet and joined a dating service hoping to find someone special. In his ad he mentioned that he was shy and a homebody, preferring to rent movies and play Scrabble to the night-life, that he was about to move out of the city to Olive Branch, Mississippi, for some peace and quiet. He never imagined the ad would lead to dating a white woman. But Rose, a casino worker recently moved from Las Vegas, didn't post a picture, didn't reveal her ethnicity, didn't even list her height and weight. She'd written in her message that those things weren't who she was, couldn't measure her soul. Looks didn't matter. Corley Schock loved the way she phrased things. He loved the fact that she didn't have to rely on an image.

It's the first time he has lived next to white people, and now he's dating a white woman. So much changed so quickly that his mother and sister still haven't even met Rose. Regardless, he's made up his mind that when his disability check comes he is going to use the money in the coffee can to buy Rose a wedding ring, make the commitment proper in the eyes of the Lord. Corley thinks it's romantic, using the money earned from donating plasma, giving part of himself for someone he loves. Not exactly donating an organ—he knows that it's only a symbol—but it's a way to express to her and everyone the way that he feels.

13.

Prince Leigh takes the stage wearing a pale blue five-button suit. The crowd cheers. He's glad his mother lived long enough to watch him become the first member of their family to graduate from college, but sad she didn't see him become a husband. Underneath his pleated pants, unseen by those at the rally and on television who stare at his chiseled brown face and large eyelashes, are a pair of boxer shorts with a "Just Married" heart ironed onto one of the legs, a present from his new wife. He doesn't want to use this opportunity to announce the secret wedding that took place in Jamaica two days ago to his fans, so he just says that he's sorry his girlfriend couldn't make it because she's back in Los Angeles promoting the release of her upcoming movie. "Her heart is with us, though." Prince Leigh winks at the crowd and takes a deep breath, lowers his head as his dimples disappear. Leigh's mother cleaned houses in Mountain Brook for a living, quit after he signed his first recording contract and then died from cardiac arrest six months later. Prince begins singing *Go Tell it On the Mountain* and the crowd joins in. It was his mother's favorite hymn.

14.
The story becomes the story.

15.
Governor George Wallace's position softened. By 1970 when a majority of Alabama's African-Americans were registered to vote, segregation was a thing of the past for Wallace—a bad odor on the breath. There was a "New South" that had emerged, and he needed to start delivering a new message.

An incident at random, which doesn't make sense: after Arthur Bremer, a mentally disturbed janitor, shot him in Maryland during his second presidential campaign, Wallace saw the country and the South for the rest of his life from a seat instead of a stance. Wheels instead of legs.

16.
Rose and Corley are playing Scrabble, laughing at the noises Rex makes while he sleeps. Rose looks up from the game wearing what she calls her 'hip' glasses: new red, pointed frames. Over Corley's shoulder on the television is a commercial about starving children in Africa. She doesn't blink. "I want to help them," she says. Her lips press tight, and her face becomes stern. Corley turns around. "I've always thought about it and always put it off, but now I want to do something."

These African children aren't conscious of the camera as George Wallace was. Swollen bellies, exposed navels that look like brown gumdrops, haloes of buzzing flies. The stare they give the camera. Emotionless. Not crying, not smiling. The way fish look. And there are always multitudes of them. Miracles of children instead of fish.

"I want to help them, Corley. We'll never have children, but I want to give something to help them. It says we can make one of them our own child. We need to do something."

17.
The police have had leads as to who may have committed the crime, but they've all come up empty. The Ku Klux Klan took responsibility for the graffiti but after further investigation that

turned out to be a lie. Then a recently fired chef in the dorm's cafeteria was questioned, but he had an alibi that checked out. Leads that have led to other leads that have led to nothing.

18.

Two female roommates are walking by Foster Auditorium, talking. They've been to parties at the KA house before, walked right past the cannon and the statue of Robert E. Lee, under the Confederate flag, went down to the basement and drank and listened to the band and talked with boys. For these two girls the General is only alive as a statue or as someone in a book. They have on shorts, the weight of heavy backpacks filled with books on their thin shoulders. Their ponytails oscillate like a horse's tail while they move. There will be a party at the KA house this Saturday night, the final one of the school year.

The blonde reporter stops them and asks if they attended the rally last night. "No ma'am," they both say, dimples forming along their cheeks. "We were studying for a final." Although she is only a few years older, the reporter thinks the girls look awfully young and coquettish. She's noticed that about a lot of these Southern girls. They're always so made up. But they are pretty, that she'll grant them. Great skin. She asks them about racism on campus. They are still smiling. "I don't know," one of them says, "I think things are better than they were. We live next door to a group of black girls and we are friendly. We sometimes goof around and listen to music together, but they hang out at their places and we hang out at ours."

"Do you know what George Wallace is famous for having done forty years ago?"

"No," one of the girls grabs her bag's straps. "Wait, he was in a wheelchair and he did something with Civil Rights, right? He helped black people."

"He had the support of the NAACP," the other girl says. "The Klan couldn't stand who he was."

"Well, something like that," the reporter says, shaking her head. She questions them some more about campus life and then as they are walking away says, "Good luck—what final?"

"History," they say in unison, giving a big smile and waving. Of course, the reporter mumbles under her breath. She thinks they are both ignorant. She feels sorry for them. Pretty faces that don't know a thing about the world outside of their own little microcosm, nothing outside of the little world they see every day.

19.

George C. Wallace served with the Army Air Corps in 1945, flying nighttime incendiary missions over Japan. After being sent back to the United States for additional training, Wallace refused to return to duty and eventually was granted a discharge due to "severe anxiety."

20.

How would Jesus have reacted to the camera? The disciples capturing images of his miracles instead of having to pen it all down. Perhaps he would have requested that they refrain from photographing him, distrusting the image like he did the word. Maybe it's not entirely untrue what was believed by some of the dead and the more "primitive" cultures that the camera steals your soul. Perhaps it's not stolen outright but rather is taken away in pieces, the way we often renege on a commitment. Slowly. Click. By. Click. By. Click, until the person is no longer, until the person's image is more real than its antecedent.

21.

Corley Schock is going to ask Rose to marry him. His disability check came today. He'll finish unpacking, and she can move into his house and they will live a happy life in spite of the fact that Schock's legs are starting to go numb periodically. His doctor thinks that one of his disks is touching a nerve. Next week he'll get a second opinion. Bending down to give Rex his food, he notices that he forgot to take the bandage off his arm last night. Corley navigates with the aid of a cane through unopened boxes over to the large front window. He has waved to his new neighbors but still hasn't gone over to meet them. They can do that as a couple, as husband and wife, he thinks, unwrapping the bandage. He can't give plasma today because the body needs two days to process new cells. After looking for a ring, he's going to go to the library and get on the Internet to try to find out how his donated plasma benefits people.

22.

There is some tension on the hall, but it's from fatigue and the stress of exams. The police have already questioned the residents. The walls are back to normal and the victims' door is cleaned. The two have gone on with finals despite the option of postponing them for a later date. The boys have both talked to their parents. They really just want all of this fuss to end, wish it had never happened. They are looking forward to going home for the summer and working to make some money.

23.

Not one eyewitness has come forward. Secretly the police have nothing, although they still tell the news that they are always investigating and that currently they are in the process of

Developing Story

checking out new leads from a variety of sources.

24.

George Wallace, while standing in front of Foster Auditorium, blocking Vivian Malone and James Hood in 1963: "This nation was never meant to be a unit of one . . . but united of the many . . . this is the exact reason our freedom loving forefathers established the states, so as to divide the right and powers among the states insuring that no central power could gain master government."

25.

It should be the job of the news to make a collage of the story. The blonde reporter is still in Tuscaloosa on Friday, awaiting the possible arrival of an African-American activist and preacher from Harlem. The incident is yeast in the making of bread, the rising of loaves. The miracle of multiplicity. Recounting past events and making them gospel for a public unable to witness the actual. She now has little problem with her lower jaw and has been boldly pressing the police for answers, visiting City Café, asking for local opinion on the story, going to Stillman College to find out what the feeling is there. The reporter is convinced that what has taken place was instigated by racial motives, by backwards thinking, and it's her job to expose those injustices. It's her job to report, to present the story.

But that evening, her producer calls, telling her to get to Los Angeles immediately, anyway she can. Due to her diligent work, she is being sent to work alongside a senior reporter. A terrorist attack has just occurred in Hollywood at a movie premiere, during the red carpet entrance. Indefinite numbers killed and injured. Prince Leigh and his new wife are in the hospital. Many other celebrities and fans have been maimed. They've finally done it; someone's finally attacked the movie-makers. There's already countless speculation as to who and why, but the one thing that is certain is the effects are devastating, the randomness unconscionable.

26.

At the KA's party people drink, releasing the anxiety built up from finals and yesterday's event. The mood of the party is subdued, the music not so loud. Students talk about what happened in California with wonder and astonishment, the way they might speak about an amazing movie or the past. California, Los Angeles especially, is a suspension of disbelief, an abstraction for these students in Alabama. As distant in space as George Wallace's stand is in time. The events out West seem so unreal and yet they affect them, make them somber and scared.

The girls don't know how well they did on their History test, but they don't care now. They are going to get drunk, try to forget everything. One of them is talking to a boy. He has a baseball cap low, bill creased, khaki shorts and sandals, Widespread Panic T-shirt. He keeps his sunglasses behind his neck. "They interviewed me," he is saying, tapping a cigarette against the back of his hand.

"Me too," the girl says. Her skin is tan and her brown hair hangs over her shoulders.

"Really? It was crazy."

"Yeah, she asked us questions like about some plaque and some guy named James Hood."

"The police?"

"No, some news lady."

"Damn. I got interviewed by the fucking cops."

"Shut up. Oh my gosh, are you serious?" Her eyes are wide.

He shakes his head and takes a drag. "Yeah, they asked me if this guy that I worked with on an English project and I had any sort of altercations, like any disagreements. I guess they thought I might have been the person who got all KKK in the dorm."

"That's so crazy."

There is a ring and then another. The guy and girl both pause and inspect their cell phones the way movie cowboys look at their pistols.

27.

The camera seems to be a tool, an instrument, a miracle like David's slingshot. Pictures of the Hollywood incident broadcast around the globe without ceasing. The images keep coming like breaths.

28.

The three girls are all holding hands and their heads are down, feet nervously tapping the tile floor. The policewoman hands them a box of tissues. Apologetic, pleading, shaking, they've just gotten through saying what a mixed-up last couple of days they've had. They've done terribly on their tests, haven't been able to sleep. Overwhelmed by the way the whole thing blew up, they didn't know how to react, were scared to say anything. It was only a joke. They are female students, African-American residents of the dorm across the street. One of the girls had a crush on one of the boys. They knew each other from a math class and he dissed her, wouldn't give her the time of day. She and her friends thought they were playing a prank in retaliation for a love affair that never materialized. It was so stupid. They didn't think everything would turn out like this. It's been a bad dream and they want it to end. They just want to put the whole stupid thing behind them, to forget about it, to start over.

29.

Not like a camera—one click and then a shudder—an explosion is not. The moment for light, with a pause in between that seems out of place. An instant of time that is not time. Like this. A dot not the size of a period to thread a miracle through. Then it is passed, over. And everything starts back up again, in an instant it comes on. And then it's just what it was, how it happened, what it means. The chaos of mysteries, the search for the connection between reality and the right words. And forever after things are changing and the only job is to put it all back together again.

30.

In June the piece about George Wallace and the University of Alabama airs. While lying on the beach at the Cape, the reporter tells her friends that it's going to be sad and hard to watch because it will remind her of everything that happened that week. Being around terrible, tragic things is part of being a reporter, and she doesn't know if she's cut out for that kind of a life. Her jaw has started bothering her again.

The news piece loops black and white clips of students talking with color clips of students talking. They discuss change on the University of Alabama campus. Reticent and worried and angry about what's soon to occur, white people in the old shots don't see why things can't just remain the way they are. In the color footage most everyone agrees things have gotten better, but there still is a long way to go to break down this new barrier of voluntary segregation taking place. During the color interviews, several students, black and white, don't know who George Wallace, Vivian Malone or James Hood are. Because the country has been through so much, the producers chose to end the story on a more positive image. They have cut any mention of the incident in the dorm and leave the viewer with a black and a white student holding hands and candles, swaying and singing to a song being led by Prince Leigh.

31.

On his wedding night Corley Schock is woken-up by Rex's barking. He looks over at Rose who is sleeping soundly, and then puts on his robe, grabs his cane from the closet and walks to the front of the house. The dog is still barking, stepping around a shattered window. Fragments of glass surround a decapitated female doll taped to a brick. Corley holds the cane like a baseball bat, veins flaring, while he walks forward to look outside. Everything is silent except for the hum of an electric streetlight. "What is it?" Rose calls from the bedroom. "Corley, is something the matter?" He picks up the telephone receiver but the line is dead.

32.

Through the years George Wallace's view on racial issues underwent a drastic change—Saul journeying to Damascus: he was probably familiar with that story. He did ask forgiveness from many people, including Vivian Malone and James Hood. And was elected in 1982, despite being paralyzed, to his last term as governor with strong support from African-American voters.

33.

Rose turns on the coffee maker, and then begins to curse. She takes off her glasses and leans against the refrigerator, pounding her fists against the door. Then she sits down on the floor and hugs her knees. Corley doesn't know if he should trust his neighbors, so he's decided that at first light he will drive to the police station to report the crime. Despite the pain shooting through his back, Corley Schock bends down and embraces his wife, scooping her up and carrying her to the bedroom, numbness beginning to spread all along his legs. He doesn't know what to say so he just holds her. For a while the newlyweds lie close to each other, with the husband's cane nearby, in their new king-size bed. And then Corley gets up and locks Rex in his kennel. Nothing should be touched. Everything should be left the way it is now.

Meg Moceri

Eclipse Tonight

On October 15th, the town of Anishanabe would officially cease to exist. The state assembly, in its last act before adjourning for the summer, had repealed the municipal charter on the grounds that Anishanabe did not provide city services, hold government meetings, or have elections. The town would lose its post office, and would no longer appear on maps, but it would be listed as an unincorporated area of the county. Apparently by way of reassurance, Anishanabe was told it could keep its road sign on the state highway, the official green one with white letters.

At first, there was resistance. Protests and petitions and even a chartered bus to Lansing, where townspeople found themselves in league with historic preservationists and activists from around the state, many of whom had never heard of Anishanabe. The decision was not reversed.

Noel had been on that bus, had been heard by a couple of legislative subcommittees. Then he'd made the return trip home, arriving very late at night, gone straight to his IGA store, and circled in red felt tip the October 15th square on his office calendar. As for writing in some kind of explanatory note, his mind blanked. What would one write as a reminder? 'Last Day'? 'The End'? It wasn't that the town would be bulldozed or its residents evicted; Noel knew the fifteenth would pass largely unnoticed, without drama or ceremony, his neighbors resigned to their obsolescence.

In the end he left the 15th without annotation, save for the red circle. The event had loitered in the margins of the passing days, but now October was just upon them and it seemed improper—superstitious even—to ignore the date altogether.

As he did every morning, Noel unlocked the front door of the IGA and raised the shade, brittle as an ancient scroll, marked "Sorry, We're Closed," and went directly to his back office. There was the calendar, the date with its red ring, like the presentation of an illness—roseola, Lyme disease.

"Are you open?" A woman's voice, accompanied cheerfully by the old-fashioned entry bell. Noel startled. Had she been just steps behind him?

She stood in the bright rectangle of the open door. With the outdoor glare behind her he could make out only a silhouette, a blurry corona around a darkened, smallish figure.

"Come on in." He beckoned with his hand.

She didn't look like his typical customer, neither native nor tourist. She was dressed for utility, in a sweatshirt covered by a nylon windbreaker that looked well worn, not just purchased from Orvis for the trip up north. Folks dressed in designer woodswear came to his store periodically, vacationers wandering beyond the perimeters of the resort towns. Usually they just wanted something quick to eat, a soda or bag of chips, but other times they were foraging for collectibles. Last month he'd sold some of the old cereal boxes that lined the upper shelves to a couple from Indianapolis. They gave him twenty dollars for a box of Kellogg's Pep, and ten dollars for Corn Flakes with the original green rooster on the front. Thirty dollars for inedible cereal.

She shivered as she walked toward him. "Brrr. Am I your first customer?"

To keep the utility bills down, Noel kept the overhead lights off, the thermostat no higher than sixty degrees, even in deep winter. The store was arranged in the old-fashioned way, designed long before supermarkets determined the merchandising of food. Instead of long aisles and tall shelves, groceries were displayed on low, broad display cases made of oak. The doors on the meat and dairy coolers were of the same veneers, cured dark as molasses. As she came toward Noel, the woman ran her fingertips over the enormous brass handles. Then she stopped at the non-perishables and picked up a can of lima beans. "Is this stuff safe?" she asked.

"That's just for show." He kept certain rows of boxes and cans for display, next to the stocks he replenished. People got a kick out of the old labels. "The rest is regular, comes in on a regular delivery schedule. Expiration dates and everything."

She tilted an old box of cake mix toward the light to read the side panel. "Half these ingredients have been banned by the FDA. Incredible, the way we used to eat." She returned the box to the shelf and spotted the ice-chest-style soda cooler near the front window. "Look at this!" she exclaimed, as though Noel were unaware of its existence. She raised the top. Chilled water flowed around the bottles, which chimed delicately in the current. The sound made her smile, and she lifted out a dripping bottle. "This reminds me of the creek behind our house when I was growing up in Pennsylvania."

"Pennsylvania." Noel squinted at the ceiling, trying to call forth a remnant of information. "Isn't that where that woman killed her kids and then blamed it on a carjacker?"

The woman looked at him blankly. "I hadn't heard about that."

"Oh, sure, I saw it on WOR. You know, that station out of New York City? That's what I love about cable. When you live way up here, you know, you like to feel in touch."

"Lately, I've been wanting to be *out* of touch." She closed the soda chest and walked toward him. "All these nasty stories you hear on the news, they all blur together, don't you think?" She placed the bottle on the counter next to the cash register. "And I should know, because I'm a journalist myself. A freelance one, these days, so I basically get to pick and choose my assignments. I deliberately stay away from the murder-and-mayhem beat. Those days are behind me." She zipped open a pouch she wore around her waist and placed a dollar bill on the counter. He rang up the Coke and slid three quarters back to her. "What's this?" she said.

"Your change."

She picked up the coins. "You charge only twenty-five cents for a *Coke*?"

"Tastes better that way." He grinned encouragingly.

She put the soda to her lips and drank enthusiastically, with her head far back, her Adam's apple pumping busily inside her smooth throat, like something moving underneath a blanket. Noel couldn't take his eyes off the rhythm of it. She drank off nearly a third of the small bottle, then touched the ends of her fingers to her lips. "I believe you're right," she said. "About the taste."

She explained that she was on assignment with one of the airline magazines—the kind they tucked into the seat pockets—and was writing a series piece on undiscovered parts of the country.

"The article's on Isle Royale, but I want it to be more than just a travelogue. The theme is still developing, but basically it's not just about being there, it's about *getting* there. The journey, not just the destination. The stuff along the way, you know? And that"—she raised the Coke bottle in a kind of toast—"is how I happen to be here."

Except for the locals, a woman by herself in his store was rare, and Noel kept expecting someone to join her—a spouse, a friend, perhaps even a child. She'd been sent ahead as the scout to see if the deserted-looking IGA was open, and any minute her companions would enter. He glanced behind her to the door.

She looked around. "Expecting someone?"

"No, no. I was just thinking, I can't imagine people wanting to read about an old store."

"Don't underestimate yourself. People are starving for this sort of thing. Lost America. Ever heard of Celebration? I mean the town called Celebration?"

Noel shook his head.

"It's a city in Florida. Disney built it. It's modeled on the concept of pre-war town planning, with commerce and houses all within the same radius. So you can walk to the store, to the cleaners, to the corner for an ice cream cone. Like towns used to be." At Noel's puzzled look she said, "I find it grotesque myself, that kind of forced, phony replication. This—" she waved her arm around the store— "*this* is genuine. *This* is what I'm talking about."

Noel was still trying to imagine the town she had described. He wasn't sure he understood the concept, or the purpose. It did sound—how had she put it?—grotesque. But Florida itself wouldn't be so bad. Someplace warm, someplace with people always walking about. He tried to picture himself among palms.

She had moved on to another subject, the book she was working on, a collection of essays about women and nature. "I write about women on adventures, who go rappelling and sea kayaking, diving in Aruba, spelunking in Chile," she said. "I write about their organic connections with Ceres. You know, the Greeks' version of mother nature, mother earth." Noel nodded as if he heard this name in everyday conversation. "Other times," she went on, "I write about emotional adventures, the ones that take place in their own kitchens or back yards or bedrooms. I write from all perspectives: young women, old women, married and single, widows, lesbians."

"I see," Noel said, although he didn't, especially the lesbians. He could not imagine how the topic of women and nature could fill pages.

"Mind if I look around some more?"' she asked, strolling among the shelves.

"Be my guest."

He watched her closely. She looked lean and solid, and underneath her jeans he imagined muscled calves. She was no kid; late thirties, fortyish, maybe. But a well-kept forty. He thought about turning on the lights.

Near a revolving wire rack that held powdered sauce mixes, Noel's dog sat scratching itself. Not with any seriousness or vigor, but absently, languidly, as if relieving the itch were pointless. The hind leg flapped without purpose, like a steam engine crankshaft slipped off its wheel; only occasionally did it make contact with the fur. The woman knelt and took the dog's face in her hands. "You're a good baby, aren't you. Yes, you are!" He closed his eyes blissfully and raised his chin, exposing his neck to be scratched. Noel wondered what that would feel like on his own face, his own chin.

"You say you're from Pennsylvania?" Noel asked.

"Born and raised there, in Pittsburgh. I've been living in Michigan for three years now, I've got a brother in Bloomfield Hills, so I thought I'd move near him." She gave the dog's ears a final rub and stood up. "Since college, I've lived all over. Idaho, Alabama, Maryland. In school I majored in physiology and communications, I wanted to do medical writing, I thought. I did work in PR for a hospital for awhile, but that was later."

While she talked she picked items off the shelves. Noel saw that she barely looked at what she'd chosen, and when she'd filled her arms she brought everything to the counter and went back for more. Noel began ringing up the groceries while she described a meandering career path as a footwear designer, overnight radio announcer, stringer for a news syndicate.

Noel put a can of chow mein noodles into a grocery sack. "So now you're your own boss."

"That's right. A few years back my brother said, 'Come to Michigan,' so I did. Southeast Michigan's not so hot, but I've fallen in love with this part of the state. In fact, I may be looking to buy some property around here. As long as you have a computer and modem, it doesn't matter where you live, really. I e-mail and fax most of my work anyway. I've never even met some of my clients." She said this almost boastfully. "You wouldn't know of anything for sale around here, would you?"

"What are you looking for? Land to build on? Or a place already built?"

She shrugged. "Don't know yet."

"Well . . ." Noel ran his palm across the battered counter, feeling the tracks of meat cleavers and a thousand past transactions. "Why don't you come look at my place?"

He listened to his words ricochet off the high pressed tin ceiling and come back to him, thinned out of their upper and lower frequencies to a narrow band of sound, like a transmission radioed from far away.

She raised her eyebrows. They were thick and dark over her green eyes, and went up like a hirsute drawbridge. "You're selling *your* house?"

Noel was not inclined to impulsive or spontaneous remarks. Now he felt that he'd been thrown from a tenth-floor window, trying to stop his plunge in midair, like a cartoon character. "Possibly. Maybe. I've been thinking about it, thinking for a while, sort of unofficially, off the record." Off what record? He didn't even know what he meant, and he had never thought about it at all, not until the words had flown from his mouth, his ridiculous, irresponsible mouth.

The woman's face was eager. "Tell me about it. Is it nearby? How much land? Are you on any water?"

He described his 70-year-old cedar shake house, his twenty wooded acres, the trout stream that formed the south property line. As he spoke her expression grew more delighted, the green eyes widened. The flattery of her interest was irresistible.

"Would you like to see it?" he asked.

He hung the "Back in Five Minutes" sign on the front door and helped her carry the groceries to her bright red Jeep Cherokee. She had parked behind his truck, and they were the only two vehicles on the street. By this time he had learned her name: Mado. "Short for Madelyn," she told him.

"I'm Noel." He pointed toward the store's plate glass window, where his name and title were painted under the red and yellow IGA emblem. "'Noel Vertigan, Proprietor,'" he read. "Just follow me. I'm two miles straight up the highway here, and left a half mile." He opened the door of his truck. "In case we get separated."

He drove slowly down the main street. Here and there, bright yellow rectangles were tacked to windows and telephone poles, shouting out from the faded surfaces. There was one in every business, at the doomed post office, on each warped plywood sheet covering the windows of the depot; Noel had one in his store window. They were notices announcing the upcoming lunar eclipse. Mrs. Joppes, who worked in the patient records office at the regional hospital in Petoskey, had done up the bulletins on her office computer and printed them out on canary-colored paper. Facts were given: the date and time of the eclipse, bleachers to be set up near the old airstrip for public viewing of the "celestial event," the availability of refreshments. Most of the town would attend; they would bring children and thermoses.

Anishanabe sat astride the forty-fifth parallel, midway between the North Pole and the equator. When the village was platted in the 1880s, land office brochures claimed that the location suggested temperance of both local climate and character. Stability, good values, a general bonhomie, could all be derived from this fortunate equipoise. It had been a company town, a lumber boom town, sprouting up among the felled hardwoods. In its heyday it had one of the largest business districts in the county, including a large sawmill and a turning works that made croquet mallets and stakes, stairway spindles, broom handles. When the trees were gone, the lumber companies pulled out, and the sawmill closed. The turning works remained until the 1950s, then closed also. Eventually the railroad no longer had a reason to make stops. Through trains passed, every few days at first, then occasionally, then never. Down the center of the right-of-way a solid strip of weeds grew unimpeded, a ribbon of green unrolled between two iron stripes. The rails turned bright orange with rust, and grew rippled atop the decaying ties until they were finally pulled in the late 1980s. Dirt bikers and snowmobilers used the grade for recreation, where they could open their throttles unimpeded by cars or speed limits. There had been talk of making the old route part of a statewide network of bicycle trails. This possibility came up regularly in conversations at the tavern, at the store, dropped like coins into a wishing well.

Nowadays, Anishanabe survived meagerly on spurts of seasonal activity, when hunters, fishermen, and skiiers gave some commerce to the IGA and the single filling station, to the small hardware—which advertised a limited selection of firearms and tackle—and the two taverns.

Driving, Noel tried to remember the last time he had met anybody new. He'd lived in Anishanabe all his life and for forty-one years commuted to his job at the cement plant in Petoskey, an hour away. Except for the handful of merchants and a few others who ran the town's remaining businesses, anyone who lived here made their living elsewhere, like Mrs. Joppes. Since retiring from concrete, Noel had run the IGA. It was not a demanding job.

He glanced in his rear view mirror to make sure she was still behind him. He noticed that she drove her Jeep Cherokee with one hand, the other arm draped along the top of the passenger seat. It was a somewhat masculine pose, and yet there was nothing mannish about her. Tomboyish, rather—another thing altogether. He considered the way she caressed his dog, his expired groceries.

Then he was scolding himself. A woman is one thing, he thought. A little flirtation, a bit of self-flattery with his vintage store, no harm in that. But whatever had possessed him to claim he was selling his home? He was appalled at himself, at the way a notion that had never occurred to him could leap out entirely unbidden. He felt reckless and at the same time exhilarated, a kid in a science lab mixing chemicals. Hearing a horn behind him, he looked down to see that he'd accelerated past seventy. He lifted his foot off the pedal. When they reached his house he would tell her again, emphatically, that he was only *thinking* of selling.

She parked behind him in his gravel driveway and stepped out of the Cherokee, laughing. "Mr. Speed Demon! I never would have figured you for a lead foot." She pointed her key ring at the car, causing it to chirp. She smiled self-consciously. "City habit," she explained, and then stopped in the yard. He watched her green eyes scan his house. "This is *ex*quisite!" she said.

As he led her up the front porch steps, she resumed the conversation they'd begun at the store. "In my work, I also look for the erotic connotations of nature. You know, like the paintings of Georgia O'Keefe. She's most famous for her flowers, of course, how the petals resemble labia. Except where she painted the eroticism, I try to write it."

Noel was glad to be busy unlocking the front door, not looking at her, not letting her see how his face had turned a fierce red. She said the word "labia" as easily as she might say "window" or "doghouse." The front door opened and he stood aside to let her enter. "I have coffee, I have beer. Would you like anything?"

"Beer's fine." She ran her hand over the door mouldings. "This white oak is really something. And porcelain doorknobs! You've got quite a gold mine here."

More caressing. He led her to the kitchen and tried to clear a space on the yellow Formica table. He pushed aside newspapers, chipped coffee cups. Sugar granules had mixed with spilled coffee, hardening into runnels. She sat down and with her fingernail began to carve patterns in the spilled sugar.

"I'm always interested in preserving things," she said. "My hobby is kinetic sculptures. Mostly lawn and garden decor, made of scrap metal. I use anything—old washtubs, rain gutters, wheelbarrows, garden tools. I make them into fountains or birdbaths or whatever. I like to put together unlikely combinations and then stand back and watch the effect." She took the beer he held out to her, wrapping her long fingers delicately around the bottleneck. "So what do you do? When you're not running that incredible store of yours?"

It was the first time Noel had heard the IGA described as incredible. But her tone was sincere, and her face (he saw now that it had freckles. Freckles!) was turned to him with genuine interest. It occurred to him to be skeptical of her candor, that this was probably the way she spoke to strangers and friends alike, but he was not by nature cynical and he preferred another possibility—that perhaps there was something about his ordinary life that had currency.

"Do you want a glass for that?" he asked, gesturing toward the beer. He opened a cupboard and stood gazing into it and growing dismayed. Finally he pulled out a juice glass. "These are my only clean ones. I'm not much of a housekeeper."

"I can see that. Never mind, I can drink from the bottle just fine." She took a sip and looked around his kitchen. "This place needs a woman's touch."

He pulled out the chair across from her. "I never have any woman visitors. You're the first."

"First ever?"

"First in quite a long time."

"Ever married?"

He nodded.

"Your wife left you?"

His face grew hard. "She died."

"Oh." She set her beer bottle on the table, where it made a new circle in the sugar granules. "I'm sorry."

He moved a spoon a few inches to the left.

"In fact, I'm sorry twice," she added. "That she died, and for assuming that she left you."

"Well. It was some years ago."

High above the house, a flock of Canada geese bleated, announcing their passage.

"How about you?" Noel asked. "Ever married?"

"Yep. For a while. I was a gay man's attempt at a straight life. Oh, well. But don't feel bad for me. I've had more than my share of proposals. Some of them even for marriage."

"Ah."

"Getting back to the matter of your house. You want me to help you get the place in order? If you're getting ready to sell, it has to show well." With her thumbnail she worked at the corner of the label on her beer bottle. "That's realtor talk."

"You feel sorry for me, that's it? I need help that badly?"

She smiled. "No, not at all. It's something I'm good at, cleaning up." She looked around. "Plus, you've got some beautiful things here. Interesting things, collectibles. They ought to be properly taken care of, displayed, arranged. For example . . ."

She had left the table and stood with her nose an inch away from the picture that hung next to the broom closet. "This is a Maxfield Parrish print. Did you know that?"

He had never heard of Maxfield Parrish. The picture had been in the house as long as he could remember, given to them by his wife's mother.

"He was famous in the thirties and forties. He did a lot of illustrations for children's books. Mostly mythological themes, or Aesop's and Grimm's tales. This is one of his most famous. I think it's called 'The Dinky Bird,' believe it or not." She tapped the glass and then returned to the kitchen table. "I wouldn't be surprised if that's a limited edition lithograph. Hang on to it."

She had finished her beer and began to clear the table as she might her own. She picked up the bottle, a plate of crumbs and a glass from a previous meal—Noel wasn't even sure which—and the torn envelopes from utility bills. She put the dishes in the sink and opened the cupboard door underneath. "Trash?" she said.

"By the back door, there." She continued to peer under the sink. "You don't have much to clean with."

She closed the cabinet. "I've got to do some traveling and hit the library in Petoskey, but I'll come back. I can bring some cleaning supplies, help you get the place spruced up. If you like."

He had forgotten, momentarily, the reason for her presence here, and remembering startled him. He owed her the truth, but still wasn't sure of it. "Like I said, I'm only thinking of selling," he began. "I hadn't even thought about price, and the place needs a lot of work."

"That's my specialty, remember? Fixing things up, restoration. You never know, though; this is how great things get started, don't you think? But don't forget, I get right of first refusal." She winked at him. "Realtor talk again. Means I get first dibs on buying your house."

She grasped his hand, leaned in and placed her lips to his face. He felt the point of contact precisely, in the fleshy pouch between his cheekbone and jaw. The sound entered his ear like a chord.

From the porch he watched her walk to her car. He was not, never would be, past the age where he didn't watch a woman walk. Her hips were narrow, creating only the slightest flare from her waist, while her fanny—Noel's preferred term—moved economically with her stride. If it were to make a sound, it would be, he imagined, *tick-tock, tick-tock*. As she drove away she tapped her horn twice and waved out the window.

He waved back. Dustbanks rose behind her car, and for a moment it seemed she had been an apparition, the whole episode imagined. Age and isolation in a fossilizing town had finally addled his mind, and he'd hallucinated an attractive stranger who appeared out of nowhere and offered to buy his house.

No—she'd been real. When he returned for his car keys on the table, the kitchen seemed transformed by the markers of her presence: the spirals she'd drawn in the sugar, the angle of the chair pulled out, even the things missing, the absence of his customary clutter. In a panel of sunlight dust motes shimmered, animated by her movement. He picked up his keys. When he turned, the Parrish print, for years invisible to him, seemed luminous also. The figure on the swing was naked and androgynous, the features delicate, the skin porcelain and almost translucent. In the long fluid line from the base of the skull to the tips of the pointed toes, in the smudge of hair blown back, Noel felt the swing sweeping forward, as if set in motion by the visitor herself.

Noel tinkered with the radio in his office, tuning one of the big Chicago stations. The proper atmosphere often carried the distant signals up the long blue brushstroke of Lake Michigan like bright sails. He liked ambient cosmopolitan chatter in his store, the staccato banter with its cadences of urban commerce and hurry.

The entry bell jangled. He came out quickly from behind his desk, even though it could not be her, returning. When he passed the clock and saw that it was 3:30, he knew that in fact it would be Roy Myles coming in for his daily box of Dolly Madison donut holes, which he ate during his afternoon coffee break. Roy was the postmaster, and so this was one element of Noel's life that would be altered. When the post office ceased operations, Roy would begin working at the post office in Odin, twelve miles away. It was the post office all the residents of Anishanabe would use come October 15th.

Roy headed for the baked goods section. "Going to the eclipse?" he asked.

Noel nodded. "I suppose."

"Some of us are going to Odin after. We're gonna close the bars, raise a little hell, take Friday off, start the weekend early.

Auld Lang Syne. Interested?"

"Maybe. No. Gotta be at the store."

Roy laughed a sharp bark. "What's the difference?" He slid his thumb under the flap of the doughnut box and popped a white nugget into his mouth. "Mmm. They're best just this side of stale." Powdered sugar dusted his lips, making them look bloodless. "You'll come with us, then?"

"I'll let you know."

Noel rang up the donuts and stepped outside. The sky was blue veiled in gauze, and he could not remember a more prolonged or amiable Indian Summer. The breezes no longer blew the fierce heat of summer, offered instead to bear aloft the earth in soft cradles. The gentleness of the air reminded Noel of the small flat waves that stroked the shores of his favorite fishing lakes. Barely even waves, really—more like soft blankets, drawn gently up to the chin of the shore. If the heart had a season, his wife had said once, it would feel like this. The dog lay pressed against the riser of the bottom step, stretched his full length to maximize his exposure to the sun. Noel clucked his tongue on the roof of his mouth to call him to heel.

He was alone on the narrow street. Buildings poked up from the ground like last season's corn stalks, the farthest ones trembling in heat mirages. A playground sat, strangely, not adjacent to the consolidated school (one-hundred and sixteen students in twelve grades), but next to the laundromat. The swings swayed in the wind—not back and forth, as they would if occupied—but side to side. Their emptiness took Noel's breath away.

On the other side of the breeze, he knew winter waited, coiled like a snake of uncertain length and toxicity. Noel didn't mind winter, except for the final weeks when he longed for sunlight more than food. He and Olive had always talked of driving South (she would not fly), and one year they tried it but had had to turn back in Tennessee because her back hurt her so from the long hours in the car.

What kind of person has never been to Florida? Even Roy had been to Florida, for God's sake. His sister lived there, in Bradenton, in a little cinder block bungalow painted kiwi green, six miles from the beach. Roy had showed Noel pictures of her house. Every year since Olive died he'd invited Noel to join him when he drove down to visit. Noel had always found some excuse not to go. At the moment, he could think of no more excuses.

He had by now reached the boundary of the town, where the buildings ended abruptly, nothing beyond. The dog, long familiar with the route, made a tight little turn and went back the way they'd come, like a shooting gallery figure. Noel stood, taking the afternoon warmth on his skin. The sun, moving farther into the southern sky, issued its light from a point nearer the horizon. Perhaps, Noel thought, that explained his recent actions, his fugitive thoughts—the longer shadows, full of diagonals and obliques, contained other possibilities. It could make a person forget himself. In Florida, he could always feel this warm, even in winter.

The dog, puzzled that Noel was not beside him, had stopped halfway down the street and was whining over his shoulder. Noel came along.

Back at the IGA, he walked halfway to his office, then returned to the door and pushed the pearlescent buttons that operated the overhead lights. The white globes, suspended from their iron poles, appeared like a constellation; it seemed to Noel that the cans and boxes themselves glowed from within. In his office he turned up the volume on the radio. This time WGN from Chicago leaped out with flawless clarity as if the entire broadcast, the announcers and microphones, issued from his tiny office. He smiled with gratitude for the generosity of the weather. How accommodating the high air currents, to bring voices from other places his way.

She showed up three days later, smiling through the door of the IGA. Only when he saw her, felt stipples of delight run up his arms, did he realize how much he'd counted on her return. She had bags slung over both shoulders, satchels and duffels, and she carried what looked like a briefcase but was actually, she explained, a notebook computer. He asked her to the tavern for lunch.

The only other customer in the restaurant was Lloyd Sheffield. Lloyd ran the hardware and had paneled the walls of his living room with sheets of remaindered Formica.

"What a trip!" said Mado. She pulled her parka over her head, back side first. Noel watched the entire process, the hem climb up her slender back, over her neck, until her head popped out with the jubilance of a toy. "I got some great shots of the falls at Au Train. Look at this." She opened a small pouch containing a camera. "Ever see one of these? It's digital. Instead of film, the images are burned into a disk inside the camera. Then I can plug the camera into a serial port on my laptop, like this." She opened another case, this one of a soft, black leather-like material, and pulled out a computer and cord. She demonstrated for him the connection of camera to computer. As she talked, she used terms he was only vaguely familiar with: "downloading," "bitmap."

Words he had heard on commercials, or the news. When she was finished she packed away all her apparatus and delicately nipped the end of a french fry between her white teeth. "I used to oppose all this stuff on principle," she said. "But I've come to learn that you can use it to promote what you care about. Hello, there," she said, looking past Noel's shoulder.

Lloyd had appeared next to their table. Noel wiped his palms on his thighs and extended his hand. "Lloyd. What's going on?"

"This and that." His eyes flicked only briefly to Noel before they returned to settle on Mado.

"Oh. Lloyd Sheffield, Mado . . ." Noel suddenly realized he didn't know her last name.

She extended her hand. "Quartz. Really, like the mineral."

Sheffield took her hand uncertainly, as if being handed a baby, or an unfamiliar tool he wasn't sure how to operate.

"Mado's a writer," Noel explained. "She's doing some stories about what it's like here."

Sheffield raised his eyebrows, causing his hairline to retreat nearly a half inch from his brow. "What it's like *here*?"

Mado said, "Well, you know. Life unplugged."

Sheffield looked at Noel.

She tried again. "What it's like—" she patted one of her many bags—"where they don't have all *this* stuff." She turned to Noel. "I've got to get further into the U.P. I heard there's a guy near Baraga who traps for a living and sells his furs on the Internet. Talk about when worlds collide."

Lloyd nodded a courtesy nod. "Well, good luck with your article." He turned back to Noel. "You behave yourself, now."

Mado was squeezing Noel's arm. "I need to get down to the business of writing this thing. I was going to try to find a place to stay, but there really isn't a motel nearby, and I'd still like to help you with your house. Is it all right if I just stay with you?" She raised both hands in a surrender gesture. "Completely innocent. I'll sleep on the couch." Her hand continued to rest on his shirtsleeve.

Noel looked down. Her fingers between the valleys of flannel were an expedition, and he was being discovered, like a continent, like a lost civilization. A love affair between the two of them would be a form of archaeology. Love affair! At this, Noel laughed out loud, a laugh of pure delight.

Mado smiled uncertainly. "Is it funny?" She chuckled also. "I guess it is. If it'll cause trouble—with people talking, I mean—I can stay in Petoskey. I don't mind driving back and forth."

Noel wiped his eyes. "No, no trouble. I'd like . . ." He stopped, unable to put words to something as unfamiliar and grand as what he would like from a woman. "I'd like the company. Keep me company."

She smiled broadly. "Then it's settled. And we'll get started on your house." She stood and slung the computer strap over her shoulder. "It just occurred to me . . . you haven't told me where you're moving to."

Noel's life had contained no surprises. He'd always followed necessity more than any yearning or ambition. Even losing his wife had demanded little in the way of debate or decision. She'd died without a moment's warning.

He pulled crumpled dollar bills from his pocket and dropped them on the table. "I've been thinking of Florida," he said.

She could work as hard as her sturdy build suggested. She scrubbed countertops and floors, moved furniture aside and swept away years of lint. She washed walls and woodwork.

"This should all be stripped and have a new coat of polyurethane," she said from her knees on the floor as she scrubbed at baseboards. "And under these carpets, that's all oak floorboards, are you aware of that?" She peeled back a corner. "And look at the width of the boards. That probably means old growth timber. Could be from the lumber they took right off this land. How long has this house been in your family, anyway?"

Noel told her that it had been his wife's childhood home, belonging to her father, who bought it in the thirties. "Before that, I don't know its history," he said.

Each day after locking up the IGA he would arrive home to find yet another room polished, brightened, rearranged. Bouquets of late wildflowers appeared on tables, carefully arranged in Mason jars she had brought up from the cellar and washed. Draperies dulled and yellowed would vanish for a day or two, then reappear at windows with their pleats sharp and crisp.

"My God, look at this!" She was on her tiptoes on a step stool, exploring the top shelves of the front hall closet. "Old *Post* magazines!" For his record albums she expressed equal enthusiasm. "Perry Como, the Mills Brothers, Rosemary Clooney. *Save* these!" She was virtually squealing, which sent Noel's delight into dizzy orbits.

She dived into cupboards and closets, places that hadn't been touched since Olive died. She threw nothing away, did nothing to desecrate his memories. In her hands his mundane belongings became treasures. Old sewing notions, ancient jars of facial cream whose contents had hardened like a dried-up lake bottom. "These packages, these are priceless!" she cried. "Nostalgia chic, just like the stuff in your store. Do you know what these things sell for in antique shops?"

When he told her about the cereal boxes, she was furious about the price.

"Honey, you were robbed! They're worth three times as much! You need somebody like me around to protect you."

She catalogued his objects, gave him estimates of their value. She took snapshots of the house and each room. "The next time I go to town, I'll talk to a realtor, maybe get a ball park selling price," she said. "Even if I'm the buyer," she added, winking, "I want to give you a fair offer."

From the store he brought home filet mignons, which he had delivered from Petoskey. He bought charcoal, lighter fluid, a table grill. Every night he barbecued the meat, while she made gigantic salads with late-harvest produce from the roadside stands. After dinner, they watched television, or she would type into her laptop. She explained the Internet, showed him how to send e-mail, although there was no one Noel knew to receive it. She slept in the spare room, the one that Noel and Olive's two sons had shared. It still had bunk beds. At bedtime Noel lay awake, feeling her presence down the hall, trying not to think of the day she would finish her article and leave. He wondered how much longer that would be, and how he would handle that day. At last he fell asleep, hearing surf and palms. Mado was in his dream somewhere. He couldn't see her, but she penetrated his skin like warm sea air.

One evening she gave him a manicure. She knelt next to his armchair and produced a small travel kit. "Spread your fingers," she said, and began by massaging each finger, which caused Noel's eyes to close almost involuntarily. Now he knew the bliss of his dog's rubbed chin. Gently she pinched the web of skin in the trough between each finger, and smoothed moisturizer into the creases of his knuckles, working her way to his fingertips. The lotion smelled like coconut and Noel drifted again on currents of Florida. Then she took clippers and an emery board and went to work on his nails.

"Grooming is important no matter what you do," she said. "Just because you have working hands doesn't mean you should neglect their appearance."

"Never seemed practical. Working with concrete takes a lot out of your hands, so I always figured keeping them pretty was a waste of time."

"All the more reason to treat them well," she said. The nail clippers clicked off his nails in tiny white parentheses.

He felt a quickening of his flesh, like bread leavening. Passion was a distant, foreign feeling, something issued from his younger self, a former life. Since Olive, he had only felt vague arousals toward occasional women, stirrings he never bothered to pursue. He stared at the crown of Mado's bent head. As if she read his thoughts, the emery board paused in its strokes. She did not look up or change her position. The file hung motionless above his outstretched finger, then slowly resumed its back and forth motion.

"It's not just the grooming," she said, and her voice grew softer still. "Manicures are very relaxing." With the mitred end of an orange stick she nudged his cuticles. "High moons," she said approvingly. "A sign of good character." She massaged more lotion into his fingertips, swirling her thumbs over his nail beds, and smiled at a sudden association. "Speaking of moons, I like those 'Eclipse' signs all over the place. Announcing it like the town council put it on their agenda."

"We don't have a town council," Noel murmured. He was very, very drowsy. "In fact, that's one reason we won't have a town at all, after the fifteenth."

She looked up at him. "What do you mean?"

He explained the state legislature's decision, the revoked charter.

"My God, what a great angle for my article!" She corrected herself. "I mean, it's a shame in a way. But after all, you'll still be here, right? The buildings, the streets, all the people, everything still exists." She paused to inspect her progress on his hands. "I've been meaning to ask you. What does 'Anishanabe' mean, anyway?"

"It's an Ojibwa word. Technically it means 'original man.' Or native inhabitant."

"Interesting. *Relax.*" He looked down to see that he had made a fist. One by one she uncurled his fingers. "It's like I said the other day, location is becoming obsolete anyway. Not long ago I read an interview with the president of some big computer networking company. You know what he said about the Information Age? He claims it will mean 'the death of time and distance.'" She propped her head at a thoughtful angle. "Who knows—Bell said the same thing about the telephone, that it would annihilate time and space."

He let his head fall back against the chair and felt his hands growing weightless in hers. Once again he had the feeling that his life was demanding something of him that he was accustomed to giving. He'd felt it before, in the tavern with Mado at lunch. As though his life had stepped in front of him and would not let him pass until he made up his mind.

Destiny was never a concept he pondered. Larger motions of the universe were out there beyond his reach; reality was mouths to feed and grinding sand and limestone into concrete. Even Olive's death was swift and unequivocal, a brain hemorrhage felling her in her tracks as she brought the mail up the driveway. After that, Noel felt he'd been right all along, not to presume any grand scheme connected to his existence. Now he wondered if this wasn't how destiny presented itself—as a complete stranger at your door.

"There! Just like new." She held up his hands and turned them this way and that, displaying them for his own inspection. They did look younger, he noticed. Restored like his draperies and his woodwork, cleansed of years of wear and concrete dust.

He said to her, "You'll go with me, won't you?"

She looked puzzled. "Go with you where?"

"To the eclipse. To see the eclipse."

She laughed and released his hands. "Well, sure sweetie. If you want me to, I'll go."

When she announced she was leaving, two mornings later at breakfast, the news left him mute, pouring coffee at the kitchen sink.

"My deadline got moved up," she explained as she pushed a legal pad into her duffel bag. "I found an email from my editor yesterday when I logged onto the internet in Petosky. I have to get to Copper Harbor sooner than I thought."

He stood there with the percolator tilted, the spout poised over his cup like a coal chute. Because he could think of nothing to say, he asked, "What about the eclipse?"

She looked at him blankly. "Oh, that! I'll try to remember to watch it from where I am. I'll think of you. If I forget you can tell me all about it. Speaking of forgetting, I picked these up from a realtor." She pulled a sheaf of papers from her computer bag and handed him a listing agreement and a printout of figures that she explained were 'comps,' showing the prices of nearby property. "I'm getting more and more serious about this," she said. "You know, even if I buy your house, you wouldn't *necessarily* have to leave. You could stay right here, you could lease it from me until I'm ready to move in permanently. Or . . . all kinds of things could happen."

This was how she always talked with him, in little innuendos. He looked at the papers. "We can discuss all this when I get back. It's time for us to have a talk anyway." She embraced him and suddenly he didn't know what to do with his own arms. They curled clumsily around her back and hung there; he was still holding the percolator.

New notices appeared on the day of the eclipse, this time on bright orange paper. Mrs. Joppes, thinking of harvests and Halloween. "Eclipse Tonight," the flyers read. "Ball Field, Dusk." This time they also contained Lunar Facts: the moon's distance from the earth, its circumference, its mass, its age. Noel read that the moon was far older than the earth, and that the perceived line between the dark and light portions of the moon was called the terminator.

He arrived at the ball diamond just after sunset. The promised portable bleachers were in place. A tiny trailer appeared, selling hot dogs and popcorn, soft drinks and coffee. As the twilight deepened more people began to arrive, bringing children and blankets, both ragged. Residents of Anishanabe didn't assemble often, and Noel found that he was moved by the sight of them; they gathered and grouped and moved about the field in tight cells as if responding to some migratory urge. Their voices rose boldly into the chilly air, like tribal paeans to the night. Noel strolled around the field carrying a paper cup of coffee. Children bolted around him, popcorn foaming from their overstuffed mouths, like rabid dogs.

Sheffield approached him. "Where's your lady?"

"What do you mean?"

"Come on. The woman from downstate. I heard she moved in."

Noel sipped his coffee. "You heard wrong."

Sheffield cuffed him on the shoulder. "It's always the quiet ones." He moved on past.

The sky faded to a deep meditative blue, blue tinted with black, dipped from Lake Superior and spread across the thick stripe of evening. Far above where the sun had set, the moon brightened, its pocked surface boiling and spluttering, like air bubbles in cement. Noel found a place on the end of a bleacher and in the yellow light from the popcorn wagon read more moon statistics. *Because it was one of God's celestial creations, all great thinkers once assumed the moon was perfect. It was after Galileo invented the telescope that they discovered the surface rough and full of craters.* Mrs. Joppes had probably made a special trip to the library and pored through the Britannica, assembling her data.

A woman cried, "It's starting!" A bit of shade crept across the moon's chalk surface, like a tarnished penny nudged into the white sphere. Noel noticed that shadow was tinted the color of soil full of iron, like the Michigan soil beneath his feet. Like dried blood smeared on glass.

As he watched the shadow grow, Noel felt Mado's absence, and was saddened to be grateful for it. The eclipse was something he could not have shared with her, even if she were next to him, her arm tucked through his, as he had imagined it would be. From wherever she was viewing the eclipse, it would look different. If in fact she was watching at all, which was very much in doubt.

He looked to the ground, half expecting to find the 45th parallel drawn across the field. The old land brochures were right; their location was providential. At this very moment new maps were probably rolling off printing presses with Anishanabe omitted. But the line was indelible, secured in place by degrees and minutes, part of a net of latitudes and longitudes cast over the hemispheres. Noel imagined the perfect quadrants and how people dwelled so deeply within them.

"Hey buddy!" He looked around to see Sheffield shouting at him from several rows back in the bleachers. "What're you staring at the ground for? The action's up there!" Noel heard hearty laughs.

A small boy shouted, "The moon is buried!"

Noel raised his face. The moon was, indeed, tucked into a slit of sky, its shaded half just discernable from the obsidian sky, the other half glowing fiercely as it waited to receive the shadow of the planet.

Sandra Novack

Conversions on the Road to Damascus

I think, though I am unsure, that my flatmate Cass knows what I have done. She has been stalking me around our apartment for days, laying word traps, hoping I might confess. I want to remain inconspicuous about the whole affair. We are not friends, she and I. We have only lived together six months, since the start of the school year, and we are bound by the necessity of shared rent that is due to our landlord, Mr. Tannen, on the second of each month. Beyond this, I have no commitment and refuse to suffer through the cumbersome condition of affection.

She has said I am godless.

Cass tells me her first mistake was rooming with an Ethics student, that this fact alone should have alerted her to the potential for what she calls "certain problems of spiritual affinities." Cass is very dramatic when she speaks. She is an actor and a second-year-graduate student in the drama department, both of which, I tell her, are (like the rest of us) something less than a miracle of nature.

Presently, we are in the bathroom. Cass wears faded carpenter jeans with frayed holes in the knees and a white V-neck sweater. She has coarse black hair that falls below her waist. She asks if I think her boyfriend, Evan (also an actor), has got another girl. She has only been seeing Evan for two months. They are not committed, but she is obsessed. Cass has a certain weakness for imposters, actor-men. She says she adores anyone who looks like a young Robert Redford, even though she also admits Evan is an oversexed dog.

I find that when enclosed in a small room it's best to say nothing incriminating. Now would not be the time to tell her, for example, about being handcuffed to Evan's bedposts, or about his deft use of electronic devices. Cass's intuition can only take her so far. I have been very careful. After our lovemaking, I have washed Evan's smell off of me, soaped every orifice and arrived home from his apartment smelling of *Irish Spring*.

I sit on the edge of the tub while Cass spreads her legs and urinates in what I am certain is a territorial display. Her jeans rest in folds against her pale calves. She cannot be more than five feet tall in heels, but she pisses like a horse and this, along with a terrible intimacy and displacement that being in the bathroom with her brings, unsettles me.

You're awfully quiet, Moira, she says.

Her eyes, I am certain, speak of murder.

At the beginning of the school year, I once saw Cass run down a freshman (the girl on foot, Cass in her Jeep). I can only imagine what she might do to me.

She asks if I'm nervous. I tell her no, I'm not nervous, not especially, no more than usual, etc. I tell her her obsession is bound to breed psychiatric bills.

Actors are full of fictions and lies, she says. She tells me she wishes she didn't always find herself in bed with thespians, that betrayal pervades all thespian interactions, and that Evan is incapable of true love.

Whine, whine, whine.

I tell her that for any proposition to be meaningful, love or affairs alike, it must be verified. Empirical evidence, hard facts. Show me the proof of betrayal, I tell her. Then I sniff the air, somewhat tauntingly and say: Do you smell *Irish Spring*?

Cass, as is a customary habit, slides her small medallion, a picture of St. Stephen, back and forth across her necklace. (Clearly this is a neurotic gesture.) She narrows her eyes in a most predictable way.

It's true I am not without some feelings of guilt. But once you have committed the crime, there is always the business of cover-up, and I am all for that. Self-preservation in circumstances of betrayal is essential.

Evan is playing Jason opposite Cass's role of the Colchian princess in the college's production of Euripides' *Medea*. He practices his lines while naked, standing over me in bed, and sometimes when he is reading he jumps up and down, causing his penis to whirl and fly about. I roll with laughter and cover myself with blankets that are warm and smell of sex. Like many men, Evan aligns himself with the Classicist school and believes his penis is an embodiment of nobility and that he can discern truths such as love or beauty, which he then approximates with sex and nipple rings. All this should make me suspicious. The truth is I have always imagined that I would end up in bed with a man who looked like Nietzsche, a little on the morose and philological side, possibly someone who listened (as Nietzsche did) to Wagner's music. But it seems I have a terrible weakness for blue-grey eyes, good looks and clean, classical features. (I suppose Evan *does* look like a young Redford, even though I ask, during sex, if he might be a dear and put on a tape of Wagner's *Tristan und Isolde*. He looks at me strangely. I have interrupted his foreplay with my constant talking.)

The truth is I am a bit taken with Evan.

Normally I suffer from a terrible interiority of the soul that causes me to hang in the corners of familiar institutions—libraries, coffee houses, etc.—and pass judgments. But here, in Evan's bed, I feel other things: sheer whimsy over our naked bodies, an unexpected affection.

Evan kisses my belly, quotes Jason's lines. *I will listen to what new thing you want, woman, to get from me,* he says.

I am not a jealous person, but today, since he has asked, I give Evan a good-natured ribbing about having two women. I have on occasion indulged horrible images of Cass riding Evan around naked, a thought that makes me feel slightly ill, that makes me scrub harder with my soap and towel to the point where my skin turns red. I tell him I want to know which one of us—Cass or me—he prefers. I say, it must be difficult to have relations with two flatmates. I ask him if ever he has indulged a certain fantasy that he might, on some occasion, end up in bed with both of us, if only out of sheer confusion, carelessness, or the simple act of forgetting. And then where would you be? I say.

He says: I can't help myself; I always fall for my leads. He tells me that this, combined with a certain dogged appreciation for the female form, repeatedly gets him in trouble. Condemn not, but pity me instead, he tells me.

Boo-hoo, I say. Poor Evan.

After our lovemaking, which consists mainly of discourse (a carry-over from my love affair with Nietzsche as well as my own disturbed thoughts), Cass calls. There are tears and drinking involved. Apparently there has been an abundance of tears and drinking lately, as well as desperate phone calls late at night. She is obsessed, he says.

I say: What do you expect? She knows, I tell him. Evan-Jason has taken a second lover (you know who) and Cass-Medea is exacting her revenge. Suddenly I think she (Cass, Medea) is probably on her way to Evan's (Jason's) apartment as I speak. I remember the running down of the freshman. It was no laughing matter. I leap out of bed and trip over a pile of clothes and boots scattered on the floor. I search for my panties. I grope. Quickly I slip into my jeans, button my shirt, pull on my sweater. I say: All interaction breeds terror.

He says nothing. Like most men I've slept with, after sex and discourse alike, Evan has a very low attention span. He busies himself by draping a Kleenex over his penis like a toga. The whole draping ceremony pleases him, confirms his own spectacular wishes about the splendor of his body, its classicism, its containment. I rush out into the frosty air (bra stashed in my purse, along with my panties) and into the descending dark.

A person decides that she is going to have an affair with her flatmate's boyfriend and, while in theory this should be easy, the whole thing is soon mired with problems. First, there is a small pang of guilt I feel constantly, along with my unexpected interest in the classics. Also things with Cass are turning ugly. I come back to our flat and she sniffs, with canine cunning, to see if Evan's warm and spicy scent clings to my wool coat. *Irish Spring, Irish Spring*, thank goodness for the thin scent that masks our deception.

Constant supervision! I am never alone. Cass swears that if I am guilty, I will pay. She asks if I think I am beyond reproach. She says: Who do you think you are, some Superwoman? (I think she is searching for proof of my amoral nature, secretly reading my books on Nietzsche while I am attending classes.) Cass slides the small medallion back and forth across her neck. She eyes me suspiciously. She says God sees everything, Moira. And in case God fails, she says, she is also gathering evidence.

Today, while I was buying a cup of coffee, I caught her peering through the window, her eyes and hair wild, snow descending around her. She placed her gloved hand on the glass and gave me the most cunning smile. She walked me to my classes and then waited, pacing the hallway. She escorted me to the library and said she was *going that way*. Cass has never set foot near the library and cannot use the UCLID system to save her life. She watches, preys on my nervousness, and when she sees I am shaken, she laughs. It's insanity. Cass is falling off the rocking horse, cracking up.

On campus, it snows and snows and the tree limbs are coated with ice.

Peril lies at every corner.

These are the hard facts of my guilt: A month ago, Evan stopped by the flat while Cass was attending Professor Klodhaven's History of Drama seminar. Wagner was playing on the tape deck. On the coffee table lay *Beyond Good and Evil*, which I was supposed to be reading had I not been painting my toenails red and taking a quiz in Cass's *Cosmo* ("Are you a true friend?"). Evan, unconcerned with time, propped his legs on the coffee table with an easiness that irritated me greatly. He smiled (straight, white teeth, very Redford). Had I been dressed more appropriately, I might have told him I was on my way out to a class or the library. But as it happened, I wore only a tee-shirt and cut off jeans.

Evan said: I don't *believe* in either *Cosmo* quizzes or the master-slave morality of Nietzsche; both kinds of indulgences in thinking can lead to trouble. He cited various historical instances where both Nietzsche and *Cosmo* have been misapplied to horrible ends. He said if I wanted to know where the real evil lay, I should look to women. He laughed, ha ha. Really, Evan has such a backwards way of flirting.

I told him that sort of thing, oppressing women and their sexuality, felt a little old. Men have been using that kind of evil-woman nonsense since the fall. I personally was sick to death of always being mistaken for the devil.

Evan told me that he would like to see me paint my toenails while naked.

Discourse, intercourse. They are not so totally unrelated. And in my defense, the air in the flat was stifling. The less clothes the better. All winter, our heaters have cranked and cranked uncontrollably, and Mr. Tannen has painted all the windows shut.

However, of the sixteen times Evan and I have slept together since that day, and how these events came to be, I cannot say.

I do not think she has showered in days. Cass has let her hair grow ratty-looking, and she skulks around the flat with a butcher knife in her hand. I am fairly certain Medea used poison, but I do not belabor the point or break her mood. Perhaps this is only method acting and not some veiled threat against my life or an act of aggression designed as a territorial display.

She paces in a pink housecoat and (for some unknown reason) clogs, holding the knife in one hand and her script in the other. The heaters crank. I hear grating, incessant clacking noises as she moves. She is leaving scratch marks that I am sure Mr. Tannen will notice and deduct from our security deposit.

Cass throws down the knife (more scratches). I wait for a primal scream, for some other bizarre form of possession to manifest. I hold my Nietzsche book in front of me like a shield. I say: Get back! and try to laugh though really I am a little frightened by her current state, which is something vacillating between severe depression, anxiety, and unleashed rage. She only looks at me and sighs. We are in the depression, I see. Evan hasn't called, she says. She laments his loss and curses what she now calls his "paramour."

I say: Why is it the woman always get the curses? What is Evan, I say? Innocent?

That's not the *point*, she tells me. She says she *is* Medea (acting =schizophrenia=illogical progressions of discourse=psychiatric bills). Her nerves are clearly frayed.

Take the running down of the freshman, for example, an event that landed the girl in the hospital with a sprained ankle (she fell) and landed Cass on probation (the Dean was present, just arriving to his office). That whole fiasco happened because before getting into her Jeep, Cass had a fight with her boyfriend Gil (predecessor to Evan, also an actor). Cass accused Gil of flirting with the girl, an understudy, and the fight put her, in Cass's exact words, as recorded on official college documents, "on edge."

I think I am doing her a favor by sleeping with Evan.

Cass sits next to me on the futon. Evan smells of another woman, she confesses.

How many women can he have? I say. I have not slept with Evan for days and have never before considered the possibility of another woman (besides Cass) in his bed, car, on his sofa, etc. I am not a jealous person, but I feel miffed just the same.

Evan has gotten the upper hand, clearly. Cass and I are silent. It is this moment, as *Medea* suggests, when a woman takes a man for her master, that she is exiled from her home and dispossessed.

Cass haunts our apartment flat at night. I hear her clogs

scratching the floor. She sobs, speaks to herself. Until they are on stage, actors live in a kind of darkness, a limbo. For all actors, I decide, life is only a performance and events on the stage are the truth. There is no way to argue it otherwise.

Other news: I found two of my Wagner tapes mysteriously sliced in half. My Nietzsche book also is missing. She is working up to something. There is evidence of this all around.

At eight o'clock the next night Evan arrives, script in hand, dragging in slushy snow that I wipe up with a mop. When I finish, he says, Hello, Moira, and shakes my hand with great formality, as if there weren't other things besides his extended arm that I have seen protracted and stiff.

The truth is I am finding him, of late, a little unbearable.

Cass says nothing. She sits on the futon, twirling and pulling out strands of her hair which she lets drift to the floor. Dark half moons have appeared under her eyes. She is beginning to smell.

Jesus, Evan says. What's gotten into you?

She ignores his question. She glances back and forth between the two of us. Evidence, Evidence. Cass slides the small medallion back and forth. There are signs of deterioration. I down cup after cup of coffee and try to stop my hands from shaking.

Evan places his hand on Cass's knee, but she brushes it away. Adulterer, she says.

Evan is an ennobled Jason. He says, *Even if you hate me, I cannot think badly of you.* He kisses her hand.

Thespians! They are a horrible, horrible lot when method acting.

I decide early on I will have no part in the evening. I collect miscellaneous books from the table (along with a few *Cosmos*) and gather my coat. I tell them I will be at the library, but Evan, not wanting to be alone with Cass, says: Moira, you can watch.

Look, the whole thing is getting sticky, I say. I am no fan of acting, I tell him.

He says: Have you seen *Medea*? There's no telling what she might do. He laughs but clearly he is nervous. I sit, and even though I feign disinterest with a copy of *Cosmo*, I am forced to see, in the corner of my eye, Jason and his Medea embracing, her body limp, her wild eyes gazing at me. Evan, I decide, gets some kind of sick pleasure from all this. Having two women (possibly more) has made him bold. Cass begins to cry.

It's true I am beginning to feel amoral.

Later, I wake to hear Evan through the stucco walls, his groans in synchronicity with the rhythmic squeaking of the futon's springs. They have made up. He has taken advantage of Cass's affections, gotten her to shower, to possibly use soap. I peer around the corner of my doorway and see her sprawled out in the throes of passion, pleading with Evan to say he loves her. When he says nothing, she weeps into his chest. It is a sad and fearful sight, to see them, the contours of their bodies, the pliability and frailty of their flesh, the frenzied way in which they come together again and again, and how, when finished, they disconnect, spent, exhausted, still only themselves.

Medea opens in two days and runs for only one week. After the play ends, I can only hope that things become quiet.

Mr. Tannen calls the next day and says he has received complaints of lewd activity, sexual trysts, loud noises. I tell him he's got the wrong flat even though the air smells of sex and there are two used rubbers in the bathroom trash. I am on a bit of a caffeine kick. I am missing my Nietzsche book, and my music has been destroyed, not to mention other things—pride, morality, the start of affection. I say: Look, Mr. Tannen, I am in no mood for harassing phone calls. He tells me he's heard rumors about both Cass and me, that he's onto us and has our number. He says the walls are thin. He clears his throat after every sentence. After he clears his throat for the fourth time, I say: Are you touching yourself, Mr. Tannen? Are you?

He tells me I'm insane.

I can no longer look at Cass. She wears the same clothes from yesterday, and she butters a slice of burnt, crunchy toast.

In the middle of breakfast, and for what reason I don't know—love, abandonment, fear—Cass sobs uncontrollably.

I fix her chicken noodle soup which she lets grow cold. She lies on the futon watching the *Price is Right*, and when I tell her it's almost time for classes, she moans and turns under her blanket. I sit with her for a few hours and rub her arm. Then I go through mail: coupons (there is one for *Irish Spring* which I discard); a credit card offer; a letter to Cass from her old high school sweetheart who still, after all this time, writes; and a letter from Mr. Tannen to all his tenants saying that unpaid rent is subject to prosecution.

Tannen is out to get us, I say.

Tannen is a pervert, Cass moans. And Evan is no better. She lies face-down on the futon, and her voice is muffled by a pillow. When she is sick of TV, she shuts it off and stares idly out the window to the park below us.

By nine at night, there is other evidence of problems: two empty wine bottles are in the trash. I find an argument paper there, too, on Modern drama which Klodhaven has given a D.

Later, I wake to find Cass standing over me. I can almost hear her murderous thoughts as she leans closer, drunk to high heaven, a knife in hand. My heart races, my fists grip the blanket, but I am too terrified to move. Cass watches, her body and the blade of the knife pale blue from the park lights. She whispers. She speaks of betrayal in both friendship and love. She says: Some friend you are, Moira, then she quotes *Medea*, saying, *I wish I might die.* Her breath reeks of cheap wine. She slides the small medallion back and forth then stumbles, falls back on the floor, and sleeps.

I could press charges, but instead I decide it's enough that I stop seeing Evan. I cover her with blankets and return the knife to the safety of the kitchen drawer.

Some miscellaneous facts: First, when considering the ethics of power, right and wrong, good and evil, there is no place for attachment, as attachment corrupts. Nietzsche, before he became so lonely and morose, sitting around listening to Wagner, all philological and suicidal, knew this fact, prescribing to what he called a pathos of distance that grows from differences between certain classes of people (actors, ethics students, a perfect case in point). Now, as I am faced with Cass's weeping, with my own feelings of guilt, I wonder if distance is really a possibility with flatmates. There are (as Nietzsche also knew) occasional attempts at reconciliation, times when certain types of actors/thespians and non-thespian sorts come together despite their differences. It is becoming clear to me that despite Evan's rather classical detachment and Greek obsession with his penis, that despite my own cynicism and judgments and concern with literary discourse, Cass has *suffered* (just as I have suffered). That we are *alike* in our suffering. Tragedy, absurdity, and meaninglessness all abound.

On the morning that *Medea* is scheduled to open, the park's groundskeeper finds Cass lying in the snow (in her pink housecoat, in clogs) laughing wildly and trying (unsuccessfully, she is drunk) to make angels. I am driven downstairs by all the noise. When the groundskeeper tries to help her up, Cass bites him, draws blood. The police are called. The Dean is called. There is a suggestion, as she lies there shaking, that she might need help, that she is rambling incoherently and possibly an indigent, but the Dean disconfirms this, tells everyone gathered around about the incident with the Jeep and the freshman. Icy blood lines Cass's forehead (from the biting episode), and her whole body turns blue from overexposure. Someone (I don't know who) covers her with a blanket. The police escort her to a hospital (mental institution).

Later, in my desperation, I ask the check-in nurse at the institution how they are certain Cass (Medea) is not simply method acting, how they know she is not playing out a derivation on the act of revenge, abandoning the knife and poison for a form of self-destruction instead. The nurse, who looks a bit like a female-version of Nietzsche, seems alarmed by my appearance (cut off shorts, a T-shirt, no coat, hair a mess). She assures me that Cass is quite clinically depressed and a danger to herself, that she has probably been like this for years. She says: Are you a sister?

An unlikely proposition, you she-man, I say, but thank you. I want to see Cass, I say.

The nurse tells me that Cass is in an "extreme state" and that I can come back in seventy-two hours before she is released to go home to her parents. I am going to be up the creek with rent problems, but I tell her, this philosopher-nurse, that I am a millionaire.

She asks me if I need some sort of assistance.

No, I say, of course not. You've done enough, I tell her/him.

The coffeeshop is already abuzz with news of the "nervous breakdown," and the people in my department, a serious and sober bunch, say they are "concerned" that all actors possess, at some profound level, feeble minds. When I come to the table, they say, Christ, what's wrong with *you*? They look at me severely, produce judgments as I leave. I am certain I am already the butt of their ridicule.

An understudy, an up and coming freshman, has taken over Cass's part as Medea.

I speak to Evan on the phone, but we have little to say. I tell him we betrayed Cass, that our cynicism and detachment collectively have done her in. He sounds apologetic and tells me he understands. He tells me that even though he feels exhausted and sad, he will continue to play the role of Jason, as this is what Cass would have wanted. He tells me that when *Medea* closes in three days, he will sleep for years.

I am filled with some indescribable sensation, some need for

Cass and feeling of duty towards her. I drive to the hospital in my Ford (it's red), but when I arrive, Cass is being escorted out of the institution by an older couple, possible parents or grandparents, I am unsure. Cass appears, as she did that night I saw her and Evan naked, to be a wholly fragile thing. She is wearing her pink housecoat and clogs, and her father (grandfather?) has draped her with his coat. When she spots me getting out of the truck, running toward her, tripping in slushy snow, she turns her head away, denying me atonement.

    I spend most of the days and weeks afterward sitting in Cass's room, filled with regret. I tell myself, I ought to have been nicer, that a little kindness and consideration, especially with regard to flatmates (if not the world at large), goes a long way. All action, I realize, is bound in space and time, and each moment, significant and insignificant alike, is unrecoverable. This premise, I am certain, is at the root of all falls from grace and sanity alike: we cannot get back our lost time.
    I am thinking seriously about quitting school.
    I am definitely, at the very least, quitting German philosophy.
    At night, I no longer sleep. I hear Cass roaming the flat and am burdened with both dreams and nightmares, all of them involving her and, oddly enough, a school of thought Nietzsche abandoned. My dreams mimic the conversion on the road to Damascus. In them, Wagner is playing in the distance, and as I ride on my horse, the sounds of music grow weaker. Cass, on the side of the road, waits, and when I pass, she asks me why I have persecuted her. I fall, weeping. In my dreams, I lose my identity, change my name. These dreams, at the end, are filled with a certain quality of hope. In my nightmares, Cass's ghost haunts my room with a knife, a possessed, tragic (lonely) figure, and she tells me only that I will pay, that our sins follow us into eternity.
    I have begun to sit in on Cass's History of Drama class. Professor Klodhaven has noticed and eyed me suspiciously, but he has said nothing. Yesterday, when I tried to hand in a paper I'd written for Cass, one which I am certain would have earned her an A, Professor Klodhaven refused to accept the work. He looked at me as if I were deranged.
    On the fifth of the month, Mr. Tannen stops by the flat to remind me of my commitments. When he sees me, he seems to take pity. He does not look like Redford except that he has, I am sorry to say, blue-gray eyes. He tells me that he will deduct fifty dollars from my rent if I am having problems, and I am so

grateful for this kind gesture, I sleep with him. Afterward, when he tells me we can sleep together every month, I come after him with the knife I now keep under my bed.

I live in exile. The desk librarian finds me asleep in the book stacks, my head resting upon a shelf, my body slumped in a chair. Around me, there are pages and pages torn from Nietzsche's books and scattered about. The librarian demands to know who I think I am, but I cannot tell him. He turns me in to the Dean who places me on probation and orders me to see the school counselor. The counselor is a *humanist*, and so I have found my little corner of hell. In his waiting room, there are endless copies of *Cosmo*, reading material that paves the New World. I weep uncontrollably and tell him I cannot go back to the flat, that I have suffered through long, lonely nights there and fear for my sanity. He suggests only that I learn forgiveness. He says I should try to learn love.

I nod desperately and tell him I will try.

Mr. Tannen, however, is out to deter me. This morning, I received a certified letter in the mail demanding overdue rent and money for damage to the floors. With it, there was a crude, hand-written note, telling me I was the worst piece of ass he's ever had. He tells me I have cost him money, he repeats that I have ruined his floors, and if I do not remit payment, he says, he will have his day in court.

Elizabeth Orndorff

The Ginkgo Tree

The sign at the entrance said "Welcome to the Loretto Motherhouse," which she found almost obscene; then the drive wound up hill, pulling her deeper into the green hills and towering—what? elms? oaks? No more chestnuts, they were all gone. But she allowed to herself that she wouldn't know a chestnut if one fell down in front of her. She knew an evergreen from an azalea, and that was about it. The grounds were covered in trees, old ones surely, huge and luscious, framing the red brick buildings like the hair and eyelashes of a woman.

The convent of the Sisters of Loretto sat in the middle of six hundred acres of green pastures edged by tree rows. It had been sitting in the middle of these six hundred acres for one hundred and eighty years, since a priest from France had founded the order. Where it had once been a convent and college for the education of the young sisters before sending them out into the frontiers, the cities, the ghettoes, it was now a convent and retirement home for the old sisters come home to roost.

That's what Mrs. Lucas's brochure had said, the one describing the lovely campus available for her private spiritual retreat. The three-story Academic Hall had been turned into a guest dormitory. The Guest House, across from the infirmary, was smaller, more intimate. It had a kitchen and a library, filled with Catholic books, a few novels, magazines, devotionals. Then there was the art studio for Sister Jean, who created huge sculptures out of wood and iron and tiny nativities of clay and wire. A road down the western hill had little cottages reserved for visiting family members of the sisters. In the distance could be seen red barns and greenhouses. The path to the Hermitages, where one could stay in seclusion for months, wound around a pond on the north.

There was supposed to be a group of women from The Presbyterian Church in Danville. Eight of them were coming on retreat, a venture into ecumenism the church had been doing for a few years. Besides, the Catholics had all the good retreats. The Benedictines had Gethsemani, but that was a Trappist monastery, and therefore silent. Mrs. Lucas had been on retreat there once, but she had not enjoyed the quiet, especially the meals. Everyone faced in the same direction, staring out the picture windows, eating the soup and bread and cheese, so quiet she could hear their stomachs gurgle. She had not liked that.

The retreats were usually popular, but this time one by one her friends dropped out. Soccer games, family dinners, anything more fun than sitting in a convent for a weekend examining yourself to see how short you fell. She would have cancelled, too, but then her husband, who usually behaved himself, had a fit of distemper and she decided she'd prefer the company of nuns after all.

Sister Mary, the guestmistress, had instructed her, on the telephone, to park in the lot in front of the infirmary. The administrative offices, the post office, the guest registration were all located in Saint Joseph's Infirmary on the first floor. The second and third floors housed the nuns who were too sick and frail to live by themselves. More sisters lived in private rooms in the north and west wings of the infirmary that formed a quadrangle. The first floor of the west wing housed the dining hall. Yellow walls, oilcloth table covers, enough room for the wheelchairs.

Mrs. Lucas locked the car door and turned toward the infirmary before a scent of guilt stopped her. She put her key back in the lock and turned it, open. This would be her first act of faith this weekend. She wondered what her husband was fixing himself for dinner.

She walked right under the ginkgo tree without seeing it, her thoughts ricocheting between Tom and the idea of nunnery and her sore left shoulder. Inside, the narrow hall was dark and quiet, no one in sight. She stood in the middle of the space and did not move. She should wait here for someone to come get her, that's what Sister Mary had said. In the distance she could hear a television playing. What kind of television did nuns watch?

The Ginkgo Tree

News of the world outside the Motherhouse? Game shows? Wrestling?

The squeak of crepe soles awakened her. Here was Sister Mary, quite young really, maybe forty. She was dressed in a red and black plaid shirt pulled out over black slacks. She had dark hair and glasses and her right arm was covered in soft black hair. Her left arm was harder to see, but Mrs. Lucas couldn't look away. It was withered and pulled up into a curl, and the hand had only three fingers on it.

"I'll show you your room," said the nun. "Then you'll still have time for dinner."

"The others couldn't come," said Mrs. Lucas, reaching into her bag. "But I have their deposits here. I'm so sorry."

"Yes, it would be a shame to turn people away and then not have guests come."

"Are you full this weekend, Sister Mary?" Mrs. Lucas looked at the woman's face, but the dark eyes were looking elsewhere.

"Please, call me Mary."

"Are you full, Mary?"

Silence. "Only you."

Suddenly the light changed as Mary pushed open the heavy door of the infirmary, and the air was a golden color that was almost frightening.

"What is it?" Mrs. Lucas cupped her hands over her eyes. "What is that light?"

Sister Mary pointed with her bad arm. "The tree. The ginkgo tree."

Mrs. Lucas raised her eyes and closed them to the amber light that wrapped around them. She could feel the warm September sun on her face. She could see the glorious yellow through her eyelids.

She opened her eyes and looked at the ginkgo. She couldn't believe that she had not seen it before. How could she not see it? It was at least thirty feet high and thirty feet across, every little leaf clothed in its September color of the purest golden yellow.

"I've never seen such a thing," said Mrs. Lucas, raising her face again to the light. Maybe the sun had moved since she had entered the building. Now it perched squarely on the horizon and beat its glittery rays into the thousands of fan-shaped leaves of the ginkgo tree.

Mary pointed again. Why did she always use her shrunken arm? "See when the breeze blows? It ruffles every one of them." Surely, this was a sight unlike any other. The huge tree quivering in delight, casting its buttery light in a pool around them. Now what did that remind Mrs. Lucas of—yes, Little Black Sambo and the tigers who chased themselves so hard around the base of the palm tree that they turned into butter for Sambo's pancakes. That's exactly what this was like. She was standing in a pool of liquid butter and she didn't want to leave. She stretched out her arms and threw her head back.

"Can I stand here forever?"

Sister Mary watched her. "It's like this every September. It is magical, isn't it?"

Mrs. Lucas nodded. Speaking would shatter the crystal light, surely.

Sister Mary took a few steps and bent to pick up a fallen leaf. She took a long look at her only boarder, then decided to give up the secret.

"See, here's a leaf," she said. "Soon they'll all be falling." She waited, then went on. "And when they fall—when they fall—"

Mrs. Lucas looked at the nun. "Yes?"

Sister Mary cleared her throat. "When they fall, they all fall at once!"

Mrs. Lucas looked at the tree, at the twenty-seven hundred cubic feet of yellow leaves. "At once?"

Sister Mary moved a step closer. "When they start to fall, the word spreads—like wildfire. Then we all come out, every last one of us that can walk, and many that can't, and we stand under this golden, golden tree. Then the lovely leaves, like shining coins from heaven, fall all around us and upon us."

Mrs. Lucas watched Sister Mary's face. Her cheeks were pink and tears gathered in the corners of her eyes.

"And the light! The light is even more glorious—because it is filled with this motion—this motion of a hundred thousand dancing yellow ginkgos!" She stopped, waiting to see what sort of reception her story would receive.

"And in those moments—those few, precious moments—" her voice fell to a whisper and Mrs. Lucas leaned closer.

"Yes?" Mrs. Lucas cried out.

Sister Mary reached out her curled, three-fingered hand and touched Mrs. Lucas on the wrist, on the soft, bluish inside of her wrist. Then Mrs. Lucas did what she did not think she could do. She grasped Sister Mary's gnarled hand in both of her own. "And what is it like?"

Sister Mary was clearly embarrassed. She smiled and gently withdrew her hand from Mrs. Lucas's clasp. "It is nothing I can explain. But I think you will be seeing it for yourself soon enough."

"When?" said Mrs. Lucas. "When will it happen?"

Sister Mary shrugged gently and crossed herself. "Perhaps tomorrow," she said, fingering the leaf in her hand. "This is a good sign."

"What if they fall at night, or on a cloudy day, or before the sun is high?"

"They never do," said Sister Mary. "They never do."

"Perhaps," said Mrs. Lucas, wishing to apply some rationality, "it is nothing more than the right combination of things. The heat from the sun and the late afternoon breeze—"

Sister Mary smiled. "Yes," she agreed, and turned to go. "That is the way God works, is it not? The right combination of things. Now I'll show you to your room, Mrs. Lucas."

Mrs. Lucas nodded. "Would you call me? I mean, when they start to fall?"

Sister Mary waved her withered arm. "Someone will call, yes."

When the summons finally came the next day, it was not what Mrs. Lucas had expected. All morning she had wandered about the grounds, waiting. She tried to pray. She went into the chapel and even knelt, something Presbyterians were not prone to do. But the silence in the chapel had an accusing quality about it, and she soon left.

Breakfast and lunch in the dining hall were unremarkable. The food was accidental, a cup of sliced peaches, some soup from a can, a bowl of bananas, and white bread. Several of the sisters came to speak with her and Sister Frances even accepted her offer of a seat. Sister Frances had spent her working life as a social worker in Phoenix.

"Do you get to leave here?" said Mrs. Lucas. "Do you ever go into Bardstown to see a movie or have dinner?"

"Oh, we can," said Sister Frances, with a small smile. "If we want to. We have a fleet of Toyota Camrys to use."

Mrs. Lucas chewed her bread and looked at the nun. "Do you have a private room?"

"Yes."

"Do you watch television?"

"We each have our own color television and a La-Z-Boy recliner!" Sister Frances was very pleased with the arrangements.

"And you've been here for three years?"

"Yes, dear. But I went to school here over fifty years ago. When it had the school."

Mrs. Lucas watched Sister Frances spoon the peaches into her mouth. Was it possible to die of boredom at a convent in the middle of nowhere?

"May I ask you a question, Mrs. Lucas?"

Mrs. Lucas nodded, her mouth full.

"Why did you come here?"

Well, that was direct. How should she answer that? That her husband had provoked her so badly that she couldn't bear to look at his face for at least forty-eight hours? Would a nun understand that kind of answer?

"We were coming as a group, from church. But then everyone else cancelled, and I was going to, but—but at the last minute—"

"At the last minute God drew you to us."

Mrs. Lucas shrugged and looked into the pale blue eyes of the nun. "I was going to say that—that my husband was acting like a boor—"

Sister Frances arranged the items on her tray and stood up, slowly. "Same thing." She turned to walk away.

"Wait," said Mrs. Lucas. "Do you think the ginkgo tree will shed today?"

Sister Frances nodded. "I think it's very likely. That's probably why you are here."

After lunch she took a nap. Again she tried to pray, stretched out on the pink and white chenille spread, the ceiling fan clicking her into a stupor. But she felt nothing, heard nothing, no matter how hard she tried. The words would barely come. What kind of failure would she be if she couldn't put forth one prayer in the middle of a convent, by herself, on a spiritual retreat? The futility distressed her. The day was passing. She began to think of her house and the things she had left undone there. Perhaps it was all a waste of time, this retreat from the world. If the ginkgo tree didn't lose its leaves this afternoon she might as well have stayed at home and argued with Tom over whose responsibility it was to unload the dishwasher.

Mrs. Lucas was on the far western side of the lake sitting on a bench and staring at the cattails when she heard the raucous clang of an old fire bell, the kind you pulled with a rope, dropping your whole body weight into the effort. As she hurried along the path toward the infirmary she wondered which of the nuns had seen the first floating leaves start to trickle down.

Sister Mary was right. The late afternoon sun was burning low in the sky and a warm breeze blew the hair out of Mrs. Lucas's eyes.

Outside the infirmary they had begun to gather, grouped in a large circle, nuns in wheelchairs in the front, nuns on walkers, nuns clutching canes, there must have been more than a hundred of them. Their average age had to be well over eighty. Two ancient sisters stood out in the crowd, both in wheelchairs and bent almost double with great humps on their backs, straining to lift their faces from their laps. They were the only ones wearing the black habit and white wimple. Tiny little women, holding hands.

Mrs. Lucas edged into the silent group, looking for Sister Frances and Sister Mary. The leaves had begun to fall, and with every sigh of the breeze, Mary's golden coins rained down on them in the yellow, shimmering air. There was Sister Jean, the artist nun, her arms raised, her face tilted upward, her lips moving. Around her head was wrapped a red bandanna. The pretty leaves began to collect on their shoulders and in their hair. There was an undercurrent of murmuring as the nuns—what? Prayed? Savored ecstatic presence? What? She noticed that most of them were holding someone's hand.

Suddenly a nun was speaking. "The ginkgo tree, you know, is also called the maidenhair tree. A maiden's hair."

Mrs. Lucas thought of the beautiful princess in the tower weaving gold from straw for the troll Rumpelstiltskin. The light under the ginkgo tree was indescribable.

"The ginkgo tree is the last living species of its family. It thrived 200 million years ago. It came from China, in the beginning. Long before man."

There was murmuring silence while the nuns thought about 200 million years of something. It was impossible to grasp.

Another nun spoke up. "It's a gymnosperm."

Why were they doing this? thought Mrs. Lucas. Was it for her benefit? This botany lesson in the midst of pure grace?

"Naked seed," said another. "That's what gymnosperm means. Naked seed." There was a soft tinkling sound—was that a giggle? They continued the litany, each adding a line or a phrase that would flesh out the picture of what was happening to them, around them, above them.

"This is a male tree. This is a male ginkgo." There it was again, only more of them this time.

Mrs. Lucas looked around at the nuns and saw for the first time that nearly all of them were smiling. No, not smiling—grinning. Huge misshapen grins on their lined and sagging faces, eyes grinning, cheeks pulled back in joy. Some of them were humming, little tunes that bore no resemblance to anything Mrs. Lucas had ever heard. The golden leaves continued to fall.

Was that a little nun over there—dancing? Was she shuffling her feet in a little soft shoe while she clung to her walker? Could it be? Then the whole crowd of them began to move, and Mrs. Lucas had to put her hand on the woman next to her, for it made her dizzy, this gradual motion of the swaying nuns among the cascade of glitter in the air.

Laughter burst out—where had it come from? It was the two

tiny nuns in the old-fashioned habits—their clasped hands beating a rhythm up and down as they giggled and bobbed their wimpled heads, the golden leaves a pile of coins in their black laps. Then others began to laugh, and Sister Jean the artist let out a whoop and clapped her hands. Then all of them felt the fetters of restraint loosen, and the whooping and hollering began in earnest; they started to move as a group, counterclockwise around the great ginkgo tree, hesitantly then faster, but not so very fast, the leaves brushing their faces, sometimes sticking to a wet cheek for a moment, before continuing downward. The golden light was thick upon them, and they, in turn, took on its exquisite quality.

Suddenly the breeze increased, as if a sigh from the lips of God, and swirled the thick piles of leaves around their feet as they danced through. Liquid butter, thought Mrs. Lucas, pointing her toes and kicking her brogans, the tigers are here! Would they like to hear about the tigers? Perhaps they already knew.

Mrs. Lucas had never raised her voice in public in her entire life. She would rather have died than subject herself to that sort of scrutiny, that judgment. But somehow beneath the ginkgo her voice was freed and she sang out.

"We are the tigers, don't you see?" cried Mrs. Lucas. They were all looking at her so intently, smiles jumping on their faces. Yes, she thought they did see. "We're Little Black Sambo's tigers—and we're turning into melted butter!"

"Butter! Butter!" grew the murmurings, as the sisters added yet another picture. "We are melted butter!" They began to move faster around the circle.

"Yes!" came a small but excited voice. It was one of the bent-over nuns in a wheelchair. "Look at me! I'm a tiger!" She had pushed the golden leaves into the semblance of rows against the vivid black of her habit. Her companion raised their clasped hands. "Grrrrrrr," they cried. "Grrrrrr!"

Then the laughter spilled out in great heaving waves as they danced and sang and batted at the tumbling leaves in the buttery air and behaved, in general, like happy tigers.

Gradually, the number of falling leaves began to lessen. Imperceptibly at first, then noticeable for the clear blue sky between the masses of yellow. Then it became possible to distinguish individual leaves, their delicate fan-shaped lobes catching the breeze. In a few more minutes the great ginkgo would be done for the season, stripped bare of its beauty, standing knee-deep in its lovely golden hair.

But the nuns would not leave until the last leaf fluttered to the ground. Only then did the singing and the laughter start to fade into talk and soft chatter, and they began to turn away, push-

The Ginkgo Tree

ing their canes and walkers and wheelchairs through the thick leaves. Mrs. Lucas stood watching them, not wishing to leave. Then she felt a cool touch on her elbow. It was Sister Mary.

"I'm so glad you were able to see our ginkgo drop its leaves, Mrs. Lucas."

Mrs. Lucas nodded. "Can I come again next year? In September?"

"Of course, " said the nun. "You can come any time."

Mrs. Lucas stood for a moment, not knowing what to say. "I suppose tomorrow I should get back to my husband." Would Sister Mary understand that?

"I hope you have enjoyed your brief stay here."

Mrs. Lucas bent over to pick up one perfect leaf. "You know," she said. "When I came here, I know I came for the wrong reasons. I know that. And then I tried to pray—and I couldn't do that, either. I tried to find God through reflection, through meditation. I did so much want to experience God! God is so elusive, is He not?"

Three pink fingers stroked the nun's chin. "I think, perhaps, Mrs. Lucas, that that is the one thing that God is not."

"Well," said Mrs. Lucas, considering. "You live in a convent, after all. Of course you must find God quite a bit. You have practice."

Sister Mary smiled. "You are exactly right. That is a good word for it."

"Practice?"

"Yes. We practice finding God. But in reality, it is God who finds us. Our practice has merely prepared us to receive Him. It's a lot like playing the piano, isn't it? The more you do it, the better you get at it—whenever anyone should ask you to play."

"I suppose," murmured Mrs. Lucas, not entirely satisfied with such a secular explanation. She turned to go, back to the chenille bedspread and the clicking fan and the piles of devotional books. Maybe she needed to work a little harder. "Anyway, thank you so much for ringing the fire bell. The ginkgo tree—and all of you—were so lovely that I almost don't mind that—"

Sister Mary raised her curled hand to her face, as if she were thinking. "Mind?"

Mrs. Lucas sighed. "Perhaps that was the wrong—"

Sister Mary looked at the tall, spare woman. "Well," she said. "Perhaps you'll find Him on your next retreat."

Mrs. Lucas nodded and closed her eyes.

Michael Schiavone

Skin

I'm picturing leftover pizza waiting for me at home when the silent alarm flashes. Jogging toward the service desk, I spot the gurney wheeling toward me, the stink of rotten eggs rushing my nostrils. Midnight, and the smell alone tells me I won't see that green chili pizza until dawn.

"I'm not sure we did this guy a favor, Knox," the paramedic says to me, waiting for a signature. A wad of tobacco stuffs his cheek. "He's still sizzling."

"Monstrous," the orderly mutters.

I've been on shift twelve hours and my new Reeboks are killing me. The victim's a mess, a long shot at best, and I consider pronouncing him dead on arrival. My sister tends bar and she tells me how much she hates it when people stagger in right before closing time. I resent this guy for the same reason.

The burns have consumed the skin, tissue, and fat in the victim's head, face, and neck. His forehead is scorched to the skull, his hands seared down to the tendons. I caress his head and it's hard as oak, a prime indication of fourth-degree burns, one of the reasons I wanted to pronounce him DOA. Third-degree burns sear through every layer of skin, which is bad enough, but fourth-degree goes further, chewing through other tissue and fat.

"What's his name, Luther?" I ask.

I work in a small, under-funded burn unit in the Arizona desert. Luther's my first intern. We don't even have a full-time secretary.

"Jason," Luther says. "How's he still alive?"

"In my ten years, I've never seen anyone live through the ambulance ride with facial burns like this," I say, inspecting Jason's neck. "When a person's whole head is burned, the airway usually gets clogged with smoke, swells shut, and he's a goner."

"Right. A goner," Luther says, scanning a flashlight over Jason's face.

Luther inserts a feeding tube into his stomach and a tracheotomy tube into his neck to assist Jason's crippled breathing. I consider waiting around for him to succumb, certain that's what he'd want if he had a voice right now, but medical ethics would disagree.

"Luther, make sure the room temperature doesn't drop below ninety. He's lost so much skin his body temp might suddenly plummet."

"Check," Luther says, winding the thermostat. "We're going to roast in here."

At 1:00 AM, I call in Denise, the night audit manager, to perform the sacrament of anointing the sick as Jason lay charred under a spotlight. Denise is also a part-time student at a divinity school and enjoys helping us out when she can.

"God bless you both," she says, making a cross in the air.

"Thank you, Denise," I say.

I take Jason's forehead and Luther works on the cheeks. Aside from the humming spotlight above our heads, only the soft, peeling sounds of flesh disturb the silence. Stopping every twelve minutes to wipe sweat from our bodies, Luther and I remove the dead skin piece by piece, waiting for the hopeful sight of blood. Jason's skin is brown, tough like rawhide. We need blood to see life.

When I work with someone on a freshly burned victim, it oddly reminds me of how I felt working on a jigsaw puzzle with my cousins during summer vacations in Florida. After a day in the sun, we'd lie on the carpet, clean and fresh from a shower, pleasantly tired, sand still in our ears. We'd stay with the puzzle until the adults forced us into bed. That's where I am right now. I figure it has something to do with the intense quiet of the operating room or my stern state of concentration, the ironic sense of safety this place can exude. If I try hard, I can even smell the warm Atlantic breeze over the stink of rotten eggs.

I like it in here.

"He sustained third-degree, if not worse, burns to his head,"

I tell his next of kin, a distant cousin who works at a Starbucks in Sedona. "Much of his face has been lost to the fire. The ears. The nose. The hands are bad, too." I pause so the information can settle, but she's very calm, receptive, nodding her head as I speak. "We have to remove the burns or he'll have no chance of survival."

I'm relieved there isn't a hysterical wife, a sobbing father, a petrified child. When I come out and try to articulate what I've been doing in the operating room, I don't feel like a doctor anymore. It somehow makes me feel sleazy, like a lawyer at a press conference. The story I tell depends on the state of the person before me. The work I do in the operating room is personal. It's mine.

Luther pushes some forms in front of her and tells her to please sign.

"Should anyone else be notified of his condition?" I ask. "Parents? Siblings? A girlfriend?"

My stomach growls and I push my pen into my gut.

"Oh, no," she says. "Jason's always kept to himself. I'm surprised my number was in his wallet. All things considered I guess it's a good thing he's a loner." She takes a crumpled pack of American Spirit cigarettes from her jean jacket pocket. "If you have any more news, I'll be outside."

I watch her lumpy body stroll toward the exit. All Jason's got is going outside for a smoke.

"Luther, I'm taking a quick bathroom break."

"Right, boss."

I turn off the lights and take a rest in the stall. The drip from the sink acts as a pulse between my deep breaths. I'll sit here three minutes, no longer, or else my legs will cramp and my mind will soften.

I've never enjoyed greeting the victim's families, but realize now I'd come to depend on their pleading, their insistence that I save that life on the operating table at all costs. They've actually made my job simpler, providing the impetus to rescue, enabling me to dismiss any personal feelings that might distract me from the task at hand. Tonight that's absent.

"Just what are we doing here, Knox?" Luther asks me suddenly. "I mean, we're about to take this guy's whole face off."

It'd been two hours of peeling. Luther's right. We'd removed Jason's face, but the only way to save him was to extract all the dead skin.

"Keep peeling, Luther."

"I'd rather die than have my face stripped."

"Me, too. But that's not the point, is it?"

We keep going into the dawn, digging deeper and deeper for

blood. Swipe, swipe, swipe. Down to muscle, down to bone.

Sunrise. Jason has no eyelids, no eyebrows, no forehead, no cheeks, no ears. His nose is a small stub with two holes.

He's vanished.

We had to staple cadaver skin over his face in order to protect the wounds. Because his eyelids burned off, we sewed his eyes shut in order to protect the corneas. We also surgically implanted his hands into his abdomen in an effort to re-grow the burned tissue.

"For his sake, I hope he wasn't a handsome man," Luther says, sipping on a coffee, visibly shaken.

"Don't worry. You won't see this every day. This is a one in a million."

"His face," Luther says as if asking a question. "There's nothing."

"We saved him," I say, squeezing his shoulder for emphasis. "We saved him."

I bring Jason's cousin in to see him, his bloodstained, bandaged head the size of a watermelon. Only the swollen lips visible.

"What's going to happen to him?" she asks. "I mean, is he going to live?"

"It's too early to tell," I say, sensing her fleeting tone. "If he makes it, he's going to need twenty-four hour attention. The process of rehabilitation will be a lengthy one."

"Is there a place for people like him?" she asks, biting a jagged thumbnail.

"If there's no family, the state will step in."

"Look, I don't know him from Adam to be honest with you. I got three cats I can barely take care of."

She shakes my hand before she leaves as if we came to some sort of agreement. As bad as I feel for Jason, I won't dwell on her absence because I know this is how the world really is. This is what happens if you're face burns right off your head. People flee. They don't need daily reminders that we might very well be in Hell. Even that dopey girl knows that.

At home, I slip on my Birkenstocks and prepare a batch of margaritas. A pile of mail a foot high rests on the butcher block and I spot the yellow envelopes from my ex-wife's lawyer in L.A., which contain receipts I must pay per court order until she is able to support herself. I've been getting them for two years now, but it doesn't bother me too much. I have plenty of money and those envelopes are something to come home to.

I take a healthy sip of my drink, the citrus smell cooling my nostrils. The light is fierce this morning, the temperature already ninety-eight. It'll be one-hundred and fifteen by noon.

The local news says a cab driver suffering from an epileptic seizure rammed into Jason's Chevy Chevette at fifty-three miles per hour. It was at eleven-thirty last night and Jason was at a stoplight on the corner of Zia and St. Francis. Jason's car shot into flames. Authorities say the victim would have died had there not been a fire truck three blocks away doing a drill. The victim was rushed to the Red Land Burn Unit for emergency . . . . . I wake up on the couch at two that afternoon. I think about going upstairs to bed, God knows my body aches, but I need to get back to the burn unit. In the bathroom, I pop two codeine pills and brush my teeth. I clip the gray hairs in my mustache. Before I leave, I separate the yellow envelopes from the rest of the mail.

For three days, Luther and I remove more dead skin from Jason's head, arms, and legs. By the end of the week, we replace the cadaver skin on his face with a material made from shark cartilage and bovine collagen. We also remove his hands from inside his abdomen where bulbous growths of skin like tennis balls rest atop his knuckles. With Jason still unconscious (doped up on pain killers and anti-anxiety meds), I staple sections of skin from his back, buttocks, and legs over the artificial dermis on his face, head, and neck. It's a grotesque waiting game, speculating what might succumb to infection and disease, wondering how much easier this would have been for everyone if he was in a pine box instead of a burn unit.

On Sunday, my day off, I'm comparing skin tissue samples when I hear throaty noises.

"Why . . . can't . . . I . . . see?" Jason finally says.

"You were in an accident." I say, leaning closer to his face, trying to keep an even voice.

"When?"

"About a week ago."

"Is . . . it . . . bad?"

"Yes," I say, sighing. "You were burned terribly."

His voice is raspy and eerily calm. Most victims thwart themselves back into a coma when they speak for the first time.

"Burned? My face?"

"Yes."

"My hair?"

"Gone."

"Ears? My nose?"

"I'm sorry."

I place my hand lightly on his frail shoulder. He's lost sixty pounds.

"Are . . . you . . . the . . . doctor?"

"Yes. I'm Doctor Caruso. You can call me Knox. You're in the Red Land Burn Unit."

"Where?"

"Two-hundred miles south of Phoenix."

The fan above shuts off abruptly and it's suddenly dead quiet.

"What . . . do . . . I . . . look . . . like?" he asks, trying to grab me, but his hands don't work anymore. "Tell . . . me . . . something . . . now."

"I don't know," I say.

"Bullshit."

"Well, you've got several bandages on your face."

"Under . . . the . . . bandages, Knox?" he asks.

I step closer and study his face: the divots, the swelling, the lesions, the shock it has endured. I try to examine it like a curious child instead of a doctor.

"A date," I blurt out. "Your head. It looks like a date."

"A . . . date," Jason says. "What . . . else?"

"Your hands, too." I pull a chair next to his bedside and sit down. I cannot continue this conversation standing. "We're hoping they make it."

"What . . . does . . . that . . . mean?"

"Well, you could lose them."

A rush of air comes out his nose. His swollen lips pinch inward.

"I'm sorry," I say.

"I'm . . . lucky . . . to . . . be . . . alive," Jason manages. "That's . . . all . . . that . . . counts, right?"

"Yes," I say. "That's what counts."

A week later we amputate both of Jason's hands. The skin growths on the knuckles succumbed to infection and plagued both hands up to the forearms. His face was gone from the first night, we knew that, but I'd been holding out hope solely for his hands, believing that'd justify saving his life. At least he'd be able to change the channels on the television or lick his fingers after a barbeque meal. And I can't rid the image of Jason's hands dropping into the incinerator like trash. Thump, Thump. He seemed to courageously accept the grim fact of his shorn face. But his hands. When he imagined himself without hands he had to stifle the tears.

Thump, Thump.

I call Luther into my office. I'd cut his hours significantly after we amputated Jason's hands, figuring he needed a vacation from the disappointment.

"I don't think Jason's going to make it," I announce.

"Really?" Luther says, covering his mouth. "What's happening?"

"He's failing slowly. Each progress is defeated by infection. You can't protect yourself without skin. It's only a matter of time before all his vital signs signal distress."

"Man, I thought we had him. Damn."

"Do you feel it's a shame for him, or for you?" I ask.

Luther looks to the ceiling, contemplating. "For all of us, I guess."

For some reason, her lawyer only sends one receipt per envelope, the specific, mundane details of her life printed out on carbon paper and stamped a price. There's a teeth-cleaning from Gentle Dental, a three-hundred dollar tab from an herbal remedy class, an upcoming yoga retreat in Baja. I like to imagine her, attach her to each receipt, watch her flinch in the dentist's chair, take notes in the classroom with a sharp pencil, struggle to pin her feet behind her head on a white beach.

I don't miss her. But I do miss someone. Something. I miss not being alone. If my face burned off in a fire, she'd probably hop on a flight first thing. And my sister and her husband, my Mom in Dallas, Uncle Reggie and Aunt Kath, and God knows how many cousins. Acquaintances from college, med school, maybe even the Pakistani man I buy my mangoes from. There'd be people around. Not for long, no, but in the beginning there'd be company. How can it be that he has no one?

Nobody.

Now I scrutinize the hundreds of receipts tacked to the attic wall in chronological order, their display an attempt to prove to myself that I'm not alone. When I feel sorry for him, when I tell people what a shame it is about this man, I worry I'm not talking about Jason at all.

Tonight I have to change his bandages. Normally, I'd assign Luther to this task, but Jason's come to expect my presence and in his sensitive state I don't want him subject to any surprises. He usually cries when I remove the bandages, tears seeping through his stitches. Sure, it stings like Hell, but I also wonder if it's his way of expressing sorrow to me. Like he's really trying to tell me something without words. He's not a complainer, that's for certain, so I listen intently to those sounds.

Inside his room, I light the six aromatic candles surrounding Jason's bed. Bright light bothers his eyes and I've grown used to performing under candlelight. He can make out shapes, but still can't see me.

"Doc?"

"Hi, Jason," I say, blowing out the match and dropping it into the hand washing sink.

"Why . . . are . . . my . . . hands . . . wrapped . . . in . . . gauze? I'm . . . itching . . . all . . . over. I'd kill . . . for . . . a . . . finger . . . so . . . I . . . could . . . scratch, but . . . all . . . I . . . have . . . is . . . this . . . gauze. A . . . coat . . . hanger, a . . . Brill-o . . . pad, anything . . . so . . . I . . . can . . . itch—"

Jason coughs, then begins to retch. I place a bib by his chin and remind him not to talk so much, that his lungs can carry only so many words. He nods slowly and breathes deeply, falling into a light sleep.

I sit down by his bedside. The candles cast a dim flicker throughout the hot room. I put on latex gloves and place a jar of ointment on the surgical table. Then I secure a mouthguard on his upper teeth.

Peeling back the largest bandage from Jason's forehead, I simultaneously apply the ointment, softly caressing it into his skin. The ointment alleviates the pain, the sooner it reaches the scar tissue, the sooner he'll feel better. He stays silent, hardly biting down on the mouth guard.

I proceed to his cheeks.

"How are you doing, Jason?" I whisper.

"It's . . . okay," he says.

I work my way toward the grooves in his neck and shoulders, the candlelight casting our shadows above the headboard. His breath is smooth, meditative.

"Are . . . my . . . hands . . . okay?" he whispers.

Sweat weighs heavy on my hair, the scrubs stuck to my chest. I stop rubbing in the ointment.

"They're fine," I lie. "They were bleeding a bit is all, which is a good sign."

"Right," he says. "Blood . . . is . . . life."

"You're going to be well."

"Yeah," he says. "I . . . can . . . still . . . play . . . the . . . harp."

I catch him smile for the first time. Not a smile like yours or mine, because his face can't smile. It's a funny expression, like when someone smells something foul. But I know what it is.

"That's right," I say, laughing.

As I delicately trace the trails of his skin, I come to feel something like nostalgia. And it's strange, but I have the sudden urge to trade places with him, to be on the verge of death. I guess that's because I can't imaging doing anything more vital than this ever again.

For the first time I'm not sorry I saved him.

Jan Stinchcomb

Norman's Girl

Norm was chasing Natalie, though he did not know her name. He knew her smile, however, and her body—the nape of her neck, her legs, the wave of her hair. He knew her better from the back and was frankly afraid of meeting her head-on. There were lots of girls he admired from afar, but Natalie was his favorite.

She often sat at the bar just off campus, the one with the loud bands and lousy beer. She was part of a group of girls, gabbing about secret girl topics, talking in the way of girls, with the whole body, weaving their hair into the points they made. And there was always one other girl with her, Lisanne, whose vibrant personality and big breasts Norm tried to sell to his roommate, Lance.

"I can't believe this. You're asking me to go to a dive to look at some girls you'll never talk to. Get real. There's a party upstairs."

"I'd rather go to the bar. I'm leaving in ten minutes."

"Norm, come on. Don't be so weird."

And they would go back and forth until Norm convinced Lance to go with him, but only after Lance made Norm swear that he would talk to the girl.

The film for the night was *Psycho*. The professor reminded the students to pay attention to how Janet Leigh's body was filmed from the opening of the movie through the shower scene. She said a few words about the secrecy surrounding the film's initial release and the shock that the first viewers had felt. Then she turned out the lights.

"I've never seen this before," Lisanne whispered. She wasn't in the class, but she'd tagged along with Natalie, as she often did, because she liked old movies.

"Me neither," Natalie said as the movie's famous music trickled into her nerves.

It wasn't until the conversation between Norman Bates and Marion Crane that Natalie really noticed Anthony Perkins' character. She had liked the movie up to that point, of course. Like Lisanne, she enjoyed looking at the costumes and hairstyles and furniture, the Phoenix streets, all the footage from the past. The way people spoke, intonation itself, was different in the past, at least in the cinema past, and Natalie found this somehow romantic. Drifting through *Psycho*, feeling slightly scared and strangely happy, Natalie suddenly found herself sitting and eating sandwiches with Norman Bates and Marion Crane in the parlor of the Bates Motel. That was when it happened.

Norman Bates had impeccable manners and an old-fashioned shyness. He wasn't charming, exactly, but there was something else, something that was trying to break through his surface. "How creepy," Lisanne kept saying, but Natalie didn't agree. When Norman smiled, Natalie liked him. She responded to him, and she couldn't understand why Marion Crane didn't see that Norman needed her. He was trying to reach out.

It was not the first time that this had happened to Natalie. She had a long history of these crushes on characters from television and film, starting with the hero of *Speed Racer*, then Daphne from *Scooby Doo*. Natalie quickly moved on to the various horror-film villains played by Christopher Lee and Vincent Price. And then there was Spock, of course, forever waiting in syndication. When Natalie turned to books, she immediately noticed brave Justin from *Mrs. Frisby and the Rats of NIMH*. There were the weirdos, too, such as Hardy's Farmer Boldwood. It was Holden Caulfield who stole her heart in high school.

Natalie never knew when the spirit would overtake her. Inevitably, there would be a new fictional candidate, and then she would be thinking about him all of the time. It was her greatest secret, her greatest tribute, worth more than a thousand term papers.

"Oh my God, Natalie, this is scary. He's going to kill her,"

Lisanne whispered.

Natalie was all impatience. "You're missing the point." This remark, almost a reproach, made Lisanne turn and search for Natalie's eyes in the dark, wondering what they would talk about over coffee. But there was no coffee afterward, because, when the movie was over, after the professor had passed out the list of discussion questions for the next class meeting, Lisanne saw Norman Bates in the crowd of students coming toward them.

"It's him!" Lisanne squealed while scanning the auditorium to see if her opinion was shared by anyone else.

Natalie saw a tall, lanky boy with pale skin and straight dark hair walking beside a much cuter boy with a soul patch. The soul-patch boy smiled at Lisanne.

"Uncanny, isn't it? I told him not to come tonight, said he'd cause a riot. But don't worry—he doesn't really keep his mother in a fruit cellar. She lives in a condo. I've seen it. I'm Lance, by the way, and this is my very good friend and roommate, Norm."

The four of them had stopped in the auditorium, making a little island that blocked the traffic flow. Natalie, completely self-conscious, kept looking down at the floor, then shooting looks at Norm, mainly to see if he had the smile of the Norman from the film. Lisanne and Lance began to ride a wave of silly banter and big grins.

In a panic Norm told Lance that they had to be going. Lance looked at Norm as if he had gone crazy. What, didn't he see these two damsels, so friendly and willing? But Norm had already turned to go. In seconds the charm of the moment evaporated, and the opportunity was lost.

As for Natalie, she was so flustered that she told Lisanne she had a headache and left for home. She wanted to be alone.

The truth was, Norm was embarrassed, fatally embarrassed, by the resemblance, and it wasn't just the problem of his name. His mother was a widow, and, naturally, mother and son had always been close. His mother had once had a boyfriend who disappeared, but not because he was murdered, simply because he had found someone younger.

That unfortunate incident had soured his mother on men. She was approaching middle age and losing confidence in her allure, or perhaps it was a general loss of interest in romance that closed its fickle doors to her. She was a sweet woman, not the least bit overbearing, nothing like Mrs. Bates. She favored plaid shirts and jeans, yet set her hair every night and never left the house without lipstick. Norm knew his mother looked forward to grandchildren one day, but she was too practical to push for that right now. She understood that her son had to get an education and establish himself in the professional world. In the meantime, she was happy to play cards with her friends, work in her garden and see Norm during school vacations.

Another point of resemblance: they did live in an old Victorian house, not a condo, as Lance had claimed in his scramble to impress Lisanne. The house was not too far from the highway, much like the Bates Motel, and it still looked as it had decades ago, thanks to his mother's frugality. When Norm offered to repaint the house, his mother was grateful, but she chose the same dark blue with a gray trim.

Another big problem, worse than anything else, was their surname, Cate. This made him Norman Cate. "You'll have to change that when you grow up," one of his high school English teachers had joked. "It'll scare off the girls."

Norm's worst fears were confirmed when he was about fifteen and watched *Psycho* on television one night with his mother. He saw right away how much he resembled the young Anthony Perkins, and he studied the famous performance carefully to make sure that he did not accidentally mimic Norman in any way. His mother didn't see the resemblance, not at all, but that was the kind of mother she was, absolutely unwilling to see anything wrong with her child.

He began to encourage people to call him Norm. Norm Cate.

He flinched when he saw *Psycho* on the syllabus for American Cinema II, but he couldn't drop the class because of one meeting. He really needed that credit to graduate on time. He promised himself that he would act nonchalant and maybe even make a neutral comment during the class discussion of the film.

Naturally Norm was startled to run into Natalie after the movie. Because he always arrived early and sat up front, he had not realized that the girl from the bar was in his film class. And he was shocked when Lance used Norman Bates to get Lisanne's attention. Norm stood there, paralyzed with embarrassment, willing himself to shrug and act casual, maybe even to force a joke in front of the pretty girls, but nothing happened. In the back of his mind, Norm suspected that if he tried to appear likeable, if he smiled, he would become all the more—no, exactly—like Norman Bates trying to get through to Marion Crane. Or like Norman Bates trying to play it cool in front of the private detective. Like Norman Bates, guilty of murdering a beautiful woman while she showered.

The fact that Natalie kept staring at him made it worse. He had to get out of the auditorium. What was she staring at, anyway? What was she waiting for him to do? It was like she wanted something from him.

At least now he knew her name.

"So, are you going to the Mardi Gras parade as Mrs. Bates?" Lisanne asked Natalie. They were lying on the floor of Natalie's studio apartment, listening to music.

"No. I'm not going to be Mrs. Bates. Far from her."

Lisanne sat up to look at Natalie. "You're kidding. What's the matter, trouble in paradise?"

"Very funny." Natalie closed her eyes, trying to shut out Lisanne's curiosity. She knew she was in an enviable position now that she had a boyfriend. She wasn't always free to sit around drinking coffee or beer, chatting and complaining and dreaming—not that Norm would have begrudged her a night out with the girls. Norm Cate wasn't exactly a hot number, but he was everything else that was important: nice, trustworthy, and attractive in a geeky sort of way. Besides, he represented a type currently popular on their campus, the semi-intellectual nerd. Give him a pair of horn-rimmed glasses and he'd have to beat the girls off with a stick.

And he was a good boyfriend. Natalie couldn't believe how nice his manners were. He always put her needs first, helping with her coat and pushing in chairs, gestures so long out of fashion that Natalie was reluctant, even embarrassed, the first few times he offered. He had all of the Beatles' albums, some of them on LP, and he always knew when it was John singing and when it was Paul. He was majoring in English and Economics and planned to go to law school at the very same place where Natalie wanted to go to graduate school. Bingo.

They kissed and held each other close, and that seemed to be enough intensity for the time being, or so Natalie told herself. The fact was, Natalie wasn't sure how to initiate sex with Norm Cate. He didn't push his way through to Sherwood Forest (Lisanne's expression) like so many of the other boys she had been with. He liked to talk, and all she had to do was feed him a few questions about his hometown, his past, or his mother.

They hadn't ever talked about Norman Bates. Norm had skipped the class discussion of *Psycho*.

Sometimes Natalie felt like her relationship with Norm Cate, such as it was, could run on and on forever, a CD set to replay. Some day she would simply find herself naked in bed with him, then packing up for grad school, then addressing wedding invitations. It would happen that way, in the unconscious, and that was all right with Natalie. In the meantime it was nice to have set dates and phone calls, nice to be able to say that she was one of those girls who had a boyfriend. She was not looking anymore. She was not single.

But then there were other times when Natalie felt like Lisanne, unapologetically simmering, ready to rip off her clothes and challenge Norm Cate, willing to risk everything just to see what kind of a lover he would be. Worse yet, sometimes she was ready to take him by the shoulders and shake him, ask him where those polished manners came from, what his mother was like. Did they have a fruit cellar in the old house where they lived? Had he read his Sophocles, or his Freud? Hadn't he noticed that in appearance and name he resembled Norman Bates of *Psycho* fame? Didn't he want to dress like a woman and play shower games with her, Natalie, his girlfriend? Why the hell weren't they making love, like all the other couples on campus? How could he be content just holding her hand night after night?

It crossed her troubled mind that he might be gay. Then she worried, to her horror and amazement, that he might be a virgin. A virgin. What was a male virgin, anyway? Did they exist, outside of monasteries? Even Lisanne would be stumped by a virgin.

Natalie rolled over towards Lisanne, who was lost in her own daydreams. "Hey, I know what I want to be for Mardi Gras."

"Yeah?"

"Marion Crane. I'll get an old-fashioned dress and shoes. Maybe I'll even cut my hair. And I'll get a black bra and slip, like the ones she wears when Norman spies on her. Before the shower."

Lisanne smiled and nodded, sure that she knew where all of this was headed.

"Don't look at me like that," Natalie told her.

"Like what?"

"Like I'm just another collegiate bimbo."

Lisanne grinned. "Don't worry, I know that you're a very special collegiate bimbo. What's the matter?"

"I don't know if I can tell you this," Natalie began.

"It's about Norm, obviously."

"Not Norm," Natalie sighed. "Norman."

"Who?"

"You heard me. Norman."

Lisanne stared, waiting. "I don't get it."

"Norman Bates."

"Oh, you have a thing for Anthony Perkins, from the movie?

Is that why you want to be Marion?"

Natalie stared at the ceiling. For a while it seemed that she was done talking.

Lisanne went on, "You don't really mean Norman Bates, do you?"

"What if I do?" Natalie said, turning to meet her friend's eye.

At first Lisanne laughed, then, seeing how serious Natalie was, she stopped and sat up. "Well, well. This should be interesting."

"You see it too, don't you?" Natalie asked. "How much he looks like him? Norm, I mean."

"I guess. I don't know, Natalie, I was just joking, that first night. I wasn't really afraid. And now that I know him, I never think about it. But if you think so . . ."

Natalie felt naked. Embarrassed. If it was this hard to tell her best friend what she was after, then how would she ever tell Norm? He was the one she needed to talk to, yet she felt as though she couldn't. What was she supposed to do, write him a letter? Why couldn't he read her mind?

What a lot of work it was, having a boyfriend.

They had paid too much money for a room that was small and ugly, but Norm had refused to go to a motel. "This time let me take the lead," he told Natalie as he steered her by the elbow up the stairs to their room. She was dressed as Marion Crane, had even cut and dyed her hair. Outside it was raining, as it is in *Psycho* when Marion arrives at the Bates Motel. Norm hadn't dressed up for the festivities.

The day had passed like any other Tuesday, ending with a test on the French subjunctive. Natalie's head pounded from early morning until she came home to her apartment, where she found Lisanne waiting and already tipsy, having cut all her classes and donned her flapper costume early. Lisanne poured Natalie a drink and then cut Natalie's hair to look like Marion Crane's, using manicure scissors, making up for in speed what she didn't have in skill. They dyed it blond only after they had both had more to drink.

Natalie hurried into her costume so that they could get to the parade, but by the time they reached the crowded main street, she saw that there was no hope of finding Norm. Lance, dressed as a pirate, came out of the crowd and began to hit on Lisanne. Norm wasn't with him.

"I guess he got tired of waiting," Lance said. "He's probably back at your place."

Looking drugged and feeling like a fool, Natalie stumbled

along in search of a café. She caught a glimpse of herself in a storefront window and saw a blowsy and ridiculous girl. She needed a mirror and some lipstick. She needed to wake up.

She fought her way to a seat at the counter of a retro diner that had stayed open for the big night. For the first time ever she wanted a cigarette. After ordering pie and coffee, she simply waited, doing nothing, trying not to feel conspicuous. She hated being out alone on tonight of all nights. She thought of Lisanne and Lance, having effortless flapper-pirate sex, and the image made her tired and sad.

"I thought I might find you here," said a boy she had never seen before, offering his best Mardi Gras come-on, but one that made Natalie turn her head so that she caught sight of Norm, walking at his usual purposeful pace past the diner. She waved at him wildly, then realized that he would not be able to recognize her with short blonde hair. One of the other patrons kindly pounded on the window to get Norm's attention, then pointed at Natalie.

It only took a second for Norm to see that it was Natalie, and for Natalie to see that he was shocked at what Lisanne's scissors had done. But the sensation cheered her. Maybe they were heading toward their first fight, she thought. Maybe they were getting somewhere at last.

Norm came in and sat down at the pink and black counter. Their kiss was awkward, almost embarrassed. Natalie saw Norm study her hair and clothes, felt herself at the center of her boyfriend's attention, saw the Mardi Gras universe bubbling with possibility around her. *Carpe diem!* She had to get started, at the very least. So she leaned forward and whispered to him.

Norm's eyes grew round with alarm. "You mean right here? Now?"

Natalie nodded. Regret mixed with irritation brewed behind her headache.

"It's crazy. Tacky. I can't do it."

"It's what I want. Don't you care about what I want?"

Norm stared into the coffee he had ordered like he was looking for help. "Natalie, I don't think I can."

She didn't respond, refused to.

"Let's go somewhere else," he said. "Let's leave."

"I want it to happen there." She pointed at the restroom.

"Why?" He was pleading.

"It's Mardi Gras."

Natalie got up and put some money on the counter before sashaying to the restroom, a tight space, meant for one occupant. She moved slowly, giving Norm time to follow, willing herself not to rush. She was never before so grateful for a crowded room.

Norm panicked, banging into chairs and disturbing the other patrons. He entered the restroom right behind Natalie, turning red at what he imagined was the scrutiny of all present. He locked the door and even thought of barricading it with the waste basket, not that it would have done them much good. Natalie never turned around, never even looked at him in the mirror, merely closed her eyes and lifted her skirt. She was naked underneath.

This was his favorite view, Natalie from the back, and now he had her face, too, reflected in the mirror. Her mouth was open slightly, poised between a scream and a smile. Norm knew he had been given a great gift, and, like a starving man, he took the whole of it, with no hesitation, losing himself.

Someone knocked on the door before they were finished. Norm paused for a second, but Natalie only grew more excited. Afterwards they waited until their breathing had returned to normal. Natalie wouldn't let Norm wash his hands, which she held in hers as if they were two precious objects.

Out on the street the cool air felt good, like a swim. Rain began to fall. Norm and Natalie held hands as they moved along with the crowd, finally feeling a part of the celebration. They didn't speak. Natalie felt relief. Norm was worrying about unprotected sex.

After they had walked all the way down the main street, they crossed over to where Norm's car was parked. "I don't know where else to go," he said. "What do you want to do now?"

"I don't know. Shall we get a room?"

"Okay," Norm said, relieved to hear a more conventional suggestion. They had their first fight over where to go, with Norm ruling out all the obscure dives that Natalie craved, finally ending up at small place that was part of a national chain.

Once upstairs, they drank water from the tap and regretted paying what the room had cost. There was always the television, but the mini-bar was out of the question, way beyond the reach of their student budgets. Natalie took her clothes off.

"I think I should go out and get us something to eat and drink," Norm said, regaining his composure with each minute. "And we need some condoms. In the morning we'll get breakfast before class."

Natalie's future marched up to her with a polite smile. Never a delayed mortgage payment with this guy. Never late to work. It struck her as funny, especially since she was dressed as a woman from the 1950s. There had been couples like them for decades at their campus, hopeful girls and earnest young men, coming together just like all the other undergrads, only to turn into their parents, but perhaps richer, better educated. Natalie didn't think she could go through with it after all, not unless something changed.

"How about we cut class tomorrow?" Natalie suggested.

"You know I don't like to miss class."

"But I feel like going for a drive out to the coast."

"Natalie, the coast is far, and break doesn't start for weeks. What's the rush? You've been rushing all night, if I may say so." He took her hand and smiled at her, then sat down, feeling more comfortable. The room would do for the night.

"Where are you going for break?" she asked.

"I'm going to see my mom for a few days, then you and I are going off together, to do something. We already talked about this."

"I want to go home with you. I want to meet your mother," Natalie said, rolling over in bed, feeling her breasts fall and jiggle. She smiled. "I want to see what she's like. I have to make sure that she really exists."

Norm sighed and leaned back against the headboard. Mrs. Bates' cadaver turned slowly in her rocking chair, the light bulb swaying back and forth over the scene. Norm shook his head to erase the image, but it wouldn't leave his mind. Why had his mother never sold that Victorian house? Thank God there wasn't a basement.

"Well?" Natalie waited. "What's the problem? Can't I meet her?"

"Of course you can," Norm agreed, not knowing what it was his girl wanted. That was the thing about Natalie. His fantasies had never conjured someone like Natalie, impatient and impulsive, full of mischief and secrets. He didn't really trust fantasies anyway, preferring instead to masturbate to the generic offerings of pornography. His few sexual encounters (two) had been, in the final analysis, meaningless, not to mention a real etiquette dilemma. How does one take leave of a one-night stand? How many phone calls are required? How do you tell a girl that you don't really want anything to do with her? But all that was behind him now that he had Natalie.

He tried to explain things at home. "Listen, my mother isn't very progressive. We're not going to be able to sleep in the same room while we're there—"

"Of course not!" Natalie was just barely able to train the giggle out of her voice. Norm stopped and looked at her, not sure what she was up to. "I expect I'll have my own room and bath. My own shower," she went on, smoothing the now imaginary dress, pressing every curve of her body.

Norm mumbled something about a very nice guest room with

its own bath, and then he saw his mother moving about, dusting and changing sheets, getting ready for Natalie. She would be happy to have company, grateful for the change of pace. Norm saw his mother sitting in their house, balancing her checkbook, filing recipes, talking on the phone. Then he saw Natalie good-naturedly helping out in the kitchen or the garden, chatting with his mother, doing puzzles, making Mrs. Cate love her.

And he saw Natalie naked in the guest bath, imagined her naked between the cold sheets of the guest bed. He corrected the picture of Natalie, making the hair he remembered short and blonde, Marion's hair. He wondered if his girl had abandoned her underwear for the long haul, or if it was just a part of this Mardi Gras caprice. He saw Natalie coming down to breakfast nicely dressed, her smile announcing that she was naked underneath it all.

The only person that he couldn't see or even imagine in his childhood home was himself. He couldn't see where he fit in.

Natalie stood up. "What do you say, Norman? Want to take a shower?"

Norman Bates, wearing his mother's clothes and a crazy smile, appeared in the room for just an instant and lay down on the bed where Natalie had been. Norm saw him in Natalie's pupil—there was no getting around it. Against his better judgment, Norm got up and followed his girl.

Jim Tomlinson

First Husband, First Wife

It was Jerry Cole's ex-wife, Cheryl, who lifted the drugs, which were already illegal anyway. She boosted them from this fat pill lady who manages Hilltop Green Assisted Living. As Jerry waited outside behind the wheel of his rust-bucket GMC piece-of-crap pickup truck parked at the curb, as he sat there imagining how good things would be now that his luck was finally changing, Cheryl's chrome beautician cart came careening down Hilltop Green's front walk like a runaway Peterbilt. Cheryl herself followed close behind, the shoebox stash tucked under her arm for anyone with eyes to see.

She handed the box through the window, stowed the cart in back, and climbed in. Three times she slammed the door, harder each time, until finally it latched. Her face was all wadded up with stupid worry, was it right or was it wrong, this thing they were doing. He lifted the lid and grabbed three bottles out, read the labels, then pushed them close to her face. See? He said, pointing to the people's names, the dates. Isn't it just like I told you? They're dead, aren't they, long ago dead, if they were ever alive, if they aren't someone's made-up names.

Cheryl's eyes got teary. Okay, she said, okay. He said, There's no way Fat-Ass reports this stuff missing. You just relax, babe. Her fists burrowed into her lap. Okay, she said again, and she wiped her cheek on his shoulder. Don't be like that, he said. She said, I'll try, Jerry, really I will.

While he drove, Cheryl pawed through the jumble. She picked out bottles, shaking each one like a baby's rattle. She read labels out loud to him, sounding out the syllables of the chemical names. Jesus, she said, I don't recognize none of this stuff.

No problem, Jerry said, feeling juiced now that they were on the interstate. We'll get us a D.A.R.E. book, he said, sort it all out, what we can sell, what to flush.

Jerry, she yelled. Slow down! He was changing lanes, passing cars on both sides. The pickup vibrated, shuddered, the steering wheel numbing his hands. The speedometer needle was waggling a blur around eighty. He backed off the gas and dropped back to legal speed.

He'd had to let Cheryl do the actual swiping, even though she wasn't cut out for it. She worked at Hilltop Green, came and went all the time, fixing old people's hair in their rooms. She had natural access, which Jerry considered important for successful burglary. That's also how, in the first place, she came to be poking around the manager's room, how she happened upon that shoebox hidden high on a closet shelf. Cheryl had always been the kind of person who liked to look at other people's stuff. She'd open drawers and touch a few things, maybe try on shoes or jewelry, check out what's in the medicine cabinet, dab ointment, maybe sniff some perfume. That's all, though. Jacking those pills would never cross her mind, not in a million years. Jerry had to help her see that shoebox for the opportunity it was.

Even though she was the one who took the pill lady's stash, Jerry was the one who got caught. It happened when he tried to broker the Lorcet. His buyer, this muscle-bound freak with a bullet-shaped head and a dragon tattoo glommed onto his jugular, turned out to be a cop, his killer tattoo a fake. A Lexington TV reporter called Jerry a regional drug lord. A station cameraman shot video of him in his orange jail jumpsuit, leg-chains dragging as he waddled up the courthouse steps. The station ran the tape on the newscasts at six and eleven. Cheryl rented a VCR, and she tried to record it so he could see. The piece-of-crap machine screwed up, though, taping some revivalist preacher instead, a completely different channel.

While Cheryl's trial got delayed and delayed, Jerry got convicted and served eight months at Blackburn Correctional Facility. It felt like eight years. The day he was to get out was also his thirtieth birthday, which he took to be some kind of sign. When he woke up that last prison morning, his mind was filled with thoughts of change, of setting off in new directions. He thought maybe he'd start an herb farm on five acres his cousin Shuey owned. Or he'd fence those acres and raise emus, raise them for meat, sell it to restaurants. Or maybe he'd get into ginseng, what Shuey called 'sang.' The stuff grew wild in Daniel Boone National Forest, old stuff, premium stuff. Foreigners paid small fortunes for a wild-grown root shaped like an animal, a duck, a horse, or maybe a hog. Sang just grew out there, grew in plain dirt, knuckles of the stuff like shallow nuggets of gold, a waiting fortune for someone with ambition to find it. As he lay on his bunk, Jerry could almost feel it in his fingers, smell the soft, musty earth as it crumbled away to reveal the root's shape. His wasted months at Blackburn were ending today. His life was starting again. This time he'd get it right.

Cheryl had rented a motel room not two miles from Blackburn's main gate. She'd decorated it with yellow balloons and rainbow streamers. She bought the fancy Kroger cheese-and-cold-cut platter and laid it out on one bed, a washtub of ice and beer stationed at the foot. She even baked his favorite strawberry jam cake. Two blocky number candles were stuck in the coconut frosting, a three and a zero. As soon as they got to the room, Cheryl lit the candles, shut the drapes, and switched off the lights. She started singing a birthday song, the one the Beatles sing, while performing a cheerleader-style dance in the flickery light. As she did, Jerry inched over to the beer tub. Kneeling there, he uncapped his first bottle since forever, brought its cold lips to his, and pointed the bottom to the swirly motel ceiling. His mind started thinking about riverboats on the Ohio. Did they run in winter when weather got too cold to dig sang? He wondered about their casinos, what they looked for in card dealers, if a felony conviction would hurt someone's chances.

Where are you? Cheryl asked, her face near his, the smell of her bubblegum everywhere. She was still breathing hard from the dancing, but the song was over. Who? Jerry asked. Where? He looked behind him, lifted a bedspread corner, stood and looked all around as though someone else might be there. He lurched toward Cheryl and poked a hand at her ribs. She dodged, squealing, her elbows tucked for protection. He said, That really was great, babe, just great, the song. He grabbed an armload of her then and wrestled her onto the bed. He pinned her there, blowing mouth-farts across her soft, surging belly. A taste like herbs was slick on his lips and tongue. Changing his life, he decided, could wait one more day.

The candles melted down. Their flames grew wide and flickered and blistered the frosting. A sugar char smell filled the room, sweet like campfire marshmallows. Jerry rolled off the bed and blew out the blaze. As he lay back down, he said, Marry me. I did, she said. Haven't we had this talk, Jerry, maybe eighty-nine times? Monkey-like, he scrambled across her. Then marry me *again*. He said it as if it were something totally new. Never, she said. His lip pouted out, and he made a whimpering sound. She combed his hair with her fingers and kissed his neck. You'll always be my first husband, she said.

    They were kids when they married. Later, Jerry had another wife, six months, that one a real mistake. She's somewhere in Iowa now, she and the twins. After Jerry, Cheryl had two husbands, the last one, Fenton, a real bastard. One night a couple years into that marriage, she called Jerry's house, waking him, her words all mush-mouthed. Fenton, the son of a bitch, had been beating on her for no good reason, threatening her, sticking the barrel of his fancy pistol in her mouth like it was his dick. Jerry got there fast. He caught the guy scrambling out the back door, got his gun away and creased his skull with it. With his bare fists he busted up Fenton's face. Cheryl packed up what was rightfully hers, and they loaded it all into Jerry's pickup. They left Fenton on the kitchen linoleum, unconscious and bleeding a puddle. Jerry drove her back to his place and unloaded her stuff into the bedroom that used to be theirs.

    Cheryl calls herself a three-time loser when it comes to marriage, says it with a quick smile whenever talk heads that direction. She doesn't mean it, though, not really. It's instinctive, like turning with a punch to take away some of its sting.

    Jerry's better than most about hitting her. He rarely does, and then it's because of some incredibly stupid, unthinking thing she's done. And it's never with fists. Never. That's nothing compared to the good things he's done, like getting her away from Fenton. One time he gave her this absolutely perfect making-up present, a calico kitten that she named Myrtle. And now, his refusing to finger her about the drugs, even when they offered probation if he'd just testify against her. Cheryl doesn't know what love feels like, not for sure. Her history is too messy for certainty about that. But on his best days Jerry does the sweetest things anyone's ever done for her. She likes how it makes her feel, and she thinks maybe that feeling is love.

    She puts her spiral notebook in her purse for her meeting with Suggs, the lawyer assigned by the court. Usually they meet in his courthouse office, which he shares with four other public defenders. She thinks of it as an office of stalls—milking stalls, toilet stalls, small stalls, hardly room for someone to yawn. On the phone, Suggs said to meet him for breakfast this time, the restaurant across the street, *Habeas Cibus*. She's seen the place, but she's never been inside. A foreign name like that and crowds of men in striped suits make her antsy. She worries about what to wear, if the place has rules about that. A dress to be safe, she decides. Not a new one, though. Something she can wear to work afterwards and not worry about dye or chemical spots. An hour ago she got a call, an urgent shampoo and set job waiting downstairs at Rodell-Ward.

She slips a light blue, flower-print dress over her head and buttons the front in the mirror. She thinks she's pretty enough, although sometimes she thinks maybe she got pretty too young. She wishes she were brighter when it comes to people, understanding what they do and why. She has this sense that everyone else was born knowing some secret thing that they're not allowed to tell her. In her notebook she writes quotes, snatches of things people say that sound intelligent, scribbling them down like clues.

Suggs is sipping coffee in a corner booth, file folders stacked beside him. One folder—it's hers, she sees—lies open on the table, its long pages flipped open, rolled over the top and tucked under. The lawyer's necktie knot is tugged loose. The wide end lolls across the papers like a second tongue. He's writing, making check marks on the page with his fat ink pen. As Cheryl slides into the booth, the pillow seat breathes cold air on her legs. The lawyer quits what he's doing, and he caps his pen with a snap. He laces his fingers together and tucks his elbows tight against the paunch of his gut. Cheryl tries to cross her legs, bangs a knee beneath the table. Suggs steadies his sloshing cup. Leaning forward, he says, Good morning, Miss Riffle. There's a bourbon breeze in the air.

Cheryl tries to read what's under his fist-ball. She asks, Is that my case?

Indeed it is, he says. His kind of word—*indeed*. His face gives her nothing.

Let me guess, she says. The judge has to delay us again. Am I right?

Suggs flips her file closed, pats the worn cover like somebody's shoulder. He says, The judge wants this one cleared up. He thinks it's dragged on much too long.

Heat rises in Cheryl's neck. After all, they're the ones who kept delaying, kept making excuses, kept putting it off. She won't say it, though, not to Suggs. The court made him her lawyer. It's confusing, though, because he's not hers, not really. Jerry says Suggs probably fishes with the judge, that they're best buddies behind her back. More times than she can count, Jerry's hunches turn out true.

A waitress comes over and refills the lawyer's cup. She's a slip of a girl, tall and young, her forehead freckled and acne-spotted. She's pregnant—six months, maybe seven—the bulge of her belly hugged tight by a denim skirt. She sets the coffee pot down, pulls a pad from her pocket, and stands near Cheryl, a pencil stub pinched between nail-bit fingers. She asks, Can I get you something?

Coffee, Cheryl says, looking at the pot. And a Pepsi and a fried honey bun. The girl repeats it, and when Cheryl says, That's right, she writes it down. There's a jittery tension in this girl. She feels familiar to Cheryl, like someone she used to be. As the waitress starts back to the kitchen, she drops her pad. She has to stoop sideways picking it up, fumbling it twice before getting a grip and standing again. A few seconds later, she's back at the table. Red-faced, she snatches up the coffee pot she forgot. As she leaves, it occurs to Cheryl that this girl might be the kind of person who could be her friend.

Suggs blows across his coffee and slurps a noisy first sip. He says, Don't you go reminding the judge about who stretched things out.

I won't, Cheryl says. Lord knows, I'm in no rush to do prison time.

Suggs says, Let's not get ahead of ourselves, young lady. You got a lawyer here, don't forget.

She can see she's hurt his feelings. Considering he isn't billing her—she couldn't pay, couldn't afford a hired lawyer, but still, considering that he'd never so much as sent her a bill—she tries extra hard to not disrespect him. She knows how it hurts, fixing hair for free at the county home, getting yelled at by people who don't know better. That's part of the deal. But their relatives, the ones who should still have manners? That's ignorant, plain-and-simple. So what if Jerry is right? Maybe Suggs does bass fish with the judge. Still, she wouldn't want Suggs thinking she's ignorant that way.

I know I've got me a lawyer, she says. She reaches across and touches his hand. You're a good lawyer, too, she says. She has no way to know that, not really, no lawyer to compare him to. Still, it seems the right kind of thing to say.

He straightens, clears his throat. Listen, Miss Riffle, he says. If we go to trial, they have to prove this case. You understand that? They have to prove your involvement with that shoebox of drugs.

I'm the one lifted it, she says, like me and Jerry—

Suggs slaps the table. Did I ask you who took it? Did I ask you that?

She hates feeling scolded, hates how it puckers her insides, how it brings tears to her eyes for everyone looking to see. She turns toward the wall, hides her eyes with a hand.

Cheryl, he says. Miss Riffle.

She draws in an unsteady breath and turns back toward him again. His face has a pitying look. It's a look she can't stand. She studies her fingers, pinches the knuckle skin, taps each nail, rubs her thumb on the sensitive center of a palm, pressing hard.

Suggs says, We have several ways we can go with your case. You need to tell me what you want, though, so I'll know how to proceed.

Her brain feels strangely cluttered, yet empty, filled with lots of nothing. She says, What I want?

He says, What you want. His eyes look straight into hers, and she imagines he can read everything in there, can see the horrible mess she is.

I want, she says, not knowing what comes next. I want things to go back like before.

Suggs asks, Before what?

She feels the tears again. This time she can't stop them. She searches her purse for a tissue. The lawyer hands her a napkin, which she takes and turns away.

When Cheryl turns back to Suggs, having finally gotten hold of herself, her coffee, Pepsi, and fried honey bun are there on the table. She's got her own napkins now, and she uses one to wipe her face, to catch the last sniffle under her nose. I'm such a mess, she says.

He looks into what's left of his coffee. It's okay.

I'm sorry, she says.

It's okay, he says again. He picks up the folder. Flipping pages, he asks, Have you ever been evaluated?

A laugh escapes her, and she can't understand why. Evaluated? She says. Sure. Yes. All the time. Is that what you're doing now? She asks. Evaluating me? He's smiling at her, but it's not a real smile. It's not in his eyes.

He gathers up folders and stacks them on his lap. Let me talk to Judge Hawkins, he says, run something by him.

You're leaving?

He says that his next appointment is waiting two booths away. Stay here as long as you want, Suggs says. Take your time. Finish your breakfast. Bring me the check when it comes.

The parking lot at Rodell-Ward is full. Cars are parked down the street, both sides, both directions. Black limousines line the circular driveway. Their tiny green bumper flags flutter like spring leaves in a breeze. Several smokers cluster on the porch, a sunny place, talking. Cheryl drives past the stately old house and circles to the alley behind the place.

The back yard is overgrown, the path shaded by enormous live oaks. Beside the basement door, she puts down her shoulder bag, takes out a sweatshirt, and tugs it on. She shoves the right sleeve up to her elbow, reaches up and searches with a hand deep among the damp trumpet vines. Out front, the smokers' low banter floats through the air like spoken tunes. In the rough stones, Cheryl's fingers find a tiny alcove, and there the key that Mr. Rodell left for her. She unlocks the door, turns the oval brass knob, and silently opens the door. Inside, she switches on the lights.

The girl waits for Cheryl in a pea-green room, a room with a double door. It's a cold room with a sour kind of hospital smell, small like a prison cell. The girl lies waiting there, waiting on a bright metal table. She lies covered head to toe on the table, covered by a sheet the same color as the walls. Cheryl lifts the sheet, pulls it back to see the lifeless face, the shoulders, narrow, bare, the neck jogged oddly to one side, an impossible angle for a neck. The girl looks young, eleven or twelve, her skin a nutmeg color. Although her eyes are closed, a mildly surprised look is on her face. Her full lips seem poised to speak. Her untroubled forehead reflects the room's sickly green light. Her black hair has red-dyed streaks in it. Maroon tips, too. Cheryl touches the hair, rolls a few strands between finger and thumb. It's straight and shiny, but matted now. No injuries to work around. That's good. An arcade photo of the girl, alive and mugging for the camera, is tucked beside her head. Cheryl picks it up. She's younger in the photo. Her hair, not as long, is clipped in tiny bow barrettes. When he called, Rodell told her, Cheryl, you get all that red out you can. Her Momma wants it natural black.

Overhead, the upstairs floorboards creak—people standing, people shifting foot-to-foot, people filing past another someone's coffin, their voices a low murmuring, a rolling kind of sound.

Cheryl looks around, searching for paperwork. She doesn't want to know how the girl died. It doesn't matter anyway, not now. She doesn't want the dreams, either, the ones that come from knowing. She only wants a name, what to call this girl, how to think of her as she does her hair. She wishes now she'd thought to ask Rodell about a name.

She pulls the sheet back and folds it onto itself at the end of the table. The girl is long-boned, slender. Her nail polish matches the streaks in her hair. She has a slight swell of breasts, narrow hips, first signs of private hair. Last signs. She's eleven at most. Maybe ten. Her frail chest is sunken and still. Her knees are knobby, boy-like, scabbed. One knee is slightly bent as if, walking, she'd died mid-stride.

My name is Cheryl, she says out loud. She touches the soles of the girl's feet, the tender white skin of the arches. She runs a finger along her ankle and calf, past a knee, up a slender thigh. She touches the girl's hand, the fingers cold and stiff, and she imagines how it would feel, this child holding her hand like a mother's.

I'm Cheryl, she says again. I'm here to fix your hair. She leans close, her ear near the girl's lips, and she listens for a secret. In the stainless steel table, she sees side-by-side two reflections, sees parts of two faces, one cheek, one ear each, falling hair black and light brown on bright metal, one eye alive and open, one closed.

The shampoo smells like apricots. In her hands the suds feel thick and warm. She works the lather in. The girl's head moves slightly side-to-side. Cheryl rinses, and the suds drain away on the tilted table, drain down plastic tubes to plastic jugs below.

When she looks at the tangle of tubes below that table, Cheryl feels a pang low in her abdomen. She thinks of her own tubes, remembers the pair of dark-faced granny women, their treatments, the gnawing ache for days down there. She was just fourteen then, and still the women said she'd come too late. The root cures hadn't worked, they said, dishonesty in their eyes. Infections, they said, the word like spit on their lips, the devil's own worst kind. She'll bear no children now, they told her mother, not in this life. Amen, her mother answered, and she counted out ten-dollar bills into their waiting hands.

Jerry kicks at the cinderblock with his muddy boots, trying to loosen the clods stuck deep in the treads. Rust-colored mud shapes—diamonds—fly out and disappear among the trumpet vines. From heel to toe, he scrapes the soles on the block's gritty edge. After wiping his hand on the back pocket of his jeans, he grips the oval brass doorknob. Silently, he opens the door.

Inside he hears a sound, the whine of a hairdryer. It comes from a room off to his right. He's never been in this place before, not in the basement. Upstairs, yes. Never down here, though. It feels like trespassing, like burglary must feel. He moves quietly. The air feels clammy against his skin. Its sour smell makes him want to burp. He cracks open the double door. Cheryl's back is turned to him, three steps away. He'll step in behind her and before she sees him, before she even knows he's there, he'll clamp his hands on her ribs, dig them in sharp and deep, scare the b'jesus out of her. As he inches the door open, she switches off the hairdryer. The sudden silence is a roar in his ears. A hinge squeaks. She hears, gasps, turns. Her hand flies to her mouth too late to catch a small scream.

I knocked, he says, opening the door fully now.

Don't you ever, she says.

He says, You didn't answer.

The hairdryer, she says, like it's her fault.

He sees the black hair now, the face, the shoulders, the sheet. And who is this?

Cheryl's hand is on his chest, pushing. Out! She says. Now!

He's stronger and stubborn when he wants to be, and he wants to be now. Was he hurting anything? No. Besides, he has reason to be here. He grabs her wrist and pushes it aside, pushes her aside, and goes over to the table.

Jerry, get out!

He lifts the sheet, stoops and looks under it. She's just a kid, he says.

With small fists Cheryl punches his shoulder. So help me, Jerry, she says. You've got no right.

He backs away, hands up, backs to the door. What killed her? he asks. Cheryl pushes him, and this time he lets her, stumbling back into the hall.

She says, You don't belong here.

He asks, You got any idea what time it is?

You'll get lunch when I get home, she says. Fix a sandwich if you're hungry.

Your lawyer called, he says. That's why I came. That was the reason, he says, if you must know, why I came all the way out here. Jerry turns then and starts to leave.

Wait, she says. She grabs his sleeve. What'd he say?

That jackass judge wants to see you today. One o'clock. He wants me there, too.

Cheryl's face takes on its confused look. Jerry wonders if he's saying too much, talking too fast for her peanut butter brain. He shows her his wristwatch, pushes it up close to her nose. Almost twelve-thirty, babe, he says. She doesn't answer. He says, What it means is we've got thirty minutes to get there. Hurry up and finish Miss Stiff.

She says she'll be five minutes, that she's putting final touches on the girl's hair, the red streaks and maroon tips.

As soon as Jerry walks to the water fountain, Suggs comes over to where Cheryl is sitting. He says, Tell your boyfriend to keep his mouth shut once we get inside. It's a useless thing to tell Jerry, she knows, but she says, Okay. They're in the courthouse hallway, waiting on hard wooden benches. And you, Suggs says, remember you only answer what you're asked. Nothing more.

She nods.

I'll call when we're ready, Suggs says, and he goes into the judge's office. She thinks of the girl on the table, how she's lying there dead in this world, her hair whatever her mother or a stranger, a hairdresser she never knew, decides it should be. Cheryl hasn't stopped thinking of the girl, not once since leaving her there.

Jerry comes back. His footsteps sound hollow in the marble hall. He plops down on the bench, pushes close beside her and spraddles his legs. His knee nudges hers. He says, Let me show you something. From his pants pocket, he pulls a root. It's shaped like three fingers joined by a large knuckle. Tendrils stick out of the thing everywhere. She covers it with her hands.

That's ginseng, she whispers.

Not just any sang, he says, pulling it free. See that shape? Don't it look like an elephant?

She doesn't think so, but it's not something to argue about. Where'd you dig it?

He whispers, Boone Forest, over by Spivey. Spent the morning scouting around.

It's illegal, she says, digging sang there.

He slides it back into his pocket. Can't no one prove where it came from, he says. Besides, you know what foreigners pay for wild grown sang that's animal-shaped?

Jerry, she says, I want nothing to do with that.

Suit yourself, he says.

Cheryl can tell by his voice he's hurt. He may sulk about it, but she's not going along with this scheme, not while she's looking at jail. Jerry stands and stuffs his hands in his pockets. He hunches his shoulders to his ears, and he wanders down the hall. He's still standing there studying the photos on the wall a minute later when Suggs comes out and calls them into the judge's chambers.

Judge Hawkins sits pushed back from his desk. He isn't wearing his robes, just pants and white shirt and starry blue necktie. He looks shorter now, wide, his face loose like bread dough. A lawyer named Embry sits to one side. He's the gourd-shaped one who prosecuted Jerry before. Jerry gives him his dagger look. He doesn't say anything, though, not yet.

Judge Hawkins has more files than Suggs. They're stacked on his desk. He says, Let's get on with it.

Embry says, Your Honor, the Commonwealth has offered to drop several charges against Miss Riffle, in exchange for a guilty plea on count six of the indictment.

Hawkins flips pages, adjusts his glasses. And count six is what? Yes, here, second degree drug trafficking. These were prescription drugs?

Suggs says, Yes, Your Honor.

Cheryl fights the urge to explain, to tell that she's the one who stole them in the first place, a shoebox full, that she deserves as much jail time as Jerry, maybe more.

The judge says, Mr. Suggs tells me there are circumstances. He's talking to Embry, but he glances at Jerry, too. Jerry's got the root elephant out of his pocket. He holds it low, below the desk so the judge can't see. He rubs it with a thumb like he doesn't even care.

Embry says, Your Honor, we're prepared to recommend probation for Miss Riffle, two years, with a stipulation that it include behavioral evaluation and counseling.

Jerry jumps up. That's bullshit, he says. He waves the root like a floppy finger.

The judge says, Sit down, son. Put a sock in it.

Jerry says, Two years? I only got eight months.

Cheryl's on her feet. She grabs his arm, pulls him back to his chair. Probation, she whispers. The guy said probation.

Jerry's chest shrinks like a balloon taken out in the cold.

Cheryl says, I can keep my jobs? Then, remembering what her lawyer said, she clamps a hand over her mouth. She mouths a *sorry* to Suggs and sits back in her chair.

Suggs says, I'll confer with my client. We'll let you know.

I want this case cleared today, Hawkins says, standing. Five o'clock.

Embry stands, too, and says, Paperwork will be on your desk in an hour, Your Honor, ready for Miss Riffle's signature.

We'll talk in the hall, Suggs whispers to her. Jerry, you too.

What a circus, Jerry says when they're outside. Cheryl knows he's fed up about something. Tell me this, he says to Suggs. Why drag me down here, make me sit next to the bastard who sent me away. I've done my time. I never need to see him again.

Cheryl wishes he hadn't come, for his sake and for hers.

Suggs says, You both need to understand the options. There's a strange look on Suggs' face, one Cheryl can't figure out.

Jerry says, There's no contest. She'll take the parole.

It's probation, Suggs says.

Jerry says, Okay, probation. She can tell he's pissed about her lawyer playing big shot with him.

The thing about probation, Suggs says looking straight at Jerry, is she can't be having contact with convicted felons.

The hall goes silent.

Jerry says, They can't do this. Can they?

Cheryl says, Me and Jerry, we live together.

You're not married, though, Suggs says. Not now.

That makes a difference? She asks.

To the law, it does, Suggs says.

Cheryl finds a bench and sits. If I take their probation, she says, I've got to move out?

Suggs comes over and sits sideways by her. No contact means no contact, he says. His eyes are steady on hers. She wonders if he's working some kind of telepathy.

I don't know, Cheryl says, her mind a complete swirl.

Suggs says, Think about it. Talk it over, you two. He looks at his watch and says, Their offer's good till five.

The woman who seats them at *Habias Cibus* reminds Jerry of the prosecutor, Embry, the way she looks at them. She leaves them with menus and water. All Jerry wants is something to eat, something sweet and syrupy, something solid and wholesome to nourish him. Waffles, maybe, and blueberry syrup. He's had enough of weasel words, enough slanted options, enough of getting shoved from seventeen different directions. He can tell Cheryl is thinking. She hasn't said one word since they crossed the street.

The waitress, a skinny kid with scads of ripe acne on her face, comes over. She's pregnant as hell and her ring finger is naked. The girl ignores him and smiles at Cheryl, who says, Back again, as if the girl's taking attendance with her pencil and pad.

Jerry orders the waffle and coffee, Cheryl a double cheeseburger, Pepsi and fries. When he gets back from the men's room, their drinks are already there.

It's not fair, Cheryl says, peeling paper off her straw.

Damn straight, he says. He bongos the table, the chrome edge with his hands. We can't, he says, we just can't let them run our lives.

Damn straight, she says back at him. She pokes her straw into the Pepsi and ice cubes, stirring and tinkling the drink.

It gives Jerry a good feeling inside, hearing her say it. He's always thought of her as someone special, this first wife of his.

Babe, he says carefully, watching her face. Say we did get married again.

No! She says. She's not fooling about it now.

I'm just saying, he says, just saying if we did. What could they do then? Think about it, Cheryl. They'd be screwed. What could they do?

She says like a groan, Jerry, I can't. You know marriage never works for me.

He says, Maybe this time.

She laughs like it's a sad joke, and she says, Every time, I'm miserable.

He says, That was before.

Jerry, I can't, she says. Don't ask anymore.

He takes out the ginseng root, makes it hop across the paper placemat, makes it look at its reflection in the steel napkin dispenser. His mind is working on something. He catches himself humming. You tell me what then, he says.

I don't know, she says. Her eyes start to go wild. We'll go somewhere, she says, but she says it like she doesn't really believe it herself. We'll pack and move, not tell anyone, Somerset maybe or Louisville.

He laughs at her. You think they won't find you? You look for work, and you're in their computers. They'll find you, and now you're in for serious prison time. An idea is breathing inside him now, alive and wanting out.

Cheryl says, Then *what?* You tell me.

He says, Guess. She can't. He thinks and then says, Here's a hint. It's right in front of you. She isn't even looking now. He says, It's right under your nose.

Cheryl's eyes are empty. She doesn't have a clue in that head of hers, not one idea. Like always, he's the one left to do the real thinking.

The food comes, his waffle, thinner than the menu picture, a ball of butter sliding off. There's a tiny shot glass of blueberry syrup, not nearly enough. Her burger is open, surrounded by curly fries. Before she can slather on ketchup, he grabs one to try.

Okay, Jerry says when the waitress leaves. Here's what we do. We take this crap they're giving us, and we make us some lemonade. Your sister living in Richmond? We say you're living with her.

Cheryl's head tilts bird-like. She's interested. But I'm not?

Jerry says, That's the beauty. We're camped out together in Boone Forest, the two of us, and we're digging a fortune in sang. This piece here, the one I dug this morning? Twenty-five bucks, maybe thirty. This guy I know, he'll buy all we can dig. Just imagine, two of us living out there every day. We're moving around. Can you imagine it? We're moving around, and we're digging a fortune right out of the ground.

Cheryl twirls a curly fry like a corkscrew streamer and flips it into her mouth. He can tell she doesn't get it yet, doesn't see the beauty of his plan. She says, It's illegal, digging sang in a National Forest. Right?

He says, Anyone asks, we say we're campers. We'll even get a legal camp permit. We'll hang it up on our tent. Our sang stash, we'll hide it up a tree for when the rangers come poking around.

She says, There's millions of acres out there.

He says, Millions of trees.

In her face, Jerry can see the splendor of his idea, how it fills her with new hope, fills her head-to-toe with glorious possibilities. That last morning lying on his Blackburn bunk, his intuition had been right.

Cheryl closes her hamburger and flattens it with her palm and takes a bite. And Myrtle, she says through the food, imagine her out there catching a million crickets and cicadas and mice, bringing them all proud to show me.

Jerry says, Any fool knows you can't take a cat to live in the forest. A dog, maybe yes. Cats aren't like that.

She puts the burger down, wipes ketchup from her lips with the back of her hand. She says, Myrtle has to come, too. I'm all she's got. We can put her on a leash or zip her in the tent. Either way, she's got to come.

Jerry takes his fork and knife and rips the waffle into dry, ragged pieces. He says, I don't know about you, Cheryl. He says, Here I do all this for you, do it all so we can stay together. And you? You complicate things. You make up roadblocks like nothing in this world matters but you. He pushes his plate away, suddenly sick of the food. He drops his fork and knife on top and pours syrup over everything. He tips the shot glass upside-down in the mess, and he squishes it to make his point.

Cheryl straightens, sits schoolteacher stiff, and she stares at him, really stares. He knows he's gotten to her, even though she's not crying yet.

Miss Pizza-faced Waitress decides to come by right then and ask so sweetly is their food okay. They're trained to ask, he knows, so they'll get a decent tip. But he can tell for a fact that this has more to do with what's going on, the discussion about the cat. She's got this know-it-all look spread across her festered-zit face. Not for one minute does she fool Jerry. The little sneak is showing them up in this backhanded sort of way.

You want a tip? He asks straight-faced. She looks surprised, doesn't answer. Here's a tip, he says. Buy yourself some maternity clothes, he says. And get yourself a husband, too. Fast.

The girl whirls around and goes. Jerry glances over. Cheryl's face is frozen into a weird kind of mask. She doesn't get the joke, which any fool with a sense of humor would. She isn't even trying. Instead, she tilts the napkin dispenser, and she stares at her reflection until the mask starts to melt. He tries to think how to explain it to her, how it's funny, what he said to the girl about a tip. Cheryl tosses her napkin. It lands on the table like a parachute. Right away she grabs it again. Her brain, he thinks must be melting, too.

We don't even know her name, Jerry, she says. She slides out of the booth, and before he can say, Hey wait, she chases after the waitress, who's already halfway across the room. It occurs to him then how bird-brained women can be, how amazingly strange, women like his first wife and this waitress.

She catches up with the girl. Even though their backs are

turned his way, Jerry would lay odds the waitress is bawling. Sure enough, Cheryl hands the girl her napkin to use on her face. For a minute they stand right there. People coming and going from the kitchen have to walk around them. Cheryl and the girl have their heads together, almost touching as they talk. Cheryl scribbles in her notepad. She rips out the page, folds it several times, and she gives it to the girl, who squeezes it in a fist.

   Jerry drinks his coffee, and he looks around the booth for his sang root. He moves dishes, shoves aside the napkin dispenser and ketchup bottle, runs a hand along the seat's gritty vinyl crease, pushing the hand as deep as he dares. He stands and pats his pockets twice around. Nothing. He gets down and looks under the table. The root shaped like an elephant is nowhere. Jerry swears, and he slams a fist on his thigh. People turn to look. Their stares feel like ants all over his skin. He sits again, drinks his coffee, thinking.

   When Cheryl finally comes back, Jerry starts to tell her about the sang root, how it's lost. She straightens the mess on the table, stacking things. She's not really looking for it, though. That much he can tell. We should go, she says when she's finished. She bites her bottom lip the way she does when she's getting ready for something. Jerry doesn't move. I looked everywhere, he tells her, and I can't find the damn thing. Cheryl doesn't answer. She seems different now, an odd version of herself, different in a troublesome kind of way. Jerry feels a new tightness in his head. He says, The sang root is nowhere. He moves closer to her. It's gone, he says. Vanished. As he tells her this, she fools with her fingers, examines her hands on the table, the dye-stained knuckle skin, her ragged fingernails, the necked-down places where rings used to be. Not once does she look up at him. He wishes she'd just cry and be done with it, if that's what she's working up to. What she's doing instead feels too much like being alone.

Valery Varble

Moving Scars

It felt good, whatever the girls were doing to Copeland at the south end of his chair. He was pushed back in his recliner, so worn out he could hardly move. Ten straight days of double shifts, repairing boilers over at the power plant. If they didn't get finished by a certain time, they'd lose the whole contract and now there was only one day left. Almost all day he'd been checking welds. So he was just about dead to the world but he could still hear the girls giggling. They were up to something, and it made him smile a little. He didn't know that his own welds were coming apart at the seams.

Copeland was already half asleep and dreaming about something he'd heard on the radio driving home, that sometimes in the few seconds while they're yawning, paralytics could move their limbs a little. For real. There was still a lot about yawning that researchers didn't know. Could the paralytics feel themselves moving as they yawned, Copeland wondered. He was too tired to yawn, already drifting into a dream about how tired he was. It struck him that dreaming about going to sleep felt a lot like being paralyzed.

He was pushed back in the recliner that was the only part of the house that still felt like it was his. Well, no. He supposed he owned one other thing: the dirty clothes hamper. His wife had ignored it so completely that he finally understood how things were. He started in washing his own clothes although he couldn't help noticing that at least all the change sure disappeared from his pockets fast enough. And some strange stuff found its way into that hamper sometimes, buried in his work clothes. Nadine's way of making a point. She hated him working all the time. She always pretended it was just things her girls left in there by accident when they were playing. Copeland said he'd like to know why they'd ever leave him a dead bird, a little finch, dry and light as a bud. "Maybe it's like a present," Nadine said, but she wouldn't look him in the eye. "They were playing at being cats."

Yeah, maybe. It was pretty in a way, and didn't look real or even dead. The worst part of it was that it reminded him of the parakeet he'd wanted for his birthday when he was a kid. He and his brother used to get one present on their birthdays, as long as what they asked for was within reason. Copeland had wanted a parakeet so bad he vomited up his supper the night before his birthday. The next morning his father gave him a rooster, which the family needed anyway and which his dad had already named "Dinner." His dad also gave him the hatchet he'd been given as a boy. He clapped Cope on the back and promised he'd show him how to sharpen it. That night, when they'd all gone to bed, Cope felt the low, hard vibration of his parents' argument through the walls. "Well, that's just the way it goes," Cope heard his father say.

"Hey, girly," his brother whispered in the dark from the top bunk. "Only little girlies want a parakeet." His voice was so savagely sweet that Cope knew how much his brother coveted the hatchet.

Another time what showed up in the clothes hamper was a mess of melted chocolate bar and Copeland thought Nadine's girls really might've left that by accident except that it looked exactly like a piece of *merde.* If you'll excuse my French, he thought. Ha. He'd worked a job with a French pipe fitter one time, name of Lambert, and learned some words off him. He was irritable as a wasp, kept up a nonstop buzz of cussing and complaining, but he was a hell of a worker, so fast Copeland could hardly keep up with him.

So now he'd forgotten about yawning and was dreaming that sleep was a warm, flat pool. He was just about to dip his foot in to test it and he could feel the girls' giggles like light bubbles, touching his toes. Then he jerked awake. "Hey," he said, and the girls jumped back, their eyes big and solemn. He looked down, shocked: they were painting his toenails with something wet.

"Just let them do it," Nadine said from the kitchen without even looking around, her voice flat. "What difference does it make?"

Copeland looked at the three girls bunched together in their nighties, holding the fingernail polish, and felt bad for the way they still froze up at the slightest little thing. What had that bastard done to them? It was like they would stop breathing, trying to fade into the wallpaper, trying to turn invisible. Okay, he thought. Nadine was right. What could it hurt? "Okay," he told them, "I'm just gonna shut my eyes for a minute or two. Make me look pretty now." They looked at each other, giggling, covering their mouths with their hands.

When Copeland opened his eyes, however, he wasn't thrilled about the color. "It's 'Kiss-the-Petal Pink,'" Amber said, and seemed so proud about it. Copeland had never seen a petal that bright in real life, kissed or not. And he didn't especially like his feet to begin with. Out of their protective shells, they seemed blind and soft, newborn. Now they looked strange in a way that made him uneasy. "Well," he said to the girls, and cleared his throat. "Now that my toes look so pretty, I may have to get me some high heel shoes."

They giggled. "That would look dumb!" Crystal said, and the three of them bolted down the hall, nickering like little ponies.

Copeland looked at his feet. The guys'd talked about it on the job before, what they were most protective about. Some worried most about their hands or their eyes. "What do you worry about losing the most, Cope?" someone wanted to know. They were walking across the lot to their pickups. The rain had finally eased off and the air was so fresh he wanted to drink it in gulps.

"Hell," Copeland said. "You have to ask?"

They all laughed and Ritchie said, "Hey, I seen there was a 'huge tool sale' going on at Rural King. You get it there?"

"Nope, it came stock," Copeland said. "What can I say? It's a problem. I just don't want to get it caught in nothing."

"I hear you, man," Ritchie said. "Got mine caught in Wanda Caine last Friday night. The wife came home early from her choir deal and all."

"You're so full of shit, Mahoney," Jack said, shoving him. "I was with Wanda Caine last Friday night."

There was a pause as Ritchie stepped in a puddle.

"Damn right," Ritchie said. "Soon's you left, she called just begging for me to come finish the job. Didn't want to hurt your feelings or nothing, she said."

They went on like that, but Copeland was hardly listening. Feet. That's what he worried about most. Steel-toed boots were the best thing ever invented and given the choice, he would've worn them all the time. That's why when Nadine and he got married and she and the girls moved in, Copeland didn't see why he shouldn't still wear his boots in the house. He was always careful to wipe them on the mat outside the door. But Nadine wouldn't have it. Then she wanted him to put out the money for new carpeting and so he did. He could hardly believe it, though, when he saw the color she'd picked.

   White. Not antique white or off white but the whitest white anyone had ever seen. The sheer arctic glare of it was so pure and cold it made Copeland's teeth ache. "Nadine," he said, but when he took her skinny arm, he felt the bump in the bone. A bad weld. That bastard. "Sweetheart," he said, "we're gonna be snow blind." He was only half kidding. And even worse was the fact that Nadine vacuumed constantly, over and over again, the living room, the bedroom, the hall, listening to her educational tapes of the greatest this and that. Copeland wanted to say to her, seriously, "Nadine, whatever that stain is, it ain't coming out." But it wouldn't have made any difference.

   He was surprised that she didn't want money for a new sweeper but she liked the old Electrolux that had been his mother's. It was on runners and left tracks in the carpet like a small sled. It touched Copeland to see Nadine pulling it around, with her headset on like ear-muffs. She looked like a little kid. One time a couple years ago when they'd first gotten married, he'd made the mistake of tickling her. "You're forcing me," she said, gasping, and Copeland knew he was forcing her but he couldn't stop. He just wanted so badly to hear her laugh for once. But soon as he heard her shrieking with laughter so close to pain, he quit. She went limp and still across his lap, her girls huddled in a corner and Copeland felt so bad he had to go out for a while.

   That was the night he wrecked his proudest possession, an old '47 Knucklehead, and got his second DWI. He hit black ice on the way home from the Pour House and over he went. Mostly what he remembered was traveling a long way on his back and looking up at the clear night sky with all the time in the world, marveling at the bright smear of stars overhead. He came to rest in a frozen ditch but his bike went on, lunging itself knuckleheadfirst right into a tree.

   Ha.

   So they had one last day to meet their contract at the power plant. Copeland woke up tired. Nadine had clung to him most of the night like he was floating wreckage but as soon as he touched her, she rolled away to the edge of the bed. Still, he could smell her green apple shampoo on his pillow and for some reason that gave him some hope.

At the plant, the job was going okay too. Copeland was working the high metal. His buddy Gerry was below him a little ways over with a quiet guy name of Mark Mattice on the other side and Cope was up on a beam, tightening a rod. "How we doing?" Gerry shouted up.

Copeland's turnbuckle kept slipping. "'I think I can, I think I can,'" he yelled back.

"Don't tell me," Gerry laughed. "*The Little Engine That Could.*" He was an odd guy who'd actually gotten some college but everyone liked him. "Shit, my kids used to love that one."

Cope gave one more twist and felt himself step off backwards into thin air.

That peculiar sensation of falling. The same way he'd felt when he'd been dreaming about going to sleep. And there was such a long, long ways to fall.

Why was it, he wondered, that what came to his mind was Sissy? That first time they'd met, at the county fair. He'd been, what, no more than twenty-one and she was maybe seventeen, although there was a calm about her that made her seem older. They'd talked for a while and then he gave her a ride on his motorcycle out to where her old pickup was parked at the edge of a field. The long grass was already wet with dew and it licked at her ankles. "Hey, take this for a minute, okay?" she said when they drew up next to her Ford. She handed Copeland the little sack of penny candies she'd been sucking on all night so that her tongue was streaked with color and her breath against his ear smelled like lemons and peppermint.

"You always leave me holding the bag," Copeland said as she leaned back to hop off the bike, and she'd laughed. Laughed for real, and it warmed him. She was the only one who'd ever laughed at his lame jokes.

She was also the only one who'd ever asked Copeland anything about the scar on his cheek, even though it was an impressed place about the size of a matchbook cover, and spalled-looking, at that. Even later, when Nadine and he got together, Nadine never asked, and that was okay. He understood. But still, sometimes he wished she would've so that he could've told her. He wished they could've talked then about all the things in their pasts.

When Sissy asked Copeland how he'd come by the scar, she listened to his story without saying a word. "I was about seven," he told her. "I was out burning trash in the barrel, standing back from it, not even poking it with a stick or nothing." The summer dusk had been soft and thick. He remembered the slow twinkle of lightning bugs against the peony bushes next to the house and the first star over the horizon, how he'd whispered *star light, star bright* to himself. Wish I may, wish I might. And then something sputtered out of the fire, a flash of green and yellow. It came hurtling through the air and hit him in the neck.

Later he found out it was a little green plastic Army truck. Seared him like a brand. That melting plastic would hardly release from the skin. His dad had to get pliers and tear it off like a leech.

Sissy shivered. Then she touched his face lightly. "Wait," she said. "It hit you in your neck? Not here on your face?"

"Yeah, that was the funny thing. The scar moved. I guess since I was still growing, it traveled on up from my neck to my face. Going north."

"That's something," Sissy said and smiled. "I've never heard of a moving scar."

They were quiet for a moment. There were carnival sounds in the distance and the ticking of the bike's engine. Crickets.

"I know it," Copeland said finally. "But I guess it can happen."

A shower of stars fell alongside Copeland and landed when he did, skittering every which way. No, not stars. They were sparks from where Mattice was still welding above him was all. Then the shouts fell, too, clanging off the walls like loose slag. "Holy *shit*, man!" he heard Gerry say. There were faces above him, all of them worried and not one of them much to look at. Copeland closed his eyes. He just wanted to lie there in peace for a while.

"Hey, Cope, how many fingers am I holding up?" Ritchie said and Cope opened his eyes. He heard Mattice mumble that Ritchie was an asshole for giving someone the finger thataway when the guy just might be seriously hurt and all. Everyone was talking at once.

"I ain't hurt," Cope said, and hoped it was true. "Just seriously thinking and all."

"Have you given any serious thought to getting up?" Gerry wanted to know. "You scared the shit out of us, man. All I can say is you were lucky to land the way you did." He whistled, shaking his head. "Unbelievably lucky. Lucky as shit. You can move, right?"

They carefully helped him up. Gerry was right. The way Copeland landed he had been lucky, all things considered. But something was definitely wrong with his right foot and ankle. They would hardly hold his weight, and the pain was just about the worst thing he'd ever felt. Shit, he must've broken something. Shit. Well, if he could just make it down to the first aid office he could ease off his boot and take a look.

He'd hobbled about halfway there, leaning on Gerry, when all of a sudden his toes felt like struck matches, flaring into hot, bright pink. Oh, God: his toenails. He stopped, closing his eyes. Shit shit shit.

He threw off Gerry's arm and turned around. "Hey, you know what?" he said, as Gerry stared at him. "I'm good. Let's get back to work."

Gerry told him he was crazy, anyone could see there was something wrong, and all morning long everyone kept at him to go down and have Clyde Withrow check him out. "Nah," Cope kept saying. "I'm okay. I'm fine." But before too long Withrow, the LPN, came to him.

No one knew Withrow personally, but everyone knew he'd served in Korea. Even so, nothing had slackened with age; he was still built like a brick shithouse. There were also rumors he'd done some prison time. Now he squatted down next to Copeland where he was taking a break for just a minute. "Son," he said. "Let's get that boot off and take a look." He had a Marine's buzz-cut, iron bristles that would've popped a balloon.

"No," Copeland said quickly and Withrow looked at him, surprised.

There was a pause.

"There's no shame in being hurt, son," Withrow said finally but Cope was thinking that in fact there was plenty of shame in it. He pictured Nadine and the girls, how they willed themselves not to breathe. He imagined his father.

No, all he had to do was make it through the rest of the day. "It don't hurt much," he told Withrow, and this was true in a way. He could hardly even feel his ankle anymore. "We got a deadline here. Just let me get back to work," he said, and got to his feet, wincing a little.

"All right," Withrow said, shaking his head, and just then the supervisor, Mike Bigelow, came by too, to check on things. Bigelow leaned in close to Copeland, pointed his finger, and said, "You better file a report on this." He said everything like a threat, probably to make up for the fact that he wasn't much more than five feet tall.

"I will later," Cope promised.

"You call your wife?" Bigelow asked him, and that was a threat, too.

"Later," Cope told him and turned away. "I will later."

The first time Copeland had ever seen Nadine was when her station wagon had broken down on old 37. That was going on three years ago. He'd stopped to pop the hood and take a look, and ended up giving Nadine and her girls a lift. The heat was miserable that day. When they got to town he'd treated them all to double-dip cones at the Dairy Barn on the square. The four of them never said one word the whole time, just sat there licking away as fast as they could. Then the girls thanked Copeland, so shy and sweet. Later that afternoon he towed Nadine's car and fixed it, just a fuel filter was all. He filled up the radiator and checked the tires. The car started up and everything, and it ran, but it still had a flat spot, especially if you crowded it. He thought maybe the coils were going out, which is what he explained to Nadine. She needed new brakes and the transmission was just about shot, too. "How much will all that cost?" she asked and Cope thought he recognized the look in her eyes. They were married almost before he knew it.

Apart from running the sweeper, Nadine didn't much care for keeping house but she did all right. She tried. She tried making chicken and dumplings for Copeland on a regular basis since that was his favorite meal and he never had the heart to tell her he didn't much care for the dropped kind of dumplings. Hers weren't bad but he'd always preferred the rolled. And since he was working most all the time anyway, he thought it was great when Nadine said she wanted to better herself someway, maybe even go to school. She went around with her headphones on, listening to The Great Opera Classics on cassette, The Greatest Poems in English, The Great Philosophers.

"Sweetheart," Copeland said once, "why don't you tell me about whoever it is that you're learning about?"

"Kant," she said.

"Sure you can." Joke. He knew what she meant. One night while he ate supper, he'd studied the booklet that came with the tapes.

She looked at him, disgusted, and shook her head. "Can't," she said.

Now he couldn't help thinking of her at home in the quiet of the house, the unsullied white carpet like fresh fallen snow. She tiptoed even when no one was around and Copeland always wondered why. Maybe so as not to leave any tracks.

"You okay, man?" Jack asked Cope as they all walked out across the road and over the railroad tracks to the Pour House bar. They'd made the deadline, and now they were "tired and wired," as Ritchie put it, although Cope was just plain tired. He'd been trying not to limp or hobble and had just about chewed through his lip with the effort.

"Shit," he told Jack. "Since you're buying, I'm fine." He'd decided on a plan. They all knew he had two DWIs from a while back. So he was going to drink a beer to take the edge off and then act drunker than he was, like he needed to call the wife to come get him. They'd give him a hard time, but he didn't care. Nadine could take him to the doctor.

Jack bought a pitcher and they started in talking the usual crap. They'd earned a bonus and all from the company, but the fact was they were just about too worn out to celebrate. All anyone did was drink. Gerry bought the next pitcher but Cope stayed at pretty much one glass, just moving it around. He could hardly pay attention as it was, seeing black spots at the corners of his vision.

Ritchie said, "So I heard Copeland here's been reading *The Little Engine that Could.*"

Cope shrugged. "Nadine's read it out loud about forty-five times. You know. The kids' bedtime story and all." Gerry's wife drove the Bookmobile in town and no one could believe how seriously she took her job, especially her new program to get dads to read books with their kids. It was a joke in town how even the sheriff tried to avoid Gerry's wife, sneaking his patrol car down alleys or back roads with his lights off. Just when he thought he'd made it past the Shell station or the IGA without getting caught, the Bookmobile would come looming out of nowhere, flashing its headlights in the rearview mirror. Ritchie did a great impression of Gerry's wife walking to the car with her flashlight, tapping on the window. "Sir, can I see your library card?"

"I always liked, what's the one?" Gerry said. "Oh, yeah. *Where the Wild Things Are.* That's a great book. I love that book."

Ritchie poured more beer in the glasses. "I hear they're over in Carterville. Problem is, they're jail bait."

Cope was thinking that his ankle felt like mangled rebar in a huge clot of concrete. He tried not to look down, shocked that even his boot leather seemed to have swelled.

"Hey, what about *Where the Red Fern Grows*?" Jack said. "Oh man, when those dogs died, I just about lost it. The kids were blubbering, I was all choked up. Same with *the Velveteen Rabbit.* You know, when the rabbit gets real? Shit, I admit it. I just can't hardly handle that stuff."

Cope jumped when Ritchie yelled to the bartender, "Hey Randy, you might wanna get down here for this," signaling for another pitcher. "We're having us a fucking literary discussion." Copeland tried to distract himself by asking Ritchie what the hell his favorite bedtime story was.

"Wanda Caine," Ritchie said. "And her favorite's *Hop on Pop.* I tell you what. Sometimes she don't even give me enough time to get the *Cat in the Hat* first."

Jack and Gerry hooted. "You're sick, man," Jack said but Cope was impressed that Ritchie knew the names of any books at all.

"Well, you asked," Ritchie said. "Okay, then. *Green Eggs and Ham.*"

"Never made it past Dr. Seuss, huh, Ritchie?" Gerry said. "Shoulda figured that about you" and Ritchie said that his wife thought *Green Eggs and Ham* was a cookbook. "I shit you not," he said.

Cope cleared his throat. "Speaking of the wife," he said and gave a big sigh as he pushed himself up from the table, swaying a little.

Jack shook his head. "Glad I ain't you." Gerry grinned at Cope and Ritchie wished him luck as he hobbled over to the pay phone on the wall.

Copeland clung to the wall, trying to take the weight off his ankle as he listened to the clicking whirr after each dial, the drop of coins, and then the hundred-year wait until Nadine picked up the phone. His jaw ached so badly he could hardly unclench it enough to speak.

"Come and get me," he said, trying not to sound like he was pleading.

There was a pause.

"Can't," Nadine said. He could hear her breath soft against the phone.

"Please."

"Can't."

A silence between them, as empty as anything could be.

"Okay," Copeland said. "Pretty please?"

Another silence.

"Sweetheart," he said. "Try yawning. Then maybe you could actually move for a few seconds." She hung up. "See, I knew you could do it," he said to the dial tone. It took everything he had not to cry a little.

Cope went back to pick up his jacket and told his buddies he'd see them tomorrow.

Yeah, man. Be careful. Take it easy, they said.

Out in his truck, Copeland had to sit for a minute, idling. *Now then*, he told himself. After a moment he said to himself, *Okay. Just kiss the pedal.*

He yelped as the truck shot forward, and then he wasn't even halfway home when he hit the sharp curve just before Pulley's Farm Road going too fast and couldn't seem to work up the inclination to step on the brakes. He rode the crest of the embankment, sailing up into the vast horizon. Then the truck's nose dived, *cawoomph,* the rear end rose, dropped, the truck made a half-turn heading down a little hill, gouging earth all the way, and finally came to a hissing, crumpled rest against a hickory tree, which rained down nuts like he'd won a jackpot.

A little while later the sheriff, Leland Fury, helped Copeland out of the truck, shaking his head when Cope almost pitched over sideways and he had to grab his arm. Cope felt himself go white and thought he might vomit besides. "Third time's a charm, Cope," Leland said. "You know it and I know it. I'm gonna have to take you in."

Copeland wasn't drunk but he didn't care. "Thank you," he said.

The doctor at the jail was unfamiliar to Cope, a kindly old man with ears and nostrils so full of thick white hair it was like he'd stuffed them with cotton. Cope wasn't a bit surprised when he didn't hear all that well and breathed through his mouth. His black pen was scribbling an inky note on the inside of his white coat pocket. But Cope just about could've kissed him for the way he didn't even bother with the stethoscope but went straight to work neatly flaying the boot off Cope's ankle and foot with a sharp blade. He would've sworn such a thing wasn't possible but once the ankle was cut free, it hurt even worse. The doc felt it with his hands first, lightly, and then took a couple of X-rays. He paused when he saw the pink-painted toes but didn't say a word.

When he came back into the room he came over to the examination table and faced Cope directly. "It's bad, son," he said. "It would've been better if you'd just broken it."

They were silent for a moment.

"So can't you just break it?" Cope said.

As for the rest of it, his court date and such, it was like when he'd wrecked his Knucklehead, that long, icy slide that burned the jacket off his back down to his T-shirt and he hadn't even felt the heat. This was near as bad. Copeland just pled guilty to everything. Judge Serrette said he was mightily disappointed in Cope. "You have a family now, son," the Judge said, "and they were depending on you." Here he'd given Copeland one final chance and Cope had failed him about as miserably as it was possible to fail another person. Even worse, Copeland had failed himself. Now he was duty-bound, the Judge said, to see to it that Cope straightened out. "I'm doing you a favor even though you might not see it that way right now: eighty-four days in the penitentiary over at Vienna. That might give you some time to take a good hard look at your character. In a place like that, you might gain some perspective. It might not be easy and it certainly won't be enjoyable but I know that someday you'll thank me for it."

Nadine cried but her face was empty. Cope felt the same way. Still, she'd cried and that gave him some hope.

Eighty-four days. When Cope went in, he hoped the scar on his face made him look mean if not dangerous. His new motto was Better Scarred than Scared. Ha. Trouble was, his cellmate, DeMoine Scofield, in for possession, had a worse scar on his face than Cope's. It was big and deep, twisted like rope. He couldn't smile on one side even if he'd wanted to, and apparently he didn't. He had to've gotten it in a fight, cut open with a buck knife or else something serrated.

"Nah," he told Cope finally. "June bug." He'd been on his motorcycle when the June bug hit him and it had rivened his face from his nose to his ear. "You must've been hauling ass," Cope said, and DeMoine said he'd been doing at least a hundred. "I seen the curve of the earth," he said. They got out their pictures. Come to find out he had an old '67 Shovelhead. Cope said he didn't know they were coming from the factory at that time still with a pan bottom. He asked him if that mousetrap clutch system's spring mechanism had ever snapped his finger when he tried to adjust the rod. DeMoine laughed. He showed Cope where he'd made some modifications. Cope showed him his old '47, stock except for the seat and a few other small things. "I bet that was a one-kicker all the way," DeMoine said, shaking his head. "I wouldn't trade my Shovel for nothing, but the '47s were the top. Just look at that."

All of that got Cope to remembering. He lay awake that night, smiling to think how Sissy'd finally worn him down, and it hadn't taken very long, either. He showed her the clutch and the brakes, and how to shift. She was slim and hard, not the kind of girl Cope was drawn to as a rule, and her hands were small on the handlebars. "I'm not going to spill it," she insisted when he pointed out the size of her hands. "Look, they're every bit big enough to pull in the clutch."

"Can they pull in the handbrake, that's all I care about," Cope said, and she laughed. Sure enough, she popped the clutch right off and the bike almost threw her but she righted herself, hardly wobbling at all. Copeland tried to relax, pulled a foxtail out of the ditch to chew on, hung his thumbs in his pockets. She went a little ways up the road toward the silo, then slowed to a stop and waited for him. The road was bone-white in the dark, soft with a powdery dust that lifted like smoke. She'd already teased Cope that he didn't have to be so nervous; she didn't have a dad who toted a loaded shotgun. No dad at all, as a matter of fact. It was her great-grandparents' farm, she'd told him, but he couldn't stop looking over his shoulder at the house all the same, the porch full of shadows, the dark windows watching them, even the upstairs one she said was her own room. "Don't worry," Sissy had said, shrugging. "They're farmers. They were asleep hours ago."

By the time Cope reached her, she had her T-shirt off and no bra. "Whoa, girl," he said, surprised, and she shrugged. "I've always envied boys this," she said. She was small-breasted but pretty, especially when she flashed her quick, stubborn grin. "See you later," she said, teasing him again. She stuffed her shirt in her back pocket, and carefully eased the bike down the road again. "Hey," Cope called out, not sure what he wanted to say to her but she didn't hear him anyway. He watched as she went down the straightaway, then rounded a curve past the silo where the fields turned into woods. She was doing fine, better than fine. In fact, she reminded Cope of something but for a minute or two he couldn't think what it was. Then it struck him: a falling star. That long, streaming hair in the dark, the pale shirt flickering from her back pocket. He glimpsed her one last time as the road lifted and fell and then disappeared, the motorcycle's rumbling drawing steadily away.

And then it was quiet, except for the slamming of hog feeders, the sounds of the nighttime woods. Cope looked over at the house and there seemed to be a whole passel of white cats that tumbled and streaked across the lawn. Under the smell of the hogs was a scent of roses and cut grass. He could taste green in his mouth from chewing on the foxtail.

Fifteen minutes went by, then twenty-five. Where was she? Forty-five minutes passed and Cope told himself to have some faith for once in his life. Then an hour went by, and what he felt was grief, pure as salt. C'mon, he told himself, how can you know? But he knew. His bike was gone. And gone with it was the girl he wanted more than anything. He should've known that look in her eyes.

After an hour and a half Cope was filled with a feeling he couldn't explain. Release, maybe. It was something like that. He even wondered if this was how it was to die. Peacefulness. An emptiness. Just him in the dark, entire.

But then she came back. She came back and Cope was glad. "Sorry," she whispered. He held her too hard, and she stiffened, wriggling out of his hold, breathless. They went back to the fair and he won prizes for her at the midway. Of course the place was just about emptied out because the carnival was fixing to close, but all of a sudden it seemed like he couldn't lose.

In a way, prison felt a little like that night, and hard as it was, in a way Cope didn't mind. He had nothing left, seemed like, but himself. Down to basics. Maybe Nadine and he and the girls could just start over.

The other part he didn't mind was that some of the inmates were taught life-saving and CPR so they could go around the little towns and teach people basic first aid and such. Community service. Greg Schnettgoecke, the teacher, was also an EMT going on nine years, and he was always telling stories of the terrible things he'd seen. "You might think you have it bad," he said, "but life's full of tragedies you can't even begin to imagine." He came and worked with the inmates twice a week.

Nadine started coming to see Cope more often, also twice a week. She brought the girls a couple times, too, all dolled up. That made him feel better about things. But the very minute she came to visiting hours and Cope saw the way her mouth bloomed with new pink lipstick, he knew. She'd never worn anything but Chapstick with him. She also looked softer, less pointed. "I want a divorce," she said.

"I'm really sorry, man. It just happened," Greg Schnettgoecke, the EMT, told Cope. "No hard feelings."

Cope had to swallow. "Well, you'll want to get you a big clothes hamper," he said. Greg looked confused. "Joke," Cope said and he nodded. Cope shook his hand. "I hope you can make her feel safe."

For days after that, though, and even though he tried not to, Cope felt a little sick inside. He went over and over again in his memory the time Nadine and he had been just about flattened in bed for a couple of days with the flu. The kids were visiting with their grandma. He and Nadine had been weak, damp, still shivery with fever, but she'd been the one who reached for him. It was like she was hungry. He was surprised when she came. Her cry was muffled, and he wasn't sure at first if it was pleasure or pain, but for some reason the sound touched him a little. Later, when they brushed their teeth, Cope looked at the two of them in the mirror, standing next to each other, lank-haired, hollow-eyed, and he smiled, thinking, "This must be true love."

But what did he know?

Back those years ago when Sissy had said to him, "I've never heard of a moving scar," it wasn't doubt in her voice, just quiet surprise that such a thing was possible. And that reminded Cope of a funny thing. When he'd seen that flaming toy truck, in the instant before it hit his neck, what he'd felt was pure wonder. He'd thought it was a parakeet. That's why he didn't move: he didn't want to scare it away. He didn't even question that a parakeet might come flying out of the burn barrel. It was a green and yellow one, coming right to him.

"What did it feel like?" Sissy'd asked him.

"It hurt," he said.

She laughed and then shivered. "Okay, but *how*? I can't even imagine."

"Bad," Cope said. Ha.

It hurt bad.

They were quiet for a long while, looking up at the clear night sky. He hadn't really felt the burn clearly at first, but once he did feel it, he'd wanted to die.

"It's funny about scars, isn't it?" Sissy had said. They stood together on a little bridge over Darkwater creek, tossing pebbles, watching how every time there was a ripple, the moon bounced across the water like a skipped stone. She leaned back against Cope and they looked up at the sky. It was the same bridge where in two weeks' time she was supposed to meet him to go away together. And while he didn't know it yet, she wouldn't show.

"I mean, if you think about it," she said, reaching back to lightly touch his face, "they're not even real. We see them but they're really just a memory of something." She shook her head. "Something that doesn't even exist anymore, that's long gone."

In two weeks, he'd wait for Sissy until the sky was starting to pale into another day.

"But we still use them to steer ourselves by," she said and shrugged. "It makes me sad, a little. Don't you think?" She was silent for a moment and Cope thought about how pain did change people, how even the memory of pain lived on and guided the roads they chose, the directions of their lives. He wondered what he'd do the next time a bright bird came flashing toward him out of nowhere.

In two weeks, Sissy wouldn't show. He'd wait for her, telling himself to show some faith for once in his life, and then he'd end up driving away alone. But right now she was here, and his arms were around her. And what she said made a kind of sense. "I mean, when do they quit moving?" Sissy said. "Do you think they ever finally just stop, and wink out?"

And all of a sudden Cope understood. *Stars*, she'd said, not scars, and he felt an ache he couldn't explain.

"Maybe they do," he heard himself say and wondered if he believed it. Moonlight touched his face, cold as water. "Maybe they do, at that."

Philip Walzer

The Cantor and the Milkman's Wife

Nearly one hundred years ago, a miracle of great wonder and horror befell the shtetl of Plepudzna, a village as mixed up and bedraggled as its name sounds. The tale of the cantor and the milkman's wife was still whispered in the marketplaces and yeshivas of Poland decades afterwards as evidence of God's impatience with His Chosen People's wanderings from His commandments. Those who came to America and passed on the story to the newer generations added a terrible twist — how two Jews of Plepudzna nearly did to their town what Hitler accomplished fifty years later. We are a disputatious people, of course, so I offer an entirely different commentary: This is the glorious fable of a righteous man who had the wisdom to perform a most awful sin.

Now Plepudzna was hardly a garden of riches. Not located near rich farmlands or much-traveled trade routes, it subsisted mostly on the goodwill of its inhabitants and the ingenuity of its storekeepers. Isaac Beilish was the shrewdest of the lot. He could create the foulest of potions when commanded. Usually, though, his concoctions were a delight to the tongue. His sweet peach compote, flavored with a little cinnamon, a little ginger and a lot of schnapps, drew visitors even from Lvov. But the appeal didn't last. The only thing the villagers could count on for eternity was trouble and more trouble from the Gentiles. Of course Jews everywhere were a beloved target of the Christians' wrath. But the people of Plepudzna seemed to hold a special attraction for Jew-haters across Europe. From the gang of teenagers the next town over, they could expect a gift of smeared pig feces across the large wooden door of the synagogue before major holidays. The Cossacks would regularly travel to the stores, their guns and daggers raised, plundering the Jewish merchants of all their profits of the week. The Polish army was the worst, helping themselves to the women's bodies and carving the youngest into terrible pieces when they were done.

Through it all, the townspeople remained remarkably pious. "Why shouldn't we be happy?" Escher the milkman said every Friday afternoon as the women of the town scurried to fill their baskets with the ingredients for their Shabbos dinners. "We have the Sabbath to celebrate." And so they did.

Every house that night was lit with candles, the flames seeming to dance in time to the singing of Sabbath zmirot and settling with the consumption of each dinner course. The next morning, the mottled oaken pews of the town's only synagogue seated every soul, there to listen to the sweet prayers of Reb Pinzl and the rich, clear singing of the cantor.

First, a little about Reb Pinzl. One look at him, with the gray beard, the long dark caftan and the soft blue eyes, and even the hardest of skeptics could be persuaded of the purity of his soul and the rightness of his beliefs. This was a man so wise, yet so gentle, that his learning lightly washed over the townsfolk like a misty rain in the midst of a summer heat wave. Not even the tragedy that visited the town—for which the rabbi would never forgive himself—could alter his good standing.

Of the cantor—his formal name was Shmuel Grunwald, but everyone simply called him the cantor—the people knew much less. He came to the town with his wife five years before, both looking a bit pale and timid, on the recommendation of the head of the Rothschild yeshiva from Vilna where he had recently completed his studies. A slight man, with hands the size of turnips and a brown beard that never learned how to grow, the cantor looked too small and inconsequential to carry a melody. But the moment he opened his mouth during services, newcomers fell awestruck by his voice—robust and sure, deep and resonant.

So with these two men, never the best of friends but compatible religious leaders, the villagers lived with hope and comfort as they teetered from pogroms to prayers and back again.

Their routine was shattered shortly after sundown on the twenty-ninth day of April, corresponding to the twenty-seventh day of the Hebrew month of Nissan.

Velvel the tailor heard it first. "Manya," he cried to his wife, already sleeping in their rock of a bed. "I hear heaven calling."

"Sha, Soup-for-Brains." She curled back into her dream, and Velvel went off for a glass of hot tea.

A few minutes later, she drifted to the kitchen, swept Velvel into her arms and glided back to bed to listen to a miracle and perform another.

They heard the sound honey would make if it could talk. The wondrous music of baby robins and burbling waterfalls.

Everyone in Plepudzna soon heard it, and the town levitated in rapture.

Teenagers and elderly couples alike gripped each other in alleyways, on flowerbed and in pantries, their bodies crashing together with cries that echoed for hours. Reb Pinzl, like the others, consummated the moment with his wife, Hinda, with an ecstasy unmatched since their wedding night. And then he scurried into his study to put to paper the brainstorm that had flashed in his head during the peak of their encounter. It was the solution to the mysterious biblical story of the red heifer, which had baffled scholars far wiser than him and puzzled Reb Pinzl since his days in rabbinical school.

A few hours later, at the edge of midnight, the joyous noise stopped. The next morning, the Jews were still celebrating. Isaac Beilish nearly hopped to his store, giddy to fill dozens of jars with a recipe for a sweet and sour horseradish he had dreamed up that night. Tante Pesha, the seamstress, cloistered herself in her back room all morning to stitch together dozens of formal dresses with a flash of inspiration. Lavender and gold, satin and silver, all blending together with a grace and majesty unsullied by pretension. The holidays were months away, but the ladies of the town, knowing without being told of her new offerings, flocked to the shop in the afternoon to try them on and pay for them, not one needing an alteration.

Throughout Plepudzna, the people, bleary-eyed but blazing with energy, chattered endlessly, all trying to answer the question: What went on last night? Some said it was the first stirrings of the Messiah. Others, the Creator's reward for their having endured such hardship.

Reb Pinzl also wondered. He didn't have to puzzle long. Late that morning, the cantor crept into the rabbi's office.

"Shmuel, come, come," the rabbi said, hastening to find a spot in the room that wasn't covered with prayer books or rabbinical commentaries.

The cantor shook his head. He wouldn't stay for long. He stood near the door, his gaze on the floor.

"It was me last night," the cantor said, still avoiding Reb Pinzl's soft gaze. "I heard the milkman's wife humming as she put out her garbage, and suddenly we were singing folk songs together. I can't explain it, but it will not happen again, I promise you." He walked out, a sheep that had bleated an earful, before the rabbi could respond.

Which was a blessing, because Reb Pinzl—despite his years of study and ministration, his counseling of couples on all means of topics, from dietary incompatibilities to unhealthy relationships with animals—Reb Pinzl couldn't think of a word to say.

Ten minutes later, the rabbi still sat open-mouthed, pondering the strange revelation. Remember, this was not today's world, where even God-fearing Jews take a portion of their hard-earned salary to listen to men and women sing and dance —very often in immodest clothing—on the theater stage. The notion of a pious man, the congregation's musical intermediary to the Holy One, lifting his voice with a woman not his wife—it was incredible and blasphemous, threatening and otherworldly. And totally incomprehensible.

So Reb Pinzl sat and thought, and thought some more, and didn't know what to think, other than that all of God's Chosen People were weak and that the Almighty One was compassionate enough to forgive the cantor's lapse, extraordinary though it was.

And then it happened again the next night.

A purring so rich and delicious that the townspeople awoke as one, their hearts and other parts engorged with happiness as never before. So began another night of ferocious and dizzying lovemaking. Sender the shoeman, his back almost bent in two from years of polishing and soling shoes, held his wife, Bluma, above him in bed, bouncing her upon his body. When they accidentally fell to the floor, Bluma screamed, fearing he had finally paralyzed himself. But Sender merely laughed and returned to bed, his back a little straighter.

The world around these light-hearted human beings also danced in delight. The trees grew taller, the daffodils and tulips more luscious. The clouds smiled before they disappeared.

The next morning, the people once more babbled giddily. The cantor repeated his apology to Reb Pinzl and his promise never to do it again. And the rabbi remained lost in thought, forgetting his appointments of the day, ignoring the knocks on his peeling door, even failing to attend evening prayers.

So many questions gathered in Reb Pinzl's head. Starting with: What had gotten into the cantor? Yes, his wife, Sala, had remained childless and her zaftig body had ballooned since they had moved to Plepudzna. But the milkman's wife, Leah Binder, should have held no allure, her face marred by a mole jutting from her right cheek, her figure a haphazard collection of jagged edges with no beckoning curves. Her personality, too, was indistinct. The rabbi recalled only one discussion with her, after her hapless husband, Escher the milkman, ate a slice of toast on the afternoon of Yom Kippur, somehow forgetting it was a fast day. She was neither mad nor amused. She was . . . well, he couldn't really remember what she had been like that day, so little impression had she made on him. And her singing? Who could have known what charms flowed from her mouth? Like the other women, she prayed quietly in the upper section of the synagogue, even in their most fervent moments careful not to distract or outdo the men.

Next came the deeper questions. What had God intended by this? How could He have wrapped this transgression inside such a bounty? It is not for humans to know His ways, but the rabbi felt bidden to at least try to understand. Could it be that a man and a woman singing together was not such a crime? Or maybe it was to show His flock that a sin could sometimes hide behind a celebration. The rabbi exercised his head and finished more muddled than when he had started.

Like the great sages before him, Reb Pinzl believed that meditation without action was just another form of foolishness. So the final dilemma was: What would he do? This proved to be the most vexing question.

The rabbi closed his eyes and tipped back in his metal chair, having refused his congregation's repeated offers for a more comfortable seat with a cushioned back. In his mind, he could see a pair of truths, one reassuring, the other threatening. The cantor and Leah had not yet committed adultery, he felt certain. God would not allow such merrymaking to sprout from a sin so dark. For now, theirs was a pleasure of voices. But—and this was the bad news—these interludes surely would come to no good. The joys of their mouths would seep down, slithering like the serpent beckoning Eve, calling to their physical beings. Soon, he could see, they would lie down in trembling passion like the rest of the townsfolk.

Eyes still shut, Reb Pinzl prayed that the Holy One, Blessed Be He, give them strength and common sense to go no further—indeed, to discontinue all their private encounters. The rabbi felt obliged himself to entreat—perhaps even demand—that they halt their rendezvous. A spiritual leader should lead his people—should he not?—away from spiritual neglect and toward greater observance of His commandments. Not even the great dueling Torah commentators Hillel and Shammai could have found room for argument there.

And yet . . . the town floated in sweet serenity as never before. Did not the inhabitants deserve this small moment of sunshine after so many years of persecution? Why, only last year, the marauding Russians slew more than twenty of their flock, including all three sons of Perchik the butcher. Yesterday, for the first time since then, the rabbi had seen a glimmer of light in Perchik's face. How could he not rejoice?

This religion of theirs, Reb Pinzl knew, was hardly ascetic. Jews were supposed to exult in life. Joyous music was not to be shunned. Didn't he nearly blister his hands every Friday night banging the table while bellowing the grace after meals? Physical contact between husband and wife glorified God, too. Could it be, Reb Pinzl wondered, that the exquisite sounds and pleasure shared by so many from Plepudzna carried greater good than the evil committed by the two straying singers?

So, gentle Reb Pinzl, always looking to blunt the harsh edges of the Torah with the softness of his heart, held his tongue and hoped for a satisfactory resolution to this strange affair.

And day after day it continued, the heavenly music growing more pure and velvety with each note, the landscape growing more lush, the villagers ever more contented and productive.

Reb Pinzl assumed the spirit would also elevate the Sabbath service. He was right. The villagers all arrived punctually, miraculously avoided gossip, and joined in the prayers with a lusty singing that lifted the rabbi's soul. The cantor, looking heartier and fuller of frame, led them with unparalleled vigor. Though the women's section also was louder than before, Reb Pinzl could not discern the voice of the milkman's wife, who sat radiant in a simple white dress.

Just when the townspeople were getting used to this Eden in Europe, this meshuggeneh magic, their world turned upside down again.

This time, Hanka the widow washwoman first heard it, a few nights after the Sabbath. A cry so ghastly, so fearsome, that the gray whiskers sprouting above her upper lip grew half an inch. Her nails hardened and curved farther around her toes; two more of her teeth fell out.

She bolted awake, a pain piercing her chest. "God in Heaven, what have you done to me?" Hanka cried, thinking she was about to be carried to the next world. She remained in this one, but felt a force, cold and fierce, slamming her back down in bed, where she remained, unable to sleep or move, until dawn.

The passions that had fired the men and women, boys and girls, even the two yeshiva boys whose private relationship had yet to be discovered, were extinguished in an instant. Their breasts and penises shriveled; couples uncoupled in disgust and fell to bickering about last night's brisket, which had seemed so tender just hours ago, or the arrangement of the furniture in the sitting room.

A sour odor pervaded the town the next day, replacing the mirth and delight. The brothers Simeon and Lester, best friends and partners in their late father's furniture store, haggled for hours over the sale price of a cherry wood side table, then decided to close the business for good. Everything turned bitter in Isaac Beilish's confection shop, even the fruit slices bathed in sugar.

Nor was Reb Pinzl spared. He forgot to say the morning prayer thanking God for letting him arise another day on this earth. For breakfast, he cavalierly used a meat dish for his hot cereal, violating the kosher laws for the first time in his life.

When he came to his senses, the rabbi hastily prayed and threw the bowl, which he had rendered unusable, into the garbage pail. His head ached with the sudden knowledge of what had caused his trouble: the cantor and the milkman's wife had taken their relationship to a forbidden realm the evening before.

Reb Pinzl hastened to his closet of an office. But before he unlocked his door, he went to the room at the end of the hall and knocked loud and insistent. No cantor.

Back and forth he went, from his office, to the cantor's, every ten minutes. Finally, close to noon, he found the cantor.

"What happened last night?"

The cantor could not mask the smile that trickled across his face. The rabbi read that as tantamount to a confession. Next, he assumed, would come a recantation or a tearful breast-beating. Instead, the cantor told the rabbi: "After the first folk song, we stopped."

"That was all?"

"Nothing more."

The lie wounded Reb Pinzl. The rabbi took on the stern voice that he used with bar mitzvah boys who dallied with their Torah study. "Don't dissemble, Shmuel," he scolded.

The cantor, now blank-faced, looked down at his disheveled desk. "Nothing more," he repeated.

The rabbi stared at the cantor until he glanced back. "Shmuel, I beg of you, stop this craziness," Reb Pinzl said. "The health of the village rests on your good sense."

"You're right, my friend," the cantor said, daring to look straight at the rabbi.

When he heard those words "my friend"—a phrase neither had ever used with the other—the rabbi knew his premonition had been confirmed. He closed the door and walked back to his office, where he stood, prayer book in hand, and swayed, beseeching the Almighty to restore peace to the town and holiness to the cantor. After he was done, he felt his head. He was losing his hair in a curious pattern circling his skullcap.

That night, the shrieking grew even more fierce. Three of the town's old women lost their hearing. The vibrations caused chaos in Isaac Beilish's shop, the spice rack tumbling down, the jars filled with caramels and chocolate-covered cherries shattering.

The following day, the townspeople grew grumpier. Their surroundings darkened, too; the sun hid behind the clouds, turning Plepudzna blacker than midnight. The trees began shedding leaves in the middle of spring. Flowers wilted in even the most fruitful of gardens, their petals turning a putrid shade of brown.

Reb Pinzl banged on the door to the cantor's room with a fury he did not know could rise up in him. There was no response.

Dreading what he might find, the rabbi walked to the cantor's house across the town, nearly colliding with five people in the dark. The cantor's wife, shadow-faced and somber, answered the door.

"Hello, Sala," the rabbi said, unable to avoid a false note of cheerfulness. "Is Shmuel here?"

She shook her head violently and started edging the door closed.

"Please tell him I'm looking for him," the rabbi said, turning more serious.

Sala bit her lip and started shaking. Her eyes reflecting surrender, she said, "I drove him to this. I never could carry a tune."

She broke down and ran inside the house.

The rabbi left, his heart stretched thin with despair.

Next, he went to Escher the milkman's house—a sad affair, with shutters dangling from loose nails, horse manure coating the walkway. Reb Pinzl expected to find the wife there, maybe even the cantor, but not Escher. So he was surprised to see the milkman's lopsided wagon sitting near the door.

The rabbi knocked, and Escher appeared, his chin splotched white from the bowl of strawberries and cream he had been eating.

"I'm having an early lunch today," he said, beaming with pride.

God bless him, he still lives in his imaginary world of harmony, Reb Pinzl thought. So should we all.

"Escher, good day today," the rabbi said. "I would like to speak to your wife about an urgent matter."

Escher scowled. "She did not pay our fees to the synagogue?" He got down to his knees. "Please, your most gracious Pinzl. Do not force us to leave the sanctuary. We are good Jews, if a little forgetful."

"No, no. That is not the matter at all. Is she here?"

Escher rose, relieved. "She said she went shopping," he said, then shook his head in wonder. "She usually goes shopping on Tuesdays, so I was a little surprised. But she said she needed some more food today. Milk, of course, she doesn't have to get," he said, breaking into a bear laugh.

Reb Pinzl did not join his laugh and let himself out to avoid hearing more of Escher's inanities.

The rabbi could not find the cantor for the rest of the day. Or the next.

Plepudzna sank into further decay. Oak trees, suddenly spineless, fell to the ground. Teenagers turned white-haired. Three couples, floating with joy just last week, came to the rabbi asking for a divorce. He told them to wait, but he, too, had a feverish urge to return home and scold his wife for no apparent reason.

And the anti-Semites returned. They shattered the windows in three stores, raped the seamstress' daughter, Ofra, and cut off her hair.

Reb Pinzl fell to tears in his office and at home, rejecting Hinda's comforts.

O Lord, he wailed during evening prayers. Why are You so troubling this town? Have we lost favor in Your eyes? Please give us the strength to conquer the evil inclination. Show me how to draw closer to Your ways.

He strained his being toward piety, but heard only silence.

On Sabbath morning, the rabbi walked with fear to the synagogue. He couldn't imagine this holiest day of the week going untouched by the plague consuming Plepudzna.

When he walked in, he encountered the first confirmation—a stench so fetid and overwhelming that he ran sick to the bathroom, soiling the bottoms of his trousers. His congregants followed his path as they entered, turning the smell even fouler.

It was as if they had been taken by a madman's spell, all memory of the grandeur of the day blotted from their minds. Men came to synagogue unshaven, in their undershirts; women in their housedresses, their hair unkempt. One old widow wore nothing but a corset—normally an unpleasant sight, but nobody seemed to notice.

They joked and picked their noses throughout the service, ignoring the rabbi's repeated attempts to shush them. And their singing—it was as if they had been Christians plucked into the synagogue for the first time. They had forgotten the choruses and melodies of prayers, the pronunciation of Hebrew words.

Even in this cacophony, two voices rang out with clarity— those of the cantor and the milkman's wife. The cantor, looking fuller and taller than ever before, also sang with incomparable strength and richness. The milkman's wife had lost her mole; her body had grown softer and shapelier. And from her voice came a sound delicate and pure. The women, unaccustomed to such expression in their section, cleared a space around her and looked at her in astonishment. The cantor's wife shrank to the background.

Bypassing his customary greetings after the conclusion of the service, the rabbi quickly left with Hinda. They also bypassed their Saturday afternoon respite in bed.

Reb Pinzl closeted himself in the study of his house. He paged through the tractates, vainly looking for guidance. He pounded his desk in defiance. It was a sin to let sadness and anger creep into this day of rest, but how could he avoid it?

As they say, one sin leads to another. In the depths of his despair, the rabbi conjured a plot crazed and inspired. He would immobilize the cantor's voice to save the town from ruin. Reb Pinzl put on his overcoat, which did little to protect him from the doubts that seemed to pound upon him from the heavens: He had become no better than his most flawed congregants. Was there no end to the commandments he would break on this most treasured of days? But: how much more of this horror could his beloved town endure? Sometimes, he reasoned—not without heartache—a man must dip into impurity to redeem others from greater misfortune.

His mind leaping between terror and hopefulness, he made his way to Isaac Beilish's house.

Isaac, upon hearing the rabbi's idea, offered no objections. His faith in Reb Pinzl's wisdom neutralized any hesitations he had about the scheme. Isaac hastened to his shop and set to work on the potion that the rabbi had requested.

Reb Pinzl had suggested a few ingredients, but left the details to Isaac's expertise. Rubbing alcohol and ground peppercorns, paprika and soap flakes. But what to make it palatable? Isaac laid out before him an array of sweeteners—bay leaves, cinnamon, dried pineapple bits, and licorice sticks. The challenge, unusual for him, was to perfect the mixture without ever tasting it.

An hour later, he returned to the rabbi's house with a jar of the homemade solution.

That night, after Hinda fell asleep, Reb Pinzl set out a paper bag and a sheet of note paper. Trying to adopt a feminine script, he wrote, "Drink this, my love, and your voice and manhood will grow even more powerful." God pardon me, the rabbi thought.

He put the jar and note in the bag and hurried, in the dark, to the synagogue. The rabbi left the bag in front of the door to the cantor's office. The cantor would be there the next morning, tutoring the children—unless he had lost sight of all of his responsibilities.

The town suffered another horrible night. A wall of rain nearly drowned Escher's cows. The sleepless inhabitants roamed the streets, shoving and poking one another, men even harassing ladies. Tante Pesha took refuge in her shop, where she dropped to her knees in shock at the sight of all of her creations stained blood-red and shorn into tatters.

In the morning, Reb Pinzl beat his chest and prayed fiercely for forgiveness, even though the Day of Atonement was four months away. The rabbi remained in his room in the synagogue all morning, no better, he feared, than a voyeur. Just waiting to see if his plan would re-establish peace in this town or inflict further disarray.

At a quarter to eleven, he found out. A rasp, a gurgle and a high-pitched yelp reverberated through the building. The cantor ran out of his office, leaving a bar mitzvah boy wondering if his shenanigans had brought on a nervous breakdown in his teacher.

And at that moment, the town returned to normal, neither bathed in a glow of rhapsody nor strewn about in a tempest.

Reb Pinzl still worried, though, for the cantor's sake. Isaac Beilish had told him the effects would wear off in a day or two. But by midweek, still no one had seen the cantor.

Finally, on Friday, the rabbi heard a timid knock on his door at the synagogue. He opened it, dumbfounded by the sight. There was the cantor, a foot shorter, a virtual cadaver, spent and hollow, his throat wrapped in a white handkerchief.

"How could you do this?" he croaked, barely audible. "It is a secret to no one that I have transgressed. But my crimes do not merit this punish—" His sentence ended prematurely with a harsh bubbling noise that both terrified and nauseated Reb Pinzl.

"I never intended for you to lose your gifts permanently," the rabbi said, stinging with guilt. "I, too, must atone the rest of my days for the harm I have caused."

The cantor left, appearing to shrink to a midget's size with his remaining steps in the synagogue.

The people of Plepudzna never saw him again.

Some said he became a put-upon teacher of unruly yeshiva boys in Moscow; others an unsuccessful jewelry salesman in New York City. One heard he had recovered his voice and become the musical leader of the majestic synagogue in Romania. But after Kleiner the traveling salesman journeyed to Budapest, he reported that the cantor there was a towering stick of a man, surely not the same person.

Sala, the cantor's wife, was declared free to remarry by the rabbi six years after her husband vanished. She found Marek

Shulsen, a dark-complexioned poet and silversmith who had settled in the town looking for inspiration. He brought her much joy and five children, including a son, Pesach, who grew rich and famous as a cabaret singer in Munich.

Leah Binder, the milkman's wife, receded into the life of Plepudzna just as she had begun. Her mole reappeared; her curves disappeared. Never again did the town hear her precious singing. Her husband, Escher, oblivious to the drama that nearly broke his marriage apart, continued to the end of his days delivering milk and snorting with laughter, a contented fool.

And what of Reb Pinzl?

The town raised him even higher as the hero who had saved it from destruction. The rabbi, however, spoke not another word of his unholy plot, and the shadow of his wrongdoing never left him. After the cantor's disappearance he rent his clothes, as if in mourning. Every day for the rest of his years, he prayed for God's mercy for destroying another's life—though he never regretted his actions.

His mind escaped his troubles only when the town fell into his own terrible troubles, beginning with the Polish army's incursion three months after the cantor's departure. Every third boy or man, including Isaac Beilish, was taken away for military service, never to be heard from again. Which only added to Reb Pinzl's lacerating grief. Until his last prayers, he couldn't dispel the suspicion that Isaac had been punished for participating in the rabbi's scheme.

God granted Reb Pinzl a long life, ninety-six years and twenty-two days. The rabbi was taken gently in his sleep three and a half months before the Germans invaded Plepudzna. The modern-day commentators—what is left of them—naturally have come to no consensus about his death. For the disbelievers, a sour bunch, his end shattered the illusion of his great wisdom and goodness—as if Reb Pinzl willingly abandoned his town to its desecration—and proved the folly of God's dominion over the earth. His wide-eyed disciples believe his influence burned on, uninterrupted, from his perch in heaven, where they say he directed a young Polish Jew to stab a Nazi in the throat with a Torah pointer.

I say simply: Reb Pinzl's death was a blessing from the One Above, who saw fit to shelter the rabbi from a monstrosity not even he could tame. May his memory inspire wondrous misdeeds to safeguard future generations.

Susan Vita Weiss

Dresses for the Melons

He had learned to sew by watching his mother. As a boy, he'd sat on the floor near her chair while she mended, the needle weaving in and out of the cloth followed by a shortening trail of thread. Her quick stitches were as regular and even as those formed, much later, by her sewing machine with so much more commotion. McKee's mother had not intentionally taught him to sew; still, her movements were recorded in his mind so that, years after, though he'd never practiced, he was able to open his wife's sewing basket and neatly hem the unraveling edge of a tablecloth.

He sewed plain curtains for their bedroom window, covered, until then, only with a shade. Next he sewed curtains for the kitchen—these a more ambitious design with a ruffled border. His wife, Madeline, seemed mildly pleased that these decorative touches had been accomplished without requiring any effort from her.

Dresses for the Melons

"I guess we should get divorced," she said to McKee not quite five years after they were married. Her face was as illegible to him as a page of Greek.

"Why, Madeline?"

"It's just . . . I don't know, I have the feeling that anyone would do. If not me, then the next person who comes along."

McKee obliged her by moving out of the house without any protest. He left the curtains he'd made behind since "they're custom fit to these windows, Madeline," he told her.

The high-rise apartment where McKee relocated had four rooms, all of them so small that he wondered if he wouldn't have done better with two larger rooms. Right away he made curtains for all of the windows, the needle weaving in and out of the cloth, in and out. He regretted now that he'd allowed his mother's sewing machine, when she died, to be claimed by one of his cousins.

He sewed two small pillows for the living room couch and half a dozen more to decorate his bed. Carlton, who moved in with McKee that first year, complained, "It's too much of a bother to put all of these back on the bed in the morning." By then McKee had added another four pillows to the heap.

"But I'm the one who usually makes the bed," he said.

Carlton tossed one after another of the assorted plump pillows aside onto the floor. "Well then I mean . . . taking them all off the bed every night. . . ."

McKee had sewn the French-blue chenille bedspread, too, managing to disguise the seams that joined three widths of the fabric together so they were nearly invisible. Finally he had purchased a machine, one that was capable of twenty-some different types of stitches but that, since it was second-hand, cost half of its original price.

"That thing gets in the way of the view," Carlton pointed out once.

"I didn't think about that," McKee said but noticed then that the sewing machine interrupted the skyline.

So McKee carried the machine into the smallest of the four small rooms, having decided to make it into a sewing room. He even emptied part of the bookcase, leaving books scattered on the floor, and organized his spools of threads and bobbins and leftover material on the shelf.

"That's better," Carlton said, looking in from the doorway. "But you're not going to leave those books there, are you?"

McKee began stacking the books into leaning towers on the floor.

"We'd better start clearing those pillows away now," Carlton said. "Otherwise we won't get to bed until dawn."

When Carlton decided, after less than a year, that he'd rather not live with McKee anymore, McKee kept the apartment since his name was on the lease. In two months the lease expired; for less rent than he'd paid for the four cramped rooms, McKee was able to rent half of a twin just outside the city. A back yard the size of a quilt was separated from its double by a painted wooden fence in disrepair, narrow gaps here and there where slats were missing. To McKee the fence looked like a smile in need of dental work.

The next spring, some months after he had moved in, unexpected sprouts and stalks emerged from the soil. McKee permitted them to thrive until he could identify them: a daffodil, a columbine. The resurrection of a previous tenant's garden, he supposed.

"You got to rent a Rototiller and dig it all up. Then you can start fresh," said his neighbor, a short, balding man whose age McKee could not imagine.

"What's the soil like?" he asked the man.

"It's all stuck together, held together with old roots."

"But I mean, do you know if it's acidic?"

McKee's neighbor worked his face into a frown. "What're you figurin' to do?"

McKee kneeled in the dirt, crumbling a fisted clod between his thumb and fingers. The earth retained some moisture from the last rain at least a week before.

That same Saturday, McKee bought several flats of seedlings from a nursery he found after driving around for more than an hour. He selected each individual plant from among the dozens for sale, rearranging them in their plastic cubicles so that every one he took home with him showed signs of recent growth.

The cucumbers blossomed first. With fine, spiraled tendrils they grabbed onto the web of string that McKee had constructed to support them. The tomato plants grew steadily, a little at a time, yet one morning they seemed suddenly to have doubled in size, and soon McKee discovered miniature cucumbers developing among the cucumber leaves. Even the melons he'd planted had produced infant fruits, each a small miracle to McKee. At night, if he turned on the floodlight aimed at his back yard, he could see not any particular plant but the collective prosperity of the whole garden.

He'd read about what pests to beware of, gelatinous creepers and bristly foes that he picked off the leaves every few days. As the summer advanced and the number of leaves and their sizes increased, McKee needed at least an hour to search for bugs.

One Friday evening after he'd conducted his inspection, he removed the tape measure he used for sewing out of his pocket and measured each young melon. The pale rinds were smooth and flawless, and so new.

McKee spent the rest of that weekend sewing dresses for the melons. He first sketched a simple design then drew patterns for the pieces, reducing them to fit the smallest of the crop and enlarging them to fit the bigger melons. McKee had saved scraps of fabric from the curtains he'd made and from all the pillows, and he edged the bottoms of the puffed sleeves with white piqué, bands to match the white piqué collars.

In the evening, when he finished sewing, McKee switched on the floodlight and carried the tiny garments out to the yard. As he was putting one on each of the melons, he happened to glimpse the cucumbers in their prickly skins. In the two hours before he went to bed, he sewed a number of floral sheaths, each like a single pants leg with a cuff at the bottom. The next evening, as McKee was slipping them onto the cucumbers, he noticed the naked cabbages.

The butternut squashes, too. During that week, McKee barely tended to his garden except for one hurried examination of the leaves. Instead he sewed clothing for all the other vegetables. The tomatoes especially challenged him: soft, fragile flesh, already large, so too much more weight might disconnect them from their stems. For his butternut squashes he created gathered skirts that opened out over the bulbous ends.

After a full week of seamstressing every evening and on his days off, McKee completed a wardrobe for his entire garden. Every fruit and vegetable was now clothed, and any new ones that appeared could be given the hand-me-downs of the more mature produce once it was harvested. The garden, as McKee viewed it from his back doorway, looked like the nearby church yard when all of the well-groomed girls and boys were dismissed from Sunday school.

Not even two weeks later, though, he discovered during a routine leaf inspection that some of the watermelons had almost outgrown their dresses. McKee had never really expected the melon plants to yield any fruit even though they were a hybrid developed for temperate climates. As they continued to get bigger, the dresses might be forced open at the seams or, worse, might constrict the melons' growth.

So McKee undressed the melons, admiring the craft required to shape the tabs of the little collars. The fabric had weathered rainfalls and the daily waterings he fed the garden. Such fine pieces of clothing, he thought, yet they had been in service for such a short time. McKee folded each one in half crosswise at the waist, planning to store the dresses until the next growing season, when he hoped to use them again.

He noticed then that many of the butternut squashes, too, were becoming too large for their clothes, and the cucumbers, the cabbages, for theirs. McKee, while squatting at the edge of the garden, conceived of a rotation system and took hold of one stout squash close to choking in its skirt. He handled it carefully so it wouldn't break off prematurely from its stem when he began to tug insistently at the skirt until it came off. Then, deciding which of the discarded watermelon dresses was the right size for the squash, he put it on from the bottom, fastening the small hook at the neckline once the dress was in place. McKee fussed with the skirt, the empty sleeves—turning, twisting, fluffing—and though the dress was more suited to the shape of the melons, he concluded that it didn't look too bad on the squash.

The outgrown squash skirts lay nicely on top of the cabbage heads like wide-brimmed hats; in turn, the broad sashes that he'd made for the cabbages, as they became too small, could be wrapped around the ripening cucumbers. McKee could think of no further use for the cucumbers' cast-off clothing, though. The long, narrow sheaths couldn't be adapted to the profusion of tense green tomatoes. Anyway, the small bows worn by the tomatoes where they attached to the plants could simply be loosened when they became too tight.

McKee's house was on a corner. The outside edge of the yard was bordered, not with the same picket fencing that split the lot in two, but with ugly chain link. Anyone could see McKee's well-dressed garden from the street.

His autistic nephew Sam, who was sometimes dropped off at the house by McKee's sister, seemed unaware of the existence of the yard, much less the garden. And though McKee's ex-wife still called him—their finances were entangled—she'd never been to his house, never seen the fashionable vegetables dangling from the vines.

Neither had Carlton. McKee continued to see him at work and couldn't understand why Carlton seemed to harbor so much anger toward him. Was it because of all the pillows on the bed? Soon after Carlton moved out, McKee had bound the pillows together with hidden stitches so all of them could be moved together as a unit.

So far McKee had received one written warning for leaving the office early though he always completed his work. The daylight hours were dwindling now as the end of summer neared, and he had yet to finish the dress he was making for the largest watermelon.

The melon was so big that McKee had bought a dress pattern intended for a baby then modified the style and added certain details of his own: a velvet bow between the tabs of the collar and a ruffle of eyelet sewed to the underside of the hem. Despite the warning he'd received at work, McKee left early on a Friday, confident that he wouldn't be fired since no one else was experienced in the system of inventory control. He needed his job, relied on his income to pay the rent and to purchase fabrics and the ribbons and trims.

McKee completed the last dress in time to put it on the melon in the steel-blue light remaining of the day. That evening he cut a short article out of the newspaper, the section devoted to local news. In the morning he drove to the address printed at the end of the article, a main road in a rural town rather far from where he lived.

The county extension office was a low structure that appeared so temporary that McKee thought a hefty wind might overturn it. Inside, he filled out an application form to officially enter his watermelons in the County Harvest Show. Only the melons and the butternut squashes. McKee was limited by just two short lines on the form and by explicit directions that ordered him not to exceed the allotted space.

"OK. Bring us the best you got," the woman who'd given McKee the form said to him.

The show was scheduled for exactly two weeks from that day. The judging would be held in the morning, the winners announced, then all of the entries exhibited in the barn-like building nearby for a week after the competition.

McKee was familiar with each fruit and vegetable in his garden, and as he drove home, he thought about which to enter in the Harvest Show. Instead of choosing the largest melons, he selected three that still fit into the dresses he'd designed and preferred to those made from a pattern. He decided to enter his smaller squashes even if they weren't really ripe. The bigger ones were wearing hand-me-downs from the melons, and the dress, he realized, would seem like a uniform.

The Friday before the show, at work, McKee mentioned to Carlton that he was entering a gardening competition and invited him to attend.

"So you're into gardening now?" was all that Carlton said.

The county exhibit building, from outside, looked like a large mobile home, but inside it resembled a barn. After waiting in line, McKee set his boxes on the table. The same woman who'd accepted his application two weeks earlier now asked him his name then riffled through some papers and assigned him a number.

"Fifty-seven. That's you."

She wrote the number on both boxes with a broad-tipped marker and slid the boxes aside without glancing inside them.

McKee had been watching the woman's face, hoping for a preview of the judges' reaction to his harvest.

"Come on, come on," she said, shooing him away. "We got quite a line here by now."

McKee started toward the white-bright sunlight framed by the open door across the room. Some of the entries were already displayed and labeled, he noticed as he walked past the long tables in rows.

Behind the building, other gardeners were standing, waiting, pacing, most of them alone but some in pairs or surrounded by a whirlwind of children. Among McKee's rivals were a couple of men wearing overalls, and he wondered if they were professional farmers that should be kept from competing. Someone inside pulled the rear door to the building closed. McKee looked at his watch; the judging was no doubt about to begin.

McKee stood, unmoving, in a small portion of shade on the otherwise sunny grounds. Soon he became conscious of a voice, first, then of a man his own age dressed in dusty clothes and with a head shaped like a tomato.

"What?" McKee didn't know how long the man had been talking.

"I said this is nerve-wracking, isn't it? Hi, my name's Thomas."

When McKee shook Thomas's hand, he felt well-established calluses on Thomas's palm and fingers, probably from gripping gardening tools.

"This is my first time," Thomas said.

"Mine too."

The two men nodded. Minutes later, McKee saw Thomas roaming into the distance.

More people now were pacing in unrelated patterns, risking collisions with each other. McKee prodded the bare ground with the toe of his shoe. When the door to the exhibit hall opened, everyone converged close to the building. Even Thomas suddenly reappeared.

"You all can come on in," they were told.

Already inside the exhibit hall were other gardeners who must have been summoned from elsewhere. McKee scanned the room. His entries should have been easy to spot since none of the other fruits and vegetables were clothed, he noted right away. Not finding them, he began to walk between the tables. "Number fifty-seven," he reminded himself. But the entries weren't displayed according to numbers or to any logic that McKee could perceive, and he kept walking up and back the enormous room. Once or twice his eye was attracted by a rich red or blue ribbon embossed with gold letters and he read the nearby number expectantly. Then he would move on.

"Fifty-seven," he read. After a delay, he recognized the number as his own but not the vegetables and melons grouped behind it. At least not at first. McKee squinted at them. Is that you? he thought. All of them had been disrobed, and their clothing was nowhere in sight.

"Excuse me." McKee located the man who had admitted everyone back into the building. "I'm looking for my clothes."

"What's that you're wearin'?" The man seemed unwilling to meet eyes with McKee.

"Oh. I didn't mean mine. Little dresses and skirts. They belong to the melons and squashes I entered." The man didn't answer, so McKee said, "Tell me where my box is, the box I brought them in."

The man turned his head, and McKee, looking in the same direction, saw a collapsed hill of cardboard cartons against the wall, each box marked with a number. Some of the boxes had been thrown onto the heap so that the sequence of numbers was preserved, while others were arranged haphazardly.

Then he saw it. Fifty-seven, off to the side as if it had toppled down from the peak. McKee seized the box and looked inside, but it was empty. Fifty-six, fifty-five, forty-three, all of them empty. In the box marked fifty-two, he discovered just one of the melons' dresses. McKee searched backward through the forties then thirties until, in the box numbered thirty-five, he found all the rest of the missing wardrobe—the dresses and the squash skirts.

Holding them close with one arm pressed to his chest, he carried carton number fifty-seven in his free hand. McKee's breathing had quickened, and with each deep intake of air, he rumbled like a coming storm. At the table where his entries were displayed, he set the carton down and lay out all the clothing on the table, then apologetically began to dress the watermelons, first. Then the squashes. Once they were clothed, he carefully placed them in the box.

McKee was almost at the door out to the gravel parking area when he suddenly spun around. His eyes like predators found the woman who'd received his entries that same morning. McKee butted his way through the crowded exhibit hall until finally he was standing in front of her. His skin felt hot, radiant. In his embrace, the box rose then fell after each exhalation.

The woman was sorting through applications and barely glanced up at him.

He tried to harden himself by tightening all his muscles, but inside him, a flutter of birds had been let loose. McKee couldn't hold in the droplets of tears seeping out from the corners of his eyes.

"What's the matter . . . with you people?"

The woman again glanced up at him briefly. "What is it?" she asked but had already returned her attention to the forms.

The number of people in the building seemed to have tripled within the last few minutes. McKee pushed through to the exit, his steps munching the gravel as he crossed the parking lot to his car. The sedative quiet of the countryside and the stillness of the air instantly started circulating with his blood. In the distance, fields were planted with agricultural experiments, and a warm bright heaven seeped into the loam.

At McKee's car, he set the box on the front seat beside him. Now that the produce had been picked, it would soon soften and rot. He contemplated the boxful of harvest with pride though none of it had won any prizes. In the garden, the next batch of melons, still growing, would inherit the dresses that he'd sewn.

TARTTS

Tartts Tell All

Naomi Benaron is the winner of the 2005 Lorian Hemingway Short Story Competition, the 2005 Juniper Creek Short Story Competition, and the 2002 Martindale Literary Prize. She was a runner-up for the 2005 William Faulkner/William Wisdom Creative Writing Competition and the 2005 PRISM International Journal Short Story Competition. She was also a finalist for the 2004 Katherine Anne Porter Prize for Fiction. Her fiction has appeared or will appear in *PRISM international Journal*, *New Millennium Writings*, *and Big Tex[t]*, *Sunspinner*, *CALYX* and *Red Rock Review*. She will receive her MFA from Antioch University Los Angeles in June 2006. She lives with a husband and two dogs in Tucson, Arizona.

Joe Benevento teaches at Truman State University. He has published stories in *The Chattachoochee Review*, *Red Wheelbarrow*, *The Chariton Review*, *Evansville Review*, *Karamu*, *Bilingual Review*, and other literary magazines.

Louella Bryant's award-winning stories, essays and poems have appeared in *Hunger Mountain*, *Vermont Life*, *Fine Print*, *Carve*, *The Teachers' Voice*, *Sacred Fire*, *Mobius*, and the anthologies *High Horse* (Fleur de Lis 2005) and *Far From Home* (Seal 2004). She is the author of two young adult novels, *The Black Bonnet*, a finalist for the Vermont Book Award, and *Father By Blood*, winner of the 1999 Silver Bay Children's Literature Award, and a picture book, *Two Tracks in the Snow*. Louella is a graduate of the George Washington University and holds the MFA in Writing from Vermont College. She teaches in the MFA in Writing program at Spalding University and instructs writing courses at the University of Vermont and Castleton State College. Louella lives in Lincoln, Vermont. Visit her website, www.louellabryant.com.

Cathleen Calbert is the author of two books of poetry: *Lessons in Space* (University of Florida Press) and *Bad Judgment* (Sarabande Books). Her third collection of poems, *Sleeping with a*

Famous Poet, is forthcoming in 2007 (CustomWords, WordTech). She has been awarded the Discovery Prize from The Nation and a Pushcart Prize. Currently, she is a Professor of English at Rhode Island College, where she directs the Creative Writing program.

Christopher Chambers' work has been published in *The Gettysburg Review*. He received two nominations for 2001 Pushcart Prize. He also earned second place in *The Atlantic Monthly* Writing Competition, 1998.

Philip Cioffari, winner of this year's Tartt First Fiction Award, teaches in the writing program at William Paterson University in New Jersey. His stories have appeared in *Playboy, North American Review, Michigan Quarterly, Northwest Review, Mangrove, Bayou, Italian Americana,* as well as many other magazines and anthologies. He is finishing work on a novel.

Jocelyn Jane Cox holds an MFA in creative writing from Sarah Lawrence College. Her fiction has appeared in *JANE Magazine, The Roanoke Review, Literal Latte, The Iconoclast,* and she has been nominated for the Pushcart Prize. She is an ice skating coach and is currently working on a book about her experiences as a competitive figure skater. She lives in New York City.

Jennifer Grow teaches fiction writing at Goucher College. She's had fiction and non-fiction published or forthcoming in T*he Writers Chronicle, The GSU Review, Hunger Mountain, Other Voices Magazine, The Sun Magazine, Indiana Review* and others. She's also been the recipient of two Individual Artist Awards from the Maryland State Arts Council, and her stories have been nominated for both the *Best New American Voices of 2001* and for a 2005 Pushcart Prize.

John Hanft has taught college literature for over 30 years and has put together a college reader for Harper and Row. He has finished a collection of short stories about the Korean War and the effects it has on America.

Jimmy Carl Harris lives to write in Birmingham, Alabama. A retired Marine Corps Sergeant Major with a doctorate from the University of Alabama, he was an assistant professor at Southeastern Louisiana University. He has received a number of writing honors, including four Hackney Literary Awards. His stories have appeared in *The Louisville Review, Appalachian Heritage, Confluence, ByLine, the Birmingham Arts Journal,* and elsewhere. His collection of short fiction, *Walking Wounded* (Iris Press, 2006) features stories about strong women, weak preachers, and brave Marines. http://www.jimmycarlharris.com

Mona Houghton teaches creative writing at California State University, Northridge. She has had stories published in *Carolina Quarterly, Crosscurrents, Bluff City,* and *West Branch.* She also has an essay, "What I Learned from a Bricoleur," in *Everyday Urbanism,* edited by Margaret Crawford and John Kaliski. A story of hers will be in the upcoming issue of *Oracle.* In 2004 her novella, *Frottage,* won first place in the Inconundrum Press Melville Novella Contest. Most recently Mona won the John Gardner Memorial Prize for Fiction for her story "A Brother, Some Sex, and an Optic Nerve." It will be published in the Summer Issue of *Harpur Palate.*

Scott McWaters lives with his wife the poet Ashley McWaters and their daughter Posey in Northport, Alabama. "Developing Story" is part of a collection *Godliness and Other Stories.* He is currently writing a prophecy about clothing and the world's end.

Meg Moceri's stories have appeared in *Crab Creek Review, Storyquarterly, Natural Bridge,* and other journals. She was a finalist in the New Millennium Awards fiction competition and the Discovery Awards from Lewis-Clark Press, and was nominated for a Pushcart Prize by the editors of *Karamu.* She lives with her husband and children in Michigan.

Sandra Novack's fiction has appeared or is forthcoming in *The Gettysburg Review, The Iowa Review, Gulf Coast, Descant, Mississippi Review, Paterson Literary Review, Northwest Review, North Dakota Quarterly, South Carolina Review,* and *Yemassee,* among many others. Her work also appeared in the anthology *Tartts: Incisive Fiction from Emerging Writers.* Her collection, *Love and Other Disasters,* was a finalist in the 2004 Spokane Prize for Short Fiction, the 2005 and 2006 Tartt First Story Collection Contest, the 2006 Lewis and Clark Discovery Award, and the 2006 Doris Bakwin Award. She placed as runner-up in the Iowa Award for 2006. Her work has been nominated for a Pushcart. She holds an MA from the University of Cincinnati and an MFA in Fiction Writing from Vermont College.

After a career in advertising, public relations and editing, Elizabeth Orndorff, of Danville, Kentucky, began writing fiction. Her stories have appeared in *Potomac Review, Palo Alto Review,* and *Silent Voices,* among others. In 2006, she was a finalist for the John Steinbeck Award given by *Reed Magazine.* In 2005, she won first prize in the *Boulevard Magazine's* short fiction competition and was nominated for a Pushcart Prize. She is the co-recipient of an Artist Enrichment Grant from the Kentucky Foundation for Women for her play *The Bathroom Cleaner,* which was given a staged reading at the 2006 Juneteenth Legacy Theatre in Louisville.

Michael Schiavone is a proud MFA dropout. His fiction has appeared or is forthcoming in *New Letters, Mississippi Review, Reed Magazine, Connecticut Review,* and *GSU Review.* For the moment, he lives in Arizona.

Jan Stinchcomb has published stories in *Words and Images* and in *Singularities: Writing from the Center of the Edge* (Plain View Press, 2001). She lives in Austin with her husband and two daughters and is currently at work on a novel.

Jim Tomlinson's debut short story collection, *Things Kept, Things Left Behind,* won the 2006 Iowa Short Fiction Award. It is being published by University of Iowa Press this fall. His work has appeared in *Five Points, Potomac Review, Shenandoah Review,* and elsewhere. Jim was awarded the 2005 Al Smith Fellowship for Fiction by the Kentucky Arts Council. He lives and writes in rural Kentucky.

Valery Varble received her Ph.D. from the University of Nebraska, Lincoln, and recently ended a two-year fellowship as the first Axton Fellow in Fiction Writing at the University of Louisville in Kentucky. Her novel-in-progress, *A Vine in the Blood,* was a finalist for the PEN/Nelson Algren Fiction Award. She has work published or forthcoming in *Ascent, Colorado Review, Prairie Schooner,* and recently won Mid-American Review's 2005 Sherwood Anderson Award for her story, "Bat."

Susan Vita Weiss writes in a small, dark room in her basement. Her stories have appeared in a range of literary journals. She received a fellowship in fiction writing from the Pennsylvania Council on the Arts and was nominated for a Pushcart Prize. Susan is founder and Coordinator of The Write Place, a program of Burlington City Arts in Burlington, Vermont, and a co-director of the Burlington Literary Festival.

Philip Walzer is a reporter at *The Virginian-Pilot* in Norfolk, Virginia. His story "The War Against the Russians" was published in *The Jewish Quarterly* in London. He will be on leave this fall to complete his first novel.

Editors

Born and raised in Montgomery, Alabama, Debbie Davis received her bachelor's degree in English from Auburn University, her master's degree from Southeastern Louisiana University, and her doctoral degree from the University of Alabama. Her major field of study is 19th century British poetry, and her dissertation was an exploration of Romantic irony in that rarely read tome by William Wordsworth, *The Excursion*. When she is not poring over manuscripts for the Livingston Press, she lectures in the Department of Languages and Literature at The University of West Alabama. In her spare time, Davis enjoys watching films, sailing, hiking, arguing about politics, hanging out with her friends, and being in the company of her family—three dogs, two cats, and her husband Rett.

Gerald Jones was born in Japan to a Japanese mother and a young, Pennsylvania private fighting in the Korean War. As a child and an adult, lived here, there, everywhere from Seattle to Brooklyn, Tiffin, Ohio to Livingston, Alabama. Received BA (English) from University of Washington, MA and PhD (both on critical theory) from Bowling Green State University. Interests include film, cultural studies (I'm still an academic), jazz, cooking, and compulsive reading. Takes in orphan animals. Married with three children. Life sounds like a Fox sit-com.

Dr. Tina Naremore Jones, associate professor of English, has been a faculty member at the University of West Alabama for 14 years. She also directs the Center for the Study of the Black Belt housed at UWA. Programs of the Center include the Sucarnochee Revue, a live national traditional music radio program; the annual Sucarnochee Folklife Festival; and a Black Belt Museum. Jones serves on the Board of Directors for the Alabama Trust for Historic Preservation and the Sumter County Fine Arts Council. Jones' interest in the Black Belt of Alabama stems largely from research gathered during the writing of her dissertation, *Stealing Away from Society's Conventions: Negotiations of Voice in the Work of Ruby Pickens Tartt*. A noted Alabama folklorist, a native of Sumter County, and member of the Alabama Women's Hall of Fame, Tartt became a gateway for Jones' study into West Alabama history. Jones also has a background in journalism and has worked with the *Western Star* newspaper in Bessemer, Alabama, and currently serves as the faculty advisor for UWA's weekly student newspaper, *The Life* and Co-Director of the Livingston Press. She was the co-editor with Dr. Joe Taylor of the anthology *Belles' Letters: Contemporary Stories of Alabama Women*, and one of four editors for *Tartts: Incisive Fiction from Emerging Writers*.

Joe Taylor co-edited *Belles' Letters: Contemporary Stories of Alabama Women* and the first *Tartts*. He has three books of short stories published: *Some Heroes, Some Heroines, Some Others; The World's Thinnest Fat Man;* and *Oldcat and Ms Puss: A Book of Days for You and Me*. He has a story forthcoming in *Quarterly West*.